QUANTUM LENS

Douglas E. Richards

Paragon Press

Copyright © 2014 by Douglas E. Richards
Published by Paragon Press, 2014

E-mail the author at doug@san.rr.com
Friend him on Facebook at Douglas E. Richards Author, or visit his
website at www.douglaserichards.com

First Edition

PROLOGUE

Abdul Salib drove past the eastern boundary of Syria's largest city, Aleppo, which had been inhabited in one of its many iterations for over eight thousand years, and onto a narrow desert road. The encampment that was Salib's destination was only a thirty minute ride from Aleppo's edge. Save for the sound of the jeep's engine and the air being circulated throughout the vehicle, he and his two companions were entombed in silence.

The hellish desert was an endless sea of desolation, which still evoked a primal sense of unease in Salib. While human progress had defanged this arid wasteland considerably, traversing its scorched sands added to the tense air of foreboding that had already enveloped the three men inside the jeep.

Salib had no idea what they might be up against. But he had heard things. Impossible things. Terrible things.

He knew he had been chosen for the assignment because he was highly intelligent and level headed, not given to fits of superstition or religious zealotry. Still, given what he had heard, his usual calm and resolve had given way to a seeping fear he couldn't quite shake.

The man they had come to meet, Omar Haddad, had no discernible past. He had been a *nobody*. No more noteworthy than any one of billions around the globe who lived their meaningless lives, and left not the slightest footprint in the sands of time. But between one step and the next, Haddad had gone from leaving *no* footprint to leaving one the size of a *crater*. What size impact would his next footfall reveal?

But what did he want? And how had he amassed so much power so quickly?

Salib ran the jeep off the road and stopped it next to several dozen vehicles parked in a makeshift lot on a random stretch of flat desert.

Fifty yards away lay their destination, an encampment at the foot of a sizable oasis, consisting of dozens of oversized tents, inhabited by fervent followers of the man who had set up camp in the largest of the tents, in the center of the encampment. In a tent so enormous it could house a hundred men.

Or a single man pretending to be a god.

A man who was quickly becoming dangerous. Omar Haddad's following was spreading like a virulent, highly contagious virus. His believers were passionate and steadfast, and also terrified that if they crossed him he would strike them down with a horrible vengeance. He thought of himself as more than a prophet. As somehow divine. As an extension of Allah.

Omar Haddad had managed to amass a following so absolutely devoted to him, and growing so quickly, that he had snatched the undivided attention of Syria's new President, Khalil Najjar. And Najjar's attention and unease were further intensified when the president took steps to investigate. No threats could discourage Haddad's followers. Najjar had overseen the torture of several, but they refused to renounce Haddad, lest they lose their place in the afterlife.

Belief had seized these followers so totally that Najjar and the ruling party knew they needed to stop Haddad quickly. If this epidemic was not contained, all could be lost.

Even so, President Najjar was a ruthless man with nearly unbridled power, and had fully expected to get control of the situation quite rapidly. Yes, Haddad was becoming worrisome, but Najjar could make him go away with the snap of his fingers.

So he had sent an envoy to meet with Omar Haddad. To explain that his claims to be a prophet, or a messiah, or even an extension of Allah were blasphemous and would not be tolerated. That his throngs of passionate followers would need to be set straight. That Haddad needed to renounce himself as a con-man and charlatan, or suffer lethal consequences.

Najjar's envoy had made a pilgrimage to the very tent complex Salib was now eyeing in the distance. A pilgrimage many others had also made for months now, on days Haddad had designated for those of influence to seek the divine. The cult leader was completely un-protected within his encampment, and visitors were not checked for weapons.

Salib had no doubt that Haddad's influential guests were impressed with this confidence. And the simple encampment in the desert, at the base of an oasis, was a theatrical masterstroke. If you wanted to stir religious fervor, nothing harkened back to the days of Muhammad better than a simple man, unprotected, in a white tent, with a hellish desert in front of him and lush palm trees and springs behind him.

The envoy Najjar had sent to *encourage* Haddad to desist had possessed overwhelming force, with instructions not to spare any of it if Haddad proved to be stubborn. Najjar had fully expected the cult leader *not* to cooperate, given how delusional he had become, and for this to be the last the president would ever hear from him.

Unfortunately, this was not the case. Instead, it was the last Najjar would ever hear—not from Omar Haddad—but from the *envoy* he had sent. Not a single member ever returned. Ever. And no one had even the slightest idea of what had become of them.

So Najjar had sent another envoy, larger and better armed, who were instructed to be quick to deploy their superior weaponry, and warned of the fate of the first envoy to ensure they did not let down their guard. They, too, were happily escorted into the Bermuda Triangle that was Haddad's tent. And they, too, were never heard from again.

Even more maddening to Najjar, Haddad had ignored him. He hadn't contacted him in outrage. He hadn't gloated or complained. It was as though the envoys had been flies that he had swatted absent-mindedly. Haddad had gone about his business, seemingly uncon-cerned by what move President Najjar might make in the aftermath of the disappearances of his envoys.

But despite the theatricality of Haddad's tent, he was intent on establishing a larger base of operations. He had recently purchased a palatial estate once owned by the wealthiest citizen in Syria, on doz-ens of acres of land, with an advanced security perimeter.

So far Najjar hadn't thwarted Haddad's effort to build out his vast stronghold. Because no matter how well fortified Haddad became, his fortress would not protect him against Syria's proud air force. Against scorched-earth attacks spearheaded by jet fighters whose terrible guns and missiles could not be denied.

Salib frowned. On the other hand, it was probable that Haddad had infiltrated the military, and that his devoted followers within would intercept any such order to annihilate him, with unpredictable consequences. President Najjar was well aware that a military strike could backfire.

So Najjar had chosen a different approach this time. A peaceful one. He was rattled. And he needed to understand what it was that was growing like a plague in the desert. So he had sent Salib this time. With an olive branch. And without any weapons.

Salib and his two companions arrived at the entrance to the tent, which was flanked by two of Haddad's followers wearing white robes. Salib explained to the men who they were, and that they sought counsel with the Great One, as they had been instructed to do. One of the men entered the tent and returned only a few minutes later, motioning them to come inside.

Salib glanced at his two companions, both of whom wore expressions that might have been sunnier had they been told they would be rolled across a pit of scorpions, and swallowed hard.

They entered the tent, and Haddad's disciples stayed outside and reclosed the fabric entrance. Thirty feet in front of them, Haddad was standing alone against one tent-wall, in immaculate white robes and headdress. His dark beard was close-cropped and neatly trimmed, and he seemed to radiate purity and simplicity. He looked almost glowing, both in his scrubbed cleanliness and the overwhelming confidence that seemed to blaze from his every pore.

White marble pedestals had been placed at the entrance and in the four corners of the large tent, and on top of each was a golden cage, imprisoning a tiny bird within, either yellow or orange red. Salib wondered if the birds served a symbolic purpose, but had no time to contemplate this further.

Salib and his two companions introduced themselves, and Omar Haddad looked them over, seeming to be in no hurry to begin the proceedings.

"Thank you for granting us this audience, um . . . Great One," said Salib in Arabic, bowing slightly. "As we told your disciples, we are an envoy from President Najjar."

Haddad smiled serenely. "No weapons this time?" he said in amusement.

Salib forced a smile in return. "No weapons, Great One. We come in peace. Forgive me for asking, but are we addressing you properly? We were told *Great One* was acceptable. But we also understand that many of your followers are calling you Mahid, or the Twelfth Imam. Is this how you would prefer to be addressed?"

Haddad shook his head. "No. I am different, and greater, than Mahid. But a misguided belief among my followers that I contain his spirit is to be understood. I am *The Hand of Allah*. But you may call me simply, *Al Yad*. Great One is acceptable as well."

Salib nodded. *Al Yad: The Hand*. Another nice theatrical touch. The man certainly didn't suffer from low self-esteem.

Salib also appreciated Haddad's creativity and audacity in carving out a novel place in divinity, created from whole cloth rather than adopted from prophecy. He couldn't claim to be Mahid, The Guided One, whom many believed to be the messiah. Too many different interpretations of this prophecy. And he couldn't pass himself off as Allah, of course. So he had chosen to create a mythical niche for himself, somewhere between the two.

"Forgive me, Great One," said Abdul Salib, "but I would like to come straight to the point of our visit."

The man before them nodded.

"We are here to ask your intentions. To be blunt, Al Yad, what are your goals? What are you trying to accomplish? What do you *want?*"

A cold, humorless smile crossed Al Yad's face. "What I *want* is to be left in peace to build my church. I am not thine enemy. I shall build a following and then, in the fullness of time, I shall destroy all infidels. I shall turn the streets of the unbelievers into crimson rivers of blood, and their cities into smoldering ash-heaps. Only true believers in Islam shall be spared."

Which meant true believers in *him*, Salib knew. He noticed that Haddad had even begun speaking using a smattering of biblical verbiage. *Thine* enemy. *Shall*. This man was seriously deluded.

But Salib had heard stories . . . . It was hard to believe them, but it was also hard to believe so many people would follow Haddad just based on theatrics and charisma alone. And the disappearances of the armed envoys was a nice trick that not even the best magicians in Vegas could manage.

Salib didn't bother glancing to either side of him to see the reaction of his companions. They were there simply to act as further eyes and ears, witnesses to the proceedings, and had been instructed to remain silent unless spoken to. This was Salib's show.

Salib cleared his throat. "These goals are all quite laudable, Al Yad," he said. "Praise be to Allah. But at the same time, you must understand why they might be troubling to President Najjar. It is harder to govern when someone is capturing the hearts and minds of so many people."

Al Yad shrugged, but remained silent. Not his problem, said the man's body language.

"Join us, Al Yad. President Najjar is prepared to make you his second in command. A sanctioned spiritual leader. He is prepared to let you continue to build your church."

"*Let me?*" snapped Al Yad sharply.

"Forgive me, Great One," said Salib immediately. "A poor choice of words. I meant he is prepared to assist you, to encourage you, to continue your excellent work. Together you can ensure a better life for yourself, and for our beloved religion and country."

"I am the Hand of Allah" he said simply. "What need have I for any assistance?"

"None, Al Yad. But as powerful as you are, this is an excellent offer. Second in command of all of Syria."

"I shall soon be *first* in command of all the world. A world cleansed of infidels and reshaped to my liking. Next to this, your president may as well be offering me a job as janitor."

Abdul Salib swallowed hard. "Shall I tell the president that you will be rejecting his offer, then, Al Yad?"

"You shall."

Salib thought about what might have happened to the last two envoys, who had brought weapons and had almost certainly tried to use them. And he tried to put out of his mind some of the stories he had heard about this man. So far the exchange had been cordial, but Salib was more afraid than he had ever been. And it wasn't just the rumors. There was an unmistakable air of menace to this man, as though he had the will, and somehow the means, to snuff out lives at his slightest whim.

It was cool in the tent, but Salib was sweating profusely under his ceremonial robes. He had an unsinkable feeling that his life depended on how carefully he was able to choose his next words. How carefully he was able to deliver the message Najjar had instructed him to deliver if, as expected, Omar Haddad rejected his offer—which wasn't made in good faith in any event. Had Haddad accepted, Najjar would only pretend to bring him into the fold, studying him up close to learn what made him tick, so he could determine the cleanest way to dispose of him.

"The president will be, um . . . disappointed, Great One. I am but a humble messenger, of course, but I can't guarantee that he won't take this as a . . . personal insult."

"Let him."

"If he takes your refusal as an insult, Al Yad, he may feel the need to retaliate."

Haddad smiled broadly. "He may feel the *need* all he wants. But he is just a man," he whispered dismissively. "And I am beyond the reach of any retaliation he might choose to mete out. Am I not The Hand of Allah?" he demanded.

The usually commanding Salib flinched. "You are, indeed, oh Great One," he said.

Salib took a deep mental breath and tried to keep any tremor from his voice, which suddenly was more of a challenge than he would have liked to admit. "Forgive me, once again, Al Yad. But I would be remiss if I didn't point out that President Najjar has control of Syria's Air Force. Speaking hypothetically, of course, but he has instructed me to remind you that one word from him and this section of desert could be turned into . . . glass."

A smile slowly grew across Omar Haddad's face.

The man was actually *amused* by this threat. This offhand dismissal was more chilling to Salib than any other reaction Haddad might have had.

"Perhaps it would be of educational value for him to try," said Al Yad simply, shrugging.

The last thing Najjar wanted was to use this kind of extreme force against this man, and the cult leader seemed savvy enough to know it. He was gambling that Najjar wouldn't unleash his air-force, whose loyalties were uncertain, against someone who hadn't made a single move against the government, or spoken out against the current regime in any way.

And this Al Yad had built a cult so fanatically devoted to him, so certain of his divinity, that attacking him, martyring him, would be highly dangerous. One might think his followers would take the fact that he could be killed as a sign he was an imposter, but President Najjar was convinced otherwise.

"Great One, I have one last point the president asked me—"

"*Enough!*" shouted Al Yad, his eyes burning with a sudden, fiery malevolence. "I grow *weary* of this nonsense," he added, the chill of his tone in perfect contrast to his blazing stare. "The time for a lesson is now at hand."

The sand began to shake violently around the cult leader's sandals, as if an earthquake were concentrated beneath his feet, threatening to rip a tear deep into the earth.

Salib's eyes widened. Reports of such seemingly supernatural occurrences had been widespread.

Al Yad stood calmly within the center of the maelstrom, continuing to focus a hellish glare on his three visitors.

Suddenly, Al Yad began to rise gently into the air.

Salib and his two companions gasped!

All three had a primal urge to either flee or fall to their knees. But they were somehow frozen in place.

The man continued to levitate effortlessly, majestically, until his feet were fifteen feet above the ground. He hovered above them, his head nearly touching the roof of the tent, as the sand beneath him settled down and became utterly still once again.

Salib sensed an almost electric energy radiating from the man, and his self confident glow seemed to intensify. Salib felt himself trembling before this raw demonstration of power. But was it divine?

Haddad's followers had claimed he was capable of feats far greater even than this, and Salib and the president had concluded that the man must have apprenticed with a master magician, and had a flair for elaborate illusions.

But seeing one of these *illusions* in person was astonishing, and it drilled into a quivering vein of terror within Salib he had not known he possessed. His usually large reserve of courage had been stripped away as though he were a game animal being skinned by a hunter, revealing the soft, quivering flesh underneath, soaked, not with blood, but with an irrational sense of dread he couldn't shake.

No wonder Al Yad's followers believed in him so fervently. Believed he truly was The Hand of God. Intellectually, it was easy to argue that this was trickery. But emotionally, *viscerally* . . . this was another story entirely.

"I have a message for you to deliver, Abdul Salib," said Al Yad, and all three emissaries had their heads tilted back and their gaze locked onto their host, transfixed, their eyes unblinking and their mouths slightly agape. Al Yad didn't raise his voice, but he somehow raised his intensity level, and his words held his visitors spellbound. "For your President Najjar."

The ground began shaking again, but this time even more fiercely and throughout the entire tent, as though they had been hit by both an earthquake and sandstorm simultaneously. All five birds whistled in alarm and hopped around their tiny quarters in distress. Two of the vibrating pedestals crashed to the ground, sending golden cages tumbling onto the now-living sand, and a jet-engine roar built quickly in the tent, pounding into human ears with nearly eardrum-bursting force.

"Tell your president I shall accept no further audiences with his people," shouted Al Yad, powerfully enough to be heard over the tremendous din. "Nor shall I allow further interference with my activities. I am The Hand of God!" he thundered down to them, and the anger in his tone seemed to cause the tent to shake ever more vigorously. "If he chooses to ignore my word, I will smite him with such a righteous, terrible vengeance, that only Allah will be able to recognize his remains."

A blast of slick spray splattered Salib's face from his left, shocking him so much he barely suppressed a scream. He instinctively threw himself into a crouch. To his left, the man he had known as Falah Malik fell to the sand beside him, his head no longer attached to his shoulders. Blood poured from his neck as if it were a hose.

Salib's eyes shifted quickly to his right, just in time to see the head of his other companion explode like a watermelon packed with dynamite, spraying additional blood and tissue onto his hair and face.

Salib fell to the sand, choking back vomit.

No weapons had been fired, and no one else had entered the tent.

The ground abruptly stopped shaking, and the roar ceased. The utter silence was as terrifying to Salib as what it had replaced.

"Go!" commanded Al Yad, waving his arms impatiently, as if unable to believe Salib was still in the tent. "And tell your weakling president what The Hand of God has wrought here."

Still hovering in midair, the man once known as Omar Haddad turned, so that his back was to his sole surviving visitor. Salib was on his knees in the sand, covered in gore, and still reeling from what he had witnessed.

"And know that you have only seen a *hint* of the wrath I'm prepared to unleash," finished Al Yad icily.

As Abdul Salib stumbled frantically toward the entrance to the tent, he realized that he didn't doubt this declaration for an instant.

PART ONE

"All truth passes through three stages. First, it is ridiculed. Second, it is violently opposed. Third, it is accepted as being self-evident. "

—Arthur Schopenhauer

1

Five months later:

Alyssa Aronson stared intently at the digital clock on the bottom of her television screen, feeling a mix of emotions including hope, anxiety, and curiosity. But mostly she felt like an idiot. A pathetic idiot.

Internet dating? Had it really come to this?

A part of her knew that Internet dating was actually far superior to how dating had been done throughout much of modern history. Through random chance meetings, fix-ups, and the bar scene and party circuit. This was more scientific. More capable of actually matching people based on their interests and personalities. And there was no stigma to it. It was the Internet age and everyone was doing it.

But even though she knew all of this intellectually, still, at an emotional level it smacked somehow of . . . desperation.

On the other hand, she had realized recently that she *was* desperate. Yes, she was still only twenty-eight, but her genes had kicked into gear lately, and she had become more concerned with entering a relationship than ever. She used to roll her eyes when the phrase "biological clock" was used, but just because she was an expert in human behavior and motivation didn't mean she could circumvent the impulses hardwired into her.

One could possess the most incredible combination of superior genes in the history of humanity, but if one was unsuccessful at mating, these superior genes died with their owner. Alternatively, if someone was good at finding mates and reproducing, and absolutely *nothing* else, his or her *inferior* genes would survive.

So if genes needed to ensure that sex, and in some cases the insatiable drive for it, were so interwoven into the fabric of the psyche that mating could not be ignored, and was even critical for proper mental health and bodily functioning, they would do so. And if genes needed to take over the mind, force one to pursue the opposite sex almost against one's will, or destroy all rationality—which, after all, a potent chemical potion released into the bloodstream after sex helped to ensure would happen during romantic love—they would do so with single-minded ruthlessness.

Alyssa was broken from her reverie by a polite, almost tentative rap at her door. She glanced at the screen, which read 11:30 exactly. *When Theo Grant says he'll pick you up on Saturday at 11:30, he means Saturday at 11:30.*

She took one last glance at the hallway mirror. She didn't know why, since she was pretty sure the mirror would show her the same image it had shown her thirty seconds earlier.

She gazed upon a woman with a light complexion and perfect skin, who was only 5'4 in height but refused to wear heels, believing these were torture devices invented during the dark ages. Her clothing was simple and tasteful, and she wore minimal jewelry and makeup. She was fit and had curves in all the right places, with shoulder-length, brownish-blonde hair, and a face that was feminine, and, of course, well above average. If she did say so herself.

She grinned as this thought flashed through her mind. It was a recurring joke she had with herself. She was well steeped in the data behind what many called the *Lake Wobegone Effect*, named after the fictional town popularized by Garrison Keillor. According to Keillor, this was a town where, "All the women are strong, all the men are good looking, and all the children are above average."

While tongue-in-cheek, this statement was more insightful even than Keillor may have realized, as numerous studies had since documented that humans had a clear tendency to overestimate themselves on almost every dimension.

Ask a group of people if they were *below average*, *average*, or *above average* on anything—driving skills, productivity, intelligence, parenting, and so on—and seventy to ninety percent were convinced they were *above* average. So people were obviously good at fooling themselves, especially when it came to their own greatness. Thinking about this never failed to crack her up, but this shouldn't surprise her because, after all, she possessed a sense of humor that was, well . . . above average.

Alyssa took a deep breath, patted her pockets to feel the reassuring presence of pepper-spray in one and a small stun-gun in the other, and opened her front door.

Theo Grant looked exactly like his picture, which was a promising start. He stood five inches taller than her, had black hair, cut short, and a friendly face that seemed calm, confident, and serene.

Some of the responses she had read on his profile page had had a Zen-like air to them, at least in her opinion. Under "favorite quotes" he had chosen one by T.S. Elliot: "And the end of all our exploring will be to arrive where we started, and know the place for the first time."

Wow. Either Theo Grant had been in a Zen mood when he had chosen this quote, or he had been stoned out of his mind.

A warm smile came over the face of the man standing before her, one she believed to be genuine, and he extended his hand. "Nice to meet you in person, Alyssa," he said pleasantly.

"You too . . . Theo," she said, trying out his name for the first time. His profile said he was thirty three, and she believed this number to be accurate.

"Are you ready?" said Grant.

She nodded, closing the door gently behind her.

They walked the short distance to her driveway, upon which a gleaming silver Mercedes was parked, and Grant opened the passenger door, waited for her to seat herself, and then carefully closed it once again.

Punctuality *and* gentlemanliness. Neither were the most critical attributes on her list, but the guy was off to a good start. The real question was, would she enjoy his company as much as she thought based on his profile? And if she did, would he return the interest?

"Nice car," said Alyssa.

"Thanks. But it's a rental. I just moved here, and haven't had the chance to buy a car."

She had known about his recent relocation from his profile. "Do you always rent a Mercedes?"

Grant smiled sheepishly. "I wish you hadn't asked that. Alas, I'm forced to admit that I usually rent subcompacts from companies like *Dirt Cheap Rentals*, or *Fly By Night Cars*." His smile expanded. "Sure didn't take you long to penetrate my feeble attempt to create the illusion of wealth."

Alyssa laughed out loud. "Maybe so, but you do get high marks for honesty."

"Yeah, that's my charm. I'm *painfully* honest." He turned the key in the ignition and then tilted his head toward her once again. "I only rent luxury cars when I'm going on an Internet date with a bright, accomplished woman who is . . . you know, " he added with a wry expression, "above average in every way."

A hint of a smile crossed her face. Apparently, she wasn't the only one who had zeroed in on the "favorite quote" section of the other's dating profile. "And how often is that?" she asked.

Grant pulled the car onto a narrow private road that led to and from Alyssa's secluded home, which was nestled in front of the tree line of a thriving woods. He raised his eyebrows. "How often do I go on Internet dates in general? Or how often do I go on Internet dates with bright, accomplished, fellow Garrison Keillor fans?"

"In general," she replied.

"Let me think about that for a minute," he said, removing his right hand from the steering wheel and rapidly extending his fingers in sequence, as if counting in groups of five. "Well, assuming my math is correct . . . this would be my first."

Alyssa realized she was liking this Theo Grant already. His sense of humor had come through immediately, and the pretend counting on his fingers was a nice touch. "My first, also," she admitted.

They made their way to the French restaurant Grant had chosen, continuing to make conversation that was surprisingly natural and unforced. Although perhaps this shouldn't have been surprising. The reason she had agreed to go on a date with this man was because he was outgoing, loved the woods as much as she did, and loved both science and science fiction. He had been a freelance science writer for many years, and was especially fascinated by quantum physics, as was she.

When they arrived at the elegant restaurant, *La Petit Gourmet*, in downtown Bloomington, Grant pulled out Alyssa's chair and then slid it toward the table after she was seated. Okay, now she was beginning to become impressed. *Who did that anymore?*

The waiter took their order while they chatted. They were both well versed in the latest mind-blowing science and technology and the conversation took on a life of its own. Grant loved what he did, but it wasn't the most lucrative. So he had decided to move to Bloomington, Indiana, because he had graduated from Indiana University years before and had an affinity for the town. And few areas of the country were as affordable as this one, or were as packed with lush and spectacular woods.

Alyssa found him charming, funny, exceedingly knowledgeable about a far range of sciences, as might be expected of someone who wrote on different scientific topics for a living, and self-effacing. And maybe, somehow, just a touch mysterious, although she wasn't sure why she had this impression.

This date could not be going any better. Since a two-year relationship had ended several years earlier, Alyssa had been on maybe a dozen first-dates, but precious few second dates. But she found herself drawn to this man in a way she hadn't been with any of the others. Maybe her track record was about to change.

She tried to steer the conversation away from herself, so she could avoid lying for as long as possible, but finally, the inevitable happened. Grant used his spoon to tear a hole through the cheese that covered his French onion soup appetizer and gazed at her calmly. "You have an impressive knowledge of physics and cosmology," he said appreciatively. "But from your profile, I thought you were more in the medical end of things."

"I am. I just think these other subjects are fascinating."

"So what *do* you study in that university lab of yours?"

Alyssa resisted the urge to frown. She hated lying, but there was no other way. Because the truth was she *didn't* have an appointment with Indiana University. She had a lab at the outskirts of campus, and she said she was with IU, but this was not true.

The truth was that she was in a branch of the military called PsyOps. The *Black Ops* end of PsyOps, which she was prohibited from disclosing to anyone outside of those who already knew, including a spouse.

The truth was she was one of the world's leading experts on hypnotic drugs and hypnosis. On the human mind, the human subconscious. On human behavior. On how to take suggestion to the next level.

Or summed up, she was an expert on human brainwashing. She studied horrible, mind-altering cousins of LSD, sodium amobarbital, chloral hydrate, and scopolamine, alone and in combinations, looking for the best way to strip people of their will, rewrite their subconscious, and bend them to the will of the hypnotist.

Alyssa sighed deeply. "Turns out I'm a mad scientist. I perform experiments so unspeakable, if I told you about them, not only would I have to kill *you*, but everyone in this restaurant."

Grant smiled and shook his head. "Good one," he said in amusement. "But I don't believe that for an instant."

Nice guy, she thought. Too bad he was such a poor judge of character.

2

Alyssa looked into the serene continence of Theo Grant's face as he took his first spoonful of French onion soup and forced herself to smile. "Okay, the boring truth is that I study human behavior," she said, a disclosure that had the singular advantage of being at least partially true.

Watching his puppy-dog acceptance of this statement was almost too depressing to bear. It was *hopeless*. She was relationship kryptonite, forever unable to share the most important part of her life with a romantic interest. How could a relationship based on lies ever succeed?

And the necessity of keeping the majority of her life secret was only the last hurdle to overcome. She was an MD/PhD in neurology from Princeton University, which was intimidating to most men. At least Theo Grant had specified on his profile page that he liked his women bright, well-read, and accomplished.

And she had to be cautious even with the bits of her expertise she *could* share, the encyclopedic body of research she had mastered on personality, behavior, and the subconscious. Like a man dating a psychiatrist, always wondering if he was being psychoanalyzed, few men could avoid feeling overly self-conscious about their behavior in her presence.

And even if she *were* authorized to tell Theo Grant what she really did, she couldn't anyway. Who could blame any man for freaking out upon discovering that she was one of the world's leading experts in narco-hypnosis. For wondering if she might turn him into a slave. For wondering if they got into a fight, or broke up, god forbid, if he would find himself clucking like a chicken every time he heard the word, *asshole*, or some other trigger that she had devised.

The fact that this wouldn't happen—couldn't happen—wouldn't matter. As an expert, she was well aware of the crippling limitations of narco-hypnosis. But a non-expert would be difficult to convince, especially given the huge volume of misinformation about the subject that many accepted as fact.

She still couldn't believe she really worked for Black Ops. This twist of fate was so improbable as to be absurd. She had been cursed with a keen interest in science, and the more she read about research into human personality, and especially the power of the subconscious mind, the more entranced she became.

So she had decided to pursue an MD/PhD with intentions of joining a university lab. The thought of joining the clandestine services had never once crossed her mind. Who sets out to join PsyOps? Or Black Ops? Or, horror of all horrors, both at once?

The beginning of the end had occurred when she had written a paper in medical school, proposing a revolutionary theory on the workings of the subconscious. It was denied for publication almost immediately. No one would touch it. So she had published the paper on her personal blog, where it had been savaged by the scientific community. Her ideas flew in the face of conventional dogma. They were absurd. Ridiculous.

Just as she was reeling from this reaction, she was contacted by PsyOps. She was told that her theories were not absurd. In fact, her ideas mirrored, and even extended, their own thinking.

And then, in typical PsyOps fashion, they had helped to fan the flames of the scientific evisceration of her ideas, just to discredit them further, since the clandestine services of other countries could read papers online just like anyone else.

The recruiter touted her as a genius, with incredible intuition, and offered to allow her to run a lab of her own, with several assistants. At a salary many times what she could expect to earn in academia.

It was an elegant piece of PsyOpera. Destroy her chances at a mainstream research career, while offering her the chance to have unlimited resources to pursue her theories. They really knew how to make it impossible to say no. A potent mixture of seduction . . . and *destruction*.

But she had had one condition. She wouldn't study narco-hypnosis to control others, just to learn how to prevent it, how to undo it, if it were ever used against America or her allies. The recruiter had agreed immediately, insisting this was the case anyway.

Trying to control others through the use of drugs was banned by international treaty. But just as biological and chemical warfare agents were banned, and the US would never use them, the US government still maintained secret programs in these areas to keep abreast of what others might be doing.

So she had joined up. Her life as she had known it had ended two years previously, at the age of twenty-six. She had to admit, the work was invigorating, fascinating, and fulfilling. And important. Controlling people was proving impossible, thankfully. But she had helped make advances in enhancing the placebo effect, something she was convinced could revolutionize medicine.

But she hadn't fully realized the consequences to her social life of doing clandestine research, and how much more difficult it would be to find the right man, and make it work, than it had already been.

She had a great relationship with her mother, but her relationship with her father was even better. He was a kind and caring man who had always adored her. When she complained that she scared men away, he would tell her that this was because she was extraordinary. Beautiful, smart, witty, and accomplished. Too smart and accomplished for most, he would tell her. It would take a truly extraordinary man to fully appreciate her. But to this man, she would be irresistible. The perfect woman.

Her father was perceptive enough to know how he sounded. Like a father whose daughter failed to make the cheerleading squad, and who tried to cheer her up by telling her a tall tale, that it was because she was *too* pretty, and the other girls were *jealous*. But in her case, he insisted he wasn't lying to cheer her up, and this wasn't the prognosis of a biased father who had a blind spot for his daughter. It was an absolute fact. He knew what he knew, and in due time she would come to realize the accuracy of his prophecy.

There was something about this Theo Grant. She already had a feeling that he was a man who was truly extraordinary. More so than any man she had ever dated.

Perhaps her father's prophecy would finally be put to the test.

3

The lone resident of the table was tall and athletic-looking. He finished ordering lunch and shook his head in disbelief. How had he drawn *this* assignment?

He was a black belt in two different martial arts, could create a bomb out of household ingredients and shape it to blow a door off its hinges, and could send a bullet into a rolling soccer ball at thirty yards—while coming out of a tuck and roll.

What he *couldn't* do was blend in while dining alone at a fancy French restaurant.

At least that's how it seemed to him. He felt like a screaming siren attached to a flashing neon sign.

A small receiver imbedded in his ear asked for an update. He glanced around to be sure no one was watching or within earshot and lowered his head so he would be closer to the tiny mike imbedded in his lapel. "Their conversation appears lively," he whispered, feeling like an idiot. "But they're too far away to hear details. He's still finishing his French onion soup. Do you copy that?"

"Yes."

"The service is leisurely and unrushed," he continued. "Confidence is high that you have an hour, at bare minimum. Probably closer to two."

"Any chance you've been made?"

"Always a chance. But doubtful. I'm a ways away from them, and they only have eyes for each other. Not even a glance in this direction. Seems to be quite the first date. I'll keep you fully updated," he finished.

Sure. Important updates to come. Would they order coffee and dessert, or would they not? The tension was nearly unbearable, he thought, as a wry smile came to his face.

"Don't you think this is overkill?" he whispered into the mike.

"Probably," came the reply. "But we're going to find out soon enough."

4

Theo Grant bit off the tip of a breadstick and considered Alyssa thoughtfully as the waitress set their entrées in front of them, each a colorful work of art. "Human behavior," he repeated. "Sounds intriguing. I've read a little about this myself, although I'm nowhere near the expert you are." He gestured at her. "So if you had to give a thirty-thousand foot overview of human behavior, what would you say?"

Alyssa Aronson paused for a moment in thought. "I guess if I wanted to keep it to one sentence, I'd say that much more of our behavior is genetic, is baked in at birth, than most people could possibly guess."

"Interesting," said Grant. "Do we know this for sure, or is this just surmised?"

"No, we're about as sure as we can be, courtesy of mother nature. For decades the prevailing wisdom was that we are all blank slates when we leave the womb, waiting to be written upon by parents and society. That we have no innate tenants to our personalities. Some proponents of this theory, called behaviorism, insisted they could take a group of babies and mold them in any way they wanted. Make a boy hate guns and love dolls. Turn someone from shy to gregarious."

Grant looked amused. "I'm guessing none of them ever actually tried to raise any children. Or had any siblings for that matter."

Alyssa laughed.

"From your initial overview," he added, "I take it this theory has been discredited. So what changed?"

"The rise of identical twins," she replied. "In 1979, a newspaper in Minneapolis published a story about identical twins who were separated at birth. They were raised by different families in different cities, and each had no idea the other existed. At the age of forty, in a freak occurrence, they ran into each other and realized what had happened. A psychologist, Thomas Bouchard, read the story and began to study the twins.

"It turned out that they had an incredible host of similarities. They were of similar weight, both smoked—the same brand of cigarette—both were into carpentry, liked racing, and hated baseball. Both had the same hand gestures, gait, and mannerisms. And so on. It was uncanny. The story went national, and the twins even ended up on the Tonight Show with Johnny Carson."

Alyssa took a sip of the red wine she had ordered with lunch. She didn't typically drink at lunch, but she didn't typically go on a first date to a fancy French restaurant either. Sometimes exceptions had to be made.

"The publicity this generated opened the floodgates," she continued. "Dozens of identical twins who were separated at birth contacted Bouchard. Since then, studies on thousands of such twin pairs have been conducted around the world."

"There have been that many twins separated at birth?"

"Yes. About one in two hundred and fifty births result in identical twins. So there are more than a million pairs of identical twins in the US alone."

Grant whistled. "No kidding."

"Turns out that far more about our behaviors and proclivities are determined by our genes than we ever realized. That doesn't mean that environment doesn't also play a large role, because it does. Parenting still does matter. Environment still does matter. But less than had been thought.

"Separate identical twins, who have identical genes, at birth. Have Gandhi raise one of them and Hitler the other. And on a number of personality traits, they will be, on average, quite similar to each other. Despite being raised by very different parents, in very different environments. More similar to each other than are siblings who are raised *together*, with the same parents, and in a similar environment. But who *don't* have identical genes."

"Okay, so genes matter a lot more than people thought. But what traits, in particular, are we talking about here?"

"Just about all of them," she said. "Some you might expect to be more on the genetic side, like the propensity to be heavy or thin. Others you'd never guess in a million years. Like happiness. Or political philosophy. Conservatism versus liberalism."

"No way," said Grant in disbelief. "You're saying political viewpoint is genetic?"

"Not entirely. But on average, genetic makeup plays a very important role. My own family is a great example of this. I have one brother who is a staunch conservative and one who is liberal. Same identical parents. Same lessons taught. Same cable news channel watched by my parents while they were growing up. Think about siblings you've known over the years, raised by the same parents in the same home, and it won't take long for you to realize how incredibly different they can be on so many levels. And with respect to any number of traits: personality, work ethic, respect for authority, and so on. Since they're in a similar environment, but have different genes, it's likely that genetics plays an important role in many of these behaviors. And sure enough, if you take identical twins with the same exact genes, and raise one in a liberal family and the other in a conservative family, they have a better chance than not of either *both* being liberal, or *both* conservative."

"I'll be damned," said Grant. "I'd have bet my life political persuasion was entirely about parenting and environment."

"Good thing you didn't bet, then," noted Alyssa with a twinkle in her eye.

"No kidding," said Grant good-naturedly. "But you also mentioned happiness," he added. "So that's genetic also? I'd think this would be the most related to environment of anything. Even more so than politics."

"Most people do. But genes play a major role in our happiness, and the level of our subjective well-being. We have a preset proclivity for it."

"That doesn't make sense to me. If a guy makes a killing in the stock market, he's going to be happy. If he falls in love. Happy. If he gets fired from his job. Not happy. All of these are environmental."

"For the short term, yes, positive events will have a positive impact on his happiness. But not for long. We tend to overestimate how long a financial windfall will make us happier. And we also overestimate how long getting fired will make us *less* happy. But we adjust to both. Go back to a baseline. It's called hedonic adaptation."

Grant nodded but said nothing.

"If I told you that one man won a fortune in the lottery," continued Alyssa, "and another lost his legs, this would tell you very little about which man is the happiest a year from now, since both would revert to their baseline states. Again, in the short term, the lottery winner's happiness will skyrocket and the amputee's happiness will plummet."

"But it isn't all genes, right?"

"Not by any means."

"So if money doesn't factor in, what does?"

"Money does factor in, but not all that profoundly. And even then, only up until an income of about seventy-five thousand dollars a year. Enough so that if your car breaks down you can get it fixed, and so on. But anyone earning seventy-five grand or more has just as much chance as being as happy, or unhappy, as a billionaire. Really. The most important environmental determinants that come into play are the quality of relationships with friends and family. And challenging ourselves, pursuing what we are passionate about, and achieving. What really makes a life rewarding is facing challenges, overcoming them, and growing as a person." She paused. "Ironically, in the long run, winning the lottery can significantly *decrease* a person's happiness."

"Well yeah. Who *wouldn't* be miserable after winning twenty million dollars?" said Grant sarcastically.

Alyssa laughed. "You'd be surprised," she said. "Not every lottery winner becomes less happy, but a lot of them do. Some quit their jobs and find they have too much time on their hands. They suffer from boredom and loss of purpose. And they often lose relationships. They move out of their neighborhoods. And jealousy, greed, unequal wealth, and so on, can cause personal relationships to deteriorate."

Grant raised his hands in surrender. "Remind me never to doubt you again," he said with a grin. "Very impressive."

Alyssa returned the smile. "Well, I do study this for a living," she said, her eyes sparkling happily.

They continued a lively discussion on a range of additional topics for another hour, long after they had finished eating. Neither was in a hurry to get up from the table.

Theo Grant made her feel as though she were the most interesting woman alive. And after they had discussed behavior, she insisted on talking about his interests once again, and she continued to find him fascinating himself, and lightning fast on the uptake.

Finally, they returned to Alyssa's home, and Grant walked her to her door. Alyssa got the sense that he had no timetable for pushing a physical relationship. He seemed confident, relaxed, and still a little Zen. She decided he would be content whether she invited him in or not, which made her want to do so even more.

"Why don't you come in," she said, "and we can continue to get to know each other over a glass of . . . iced tea."

She had been about to say *wine*, but had thought better of it. She had already finished two full glasses at the restaurant, and she didn't want to lose her inhibitions, or good sense, altogether. At twenty-eight it was a bit silly to be worried about reputation for jumping in the sack too early—God, and surely Theo Grant, knew she had long since lost her virginity. Still, she could at least wait for a second date, even if this was, hands down, the best first date she had ever been on.

Not that she could even guarantee he would ask her on a second. She thought the chemistry between them was extraordinary, but even *her* intuition and knowledge of human nature were far from perfect. She understood it in the aggregate, but in any given situation, who knew?

Grant happily accepted the invitation and stepped inside. Alyssa gave him a quick tour, and then sat him in her living room while she prepared iced tea. Just as she returned with two glasses, the doorbell sounded. Two quick rings.

Alyssa handed Theo Grant both glasses and said, "Let me just check who's at the door, and I'll be right back. Won't take a minute."

Grant nodded and Alyssa exited the room, turned the corner, and walked briskly to her door. She looked through the peephole. A brown-clad delivery man was on the other side, holding a small package that required her signature.

She threw open the door hurriedly, wanting to get back to Grant as quickly as possible.

But the man was gone. He must have left just as she was turning the handle on the door. Apparently the package hadn't required her signature after all, since he had left it for her. She stepped outside and bent down to get it.

A man lunged at her from out of nowhere.

Her visitor hadn't left, after all.

It was an ambush.

Two thick arms snatched her off her feet, while a massive, calloused hand clamped tightly over her mouth and nose. She issued a scream of such shock and terror it should have awoken the dead. But as it was, it was so muffled by the thick hand that she was barely able to hear it herself.

Her attempted scream had stolen all of her breath, and she fought desperately to take another. But the hand was suffocating her.

Her lungs began to burn, and she knew that if she didn't fill them once again, she'd be dead in a matter of seconds.

5

Alyssa's abductor seemed to realize she couldn't breathe and slid his hand lower, uncovering her nose, while keeping an iron clamp over her mouth. She sucked in as much air as she could through her nose, breathing in and out in rapid succession, her lungs and blood-stream seizing on the still limited oxygen desperately.

"Stop struggling," whispered her abductor, moving quickly away from the door. "I'm not going to hurt you."

The man was huge, a block of pale granite well over six feet tall with the density of lead. He kept her completely immobile, despite her struggles, while lifting her as easily as she might lift a backpack.

He rushed off toward her backyard and the woods beyond, while a team of six commandos emerged from all sides of her house, armed for a war. The timing of her exit from the scene and their entry was remarkable in its precision.

What was going on?

Where was she being taken? And what did they want in her house?

This had to be some kind of nightmare from which she would soon awaken, but as her abductor continued to rush her deeper into the woods, it was impossible to deny the reality of what was happening.

Alyssa had the highest security clearance possible, and access to a considerable volume of eyes-only research. Did they know it was never allowed to leave the lab? Even if she had managed to break the rules, the computer data would be so heavily encrypted they would never get at it.

Which explained why she was still alive. She was their insurance policy. In case they didn't find what they were after, or needed her to retrieve it.

She had to find a way to warn Grant!

Whatever their interests in her work, what would they do when they realized someone else was in her house? Would they kill him? Would they swat him away like a fly and go about their business, whatever it was? Grant was a sweet, tranquil man who just happened to be at the wrong place at the wrong time.

Alyssa thought about reaching for her pepper spray or stun gun, still in her pockets, but the one arm her abductor was using to crush her body against his torso pinned her arms as tightly as if they were in a vise.

She tried to scream again but nothing came out, and she knew that by now, if their goal was entry into her house, this had long since been accomplished.

"I'm going to let you go now," said the block of human granite, setting her down and removing his hand from her mouth. She considered running or shooting him with her stun gun, but decided against it. She was outmatched, in size and skill.

"I was tasked to remove you from the area," he explained. "I expect no shots to be fired, but just in case, you're now out of harm's way."

"Tasked? By whom?" she demanded. "Are you mad? What's this about?"

He ignored her questions. "They'll let me know when the target is in custody, and we can return," he told her. "Should be any second."

"*What target?*"

"The man you were with."

What? They were after Theo Grant?

But before she could even begin to digest this stunning news, all hell broke loose fifty yards to the north. Machine gun fire began sounding, and as near as she could tell, it was continuous fire from multiple locations.

Alyssa glared at the man beside her. "Is that what you call *no shots being fired?*"

He opened his mouth to reply when an explosion erupted in the direction of her lawn.

"Wait here," said her abductor, pulling an automatic pistol from his belt and dashing off through the trees.

Alyssa hesitated for only a few seconds before running to follow. She wasn't about to put herself in the middle of a firefight, but she wasn't going to wait in the woods like a deer in headlights while World War III was taking place at her house.

She arrived at the edge of the woods, at an angle to her house that allowed her to observe the front of it. *What the hell?*

It had become even more of a war zone than she had anticipated. Commandos were sprawled all over her yard in various poses, like little green plastic army men carefully set up around a model house and then toppled over, with a surprising lack of blood to be found anywhere. Light was streaming into her house through uncountable holes.

Rocket launchers were on the ground next to two of the unconscious or dead soldiers. *Rocket launchers?* She had seen a movie depicting the raid on Osama Bin Laden years earlier, and what she was seeing immediately brought this to mind.

Grant's Mercedes was also on its back, a burning pile of wreckage, and Alyssa was near certain it had been the causality of one of the rocket launchers.

Her house, the car, and even her yard were burning outright, and smoke and the smell of sulfur pervaded the air. Shiny silver casings from a seemingly limitless number of rounds that had been fired were strewn about her lawn.

As she was taking in this war zone at a single glance, Theo Grant emerged from behind the burning car, his eyes frantically scanning the area. "Alyssa!" he shouted out at the top of his lungs. "Alyssa, where are you?" He seemed more worried about her welfare than his own, which was almost as shocking as the fact that he was even alive.

She shook her head as if to clear it. How was Theo Grant the last man standing?

Alyssa was out of his line of sight as she emerged from the tree line. But before she could respond to his desperate call, two more commandos appeared in front of him and began firing. She felt a sting and looked down to see blood running down her arm.

She had been hit! She was in the direct line of fire from one of the machine guns.

Hundreds of rounds were sprayed from the gun, its owner unaware that she was behind Grant, and so much bark flew through the air it seemed like the trees around her were being put through a wood-chipper.

Her only chance of survival was to take cover behind the trees once again.

She darted back into the woods as gunfire continued to kick up dirt and bark around her. In a blind panic, she tripped over a large root and cracked her head against the thick trunk of an oak tree.

She fell to its base as gunfire continued to sound.

An image of Theo Grant flashed into her mind's eye, and from the deep recesses of her subconscious a flash of dark humor emerged. *If I survive this,* came the stray thought, *I'm really going to have to reevaluate that whole, best first date ever, status.*

And with that, Alyssa Aronson's eyelids fell closed, the machine gun fire faded into the background as if it were a dream, and she lapsed into oblivion.

6

Alyssa's eyes fluttered open.

She was alive!

She was in a conference room, one she immediately recognized. It was *her* conference room. From work. In the ten-thousand square foot building near the university that housed her lab and offices.

She shook her head to clear away the remaining cobwebs. Her arm had been bandaged and felt fine. The shot must have just grazed her.

Of course she was alive, she now realized. This wasn't the first time she had come to.

She recalled regaining consciousness in the woods behind her house, brought back to life with a start by smelling salts held under her nose by a medic standing over her. The ammonia gas the salts had released had performed the same magic they had demonstrated since Roman times, triggering the inhalation reflex and activating her sympathetic nervous system.

The medic had examined her pupils, taken vital signs measurements, had her move in various ways, and had asked her questions to get a sense of her mental acuity. After ten minutes of putting her through his paces, he announced that she would make a full recovery, and handed her a pill.

Apparently a sedative, she thought with a frown.

A man rapped at the conference room door and then entered. She eyed him but didn't say anything.

"You're awake about ten minutes sooner than expected," he said, checking his watch. "I'm Major Greg Elovic," he added, holding out his hand.

Alyssa ignored it. "You gave me a *sedative*?" she said accusingly.

Elovic pulled his hand back and seated himself across from her. "The medic on the scene thought it would be best. Give your body a chance to sleep it off some more. And give him a chance to examine you more thoroughly."

Bullshit, she thought. She had never met this man in person, but she knew who he was. A major in the Black Ops chain of command. But a major with broad responsibilities. He wasn't really in the PsyOps chain of command, per se, but above it. And his rank didn't fully reflect the scope of his responsibilities and the power he commanded.

It occurred to Alyssa with a start that he must have come to Bloomington just for her. They had sedated her to be sure she couldn't receive or provide intelligence until his arrival. She knew how these bastard's thought.

"How long was I out?" she said simply.

"Four hours," replied the major. "How are you feeling?" he asked, but in such a way that she knew he didn't really care about her answer.

"Are you going to tell me what's going on? Who the hell were those men? How did my home become a war zone?"

Elovic winced. "They were ours," he said without preamble, quickly ripping off a band-aid he knew would tear out hair along the way. "And I was the one who ordered them in."

"*Ours?*" she said incredulously. "You unleashed an army with more firepower than the Bin Laden raid on a private home in Bloomington, Indiana? What are you telling me, that I just went on a first date with Bin Laden's second coming?"

"I wouldn't say that. But he is definitely what you might call . . . a person of great interest to us."

"Don't you mean, he *was* a person of great interest?"

The major shook his head. "I said it right the first time."

Alyssa Aronson shrank back in disbelief. "Are you telling me he *survived* that barrage? I didn't see what happened. I was too busy bleeding and trying to avoid getting killed by, incredibly enough, *friendly fire*. But Grant was their *target*. No way he survives that. There were so many bullets flying, a *mosquito* couldn't have survived in his position."

"And yet he did," replied Elovic with a deep frown. "And he escaped, as well. We had a shot at him once before. Four months ago. Our forces had instructions to capture him, and several of our best men had him cornered. But he slipped that noose. We're still not quite sure how he did it. We actually assumed he had been caught in an explosion and was no longer with us. Anyway, this time, we decided to come at him with overwhelming force."

"And decided to ditch the *capture* part."

The major frowned. "No, the orders were the same. *Capture.* Again, I'm not sure what happened, but it was a major cluster fuck. I don't know who fired the first shot, but if I ever find out, that man will wish he had never been born. But as you saw, things got out of control quickly. Under the circumstances, you're right. There is no way he survives. No way he escapes. But he did."

Incredible, she thought. More than incredible. Impossible. "How?"

"We don't know. The men got off enough rounds to kill an army. They all ended up unconscious, but not injured in any way. We think he may have used a new weapon. Some kind of concussive technology. Most likely sonic. Compressed sound waves knocking out all conscious life within a certain radius of him."

"You'd think I would have heard or felt something then, or have been affected in some way. I was almost certainly within this radius."

"Look, we're at a total loss. Which is one of the reasons we're so interested in this guy. To be honest, the fact that he did escape is a blessing in disguise. I gave strict orders that he was not to be harmed. He doesn't do us any good dead."

"So you've been tracking him?" said Alyssa coldly, finding it hard to adjust to the reality that Grant wasn't just the harmless man who had so effortlessly won her over. "So why did you wait until he showed up at my house to make another attempt to get him? Did there just happen to be a special forces convention in Bloomington, Indiana?"

The stone-faced major laughed. Alyssa was surprised that his face didn't shatter from being twisted into such an unfamiliar position. "As I told you, we thought he was killed four months ago. So we weren't following him, only to randomly decide to hit him today. We only discovered he was still at large yesterday. He only reemerged on our radar *when he made a date with you.*"

She was an idiot, she realized. Just fricking great!

"Really?" she said, outraged. "My dating life is being monitored?"

"I'm afraid so. Good thing, too, don't you think? It's for your own protection. It's not likely anyone could ever learn who you are and what you do, but it's not impossible. Our intent isn't voyeurism. But new relationships being forged by anyone on sensitive black projects are monitored. Anyone trying to get close to you, male or female, friend or lover, is scrutinized. Unless there is good reason to suspect someone is trying to approach you under false pretenses, they're cleared, and you can have whatever relationship you want with them. I know you're not a field agent, but you've been trained. You know the Honey Trap has probably been used to get information more successfully than any other technique throughout history. On both men *and* women."

Alyssa clenched her fists upon hearing a term she considered odious. She was in a poison mood and was barely able to avoid taking it out on the major. And who could blame her? Too many commandos and ugly revelations for one day.

Of course it had been a Honey Trap, the term used by the clandestine services when they sent in an appealing agent to seduce a mark, get them to fall in love or in lust, and then use this level of trust to exploit them, or put them in compromising positions so they could be blackmailed into revealing state secrets. But she had always thought this was mostly effective with male targets, who were more susceptible to the manipulations of a hot woman fawning over them, and the lure of sex.

The whole idea of the Honey Trap was abhorrent to her.

Sleep with a man after he gives you a thousand dollar necklace, and you're a girlfriend. Sleep with a man after he gives you a thousand dollars *in cash*, and you're a prostitute, and can be arrested. Sleep with *ten men*, simultaneously, for a thousand dollars in cash—as long as this encounter is being filmed—and you're a porn star, doing nothing illegal. And sleep with a man, not for money, but for information or leverage at the behest of a spy agency, and you're considered by many to be a hero. By the same people who would arrest you if you screwed the same man for money rather than secrets. Human behavior was never dull, that was for sure.

But knowing she had fallen for Theo Grant's charming act was filling her with hatred and bile. He had studied her. Sized her up.

Of course they were compatible. Of course he shared her interests. He had made *certain* of it.

She had begun to view him as quite possibly the perfect man for her. She should have known that when someone seemed too good to be true . . .

And now, learning that she was simply a mark he had targeted, twisted every positive feeling she had for him into its grotesque, funhouse mirror image. The more delighted she had been by his praise, the more disgusted she now was with herself for having fallen for it. The more she had liked him then, the more she *despised* him now.

And she had liked him more than she cared to admit, even to herself. Hell hath no fury like a woman scorned. But she had been scorned in the past, and what she was feeling now made the fury she had felt then *pale* by comparison.

"So who is this . . ." she paused and considered several choice expletives, but managed to retain enough of her professionalism not to use them. "Person of interest?"

"When you set up a date with him, our computers automatically took note and ran his face through all the databases. He didn't show up anywhere, which is almost impossible in this day and age. So he was flagged for human eyes. And he was identified. We're not sure how the computers missed him, but since he's someone I had tracked previously, the identification ended up on my desk."

Elovic changed his position at the conference table and locked his eyes onto Alyssa's. "His real name is Brennan Craft. He grew up in Clearlake, Iowa."

"Brennan?"

"Usually it's a last name. But it's not unheard of as a first. He goes by Bren."

Alyssa nodded. *So long forever, Theo Grant*, she thought angrily. *You and Brennan Craft can both burn in hell.*

7

Al Yad had had no trouble moving into his new headquarters, trading in his tent for a residence kings of old would envy. As he had expected, President Khalil Najjar was too much of a simpering coward to attempt to block the move. But in this case, cowardice happened to be good judgment, since he now had an inkling of Al Yad's capabilities, and didn't know who he could trust in his own military.

Despite the opulence of his residence, which was nothing less than a palace, Al Yad had chosen to continue his theme of simplicity and purity. He allowed no fountains or statuary of any kind. His furnishings were simple and few, and everything around him was white, including his robes and headdress.

He had been meeting in the palace's main chamber with a man named Ahmad, one of His most trusted lieutenants, for almost an hour, reviewing mundane items such as the number of new followers, logistical concerns, and his financial holdings.

Al Yad's wealthy followers provided a forty percent tithe to him, and he was certain they considered this their greatest honor. What man wouldn't be honored to be of service to the Great One, to an appendage of Allah on earth.

Even though Al Yad could increase his funds by calling upon his grateful followers at any time, Ahmad thought it wise for him to keep track of his holdings and investments. But the *smallness* of the exercise was becoming infuriating to him. It was beneath him. He was a *god*, and shouldn't have to deal with such mundane matters.

But what was really getting under his skin, rubbing his every nerve raw, was that he was still unable to fulfill his divine destiny. He had spent more and more time thinking, deploying men around the globe, weighing options, but until he solved the ultimate thorn in his side, he couldn't unleash his true and terrible might on the world.

Allah had often extolled the virtue of patience, and Al Yad continued to remind himself of this. And he had thrown off the shackles of his humanity to become a god, and was now immortal. So what were a few years of delay to a god? A mere blink of an eye.

Still, as Ahmad continued to ramble on, the affront of being unable to assume his rightful place atop a paradise of his own creation, respected as a god by every being on the planet, *galled* him. Finally, he could contain his justified fury no longer. "*Enough!*" he shouted, interrupting his aide in mid sentence. "These are trivialities. I need to speak of greater things."

Al Yad paused in thought. "Tell me, Ahmad, what is the mood of my followers? What is in their hearts?"

Ahmad swallowed hard. "Love and respect for you, oh Great One. They have heard your vision and witnessed your power. Your glory is on high. They dream of the promised land that you will lead them to. When you wipe the scourge of the infidel from the planet."

Al Yad found himself annoyed. Ahmad had adopted his speech patterns, which was blasphemous. As a god, he was expected to speak poetically, but as a lowly man, Ahmad would do well not to assume he could also. "And do they voice any concerns? Complaints?"

"*None*, Al Yad," said Ahmad hurriedly, as if the very thought of this was abhorrent to him. "You are the Great One. They only count their blessings that they are lucky enough to live during the age of your coming."

"You are not being honest with me, Ahmad."

Ahmad's face began to glisten from perspiration, even though the palatial room was perfectly climate controlled. He trembled, ever so slightly. "I would never lie to you, oh Great One."

"And yet men are men. They have concerns. And they have complaints. There are temptations and dark places in men's souls conjured by the king of evil to test their beliefs and resolve. So you shall tell me their chief concern, right now. Or I shall smite you where you stand. I shall crush your heart into paste."

Ahmad's tremor increased to a noticeable level. "Yes, oh Great One," he said, terror etched into every line on his face. "Just a few, a very few of them, and only on rare occasion," he began, suddenly finding it difficult to breathe. "One or two, perhaps, have wondered why we have yet to carry out your glorious vision of our future. They have seen your might and wisdom, oh Great One. And they are eager to see the world transformed as you have foretold."

And this was the crux of it, thought Al Yad. *He* could afford to be patient. *He* was a god.

But his followers wanted him to strike. And he was not about to explain to them what was holding him back. He would have to ratchet up his hold on them. He would have to make it clear that his divine judgment was *never* to be questioned. He would make it clear, violently so, that he would strike when *he* decided to strike, and not a moment sooner.

Al Yad was well aware his reputation was growing. World governments had begun to fear him. He would explain to his followers that he wished to let this fear build further. And only when it had reached its apex would he unleash his wrath upon the world.

But he would have to provide further demonstrations of his power. Make sure his followers continued to understand he expected absolute fealty, and that he saw them as insects, his to crush at his whim.

"And do you agree with them, Ahmad?" he asked evenly.

Ahmad became paralyzed. Al Yad watched him squirm, knowing he was trying to decide if this was a test. But what was being tested? His loyalty? Or his honesty? "Of course not, Great One," he said, having chosen loyalty. "I would never question The Hand of God."

Al Yad was about to respond when Tariq Bahar rushed into the chamber, narrowly missing a collision with a bird and cage sitting on a pedestal at the entrance to the room. Bahar was Al Yad's head of military and intelligence. The man had recruited a legion of mercenaries and true believers around the world, pressing them into serving the Great One.

Al Yad welcomed the sight of him. Unlike Ahmad, a simple functionary, interchangeable with thousands of others, Tariq Bahar was highly skilled, and highly useful.

"A thousand apologies, Al Yad," said Bahar. "I didn't realize you were occupied. I will come back another time."

"Speak," demanded Al Yad.

Tariq Bahar glanced meaningfully at Ahmad. "This is very exciting, but sensitive information, Great One. Perhaps it would be better if we were to speak of it alone."

Al Yad glared at the man. "I said to report," he whispered. "I won't ask again."

"We've narrowed Shaitan to a geographic territory," said Bahar without hesitation. "And we have a further lead." He went on to explain in detail, including his recommendation for how they should proceed. "Request permission to follow up personally," he finished. "Immediately."

Al Yad was pleased by the news. It still didn't solve his problem entirely, but finding his nemesis was at least a step in the right direction.

Under other circumstances, his improving mood might have saved his aide's life. But Ahmad had heard things he should not have heard. Al Yad sighed. At least the man would enter the afterlife knowing he had served him to the best of his capacity. As an example for others. What better sacrifice could a man make?

Al Yad gestured toward Tariq Bahar. "Permission granted," he said. "I know you're eager to get started, and I'm just as eager. But remain here a few moments longer."

Al Yad turned to his aide. "Ahmad, I am unhappy with your lack of faith in me," he said simply. "But there is still a way for you to help our cause."

"Anything," pleaded Ahmad.

Al Yad nodded. There was a sound like a concentrated concussive blast and Ahmad's eye's bulged from their sockets. The man clutched at his chest for just a moment before toppling to the marble floor. Bahar was startled by this event but managed to keep his face impassive.

"I burst his heart," Al Yad told his head of military and intelligence. "He doubted my judgment. He wondered why we have yet to strike at the infidel."

While this was not technically true, this narrative would better serve his needs. "Ahmad was a trusted aide, as you know. But I demand total, unquestioning loyalty," he explained. "So before you go, make sure my followers get an accurate account of what happened here. Make sure they understand the price of disbelief."

"As you command, oh Great One," said Tariq Bahar.

Al Yad gestured at Ahmad's body on the floor with a look of distaste. "And have someone clean up this mess," he said evenly.

8

So Theo Grant was really Brennan Craft, thought Alyssa. Which wasn't the least bit helpful. This name meant nothing to her.

A dozen questions ricocheted around her skull. She rose from the conference room table and pulled a bottle of water from a small refrigerator in the corner, not offering one to Major Elovic.

She returned to her chair across from the major and stared at him accusingly. "So when I was with this Craft," she said finally. "Were you listening in? Did you eavesdrop on our entire conversation?"

Elovic shook his head. "I would have liked to," he replied candidly. "But there wasn't enough time. I didn't get wind of your . . . date, until this morning."

"That still gave you plenty of time to give me a heads up," snapped Alyssa. "You knew this bastard's game and you didn't *warn* me?"

"I couldn't. I wasn't willing to risk that you might accidentally tip him off. Brennan Craft is too valuable. But rest assured, you were never in any danger. The strike team wasn't quite ready when Craft picked you up, but we were confident he wouldn't try anything—at least until he brought you back to your house."

Alyssa tore the cap from the bottle of water and took an angry gulp. They were *confident*. How very comforting.

"And you did a great job of distracting him while we prepared," added the major.

Yeah, she thought wryly, she was distracting him. *That* was her goal. Anything for her country, even when she didn't know she was doing it.

And she was never in any danger? That was the most ridiculous statement she had ever heard. According to the major, neither was Craft. Until all hell broke loose. And barely surviving a curtain of bullets being sent in her direction didn't qualify as danger-free.

Alyssa glared at Elovic for several long seconds, but decided not to confront him. "So tell me about this Brennan Craft."

"Uneventful childhood. His dad died when he was fourteen, and his mother raised him after that. Good kid. Brilliant. One of only four kids from Iowa to get a perfect score on his SATs the year he took them. As far as we can tell, well adjusted and stayed out of trouble." He paused. "Loved physics and science and was accomplished in these disciplines, even in his early teens. And a computer programming prodigy. The Mozart of computer code. Could have gone to Harvard or MIT. Any guesses where he did go?"

Alyssa shook her head. "Not a one."

"The theological seminary. To become a Catholic priest."

This did take her by surprise. "No kidding?"

"No kidding. But this was where he began causing trouble. Near as we can reconstruct, he went into the seminary because he was raised a devout Catholic, and his mother always dreamed her son would be a priest. By all accounts he was very spiritual as well. So when he promised her on her death bed to go into the priesthood, he followed through, even though we believe he had reservations."

"So far you're not exactly painting the picture of America's Most Wanted here."

"He butted heads with the establishment almost immediately. He wrote letters asking the church to seriously consider abolishing the no sex, no marriage rule of the priesthood."

"Was he having an affair at the time?" asked Alyssa.

"We don't think so. But we know he was brilliant and quickly became versed in all aspects of the science of human sexuality. He argued that science had shown the criticality of forging physical relationships in achieving a healthy brain chemistry. Infants not touched enough growing up became severely damaged. Not just sex, but even touch, releases all kinds of chemicals and has all kinds of effects on the brain. I read his letters, but I don't remember the chemistry and neurology he cited." He raised his eyebrows. "I imagine you're familiar with this data, though."

"Yes. And I agree with him. The running joke is that the lack of sex makes people more intense, winds them up, messes with their heads. But it's not a joke. It's a critical need, and in my view, something whose contribution to the human condition and mental health can't be minimized."

Major Elovic smiled. "You and Brennan Craft really do have a lot in common," he said.

"No we don't!" snapped Alyssa angrily. "He just made sure he filled out his online dating profile to match my interests. The match was too good to have been real."

"That's the odd thing," said the major, tilting his head. "It *was* real. Craft misled you about his intentions, but as far as I can tell, not about his interests and the personality type he prefers. He may have been using you, but you two really are highly compatible. At least on paper."

Alyssa scowled, unsure if this information made her feel better or worse.

"With respect to the abolishment of celibacy rules," continued Elovic, repositioning himself in the black mesh office chair in which he was sitting, "Craft also laid out a comprehensive argument that this policy might have the unintended effect of attracting those struggling with their sexuality."

"In what way?"

"He argued that young men who were devout and spiritual like he was, but who had a healthy appetite for sex, and a desire to have a family someday, would be less likely to go into the seminary with the celibacy rule in place. For some this would be one sacrifice too many. But imagine a young man who had an *unhealthy* interest in young children, and who was trying to suppress this. This man might see taking a vow of celibacy as a tool to help him battle these inner demons. And not always successfully."

"I see," said Alyssa. It was an interesting thesis. Even if this were true only one percent of the time, it would lead to an enrichment of this type in the institution. And denying members something that was so integral to the human condition, with known mental and physical health benefits, was likely to result in any number of unintended consequences.

"I'm not really doing his arguments justice," added Elovic. "Craft is a brilliant writer and logician, and he was very persuasive."

"Did the church take him seriously?"

"Not so much. Finally, frustrated that he couldn't at least get a hearing, or generate more of a debate within the church, he left. After only being a priest for eighteen months."

Elovic walked to the refrigerator and removed a bottle of water of his own. "But he didn't lose his virginity until a month after he left the church," he said, as he closed the refrigerator door. "I have to give him that. He may not have agreed with celibacy, but he apparently stuck by it."

"Now how would you possibly know when he lost his virginity?" asked Alyssa.

"He wrote about it. Tried to continue the argument on a personal blog, but got nowhere with that as well."

"Now that is a blog I'd like to see," said Alyssa, smiling for the first time since the attack on her home. Her bitter demeanor was finally retreating. She was relatively cheerful and full of humor by nature, and could only maintain a state of rage for so long.

"I'll e-mail the link to you," said the major. "But Craft described his first sexual encounter as utterly mind-blowing. Earth-shattering. Life affirming."

Alyssa couldn't help but wonder what this enthusiastic encounter had been like for the *woman* involved, whom Craft had clearly made the center of the universe after denying himself for so long. It might have been awful, but she suspected it had been amazing.

"Meanwhile, he began taking classes in quantum physics," continued the major, having returned to his seat. "Didn't care about a degree, but by all accounts became an expert. World class in the field."

"I guess quantum mechanics is an interest we really do have in common," noted Alyssa. "Although he pretended to only have a layman's knowledge of it, like I do."

Elovic scratched his head. "So what is that, exactly?" he said. "Craft was at the top of the field, so I should probably at least know the gist of it."

"Even after reading several books on the subject," said Alyssa, "a gist is about all I can give you." She paused to gather her thoughts. "First, you should know it's the most successful theory in the history of science. It's predictions have been verified over and over with uncanny accuracy. And something like thirty percent of our economy stems from our knowledge of this field. Computers, cell phones, MRIs, lasers. You name it."

Elovic leaned back in his chair with a thoughtful expression.

"Relativity works in the realm of the large. It deals with gravity and mass and speed. Quantum mechanics deals with the very small. Elementary particles. Like electrons. Both paint a picture of a universe that seems ridiculous. Crazier than something out of a fantasy novel."

"For instance?" prompted Elovic.

"Relativity shows that as an object speeds up, time itself passes more and more slowly for it. At the speed of light, time stops altogether."

"You're right. It does sound like something some crazy person made up."

"It's been confirmed beyond a shadow of a doubt. Time moves at a different rate for our GPS satellites in orbit than it does down here. Einstein's equations correct for this discrepancy. Perfectly. This really is how the universe works. The reason it's so counterintuitive is that we'd have to travel millions and millions of times faster than we do to notice it." She paused. "As for quantum effects, these are best experienced at the subatomic level. Another realm for which humans have no exposure or experience."

She tilted her head in thought. "It's like a fish professor teaching other fish—you know, a *school* of fish," she added, grinning at her own joke, "his theory of air. The fish instructor could prove it all he wanted, but no matter how smart a fish, the concept would always be counterintuitive to a creature who had only ever experienced water."

"Good analogy," said Elovic.

Alyssa took a deep breath. Quantum theory was all but impossible to explain well in a short time. It didn't make a lick of sense. It was so crazy it made relativity look sane.

She began by describing what many believed to be the most important experiment ever done in the field: the double slit experiment.

Cut two slits side by side in a metal plate, and put a screen behind the plate. Now send a stream of photons through the slits, and observe the light pattern you get on the screen.

If the photons behaved like particles, you would expect to see two lines on the screen, right behind the two slits. If the photons behaved like waves, the peaks and troughs of the waves traveling through the two slits would interfere with each other, and create a pattern more like a barcode. It was a very simple experiment, and it was expected to yield a very simple result.

But it didn't. It yielded an *impossible* result.

If you did the experiment, you got a wave pattern. A barcode. Fair enough. But if you shot electrons through—or any other particles, for that matter—*one at a time*, you *still* got a wave pattern.

This just wasn't possible. How could photons interfere with each other if they were going through the slits single file? A single photon or electron couldn't split, go through both slits as a wave, and interfere with *itself*. Yet it did.

Stranger still, if you tried to cheat by *watching* the slits to catch photons splitting and going through both, they *didn't* anymore. Suddenly, you got the two-line pattern characteristic of particles. Nature seemed to know when you were looking.

This was only the beginning of the crazy effects of quantum mechanics. Particles could be joined, entangled, and have some kind of instantaneous metaphysical connection, even across the entire universe. Particles could be at an infinity of places at once, and popped into and out of existence randomly, creating a froth of particles and energy in the vacuum of space.

The longest-standing theory to account for this was that a particle could be *anywhere* until it was observed. When it was, it immediately *collapsed* to a discrete location. On some level, the reality of the universe depended on conscious observers.

The implications of this had been causing physicists to pull out their hair for over a century, and called into question humankind's fundamental understanding of the nature of reality. If an observer could alter the universe by his observation, then didn't the universe *require* consciousness to even exist?

When Alyssa had finished her brief explanation, like everyone else ever introduced to the subject, Elovic had trouble believing it. But she knew that further explanation wouldn't help. It was time to get back to Brennan Craft.

"You said Craft became an expert in quantum physics," said Alyssa. "According to whom?"

"According to everybody. The people at all the top universities are familiar with his work. Many call it groundbreaking."

"And he never got a formal degree?"

"No."

Alyssa considered this. Craft was clearly a once-in-a-generation intellect. Reaching the pinnacle of a scientific field like quantum mechanics without any formal training was almost unheard of.

"During this time he also whipped up a computer algorithm," continued Elovic. "I won't describe what it did, because I don't quite understand it. But suffice it to say it was a breakthrough in data handling, analysis, and storage. Which he sold to Eben Martin."

"*The* Eben Martin?" said Alyssa. "The billionaire?" But even as she said it she knew it was a dumb question. He was the only *Eben* she had ever heard of—which he pronounced *ehben*, with a soft *E*.

"Yes, except he wasn't a billionaire then. Eben Martin founded Informatics Solutions based on Craft's algorithm. Craft didn't want money. Instead, he received shares in Informatics Solutions. A year later he cashed them in for fifty million dollars."

Alyssa's mouth fell open. "Fifty million dollars?" she repeated.

"Maybe I should have said, *only* fifty million dollars. Had he waited a few years longer, his stock would have been worth *billions*."

"And he pretended to be poor," mumbled Alyssa.

"He didn't make you pick up the check, did he?" said Elovic wryly.

Not waiting for a response, he continued. "So after becoming an acknowledged leader in the field, and then in his spare time creating intellectual property that set him up for life, Craft suddenly went silent. We think this is when he began going off the rails. We suspect schizophrenia, like the Unabomber, who was an unparalleled mathematical genius before he became paranoid and delusional. Anyway, Craft began reading numerous spiritual and metaphysical texts. He emerged a few years later as a disciple of a scientist named Bernard Haisch."

Alyssa looked at him questioningly.

"In addition to being a highly accomplished scientist, well published and well respected, Haisch wrote a book in 1997 called *The God Theory*. Craft became enthralled with this theory."

"Was Haisch trying to start his own religion?"

"No. He just wrote a book with his ideas. Why?"

"You used the word, *disciple.*"

"You're right. Student might be better. And actually, since Craft never even met this Haisch, student isn't right either. Let's say proponent. Believer."

"The God Theory?"

"Yeah. I haven't read it, but I'm told it has something to do with all of us being a part of God. That we and the universe are a result of subtraction rather than addition. I don't know it well enough to do it justice, but I do know Craft fell for it in a big way."

The major downed the last of his water and placed the empty bottle on the table. "And then, inexplicably, he spent two years immersed in the world of something called *Inedia*. Have you heard of it?"

"No."

"It's Latin for 'fasting.' People who subscribe to this—I'm going to call it, cult, for want of a better word—believe that food isn't really necessary. Reportedly, Inedia adherents have fasted for decades and are still alive and kicking."

"Don't you think they're probably, you know . . . *cheating* now and then," said Alyssa, rolling her eyes.

"I do, yes. But people into this sort of thing swear they know of cases that were documented and carefully monitored. Another term for this phenomenon is *Breatharianism*. Whatever you call it, they believe that there is no need for traditional nutrition. That they can be sustained by light alone, or through something called *prana*, which I understand is the vital life force from Hinduism."

"Okay, so first The God Theory, then fasting. So the guy has some eclectic interests, that appear to be getting stranger and stranger."

"But this last interest he acted on," noted Elovic. "He began fasting himself. Had to be rushed to the emergency room several times over a period of six months and given IV's or he would have died."

"Sort of disproved the subject of his fascination, didn't he?"

"You would think. But you'd be wrong. Because after this, he traveled the globe—ending up in Afghanistan, of all places—seeking out people who had reportedly survived extended fasts. We've done some research, and let me tell you, some of these fasters were beyond lunatics. Saying they were delusional, deranged, schizophrenic—whatever—would be being very generous."

"But that didn't dissuade this Craft."

"Not a bit. He spent years at this. Probably because he had become totally unhinged himself."

Alysssa frowned. "He may be unhinged, but he can fool you. He seemed to me to be the most together man I have ever met. Sane, rational, charming."

"A lot of people who are seriously delusional can pull this off when pursuing a goal. Suppress their crazy, so to speak." Elovic paused. "We know he also purchased a number of very expensive scales. The kind that weigh fractions of ounces. So maybe he was selling drugs as well. Not exactly unheard of in Afghanistan," noted the major. "We only found out any of this after he became a person of interest. None of his activities that I've described would warrant any attention from us."

"So what did put him on your radar?"

"You ever hear of someone named Omar Haddad?"

"Am I supposed to have?"

"No. Stupid question. There is no way you could have. He's Syrian. Saying that his past is unremarkable would be giving him too much credit. But recently he's been going by two names. *The Great One.* And *Al Yad.* Which translates to *The Hand,* by the way. Short for *The Hand of Allah.* I'm told *yad* means hand in Hebrew as well as Arabic."

"Sounds like a real nut job."

"Yes. But a nut job whose power and influence is growing at unprecedented speed. He's gathered a huge following. It is our understanding that the Syrian government is considering asking for our help to rein him in."

"You're kidding, right? The Syrians asking their least favorite country, the Great Satan, to help them? With a domestic dispute? Why would they need help reining in one of their own?"

"We don't know. But reports are that they've tried themselves. We aren't clear on all of the details, but Al Yad has them spooked. And given his speedy rise to prominence, he has us spooked also. His followers really do think he's divine, either a messiah or some kind of extension of god. His rhetoric is off the charts. He will destroy the West, destroy the infidels. The streets will run with blood. He will cleanse the population, and only those who accept him as the Hand of God will be allowed to live as he reshapes the planet to his whim. That sort of thing."

The major leaned in toward Alyssa. "He's now the State Department's number one priority. We don't know what to make of him, but people are scared. And I mean terrorists in Syria. Terrified of him."

"Has he committed any major terrorist acts?"

"That's just it. None. At least none of which we're aware. And this makes no sense given his following. And his rhetoric, which is so venomous he makes Hitler look like a tree-hugging pacifist. We've been pulling out the stops to get a handle on him, and we've gotten nowhere. We've heard rumors, but no one has gotten near him. I can't go into all of our eyes-only intel, but he has a lot of people very worried."

"So what has this got to do with Craft?"

"Maybe nothing. Maybe everything. In researching Haddad's past, pulling satellite surveillance imagery looking for him before he showed up on the international scene as Al Yad, we found a number of shots with him and Craft together. Seems they were buddies."

Alyssa pondered this for several seconds. "So you see Craft as a way to get a handle on this Al Yad? The only way right now?"

"Exactly. The man you just went out with. The man who miraculously slipped our net at your house. He might just be the key to unlocking the enigma that Omar Haddad—Al Yad—represents."

The major frowned and blew out a long breath. "And if even a fraction of the rumors we've heard about this Al Yad are true, he's the most dangerous man on the planet."

9

Brennan Craft raced through the woods that abutted the home of Alyssa Aronson.

Wow, that was really, really stupid, he thought, but in an effort to stay centered he forced a wry smile on his face and tried not to beat up on himself. *Okay, so I'm not perfect. If I were, life wouldn't be nearly as interesting.*

This pep talk didn't help as much as he had hoped. Telling himself not to worry about this mistake couldn't entirely divorce him from the reality of normal human wiring.

It was so obvious in retrospect. *Of course* the clandestine services were going to monitor key members with top-secret clearance who put their profiles, fabricated or otherwise, on wide open dating sites. And who could blame them, really? You'd have to be suspicious of strangers trying to work their way into the lives of key personnel, hoping to gain leverage, exploit them, or learn secrets. Had he thought he was the only one who ever had this idea?

Stupid!

He forced himself to look on the bright side. He had chosen Alyssa Aronson because of the handful of those with her expertise, she was the one he thought he could get close to. Develop a relationship with. And he had been right. He had truly hit the jackpot.

Their date could not have gone better. Within a few weeks he had no doubt he could have won her trust, and then confided in her. Made her an ally.

But now . . . .

Now she would be wary of him. No, that wasn't strong enough. She would likely *hate* him.

Even so, he took their compatibility as a sign. They were meant to work together.

But he had certainly made things more challenging for himself.

The powers that be had thought he was dead. Now they knew he wasn't. The good news is that he had hacked all the right computers and changed the software for the government's biometric algorithms. He knew the exact pattern of his face—the features, skin texture, and so on—to which the recognition software would respond.

So he didn't modify the endless cameras operating around the country—that would have been impossible. And he didn't remove himself from the system. His face was very much present. He just made a subtle change in coding so that any image of him that would otherwise score a hit in the system would be corrupted just enough to miss matching up. And even now, when they realized he had done this, he was confident they would never be able to find the subtle change he had made.

But while he had reprogrammed computer recognition software, he couldn't reprogram the human brain. He was still vulnerable to a single pair of eyes.

Still, the people chasing him had become too reliant on traffic cams, store cams, and the like to help catch their prey. Which meant they'd be unlikely to send their people to areas they could easily surveil with cameras. So if he stayed in plain sight of cameras at all time, he had less chance of running into a pair of eyes that could identify him.

Craft emerged from the woods and checked his phone to get his bearings. He had made a major blunder, but he was confident he could find a way to recover. And while he had been running through the woods he had devised a plan.

He walked to a nearby diner and called a cab, which he instructed to take him to Indianapolis International Airport a little less than an hour away. When he arrived, he paid his fare, smiled, and entered the terminal, where he purchased clothing at a small shop, and changed into it.

He then rented a car under an assumed name, secure in the knowledge that his computer tampering would make certain this didn't trigger any alarms.

Less than an hour later he was parked in a lot at Indiana University, a heavily wooded campus with magnificent limestone buildings that wouldn't have looked out of place at Hogwarts. They would expect him to flee. Instead, he would stay right in the heart of Bloomington.

But he wasn't doing this for tactical reasons only. He still had his sites on Alyssa Aronson and wanted to be very close. And he needed access to the most advanced computer in the region, which was certainly at the university. Named Big Red II, IU's supercomputer was housed in their Cyber Infrastructure Building, and possessed an incomprehensible processing speed of one thousand trillion floating-point operations per second.

Within minutes Craft had located one of three computer rooms on campus, filled with dozens of terminals tied into the central university computer. Craft could tap into Big Red II from the central computer without much difficulty. There were large windows encircling the room, making it somewhat of a fishbowl, but this couldn't be helped.

Only a handful of students were scattered around the room on this Saturday afternoon—most of the terminals were empty. The door was locked, requiring a keycard for entry. Craft rapped on the door repeatedly until the closest student, an unshaven young man wearing a gold and blue sweatshirt that read *Alpha Epsilon Pi*, finally responded, and pulled open the door.

"Hi," said Brennan Craft. "I'm visiting my nephew. He's working on a group project in the next building over."

The student's eyes narrowed, and Craft knew he wanted him to get to the point.

"Anyway," continued Craft, "for some reason my phone isn't connecting to the web. Would you mind letting me in to work on a computer while I wait for him to finish up?"

"Sure," said the kid amicably. "But you won't be able to access anything without a student ID and password."

Craft smiled. He had no doubt he could hack onto these terminals in short order. "Actually, I know Luke's—my nephew's—password. So I'll be okay."

The student shrugged and opened the door wider so Craft could enter.

Craft chose the most isolated work station he could find, one with a monitor that couldn't be seen from outside of the room. He knew it would take some time for him to accomplish all of his goals. As good as he was with computers, there were still limits.

But he had no doubt that if he stayed steady, he would end up where he needed to be. Within a day or two, he would be able to co-opt DOD and NSA computers to allow him to conduct surveillance on Alyssa Aronson. Track her. Learn even more about her. Find out how her superiors were reacting to his reemergence.

NSA computers were the best protected in the world. But he had hacked them before, and he was one of only a few people in the world skilled enough to leave a hidden passageway back inside. One capable of surviving countless security scans and updates.

Even so, he would have to dig in at his current location. First hacking the university computer to create a skeleton passkey and parking permit, and then using the offices of professors on sabbatical. He could bring in bedding and food late at night, and could use the university's public restrooms to brush his teeth. But he also suspected he could find a building with at least one private shower. It was just a matter of hacking all of the floor plans.

He would sleep here, shower here, and eat here. But mostly, he would work here. Tirelessly. He had dug himself a hole, and he would find a way to dig out of it. He would track Alyssa Aronson and carefully determine his next course of action.

And he would learn about the recent activities of a man named Omar Haddad. Craft knew he had screwed up. Huge.

But now it was time to find out if his blunder had awakened just one sleeping giant. Or two.

10

Alyssa Aronson left the major in her conference room while she used the restroom.

She had finally learned what the raid on Craft had been about. Elovic had desperately wanted to interview him in the hope of getting a handle on this Al Yad character. But the major hadn't been at all certain Craft could help him. Elovic had just *hoped* he could. So could this really justify his actions?

She returned to the conference room and retrieved a second bottle of water from the refrigerator. It had been a very long day. Without any hyperbole, the most eventful in her entire life. Getting snatched from her porch, being witness to a special forces raid on her lawn, and getting shot, each, by itself, would have qualified the day for this distinction.

When Alyssa returned to her spot across from the major, he was studying his phone, but quickly returned it to his pocket and faced her.

Alyssa sighed. "Okay," she said. "So let me get this right. You need to speak with Craft and find out what he knows about Al Yad. But Craft, himself, hasn't done anything wrong or illegal. Correct?"

Elovic nodded. "For that matter, we aren't aware of any terrorist acts committed by Al Yad. But so what? Hitler was still Hitler before he invaded Poland. It's going to happen. And when it does, it's going to happen in a very big, very dramatic way."

"You changed the subject, Major. I was talking about Craft. You've made it very clear why this Al Yad person is important. But what happened this afternoon at my house—this is the kind of thing that gives the Black Ops, and the military, a bad name. And bad isn't even the right word. Look, I'm furious that Brennan Craft tried to use me. But unless I missed something, he's a US citizen, and doesn't even have an outstanding *parking* ticket. Yet he found himself the target of a special ops commando team, *on domestic soil.* Is there any way to abuse power, or a US citizen, any more absolutely?"

Elovic shook his head. "It wasn't supposed to go down like this. Really. We were going for containment. I don't know how it got out of hand. And I do realize, even containment was pushing it."

"You think?"

"But if things had gone according to plan," said the major. "If no shots had been fired, and we just had a conversation with him . . . . I mean, at some point, the ends do justify the means. This Al Yad is going to kill many thousands—possibly many *millions*—if we don't get a handle on him. I can *feel* it."

"Even though he hasn't committed any terrorist acts as of yet?"

"We don't know what he's waiting for. Which in some ways is even more worrisome than if he *had* been committing terrorist acts. We're somehow missing the big picture. But the carnage will come. This guy is too deranged, and too reckless, for it not to."

Alyssa found herself not easily swayed by the *ends justify the means* argument. How many atrocities had been papered over using this same argument?

"And there is something else," continued the major. " Something that, even if Al Yad wasn't in the picture, could justify us forcing a conversation with Brennan Craft."

"What's that?"

"When we were getting information on Craft, we uncovered some of his Internet search history in the cloud. He's done a lot of research lately into world governments. Autocracies, totalitarian regimes, theocracies, and democracies. He's studied revolutions. How to topple governments in the most efficient manner. Weak spots. Tipping points. How to manage governments with the fewest people. As though he were preparing to take over the entire world with minimal resources and organization."

"Are you *sure* you're not just making this up as you go along?" muttered Alyssa sarcastically. "Let me make sure I have everything. Brennan 'Bren' Craft goes from brilliant scientist high schooler to reluctant priest," she began, ticking each point off on her fingers. "From there to quantum physics genius. During which time he uses his software skills to become a multimillionaire. Followed immediately by disciple of The God Theory." She tilted her head in thought, making sure she wasn't missing anything. "And then, that fasting thing."

"In-E-dia," said Elovic.

"Right. Inedia. Craft then becomes an Inedia disciple, almost dying several times in the process. Finally, he's a buddy of a self-proclaimed god. Long before this god is on anyone's radar screen. Then Craft follows all of this up by becoming a student of all political systems and the best way to topple them. Have I missed anything?"

"No. You summed it up nicely. The guy is delusional, but you can't say he's not brilliant. Or that he's boring. He seems to go from one freaky pursuit to another, without rhyme or reason."

"Is that everything?" said Alyssa with a crooked smile. "He's not the star of his own reality television show or anything, is he?"

Elovic ignored her sarcasm. "There's more that we know about him, but I've covered the important details."

"So his angle has to be hypnosis, right?" said Alyssa. "He suddenly developed a thing for it. After everything else he's been interested in, why not? How did he find out who I am, and what I do?"

The major shook his head. "Good question. It's not impossible to do, but it's very, very difficult."

"So he wanted access to some of the narco-hypnotics I've helped develop, and access to my results. But instead of kidnapping me and holding me at gunpoint, why try a . . ." she paused. She really did detest, not just the concept, but even the phase, *Honey Trap*. "Why try the romantic angle?"

"You get more comprehensive, and more reliable, information with sugar than with vinegar," he replied simply. "But while Craft has been able to accomplish things that would make a master spy envious, approaching you like this on a dating site is a stupid move. Strictly amateur hour. Anyone who knows anything at all about this game would know we'd be monitoring this approach."

Alyssa frowned. "You mean, other than the hopelessly naive like me?"

Elovic clenched his teeth. "Sorry," he said, forgetting this had been news to her, as well. "But the point still applies."

"Okay. So he wanted to get the most reliable information. But even if I gave him everything, told him everything, this helps him very little."

"We know he was researching—as ridiculous as this sounds—world domination. He must think your narco-hypnotics can help. You know, Manchurian Candidate style."

Alyssa frowned. "Hypnosis is the most mythologized, exaggerated, exploited, overhyped, and over conspiracy-theoried branch of science ever," she said passionately. "Yes, my group is trying to improve it and perfect it for certain uses. But as you well know, Major, it only works on *willing* subjects. You still can't make someone do something against their own self-interest. And you can't make a person do something that he doesn't already want to do. If a man wants to lose his fear of flying, we can now make this happen with absolute perfection. As long as he really wants this to happen. But we can't make him kill his wife."

"Well, assuming he . . . you know, is *against* that."

Alyssa laughed. She didn't think Elovic had it in him to make a joke, and a successful one at that. "You can't even make him cluck like a chicken if he doesn't want to. So you certainly can't hypnotize him to become a traitor to his country. With the proper drugs and electrical brain stimulation, we can greatly enhance behaviors a subject *wants* to acquire. But you can't use hypnotism to turn someone into a zombie slave, despite what the sensationalism of the Internet, movies, and conspiracists would have you believe." She shook her head. "Craft must have had another motive."

"No he didn't. He's delusional, remember? He probably bought all of the Manchurian Candidate stuff hook, line, and sinker. We both know the science isn't there. Yet. But Craft doesn't know that."

Alyssa pursed her lips and shook her head firmly. "You didn't just have lunch with him. He is very impressive. And from the background you've given me, not only is he absolutely brilliant, but he does his homework. He might be delusional, but he gets his science right."

Elovic shrugged. "You may be right, but I can't think of any other explanation for his interest in the field."

"Me either," said Alyssa. She took a deep breath. "So now what?"

"We can't be sure," said Elovic. "But now that his Romeo approach failed," he continued, and Alyssa couldn't help but cringe as he said this, "he'll likely go to plan B."

Alyssa looked confused. "Plan B?"

"I think he'll try to take you by force."

She barely kept her mouth from falling open. "You've got to be joking. After you attacked him at my house? No way."

Elovic shook his head. "Craft needs you. We don't know why, but he went to heroic efforts to make the play he just made. He took a lot of chances to resurface in Bloomington, Indiana just to ask you on a date. I've researched his past. Here's someone who became interested in fasting and almost killed himself, twice, trying to mimic a few crackpots. He's as stubborn as he is delusional. And for some reason, you're important to him. I don't think he'll give up. I could well be wrong, but I think we need to plan accordingly."

Alyssa's stomach tightened. Would Craft really try to take her? And if so, for what purpose? The scariest thing about it was that a raving lunatic didn't have to have a rational purpose for the things he did.

She eyed the major anxiously. "So how do you plan to prevent this," she asked.

"I don't," said Major Greg Elovic, the hint of a sly smile coming over his face. "I plan to let him," he finished simply.

11

The nice thing about being holed up for an extended period, thought Brennan Craft, was that it gave one plenty of time to plan. And to think.

And he had done a considerable amount of both while at IU, in between plumbing the depths of the State Department's knowledge of Al Yad, and learning more about Alyssa Aronson.

He had been borrowing the office of a Professor Sumner Saeks for several days now while Saeks was at a chemical engineering conference, and had hijacked his desktop computer, which was now a conduit to the IU supercomputer as well as other, supposedly, well defended computers around the world.

He had also gradually discovered the best way to live as a shadow in the belly of the beast. He had learned where to find private showers, when to take them, and had managed to maintain high standards of personal hygiene.

He had just a few more things he wanted to accomplish before his reunion with Alyssa Aronson. But this reunion wouldn't be far off. It *couldn't* be far off.

A message came in through his secure e-mail address. He clicked on it eagerly, and began reading:

The great Brenan Craft. I'll be damned! How the hell are you?

I have to admit to being surprised and thrilled—overjoyed—to hear from you. I had heard through the grapevine that you had been killed four months ago. What a relief to learn that this report proved to be, shall we say, less than accurate.

And not to worry, you put plenty in your comprehensive message to convince me this is really you. Not to mention that you're the only one who could have hacked into my secure e-mail address to leave this message in the first place.

With respect to the contents of your message, they were beyond remarkable, beyond incredible, as you well know. Earth-shattering isn't a strong enough word. If this had come from any other man I wouldn't buy any of it, no matter what . . . but because it's you—what can I say? I'm prepared to be blown away.

I cannot wait to meet up with you—as soon as you give the word. In the meanwhile, I will do exactly as you ask. If you need anything else, it goes without saying that there is nothing I won't do for you.

Your friend,
Eben Martin

Brennan Craft nodded to himself. He still wasn't sure if he had set the correct steps in motion when he had written Eben Martin, but he had known there would be no turning back after he had hit the send button.

But prior to this he had done his homework. He had hacked Martin's private computer, read his e-mails, his notes, and about his activities. Just to learn what the man was like now. It had been a long time since he had communicated with Martin, and Craft wanted to get a feel for how his status of billionaire and industry titan might have changed him.

He wondered if his decision would end up being brilliant or disastrous. Given how badly he had blundered with Alyssa Aronson, he had lost a measure of confidence in himself. But only time would tell. There were just too many unknowns to even hazard a guess as to how things might turn out.

But no matter what, he had just introduced a huge variable into his ever-evolving strategic calculations.

12

Alyssa Aronson couldn't believe her ears. She glared at the Black Ops major across from her. It was Saturday, and no one had come in to disturb them. Alyssa wondered if Elovic had put out the word to the researchers that any pressing work they had could wait until Monday.

"Did you just say you plan to let Craft abduct me?" said Alyssa. "By force? Please tell me I heard that wrong."

"You just told me there was no way he'd come back for you. So you have nothing to worry about."

"Probably not. But if you *are* right, I'd like to think you don't see me as expendable."

"Expendable?" said Elovic in surprise. "Not at all. More like *invaluable*."

Alyssa digested this for a moment. "Regardless, are you telling me that if Craft tries to abduct me, you won't lift a finger to stop him?"

The major shook his head. "Of course we will. We can't make it look *too* easy. After the raid at your house, he knows we're on to him. So he'll expect us to heighten security around you. If we made the bait look too easy, he'd suspect a trap. Having you wear a sign that says, 'here I am, please kidnap me' would probably tip him off."

"I can't tell you how much I love the idea of being referred to as bait," she said.

"Look, no matter what, we'll have a homing beacon on you. And a bug. You'll be as safe as you can possibly be. And you think I'm wrong anyway. Maybe I am."

Alyssa looked at the major in disgust

"You said yourself he's never broken a law," continued Elovic. "So kidnapping you would be out of character for him. And we've seen that he doesn't kill, even under extreme provocation."

"So far. But then again, you don't have a single clue as to what makes him tick."

"We'll have two bodyguards assigned to protect you," said Elovic. "They'll have orders to prevent you from coming to any harm. By capturing anyone trying to do so, if possible. Or by killing them, if not.

"I thought you *wanted* me abducted."

"I do. But again, we have to make it look good. And if they *can* capture Craft, which would be astonishing after the crack team I sent after him failed, this is the best outcome of all. As it is though, after the events at your house, I can't imagine Craft will have much trouble dealing with them."

"Are you telling them the end game? That you want him to take me?"

"No. Who knows, maybe they'll succeed where we failed. That would be ideal. And we need them to go to heroic measures to save you. We can't risk Craft seeing through a deception, so we'll play it straight."

"Great. I'm sure these guys will appreciate not being told what's up when their lives are on the line."

"Again, we don't know they'll be in any danger. And we'll tell them everything we know about Craft's capabilities and methods. Which isn't much. Basically, we'll tell them to be careful and be prepared for anything."

Alyssa considered. "So let's assume Craft *does* come for me. And that your men can't stop him. So then he whisks me off somewhere. What then?"

"We'll set you up with a homing device, implanted in your thigh just under the skin. Press on the right spot, and you can activate a distress signal through it. And you'll have a digital recorder you can activate at any time, with a three hour capacity. Very tiny. Neither device will trouble you at all."

"Handiwork of other Black Ops research teams?"

"Yes. Very reliable. So we'll know exactly where you are. We'll have a team poised near wherever you end up. If you're in trouble you can signal a strike." Elovic shook his head. "But I don't think this will be necessary. Because I want you to be Craft's friend. Help him. Go along with whatever he wants from you. Try to work the Honey Trap in reverse if you can."

"Sure, that'll work," said Alyssa sarcastically. "Craft knows that I'm aware of his deception on our, *supposed*, date. Then he abducts me. And then I try to *seduce* him?" She rolled her eyes. "Sure, he'll believe that."

"You'd be surprised," said Elovic. "Maybe he'll think it's the Helsinki Syndrome. Maybe he won't ask too many questions. But get him in bed if you can. It's the best way to cement trust."

Alyssa knew that this was true. Oxytocin was released during intimacy, even after a short hug, and it did induce trust.

"Pretend to be falling for him," said the major. "You can cooperate fully because he can't get your narco-hypnotic agents anyway. Even if he could, unless he knows your neuronal stimulation protocols, this won't help him. So tell him what he wants to know. Be honest. He's smart enough to see through bullshit."

Alyssa Aronson remained silent.

"Learn what you can, and we'll be waiting in the wings. We haven't been able to capture and interrogate him. But for whatever reason, he tried to play you romantically. And he failed. Now it's *your* turn."

"I'll fail as well," said Alyssa evenly.

"I'm not so sure. I told you that the two of you share eerily similar interests. And there is one other thing. If you examine his past girlfriends since he left the priesthood, which I have, you'll see that you're exactly his type. You combine the physical features and personality type he most seemed to seek out in other women."

Alyssa chewed on her lower lip as she pondered what he was asking. "And what if I refuse to prostitute myself?" she said finally. "Assuming, of course, that he does capture me."

"Obviously, there is no way we can control this. If your conscience won't allow it, so be it. Ideally, you can win his trust without sleeping with him."

"And if I refuse to be the bait?"

Elovic sighed. "You *can't* refuse," he said. "You are what you are. A wounded zebra can refuse to be a lion's prey all it wants, but that won't stop the lion. *I* didn't make you vital to Brennan Craft. He came to that conclusion on his own. And, as I've said, I'm going to honestly try to protect you. But if I fail, as I expect, I'm making your life easier. I'm not asking you to hold out. I'm asking you to tell him whatever he wants to know. To gain his trust. So you can find out what *we* want to know. About him, and about his friend the Muslim god."

Alyssa rolled her eyes as Elovic's description of Al Yad brought home the absurdity of her entire situation. How did a nice Jewish girl like her get into a mess like this? There was a great joke in there somewhere.

A Jewish girl, an ex-priest, and a Muslim god go into a bar . . . .

Her state of amusement lasted for a few seconds longer, but then quickly dissipated as she considered the job ahead.

She was still furious that she had been conned so completely. The fact that Craft had toyed with her emotions, made her fall for him, made her hopeful, and was just manipulating and using her, made her want to spit blood. Could she really put this out of her mind and pretend to fall in love with him? Sleep with him?

What the hell did he want from her? And who the hell was he to put her through all of this? *Screw him,* she thought bitterly, and became even more bitter as she realized that this sentiment could end up being more literal than figurative.

13

Lieutenant Stan Wacksman stood near the entrance to the Starbucks and marveled at the steady flow of customers that ensured the roiling line, as far as he could tell, was inexhaustible. The stream of bodies parading by represented the most eclectic group of humans he had ever seen in one place. Men and women in professional business attire, most of them yakking into their phones, stood next to joggers and bicyclists in shorts and tight lycra pants. The young and the elderly stood side by side. The clean cut and the tattoo-covered. Bubbly cheerleader personalities and Goth types alike. Multiple ethnicities. All stood together in harmony. Waiting to give their orders to the blur of green-aproned employees swarming behind the counter.

What a business, thought Wacksman enviously. So that was the secret. Serve something that was relentlessly addictive, and yet legal and socially acceptable, and shatter all class, social, geographical, and political boundaries.

Make coffee, not war, he thought, as a smile spread across his rugged face.

The sea of green employees behind the long counter worked with an efficiency that a military drill instructor would envy, and names were called out every few seconds to the gathering of lost souls who had already ordered and were milling about on the other side of the cash registers, awaiting their fixes.

Wacksman's eyes shifted from individuals in the crowd to Alyssa Aronson, and then to the outside of the store, every minute or so. His partner, Lieutenant John Gorgas, was doing the same from the other end of the store.

This was their third day on protective duty, and so far it had been uneventful. But that was the nature of protection. Days of routine and even boredom, punctuated by seconds of intense life-and-death action.

Well . . . sometimes.

The truth was that just because someone was important enough, or *at-risk* enough, to need bodyguards, didn't mean that an attack was inevitable. Actually, hostiles rarely made a play for those being protected.

He and Gorgas were more like . . . car seat-belts. The vast majority of the time they served no real purpose. Even bad drivers could go *years* between accidents. But when an accident finally did occur—in that *precise* instant—a seat-belt became the only thing standing between a chance for life and a grisly death.

Alyssa was friendly, and made their duty pleasant enough. She cooperated with their standard operating procedures and visibly fought her tendency to become frustrated and impatient with delays. Wacksman gave her a lot of credit. They had been living in a safe house while her home was undergoing repairs, and she was taking the entire situation, including her new and unfamiliar surroundings, quite well.

And while she was quite attractive, undeniably a positive in Wacksman's book, she wasn't his type. She wasn't snooty—very down to earth, actually—but she was too much on the egghead side for his taste. The way she spoke, her enormous working vocabulary and effortless sophistication with the language, made this just as clear as did her medical degree. And physically, she was a little too petite. Which was actually a *good* thing. While he'd like to believe that he was professional enough to guard a woman he found enticing without letting this distract him, every man learned at a young age that the body had a mind of its own.

They had been told that a man named Brennan Craft might come after her, and to prevent this at all cost. But they had also been given other orders, not to be shared with Alyssa Aronson, that Craft's capture was more important than *her* protection, assuming such a choice should be forced upon them. Orders that didn't sit well with Stan Wacksman. So he had spoken with Gorgas, and convinced him they had no other choice but to disregard orders they deemed to be unlawful.

Wacksman had grown up in Ohio and had signed up for ROTC while attending a small college near Cincinnati. Originally, he had set his sights set on the Air Force, since his older cousin was serving in this branch as part of a missile combat crew, a group tasked with manning nuclear missile silos around the clock. These were the soldiers who were trained to authenticate orders, and then turn a key simultaneously with a partner, to destroy the world—or at least launch a nuke that would ensure other parties continued to launch theirs, leading quickly to this outcome.

Wacksman had asked his cousin, Eli, if he would really do it. And while Eli had been carefully trained and screened to ensure he would do what was required of him, he had hedged in his answer, enough so that Stan Wacksman became convinced that he wouldn't do it, after all. That he would refuse to contribute to the almost certain extinction of the species that carrying out such orders would catalyze.

Wacksman approved. Despite occasional exceptions, sanity still seemed to reign supreme among the vast majority of those who served in the military, including, at the moment, he and his partner Lieutenant Gorgas, who weren't about to make protection of this helpless woman a secondary priority.

But while Wacksman had always imagined himself in the Air Force, he had ended up going Army instead, at the advice of his cousin, who complained that manning missile silos, despite the steady barrage of drills, could be exceedingly tedious.

It had been a great decision. Wacksman was restless, and a bit of an adrenaline junkie. And he enjoyed putting his skills to the ultimate test. He didn't drink coffee because he didn't *need* to. He was wired enough as it was.

He had served in every major terrorist theater, but was currently between assignments, so he had been tapped to protect this woman, for reasons that weren't fully disclosed. Chances were that no hostiles would move against them. But if they did, he would likely need to marshal all of his training, and all of his creativity and problem solving abilities, to come out of it alive. Matching his skills against those who would seek to challenge him, for the ultimate stakes.

Now *that* would be a rush. So while he hoped that the assignment would remain routine, he couldn't deny that a part of him wanted the chance to test his mettle.

"*Alyssa!*" shouted a young girl, holding up a Tall Cafe Mocha in an instantly recognizable Starbucks container. Alyssa Aronson broke through the milling crowd like Moses parting the Red Sea and took the proffered beverage gratefully. She took a small sip, breathed a sigh of contentment, and then headed for the exit, with Gorgas following close behind.

Both bodyguards were dressed casually and tried to blend in. But not *too* hard. They had been told that if Craft did come after her, he would expect her to be guarded, at least for a week or two, so a show of force wasn't necessarily a bad thing.

Wacksman exited the store ahead of Alyssa and his partner and surveyed the area. Nothing suspicious or out of the ordinary. He hadn't expected there to be. But he knew that in the bodyguard business, you had to be careful not to let hours and hours of tranquility seduce you into lowering your guard. He wasn't about to do so. He was exceptionally well trained and alert, and he had absolute confidence that he couldn't be taken enough by surprise for an attack to succeed. Not that he expected one to take place in the middle of the parking lot of a suburban strip mall.

They arrived at a white, four-door sedan, which sported a reinforced body and bulletproof glass, and all three approached the passenger's side. Wacksman pulled the keys from his pocket and stood near the door, with Alyssa just behind him, and John Gorgas behind her. Both men surveyed the area one last time.

Alyssa had gotten used to this routine, and waited patiently to be let into the car. The area appeared clear, as expected, and Wacksman nodded at his partner. He pulled open the door, waited for Alyssa to seat herself, and then closed it again, while Gorgas let himself into the back.

As Wacksman pulled his hand away from the door, he realized his fingers were slightly wet. He rubbed his thumb and fingers together, feeling the slippery liquid. What was that? It felt exactly like motor oil.

That was odd.

He sniffed his now amber-colored fingers, but smelled nothing.

Wacksman glanced anxiously at Lieutenant Gorgas, now seated in the car behind Alyssa. Gorgas was examining his own hand with a puzzled expression.

Wacksman's heart raced frantically as he realized the truth. The world began spinning madly around him. Waves of horror hit him like a hurricane.

He was dead! And Gorgas as well. Just like that. They both had less than a minute to live.

They had been told Craft avoided deadly force, but this intel had been utter *bullshit*.

They had been totally blindsided! Craft had used a tactic they could have never predicted. Fucking VX! The most potent nerve agent ever discovered. A nightmare substance that was rarely used even in the most desperate of war zones, because it was classified as a weapon of mass destruction, and the international backlash against those discovered using it was too great.

VX was rare in a war zone. But it was *unheard* of in the middle of Bloomington *fucking* Indiana!

An image of Nicholas Cage staring at a glass globe filled with liquid VX flashed into Wacksman's mind, from an old movie he had seen: "The second you don't respect this," Cage had said, "*it kills you.*"

It wasn't fair, thought Wacksman, a tear forming in the corner of one eye. He had *incredible* respect for this substance. But he was dead, nonetheless.

VX could be heated and turned into a gas, but was a liquid at room temperature: a liquid that was readily absorbed through the skin. Craft had coated the underside of the door handles with it.

He had watched their routine. He had known that Wacksman and Gorgas would be touching the door handles, but Alyssa would not.

The tactic was utterly *despicable*. Horrifying. It was cowardly and an atrocity, even among killers.

But it was undeniably brilliant, Wacksman couldn't help but admit. And undeniably effective.

Ironically, if he were in Iran or Syria, he would survive this attack. He had identified the VX in time to counteract it. In these theaters he would have carried an auto-injector with the antidote in his ruck sack. A combination of atropine and diazepam, which, if injected immediately, would save his life. But here in the fucking heartland of America, he had no ruck. All he had was a *Starbucks*.

I'll take an atropine and diazepam latte, he thought, beginning to lose touch with reality. *And put that in a syringe please.*

He fought to cling to rationality. To steady his spinning world.

Focus!

Even in death, he was *better* than this. He forced his panic into retreat and suddenly knew what he needed to do. He needed to open the car door again. To give Alyssa Aronson the keys. Warn her not to touch the outer door handles, and tell her to drive away as fast as possible.

But as he reached for the door the contents of his stomach exploded from his mouth and onto the pavement. He had just enough time to note that John Gorgas had begun vomiting inside the car as well, and that Alyssa Aronson's face was curled up in horror, but he was unable to even mouth the word *run* to her as his entire body began convulsing.

Seconds later, Lieutenant Stan Wacksman fell to the pavement, breaking his nose in two places.

The last thought he had, before the nerve agent induced paralysis and respiratory failure, was that he couldn't believe he was really going to die in the parking lot of a strip mall in Indiana, gasping for air in a pool of his own vomit.

14

Alyssa was too paralyzed by shock to even scream. Both of the bodyguards that had been assigned to her, men she had come to know as strong, decent human beings, were retching their guts out at the same time.

An alarm sounded in her mind, cutting through her fear and concern for these two men. Were they being gassed?

What else could explain such perfect synchronization of symptoms?

But that was impossible. One of the men was inside a closed car, and the other *outside*.

Lieutenant Wacksman crashed to the ground, hard, convulsing as he did so, and Alyssa's panic intensified further. For a moment she had thought their symptoms were akin to food poisoning, but she suddenly had an even sicker feeling that what they were experiencing was far more deadly than this.

She threw open the heavy armored door. Wacksman's fall had been hard, and he was now writhing in his own vomit. She had to help him somehow.

She pulled her phone from her pants pocket to call 9-1-1 and slid out of the car. She was about to kneel down beside the lieutenant when a large man grabbed her from behind, startling her so completely she thought her heart had stopped, and knocking her phone to the pavement.

Where had he come from?

And then she realized where. He had jumped from the side of a large white commercial van that had just arrived next to them. She had been too preoccupied to even notice.

She tried to scream, but she was feeling sleepy, and vaguely noted that a damp rag was being held over her mouth. The word *chloroform* entered her addled mind for just a moment before she blacked out and was tossed, like a chord of wood, into the back of the white van.

15

Alyssa awoke with a start and her head jerked to the side of its own volition.

The man kneeling before her removed the smelling salts he had been waving under her nose and tossed them in what looked like a medical bag.

Smelling salts? Again? How many times was she going to be snatched off the ground by a man with an iron grip this week? How many times knocked unconscious and revived with smelling salts? How had her life possibly come to this?

She was on the floor of the oversized, windowless commercial van she had seen, her back against one wall, facing the sliding door. She was unrestrained, as if her abductors didn't take her the least bit seriously as a potential threat. Blood seeped into her pant leg, and from its location, whoever had taken her had already removed the tiny transmitter that Major Elovic had implanted in her thigh.

The van wasn't moving, and Alyssa decided they must be parked. The interior was lighted, but there were no windows, so she had no idea where they were.

Two men were standing before her, watching her with great interest. Neither one was Brennan Craft, but it was likely they worked for him. One was a brute of a man, who must have been injecting steroids with a horse needle for years, and who had a face that could only be described as cruel, with soulless gray eyes that were predatory and seemed to stare right through her.

The Yin to his Yang was a short, spindly man, fastidiously dressed and manicured, clean-cut and prim, with a slight olive complexion. *GQ and Tree Trunk*, she thought. Quite a mismatched pair.

"Rise and shine," said GQ, almost cheerfully. He spoke softly with an elegant accent, but one she couldn't quite place. It was somewhere within the British accent lexicon, she thought. Something about him screamed education and refinement, and Alyssa suspected he had attended school in England, and that his accent was a mixture of his native accent, whatever that was, and the Queen's English.

"What did you do to my friends?" she demanded.

"We killed them," said the thin man matter-of-factly, and this statement brought a malicious grin to his burly associate. "VX nerve poison under the door handles," he explained. "Horrible way to go," he mused, as if talking about the weather.

"Since I didn't tell you the rules," continued GQ calmly, "I went ahead and answered your question there. But that's the last time I will. You see, we're here to learn about *you*. We're not here so that you can learn about *us*. So you can ask questions, but only to help you clarify what *we* need. Not to get information to satisfy your own curiosity. Do you understand?"

"Yes."

"Good. Because my colleague here is a sadistic bastard from the depths of hell who gets an almost sexual thrill from inflicting pain."

"Yeah. And how do you get *your* jollies?" spat Alyssa, trying to burn a hole in the back of his head with a withering glare.

Tree Trunk backhanded her across the face so hard she thought her neck might snap. She turned back in time to see a predatory delight flash across his otherwise dead eyes.

"Did you not hear the part about no more questions?" said GQ. "You even confirmed you understood." He shook his head in disappointment. "Since I'm feeling charitable, I will answer. You may have figured this out, but I'm highly educated and, at the risk of appearing immodest, quite bright. And while I'm accomplished at killing people, I prefer to use my brain. So I get my *jollies,* as you so eloquently put it, from intellectual stimulation."

He gestured to Tree Trunk. "My hired hand here is a psychopath and a sadist. Not all that educated, but what are you going to do? He's in it because the only thing better to him than torturing people, is getting paid handsomely to torture people. We make an odd team, I know, but I thought he was perfect to assist me on this job. When this man works alone, people tend to be butchered. Which is fine, unless you decide you need them again in the future. And he does tend to make a mess. So I help rein in his . . . zeal. And I'm not a fan of wet-work, which he loves. So it's a marriage made in heaven."

More like Hell, thought Alyssa, but she remained silent.

"So let's begin, shall we?" he said, and Alyssa sensed if she didn't respond Tree Trunk would make her regret it.

She managed to nod at him.

"Good," said GQ happily. "Just so you know, stalling won't do you any good. We removed your homing beacon and we've scanned for transmitting bugs. We left your cell phone back where we found you. And we've driven several hours from your favorite Starbucks, with no one following. So there won't be any rescuers coming to interrupt our festivities."

Alyssa's eyes narrowed worriedly. These people were very dangerous and very sophisticated. But who were they? They must be involved with Brennan Craft. But how?

She decided she needed to risk activating the digital recorder that the major had installed inside a small fake mole glued to her upper neck, just below her right ear. It recorded, but didn't transmit, so it was undetectable. She bent her right arm to the back of her neck, and while pretending to massage it absentmindedly managed to press down on the mole before returning her hand to her lap.

"So question number one: who are you?" said GQ.

"I'm Doctor Alyssa Aronson. I'm a professor at Indiana University, although I run a lab and don't currently teach."

"What do you study?"

"Human behavior."

GQ nodded. "Yes, I've seen your website. Interesting work, but very academic. Nothing too exciting. So what are you working on that *isn't* listed on your website?"

"Nothing else. It's all broadly summarized there."

GQ gestured slightly with his head and his partner grabbed Alyssa's arm and turned it so her hand was palm up. His other hand came across her forearm with savage speed and her blouse became wet where he had touched her.

She gasped as the pain signals from this action finally reached her brain after a moment's delay.

Tree Trunk had sliced her with an exacto knife!

He had cut through her blouse like it wasn't there and across her forearm, just under her inner elbow, and parallel to it. A deep, razor-thin line bloomed red as blood began to flow, soaking into her blouse and dripping to the floor.

"You see," said GQ apologetically. "My associate can be a bit messy. The good news is that he is as precise as a surgeon. You'll be just fine. But every time you tell me an untruth, he's going to do that again, an inch closer to your wrist. I don't know how many inches of arm you have, but when he gets to the wrist . . . ." He turned his nose up in disgust. "Well, let's just say that nobody—well, other than my associate here—really wants that."

He nodded at Tree Trunk a second time and he backhanded Alyssa viciously across the face once again, this time dazing her for several seconds. Tears came to both of her eyes and began rolling down her cheeks.

GQ eyed her tears with disapproval and nodded toward the expanding red stain on her blouse. "Careful," he said with a cheerful smile. "You don't want to leak *too* many fluids."

GQ paused, as though deciding what question to ask next, when an excited gleam came to his eyes. "Do you know what I just realized?" he said. "I just realized that I've never interrogated an expert in human behavior before. So I think I'll digress a moment from the main course. I've followed the debate about enhanced interrogation techniques with great interest. I have to say, the US government sure knows how to turn a euphemism. George Orwell would be proud. *Peacekeeper* missiles. Much better than *war-mongering* missiles. But while I admire the phrase, *enhanced interrogation*, let's go with the word *torture*, shall we? It really is more accurate. I assume you're familiar with the academic debate about the usefulness of torture, correct?"

"Yes."

"Good. This might prove interesting. You have academic knowledge of the subject. And my associate and I here have what you might call, *empirical* knowledge. In fact, we're imparting that on you now, giving you firsthand experience. But no need to thank us."

Alyssa took a deep breath and forced herself not to respond.

"I wonder how many academics have actually *been* tortured," continued GQ. "Wouldn't that be a fascinating experiment? Torture an academic who writes poetically about torture not being effective—and see if you can make him reveal information he wouldn't have otherwise revealed. I guess that would be one way to win a debate on the subject."

The man smirked at the thought. "So what is the verdict?" he said to Alyssa. "I'd hate to think we're going about this interrogation incorrectly. Or that it won't be effective."

Alyssa noted that Tree Trunk looked annoyed at this digression, since he would have little likelihood of slicing her again soon.

"Torture *can* be effective," responded Alyssa. "But it depends on the circumstances. If one knew something specific—"

"Let's not use the generic word, *one*," interrupted GQ. "Why don't you use first person. Let's make this more real. And let me confess. While my associate really will work his way down your arm with his makeshift scalpel, he won't cut your wrist. Dead people don't answer questions. But he will do something horrible that you *can* survive. Like taking out an eye. Bursting an eardrum. Slicing off a thumb or two. So base your answers on this specific torture scenario."

Alyssa swallowed hard and nodded. These men were animals, and she had no doubt they would do everything they promised, and more. Tree Trunk's work with the exacto knife, and his ecstatic look when he got the chance to use it, was more than enough of a demonstration.

"Okay," she began, taking a deep breath. "First, let's take the example of something that really *isn't* a secret. My answer to the question you're posing now, about the effectiveness of torture. You can look it up yourself. So if this were a friendly interrogation, I might lie, just to make you research it yourself. Or I might tell you the truth."

"But since I'm after innocent, non-secret information, you're damn sure going to tell the truth to avoid losing an eye? Is this where you're heading?"

"Yes. Which is why I'm happy to tell you my true opinion on torture."

"I really am enjoying this," said GQ. "Two torturers and a torture victim—who has *studied* torture—having an intellectual discussion on the topic. What could be more fun?" He paused. "So that makes sense. If the information being requested isn't even secret, torture definitely works. What about information that actually *is* secret?"

"In this case, if I knew you could easily check the veracity of what I told you, torture, or the threat of torture, would likely get me to divulge it. Where other techniques would not." She tilted her head and studied his face. "But I'd have to believe you'd keep your word," she added pointedly, trying to read his body language as she did. "And not torture me anyway. Or kill me."

"A good point," said GQ. "I have to be honest with you. I can't guarantee we won't kill you after this interrogation. Much will depend on what we learn. My boss will make the final call. But I do think the chances are about ninety percent that if you cooperate, you'll get out of this alive." He raised his eyebrows. "And with all of your digits and . . . organs, intact."

Alyssa continued studying the man she thought of as GQ for several long seconds. Would he really let her go? Was he telling the truth? For some reason her instincts told her he was.

"To continue," said GQ, breaking the silence. "You said torture would *likely* get you to divulge information under the last scenario. Why just *likely*? Why not for sure?"

"If the information would lead to the deaths of people I loved, I still would not tell you. If I knew the location of a nuke, and you tortured me to tell you, so you could use it to destroy a major city, I wouldn't tell you. No matter what."

"I see. So some information is worth dying for. While other information . . . not so much."

Alyssa nodded. "Which brings me to why many say torture is not effective. If I didn't know where the nuke was, or if I knew but thought this information was worth dying to protect, I would still tell you a location. I would tell you *anything* to get the torture to stop. Even if the information was false. That's why torture is mostly ineffective. You get information, but it's unreliable. You can't be sure how much of it is garbage."

"Right," said GQ thoughtfully. "You never know when you have a Marcus McDilda on your hands."

Alyssa's eyes widened, and she was impressed despite herself. This GQ seemed suave, smart, and dangerous, but there was more to him even than this. He had just demonstrated that he did his research, and that she needed to be very careful making assumptions as to what he did or did not know. This man would not be easy to fool.

Marcus McDilda was a fighter pilot in World War II. After the US dropped its only two atomic bombs, Japan was still determined not to surrender. But McDilda was a recent prisoner of the Japanese and he was tortured to find out how many more atomic bombs the Allies possessed, and where they might be deployed.

Only a few people in the world had any knowledge of the atomic bomb program, and McDilda was not one of them. He had absolutely no idea the US had used up its entire current supply. Under torture, however, he *confessed* that the Allies had a hundred bombs, and that Tokyo was to be bombed next, in the next few days. False information that led to Japan's final capitulation.

"Thank you for giving me straight answers to this pressing academic question," said GQ. "It was a fascinating digression. But I fear it is time to return to the business at hand."

He sighed. "You were saying that everything you study is proudly described on your website. But this can't be true. Innocent university researchers doing harmless work don't tend to have two military bodyguards and travel around in sedans enhanced with hidden armor. But I'm trying very hard not to take it as a personal insult that you thought there was a chance I might have believed you. So why don't you tell me who you really are. And what you really do."

GQ smiled pleasantly. "And then we can see if you get to live another day."

16

The air in the back of the commercial van had turned stale, and Alyssa swore there was a nasty stench present she couldn't quite place. Perhaps it was just the stench of malevolence, and it was only in her imagination.

The smile vanished from GQ's angular face. "Consider your answers very carefully," he said. "I already know much of what you might tell me. So if you tell me something I know to be a lie, or that is misleading . . ." He trailed off and nodded pointedly at his silent companion, still holding a bloodied exacto knife with ill-disguised impatience. "It would be a mistake. And please note that I'm not going to be asking you the location of a nuclear bomb. So there is no reason for you to be noble and foolish."

The man may have been pure evil, but he was very, very good, and off-the-charts smart. He was as articulate as anyone she had ever met, and she was almost certain English was a second language. And he had managed the interrogation brilliantly. He had gotten her to intellectualize her situation, and he had demonstrated his cunning. By her own arguments, she should tell him whatever he wanted to know.

GQ waved a hand at her. "So, Alyssa. Let's try this again. What are you not telling me about your occupation?"

Alyssa sighed in resignation. "I don't really work for the university," she said woodenly. "I run a Black Ops science lab under the direction of PsyOps."

GQ beamed. "Much better," he said happily. "Now we're getting somewhere."

She glared at him. "Yeah, well don't get too excited. Be sure your boss knows that the US Black Ops has capabilities he can only begin to imagine. And we get very upset when one of our own is tortured or killed. It's like killing a cop. You don't want to do that because other cops take it *very* personally. So, if you let me go now, no harm, no foul. Yeah, we'll be curious about you, but you'll live a long, healthy life."

Alyssa shook her head. "But torture me or kill me, and the government will never rest until they find you." Her lip curled up into a snarl. "And it won't be pretty when they do."

GQ simply smiled serenely at her threat. "Thanks for the warning," he said in his elegant, soft-spoken voice. "But, please, do go on. What do you study in this Black Ops lab of yours?"

Alyssa glared at him again but knew better than to try to withhold this information. "Narco-hypnosis. I have chemists modify known drugs that have psychoactive effects, trying to improve them. Trying to understand how someone can be controlled against their will. So I can *prevent* this from happening. We know that other countries are working on this, so we need to understand it."

"But never with the goal of using these techniques yourself, right?"

"Right," said Alyssa.

For the first time, GQ laughed out loud. "By god, I think you really believe that. You're demonstrating a facet of human behavior I'm sure you've studied. Our capacity for self-delusion."

Alyssa bristled, but she also knew he could be right. She believed that most in the US government abided by international laws when it came to biological and chemical warfare, interrogation, and narco-hypnosis, but she wasn't so naive as to refuse to acknowledge that the potential for bastardization did exist.

"So how far have you come?" said GQ, and Alyssa found herself wondering if Tree Trunk could speak. He was clearly little more than a trained Doberman.

"I assume you mean 'we' collectively. Mine isn't the only lab working in this area. There are eight different scientific teams across the country. We study the problem from various angles and pool results."

"Okay, so how far have you and the other seven labs come?" he amended.

"We've made great strides, but not in controlling people. I've been thrilled to learn that this doesn't look possible. Ever. By anyone. Regardless of the drugs used."

"So even with designer variations of known drugs, you *still* can't control others?"

"Right."

GQ nodded at his silent companion once again.

"No!" screamed Alyssa, but the burly sadist was so quick that another incision was forming a bright red, gushing line on her arm, a short distance from where her blouse had finally stemmed the flow of blood from his earlier handiwork.

"*God damnit!*" screamed Alyssa through the fresh burst of pain that assaulted her. "I'm telling you the *truth*! You've convinced me. I'd be stupid to lie in this situation. So hook me up to a fucking lie detector. If you won't believe the truth, you'll force me to invent lies you *will* believe."

GQ thought about this for a moment. He shrugged. "You'll need to convince me further, but I'm willing to accept that you're cooperating for now. But if this last was a mistake on my part, it's a minor one. Little more than exaggerated paper cut really. Just to get your attention."

GQ's face hardened. "When I'm *really* convinced you're lying to me, you'll know it. When you no longer have opposable thumbs. But rest assured, if that were to occur, we'd make sure to cauterize the wound so you'd stay alive for further questioning." He waved a hand toward her, palm up, as though giving her the stage. "But please. Continue. Convince me."

Alyssa described the many exaggerations associated with hypnosis, and that a human mind was extremely resistant to being controlled in this way. She explained that ninety to ninety-five percent of the population was susceptible to being hypnotized, and that within this group, a wide range of susceptibility existed. And that the susceptibility of the person being hypnotized was the key factor in the success of the procedure, *not* the expertise of the hypnotist.

Hypnosis was in some ways a dream state, in the sense that logic was no longer paramount. In a dream, she explained, a person's mind was creating the dream, but at the same time that person was not consciously aware of what would come next. As though two different people were involved, one creating the dream, and one watching it.

The same applied to those who had been hypnotized. When a hypnotist told a subject to hold out her arm, and that it was getting heavier and heavier, her arm would fall. *Of course* the subject was controlling her own arm. But even so, she really did believe her arm was being forced down, outside of her control. Just like in a dream, she was controlling it, but also observing it as a spectator. As was the case during the dream state, hypnosis placed a wall between the conscious and subconscious.

GQ was brilliant, and asked probing questions, but Alyssa told him nothing but the truth. She made sure to cite research that she knew was too detailed for her to have made up on the spot. She believed that she was finally able to convince him that she was playing it straight. The fact that she hadn't been backhanded or cut by Tree Trunk was a good indication of this.

"So you're saying that hypnotic trances are real," said GQ. "That even without your drugs to induce a trance, subjects aren't just faking it, correct?"

Alyssa nodded. "Willing, susceptible subjects really do fall into a genuine trance. You can prove it experimentally."

"How?"

"Send subjects to a hypnotist one at a time. Tell some in private not to let themselves be hypnotized—but to *fake* it. After a trance is initiated in each case, have the hypnotist indicate he needs to leave the room for ten minutes. Then use a hidden camera to observe what happens to each subject when they *think* they're alone.

"Those told beforehand to *fake* a hypnotic trance will immediately drop the pretense the moment the hypnotist leaves. They'll fidget. Sit down. Check their cell phones. And so on. The ones in an actual trance will *remain* in a trance, coming out of it gradually." She paused to let him draw the proper conclusions. "If they were faking also, they would have reacted the same way the known fakers did."

GQ nodded thoughtfully. "An ingenious experiment," he said. He rubbed his chin. "What about trigger words? Are they real? Can you trigger someone to start singing when they hear a certain word, for example?"

"Post hypnotic suggestions can work, yes. But you can't hypnotize people to do something against their will, or even embarrass themselves. They have to be absolutely willing. Hypnosis can't transcend volitional capacity."

"And you're telling me hypnosis is just as useless with the host of drugs you use as it was before?"

"First of all, it isn't useless. Even without our advanced drugs and techniques. It can benefit those who are hypnotizable and willing. Those who want to quit smoking, for instance. It would be used in this way more often, but there is a powerful negative stigma associated with it. It isn't taken seriously by many in the medical community, who believe it's a sham." Alyssa paused. "And we have improved upon it. Greatly. With drugs, we can make a hundred percent of the population hypnotizable. And all of them very strongly so, instead of demonstrating a wide range of susceptibility."

Alyssa went on to explain that most of her progress was in using narco-hypnosis to enhance the placebo effect. If the mind believed a pill would work to alleviate pain or reduce inflammation, even if the pill were a sham—a sugar pill—these outcomes would still occur.

The power of the placebo effect was shocking, still not completely understood, and demonstrated the mind had capabilities that were not readily apparent. And the effect wasn't limited to pills. Osteoarthritis patients who received arthroscopic surgery, during which their joints were flushed out and cartilage removed, showed marked improvement. But patients for whom the surgery was *faked* showed the *same* degree of improvement.

In a study of patients after oral surgery, half received ultrasound—known to reduce pain and inflammation—and half only *thought* they had. Both the real and phony procedures reduced pain, and even swelling.

The power of the subconscious mind was *immense*. And inexplicable.

And the placebo effect was growing *stronger*. The pharmaceutical industry was a victim of its own successes. The more magic-seeming pills the industry developed, the more faith people had in the power of the pill. So when drug trials were conducted for new therapies, and the actual medicine was tested against a placebo—a sugar pill—the placebo effect was off the charts. The more faith people had that the fake pill would actually cure them, the more it *did*.

In drug trials, the rates of improvement for patients given a sugar pill was often many times the historical rate of improvement in the general patient population. Drugs were failing to get approval, not because they didn't show a powerful healing effect, but because the subconscious minds of those given fake pills were able to suddenly heal the condition just as powerfully.

And the evidence had become overwhelming. The placebo response had been accepted by the scientific and medical communities as settled fact for some time. The more the mind believed something was true, the more likely it was able to make it *come* true.

"Our greatest triumph," explained Alyssa, "is that we've been able to greatly enhance and strengthen the placebo effect—which was already powerful. We're able to really nail it down. Really imprint in the subconscious mind that a treatment will be effective."

"So that's it? That's everything?" said GQ.

"If you were able to gain access to my computer and all my notes, this is basically what you'd find. In far greater detail, of course."

"Anything else. Anything I wouldn't find in your computer?" he asked, raising his eyebrows. He glanced meaningfully at Tree Trunk. "And consider your answer very carefully."

Alyssa sighed. "Yes, there is something more that you wouldn't find on my computer. But not because it's more secret, just because it's preliminary. A new drug, which is very complex, very difficult to synthesize, was recently produced by our best team of chemists in

Lawrence, Kansas. We've had spectacular results with it, on the no-cebo side of the ledger. But they haven't been written up anywhere. Mostly because we ran out of the compound. The chemists are making another batch, but our lab is the last in line to get our hands on it. So it'll be six or seven weeks before we get more."

"You said the *nocebo* side of the ledger. What does that mean?"

"A nocebo is basically the opposite of a placebo. It refers to negative effects powered by the subconscious instead of positive effects. Tell a man you have a potent drug that will ensure he can't get an erection, and he won't be able to get an erection. Tell a man he'll get nauseous from a pill, and he'll get nauseous—even if it's a sugar pill. Again, the power of the mind is mysterious and immense. We've had great success getting people to believe in something positive. To do something positive. But we've had even greater success getting them to stop something they want to stop, on the negative behavior realm. This comes into play for things like nervous tics and twitches. Ones that are habitual, driven entirely by the subconscious. I was able to strip subjects of involuntary tics they've had for years. In a single session. Tics they had no hope of ever controlling consciously. With the snap of my fingers. Literally. Post hypnotic triggers work beautifully in these settings."

Alyssa was beginning to feel light headed from loss of blood, but decided she had to keep talking until GQ was fully satisfied. "I've been fighting to declassify this work. The progress we've made has been astonishing. If we revealed our techniques for harnessing the placebo effect to the medical community, this would become the most powerful therapy in existence."

"The pharmaceutical companies would find a way to discredit it," said GQ cynically. "They would lose too much money if they didn't."

"Yes, they would lose money," said Alyssa. "But I'd like to think they'd be happy that people were able to improve their health, and battle disease, by enhancing the power of their own minds to heal themselves."

GQ laughed again. "You really are hopelessly optimistic. And hopelessly naive. I know my associate here won't agree with me on this, but I'm really hoping my boss decides to let you live."

He shook his head, almost as if he couldn't believe someone like Alyssa Aronson actually existed. "So your goal is to find a way to brainwash people into becoming zombie puppets. But instead, you end up finding a way to unleash powerful cures that can outperform expensive drugs. This is so stupid, and so unlikely, it almost *has* to be true."

"It is."

GQ had been standing in the van, but dropped to the floor across from Alyssa, with his back against the sliding door. Tree Trunk maintained his vigil to Alyssa's left.

"Okay," said GQ. "I'm satisfied you're telling me the truth about your work. So let's move on," he continued, raising his eyebrows. "Tell me how you know Theo Grant."

17

A surge of electricity swept through Alyssa at the mention of Theo Grant. She had wondered when he would come up, since he was, without doubt, either behind her abduction or the reason for it.

GQ had certainly taken his time getting here, but he had finally arrived. Still seated on the floor of the van facing her, with his back against the sliding door, his posture suggested he was totally relaxed as he awaited her response. Alyssa wondered if the use of this name was a test. If so, it was a test she intended to pass.

"You mean Brennan Craft?" said Alyssa.

GQ studied her face as though it were under a microscope. "That's right," he said finally. "So when did you first hear of him? When did you first meet him?"

"A week or so ago. I read his profile on E-Matchups, an Internet dating site. He had read mine also. The computer suggested we might be compatible, and we both agreed. So we arranged for a date through the site. He picked me up for lunch four days ago."

"Don't pretend you didn't know him before then. I don't want to have to hurt you again."

"*Please*," pleaded Alyssa. "I really didn't know who he was. I still don't. I swear it! Why would I lie about that? This was the first I knew of him."

"During this lunch, did he tell you anything about himself?"

"Yes. But I learned later that everything he told me was a lie. Even his name."

"Did he say what he wanted from you?"

"No. It was just another date. As far as I knew, he just wanted to get to know me to see if we were compatible."

"He didn't ask you for anything?"

She shook her head.

"Did he do anything . . . unusual?"

Alyssa looked puzzled. "I'm not sure I know what you mean. He was an interesting conversationalist. But that was all."

GQ weighed this statement. "Did he know what you really did?"

"Not that he let on. We didn't discuss this at all. We did talk about human behavior, which is what I told him I studied."

"So how did things leave off?"

Alyssa managed to keep her face impassive. Was this just another test? Could it be they didn't know about the raid at her house?

For some reason, she was reluctant to tell him. If he didn't already know, this could be important to them. Was she really going to risk being cut again, or worse, to protect information just because she had a gut feeling that she should?

These thoughts raced through her mind in an instant, and she decided to take a chance. "He disappeared," she said bitterly, trying not to cringe or show she half expected her arm to be grabbed and a new line of blood to appear. Technically, this was the truth. He *had* disappeared.

But GQ just nodded. "No e-mails, no texts, no calls? Nothing? Did the date go poorly?"

Alyssa couldn't believe it. GQ really *didn't* know what had happened. He only knew about the date.

"I thought it went great," said Alyssa. "I was sure he would call. But the next day, a Black Ops major visited me and told me the guy I knew as Theo Grant was really Brennan Craft. Told me to stay away. That they had been monitoring my dating information and had flagged him as having a false identity. The major told me Craft was either a crackpot or trying to use me in some way." Alyssa shrugged. "Maybe he was sent by a pharmaceutical company. To stop my work on the placebo effect."

"Perhaps," said GQ noncommittally.

"The major was very concerned about the situation. He told me Craft had gone to a lot of trouble to set up this date with me. He didn't elaborate, but said Craft must have wanted something. That's

98

why the major set me up with two bodyguards. He thought Craft might try to come back and contact me again."

"And this major told you nothing about Craft? Nothing other than he wasn't who he appeared to be? And that he was concerned about Craft's intentions?"

"Nothing," said Alyssa in disgust. "I thought I deserved to know. But he told me information about Craft was beyond my pay grade."

"And the major didn't suggest why Craft might have had interest in you? What he hoped to gain?"

"No. I don't think the major knew himself. I think he wanted to know, but he was at a loss. He did say that I was Craft's type, though. I have no idea how he knew this."

"Sure," said GQ, rolling his eyes. "That's the explanation. Brennan Craft just wanted to court you. He went to all this trouble just because he wanted to get laid." GQ shook his head in amusement. "Wouldn't that be ironic."

Alyssa shrugged. "It's as good a theory as anything else I can think of," she said.

18

Alyssa Aronson regained consciousness, but her eyes remained closed as she struggled to remember where she was. After several seconds of this, she realized why she was having trouble.

Because she had no idea.

Memories of her interrogation at the hands of GQ and Tree Trunk came back to her. But how had it ended?

And then she remembered. They had used chloroform on her for a second time.

So they had let her live, after all. But now the million dollar question. Was she now their prisoner somewhere? Was it GQ's intent to keep her alive, toy with her, let Tree Trunk live out his psychopathic fantasies? Let him carve her up like a pumpkin over days or weeks?

A part of her wanted to keep her eyes shut forever. Why risk the most unpleasant of truths. Why not construct a pretend reality within the cozy confines of her mind?

But as tempting as this was, she had to know. She was agnostic, at best, but just prior to opening her eyes a prayer entered her mind, unbidden. She was proving the old adage that there were no atheists in a foxhole.

Please God, she thought. *Don't let me still be captive. Please let this nightmare be over.*

She threw her eyes open and was hit by a barrage of data immediately. She was lying on a sophisticated bed in a private hospital room, wearing a blue cotton gown, with an IV in her arm. Few places were as instantly recognizable as a hospital.

And the man sitting in the chair next to her bed, coming alert as he realized she was awake, was just as instantly recognizable.

Brennan Craft!

Alyssa shrank back, and her mind raced as fast as her heart.

Should she scream? Push an alarm for the nurse? If she didn't calm down and get her vital signs under control, given the number of sensors to which she was connected, a nurse would be rushing into the room before too long anyway.

Craft was radiating an unthreatening, soothing calm at her, and even concern for her well-being. She felt her panic recede. After all, if he had wanted to kill her, he could have done so easily while she was unconscious.

Craft winced from her negative reaction to seeing him there. "You're going to be okay," he reassured her. "And I understand why you don't exactly trust me right now." He paused for a second and then smiled disarmingly. "And by 'don't exactly trust me' I mean, "despise me with all the thrilling, unadulterated hatred of a thousand demons.'"

Craft had gotten that right. But what annoyed Alyssa the most was that she found herself responding to how he had said it. She was amused despite herself. He was so charming that she found herself liking him—even as she despised him.

"What do you want?" she growled, working the controls on the side of her bed to raise herself to a seated position facing him. "How did I get here?"

Craft opened his mouth to respond when she thought of yet another question. "What time is it?"

"The better question is, what day," he replied. "Thursday morning."

"Thursday morning?" she mumbled. Could it be? She had been abducted the morning before.

"I know you don't trust me," said Craft. "And you feel misled and betrayed. I get that. And I deserve it. But to help put your mind at ease—as much as possible given the circumstances—you should know that I'm not your enemy. And not only will I never hurt you, I will make sure that no one else ever does, either. And I couldn't be sorrier about what you've been through. None of this was supposed to happen."

She remembered him calling out for her frantically at her house, his concern for her welfare quite evident, even after having survived an exploding car and a war zone. And even though he was a certified loon, as far as anyone knew, he had yet to break any laws. All he had really done was to stay alive after some idiot had ignored orders not to fire on him.

Craft lowered his eyes. "But if we're going to become friends and allies, I'm going to have to be completely honest with you," he said.

"Friends and allies?" she repeated incredulously. She was about to say more but decided against it. He was charming and had considerable charisma, but he was also dangerously psychotic—which meant unpredictable. Disrupting whatever fantasy world he was creating might not be great for her health. Even worse than he had been for her health already. In the four days since she had met him, she had been shot, knocked unconscious by a tree, knocked unconscious by a sedative, slashed, and knocked unconscious twice by chloroform.

"So in the spirit of total disclosure," continued Craft, "let me start with this. I've had you under surveillance for several days now. Monitoring your activities. Through street and store cameras. Through your computer and cell phone. The works."

A look of horror and violation came across Alyssa's soft features, and Craft cringed from this reaction.

"Why?" she said simply. "And how?"

"As to the why, after what happened, I thought it wise. I'm sorry for invading your privacy. But, as it turned out, it's a good thing I did." He paused. "As to the how, as I'm sure you've been briefed, I'm pretty good with computers. So I was able to tap into the grid."

Craft shook his head and looked disgusted with himself. "I only wish I could have found a way to stop what happened to you. But I was taken off-guard. A camera caught you and your two . . . escorts . . . yesterday morning entering a parking lot. But after that you were out of range of any cameras. I checked back an hour later, but I wasn't able to pick up your car, or you, again anywhere. I became alarmed. Given the number of street cameras in the vicinity of that lot, there's no way you could have gone anywhere without passing by one of them within a few minutes. So I drove to the strip mall and found it swarming with police and medical personnel."

Alyssa thought back to the Starbucks parking lot. "They didn't make it, did they?" she whispered sadly.

Craft shook his head and sighed. "I'm afraid not," he said, confirming what GQ had told her. "Whoever took you was very good. And very lethal."

"How did you know where I was?"

"Despite my best efforts, I didn't um . . . reacquire you . . . until you were admitted to this hospital, and passed your first camera. We're in Covington, Kentucky, by the way."

Covington. That made sense. GQ had wanted to put some distance between themselves and Bloomington, and Covington was a little over two hours away. And it was also home to the Greater Cincinnati and Northern Kentucky International Airport.

"So you have no idea how I came to be here?"

"Actually, I do," replied Craft. "According to hospital personnel, someone found you near the banks of the Ohio river late last night. You were unconscious, had no ID or phone on you, and had lost a significant amount of blood. So an ambulance brought you here, where you've been getting stitches, antibiotics, blood—the works." He flashed her a strained smile. "Checked in as a Jane Doe. So now you're all patched up. Good as new."

"Just to be clear," said Alyssa. "You're being hunted by the military. And while you're eluding this dragnet, you managed to launch a one man surveillance operation the NSA would envy. You activated manhunt protocols allowing you to tap into every camera in existence and have them perform facial recognition analysis to identify me. And then, after you were alerted by your own personal grid that I had been picked up on a hospital camera, you decided you would saunter over for a friendly visit."

"While my visit *is* friendly, I certainly didn't *saunter*. I shattered every highway speed limit to get here. I arrived about four hours ago, and I've been letting you sleep and recuperate. But I was going to have to wake you soon anyway. Your own people are hunting for you like mad."

"And yet you found me first."

"They would have also found you when I did, but I cheated. I, um . . . intervened. I made sure the computers only reported suspected sightings to me, and not them."

Alyssa digested this for several seconds. His skills were even more impressive than advertised.

"Here," said Brennan Craft, removing a plastic department-store bag from under his chair and handing it to her.

Alyssa took it without a word and looked inside. Clothing. Women's clothing. She looked at him quizzically.

"When they put you in this hospital gown," he explained, "they saved the clothes you were wearing when they found you. But I snuck them out and disposed of them."

Alyssa looked confused, but only for a moment. "Are you worried the men who took me imbedded electronics in them?" she asked.

Craft nodded.

She had to admit, it was a wise precaution.

"I've thrown your people off the trail," he said. "But they are very good, and have access to impressive resources, so they'll find you soon. And the police want to interview you as well. They've been waiting while you sleep and recuperate, but they won't wait much longer." He paused. "So if you could put on these new clothes I bought you, we really need to get out of here."

19

Alyssa took quick inventory of her situation. What now? Nutrition and probably antibiotics were still being pumped into her, and she did still feel a little weak. But she felt good enough to leave if required.

And she had been told to cooperate with Craft. The major had *wanted* him to abduct her. And to get into bed with him—literally.

Was it possible that Craft had sent GQ after her in the first place? What if he had been behind it all?

It was true that killing her bodyguards didn't comport with his MO. But MO's could change. On the other hand, GQ had grilled her about Craft himself, scratching his head over Craft's interest in her.

But was this just a mind-game? Had Craft sent them to abduct her, and then let her go, simply so he could continue pretending to be the good guy?

Regardless, if he wanted her dead, she would be dead already. So she had no good excuse, even after what had happened, not to follow the major's instructions. But she couldn't cooperate too easily, or this would be out of character, and Craft would smell a rat.

"Are you *kidding* me?" she said with the proper tone of incredulity. "After everything I've gone through—because of you—if you expect me to just willingly waltz out of here with you, you've gotta be cr . . ." She hesitated.

Craft *was* crazy, so *calling* him crazy probably wasn't a great idea. On the other hand, for someone who was schizophrenic and delusional, he was the most rational sounding and centered man she had ever met.

"Are you searching for the word, crazy?" said Craft, grinning.

Alyssa nodded reluctantly.

"Don't worry. You're safe with me. And nothing you say or do will change that. Especially not calling me crazy. Believe me, I've been called worse."

Alyssa smiled despite herself, but she quickly forced this unwanted expression from her face.

"You know," said Craft, "there's a mischievous part of me that could really have some fun with this. But you've been through a lot, and we don't have time. So let me make this very simple for you. I don't mean to boast, but I'm *really* good with computers. And if you're as good as I am, if information is on a computer, you can get at it. So I've read your Major Elovic's report back to his superiors."

Alyssa barely managed not to gasp. Just the fact that he knew Elovic's name and position in the agency hierarchy was stunning.

"Major Elovic is using you as bait," continued Craft calmly. "He had a long-range transmitter implanted in your thigh, which your abductors found and removed, judging from the location of your injury and Elovic's inability to find you. And a digital recorder disguised as a mole, glued under your ear. Which I suspect you activated during your recent encounter."

Craft paused. "You were also given orders to cozy up to me and gather intel. In fact, the major couldn't really order you to do it, but his report says that he suggested, strongly, that you sleep with me."

The hint of a smile crossed Craft's face but he quickly suppressed it. "So I know you're willing to come with me," he continued. "Because you've been *ordered* to do so. Now, you had no idea I knew this. So it makes sense that you'd want to stay in character, put up a fight—play hard to get. But we really don't have time for this. Your people and the cops will be here soon, as I've said. I've hacked into the hospital computers while you were out and changed your room number. So anyone trying to crash the party will be looking for you in an empty room. But still, we have to go *now*. We've overstayed our welcome. I've made sure the computers won't alert the nursing staff when you remove your IV, so we should be able to slip out of here without any trouble."

Alyssa stared at him open-mouthed. Who *was* this guy?

Craft didn't wait for her agreement. He moved closer to her bed, gave her a reassuring look, and gently removed the IV from her arm.

"So I'm going to turn around," he said. "And if you could change into the clothing I brought you as quickly as possible, I'd really be grateful. Okay?"

Alyssa nodded. "Okay."

Craft looked relieved. He quickly turned his back to her as he had promised.

"But here is the good news," he called over his shoulder while she changed. "I plan to tell you anything and everything you want to know. So you'll be getting all the intel you were looking for. And because of you, I've secured my place in heaven," he added in an amused tone.

"What does *that* mean?" she asked on cue.

"It means that a beautiful woman I'm extremely attracted to— and not just physically—had instructions to sleep with me to get information. And I'm going to just *give* her the information. With no strings attached. Despite the devil on my shoulder pleading with me to do otherwise." Craft paused. "Now if that doesn't get me through the pearly gates" he added with a grin, "nothing ever will."

20

Alyssa kept her head down in case any of the nurses might recognize her, although since they weren't expecting her to be up and about, or dressed as she was, the chances were small. Even so, Craft assured her that her face and figure were memorable, although he allowed that this was probably more the case with males than females.

As they pulled out of the lot, a police car pulled in, and Craft suspected they were arriving to interview the Jane Doe they thought was still in the hospital.

The car Craft was driving was a rental. A black Ford SUV that Alyssa decided was the size of a battleship. "I thought you liked Mercedes-es," she commented, trying to decide how to make it plural. Mercedi? "Or was that more of a Theo Grant thing?" she added pointedly.

Craft grimaced. "I *am* Theo Grant," he said. "Or to put it another way, I was totally being myself the other day."

"Sure you were," said Alyssa.

"Okay, I lied about a few things. But you weren't exactly straight with me either. We both know you don't really work for IU, or just on human behavior."

Alyssa shot him a look of disgust. "Really?" she said. "You really think this can justify your actions? That's pathetic. You lied about your name and background, but more importantly, your intentions. Yes, I lied also. But I'm prohibited by US law from disclosing my research. Research that is supposed to be," she added, glaring at him as she emphasized these words, "eyes-only."

Craft frowned. "You're right," he said softly. "That *was* pathetic."

Alyssa wasn't sure how he would respond, but this wasn't what she had expected.

"So let me try again," continued Craft. "Yes, I disguised my name and background, but what you saw of my personality, and my interests, was real."

"And your intentions?

"Obviously I wasn't just a guy who randomly found your profile online. Yes, I did have long term intentions different from what I let on. But my intentions, with respect to Saturday, were real. I was hoping we could get to know each other and see if we connected."

Alyssa considered this and decided to return to the point she had originally been trying to make. "So why the SUV . . ." She trailed off, not comfortable addressing him by name.

"Bren," he said, picking up on this hesitation. "Please, call me Bren."

Her face must have betrayed her distaste because he quickly added, "I know it's a little familiar under the circumstances, but I'd really appreciate it. I'd love for us to, you know . . . bond." He flashed an easy smile. "Doesn't mean we're married or anything," he added with a light tone.

Alyssa blew out a long breath. The idea of being on a first name basis with this man was repellent to her, but she had been ordered to cooperate with him, after all. "So why the SUV . . . Bren?" she repeated. "Wouldn't a smaller car blend in better?"

Craft laughed. "We can only be spotted the old fashioned way— by a pair of eyes. So I'm hoping anyone looking for us will think the same way you are."

Interesting strategy. Counting on those searching for them to overlook such a bold choice. *Hidden in plain sight.*

"And *both* of us are off the grid right now," added Craft. "It wasn't just your people I've misdirected. Your face will no longer trigger any notices through facial recognition algorithms."

Great, thought Alyssa. She was supposed to cooperate with Craft, but she was also supposed to be broadcasting her whereabouts continuously.

"Can I assume you recorded your encounter with the men who took you?" asked Craft.

Alyssa shook her head. "I didn't get the chance."

"Come on, Alyssa, I know you don't trust me. But these were dangerous people and they could have killed you. I need to listen to your interrogation so I can better understand our situation. And be in the best position to deal with it. It's for *your* safety as well as mine. And you're far too smart not to have recorded it."

Alyssa sighed. He did make some good points. "Okay," she said. "You can listen. Why not?"

Craft pulled off the road into an abandoned lot and parked behind a building, out of sight of the street.

Alyssa pressed twice against the mole on her neck in rapid succession, and explained to Craft that the bug was transmitting, and his phone was within the ten foot range required to pick it up as a wireless network choice. She wouldn't have been all that surprised to learn he had already read the spec on the device and was well aware of this.

Craft found the bug as an optional network on his phone, selected it, and Alyssa gave him the username and password information to log on. Less than a minute later the recording was loaded onto his phone.

"I won't play this out loud," he said softly, inserting small wireless earbuds into his ears. "The last thing I want to do is put you through it a second time. So feel free to close your eyes and rest while I'm listening. I'll let you know if I have any questions."

Alyssa nodded, relieved. She hadn't realized how much she was dreading listening to this nightmarish encounter a second time. The fact that *Craft* had considered this, even when she had not, showed that he was a thoughtful man, even when he wasn't operating under false pretenses.

21

Tariq Bahar, Al Yad's head of military and intelligence, had paid Tom Manning, the over-muscled sadist who had helped him interrogate Alyssa Aronson, and they had parted ways. Bahar hoped he wouldn't need his services again. While Manning radiated such a clear air of being a cruel psychopath that no one was more intimidating during an interrogation, he was repugnant and couldn't be fully trusted.

Bahar wasn't surprised that Alyssa Aronson had jettisoned the electronics he had implanted in her clothing, but these were red herrings anyway. This was far too important to rely on electronics only. So he had put an Indian born American mercenary named Santosh Patel on her tail. Tracking her, not with electronic transmitters or street cameras, but the old fashioned way. On foot, so to speak.

Sometimes the old ways really were the best, reflected Bahar. Santosh Patel had waited patiently for Aronson to be found by the river bank, and made sure he knew to which hospital she had been taken.

This girl was the only connection they had ever discovered to a man Al Yad had been obsessed with finding since Bahar had known him. Brennan Craft. Al Yad would follow this girl to the ends of the earth if there was even a remote possibility she could lead him to the man he was desperate to find.

Al Yad seemed to feel he was in an epic struggle with Craft. That it was a clash of titans. *The Hand of God* against Satan incarnate—*Shaitan* in Arabic. Shaitan had done a miraculous job of staying in hiding.

And as much as Al Yad seemed to despise Craft, he was the only man that his boss had ever respected. Apparently, Craft had some of the same . . . abilities . . . that Al Yad had. Which would make anyone take pause, whether these abilities were conferred by Allah, as was the case with Al Yad, or by the devil.

And then Craft had arrived at the hospital!

Bahar was on a layover in London, during his return trip to Syria, when Patel had contacted him with the news. Patel had texted him a photo of Brennan Craft entering the hospital.

Tariq Bahar couldn't believe his eyes.

Brennan Craft himself. *Shaitan.* "Speak of the Devil," he had said in English, proud that he could construct this play on words in his second language, which he spoke more eloquently than most native speakers.

Once visiting hours were over for the night, Patel had placed a motion-activated electronic camera pointed at the lighted entrance to the Emergency Room, reasoning that any visitors would need to sneak into the hospital from this point, since it was accessible 24/7. Craft had arrived at the hospital at three in the morning, Kentucky time, which Patel had discovered when he retrieved the camera upon waking three hours later.

Patel had truly earned his pay this time, thought Bahar.

He had immediately instructed the mercenary to activate his team of mercs, each paid handsomely to drop everything and prepare for action. They had all managed to catch up to Patel near the hospital with all of their gear only minutes before Brennan Craft and Alyssa Aronson had left.

And they had left together. Not only that, Patel had reported the girl seemed to be leaving with Craft *willingly.*

Bahar knew he had missed something when he had interrogated Alyssa Aronson. Something big. She and Craft had obviously been in communication or he wouldn't have known where she was. She had managed to pull the wool over his eyes somehow, which wasn't easy. He had been so sure he had managed the interrogation flawlessly, but obviously he hadn't.

One of the recent converts to Al Yad's cause was an expert at conducting, and interpreting, lie detector tests, using the most advanced polygraph equipment available. But Bahar had completed only a few training sessions with the man and was not yet ready to use this technology.

If Al Yad realized just how immense a failure the interrogation had been, he would be furious, and Bahar might soon find himself a dead man.

But the Great One had not been furious upon learning of Craft's visit to the hospital, and his subsequent departure with the girl. He had been *ecstatic.* And Al Yad had just called Bahar back, and seemed to be, if possible, even more jubilant. He had finally had the chance to listen to Bahar's interrogation of Alyssa Aronson, and had been very happy with it. Instead of the wrath Bahar expected, he had been *congratulated.* And then Al Yad had radically altered his orders.

Bahar had initially been instructed to have Santosh Patel and his team maintain surveillance, until they could trace Shaitan back to his base of operations. But Al Yad had changed these orders. What could The Great One possibly have heard during Alyssa Aronson's interrogation that had altered his thinking so dramatically?

Bahar was furious that he wasn't in position to be a part of the action, but Al Yad hadn't wanted him to be in any case, telling him he was not expendable like his hired hands. So while he would not return to The States, he also would not be continuing on to Syria. He would remain in London, where he would direct proceedings.

Only a few minutes after ending the connection with Al Yad, Bahar gathered himself and put in a call to Santosh Patel. "Give me a status update," he ordered in his elegant, soft-spoken English.

"Craft has pulled into a lot," reported Patel. "Out of sight of the road. And he and the girl have just been sitting there for almost an hour now."

"You're sure they're still there?" said Bahar anxiously. "That it's not a ruse? Perhaps they detected you following."

Bahar had already dodged a bullet, but if they screwed this up, failed to deliver the Great One's prize, his chances of living out the week were very small.

"I'm *sure*," said Patel. "And they didn't detect us."

Bahar sensed the mercenary was insulted by the question. Not that he cared.

"You had me activate four other members of my team for a baby-sitting mission," Patel reminded him. "My men are all in different cars, in different locations, with me as central command. With five of us tracking them, coordinating switch offs, they'll never detect us. And there is no way we lose them. Not with this kind of manpower."

"Conference your team in on this call," said Bahar

He waited impatiently as Patel did so and the members of the team reported in one by one. When all five were on the line, Bahar began. "I have new orders," he said. "This is no longer a surveillance mission. It has become more . . . active."

Tariq Bahar paused. "In short: I want Alyssa Aronson. Bad. And I want her alive. Repeat, she must be taken alive. I don't care what you have to do to get her. But there are some special instructions, so pay careful attention."

Bahar considered how best to phrase things. "First," he continued, "you won't be able to take Craft down no matter what you throw at him. So you'll need to attack them, get them separated, and then take the girl. The moment you catch them somewhat isolated, mount your attack. But don't wait too long. If you haven't seen a good opening within eight hours, attack anyway, even if they're in public. This is *that* important. Each of you confirm you heard me clearly and understand these instructions."

Each did as he asked in turn. When they had all acknowledge the orders, Santosh Patel said, "I need to point out that mounting an attack like this in public is very risky."

"Bring me the girl, alive, and I'll pay each of you five times your usual rate."

There was silence on the line for several seconds, and Bahar could imagine each of the five mercenaries drooling over their phones.

"This seems fair," said Patel finally. "Please continue."

"Good. But just so you know, getting the girl will be as difficult as anything you've ever done. This is important, so I'll repeat myself. You'll need to create a diversion so she separates from Craft. And when you grab her—make sure Craft is so distracted that he doesn't *see* you do it. Listen very carefully," he insisted. "The moment you let Craft see you, you'll be unconscious or dead."

Bahar paused for a moment to let this register with the five mercenaries. "Let me repeat that," said Bahar. "The second Craft gets a line of sight on you, he'll take you out. Period. Even if he's seeing you through binoculars. So if he turns in your direction, you better be sure you're not in sight at the time."

"I don't understand," said Patel. "And I'm sure I speak for my entire team on this. You said binoculars, you didn't say sniper scope. If he's looking at us through binoculars, how will he possibly be able to get off a clean shot?"

"I need you to trust me on this," said Bahar. "He won't need to shoot you. Just see you. He has a new weapon. One you've never encountered before."

"A weapon that takes anyone out, the second he sees them?" said Santosh Patel skeptically.

"Take my word on this one. If you doubt me, send one of your men to test it. Let Craft see him. And see how long he remains standing."

There was another silence on the line. "That won't be necessary," said Patel finally. "We'll take your word for it. But this will complicate the mission."

"I'm well aware," said Bahar. "And you also need to treat the girl like delicate crystal. If she dies, my boss won't rest until you die as well. And your family and friends. Trust me, you do not want to disappoint my boss on this one. In fact, you had better be armed with rubber bullets and other non-lethal equipment."

"Five times our normal fee?" said Patel.

Tariq Bahar had worked with these men before, and they had established a strong basis for trust. They knew that Bahar's word was his bond. "Five times," confirmed Bahar. "But you'd better take what I've told you to heart. And you'll need to be at your very best."

"Don't worry," said Patel confidently. "We know what you want. We will create a diversion. Pretend to attack Craft until they are separated. And then take the girl. Alive. And we'll stay out of Craft's sight."

"Good. And disengage the moment you have her. Craft will go to heroic efforts to stop you. And he is far more formidable than you might think."

"Uh huh," said Patel, unable to fully conceal his skepticism. "So the girl needs to live. What about Craft? What if *he* dies?"

If only, thought Bahar. Al Yad would give them their weight in diamonds if this were to happen. But he couldn't tell Patel that. If he did, they would focus on killing Craft, which they didn't fully understand could not be done, rather than getting the girl.

"Craft is incidental," replied Bahar. "I don't care if he lives or dies."

He thought about ordering them to tail Craft again after they had taken the girl, but he knew it would be futility itself. Craft would never allow it once they had revealed themselves.

"Just bring me Alyssa Aronson," said Bahar. "Alive and well."

"Roger that," said Santosh Patel.

22

The recording lasted for over an hour. Craft stopped to ask Alyssa questions on occasion, but rarely. At one point in the recording, she had no idea where, she thought she saw Craft's eyes light up, gleam with an almost neon intensity, but she might have been imagining it.

When Craft finished, he turned to her and said, "I am so sorry you had to go through that, Alyssa," and his voice was a mixture of outrage and barely contained fury.

They got back on the road and drove in silence for several minutes, each alone with their thoughts. Craft took a left at a busy intersection at the behest of the SUV's navigation system.

"Where are we going?" asked Alyssa.

"Breakfast," said Craft. "You've been through the wringer. I thought you'd be up for some nutrition you don't have to get through an IV."

Alyssa smiled thinly. He was right. She *was* hungry. And sitting down over some eggs and toast did seem civilized after what she had gone through.

"So you'll tell me anything I want to know?" said Alyssa.

"Anything. I doubt you'll believe this, but that was always the plan. I had just hoped for us to get closer first. So you would be more open minded to what I might tell you."

Alyssa thought about this. "And in return, I suppose you want me to tell you everything *you* want to know?"

But even as she said it she realized that her computer system was cake for this guy compared to those he had already demonstrated he could crack. That's how he must have learned of her research in the first place. He already knew everything there was to know about her.

Well, almost everything. There were key components that she hadn't put in the computer—secret sauce that he would need to know to replicate her work precisely. Which is probably what he had discovered and why he needed her now.

"You don't have to tell me anything," replied Craft. "I already know enough to know that you're perfect. Beyond my wildest hopes perfect."

"Perfect for *what*?" she said. "What do you want with me?"

Craft sighed. "That's a bit complicated. I'm not trying to be evasive. But you have to know a lot more to have any chance of understanding my answer. Or believing it. So why don't we start elsewhere and come back to this." He smiled wistfully. "Believe me, it's critically important to me that you know how you fit in."

"Okay," said Alyssa. "Fair enough." She studied his profile for several seconds as he drove. "So tell me about yourself. Let's start there. Pretend I know nothing about you, and start when you were a kid."

Craft quickly described his upbringing in Iowa. It seemed normal enough to Alyssa. He had led a baseball, soccer, and skinned knees sort of childhood. Well, except for the part about having taught himself algebra in the third grade because he had found it so interesting. He mentioned this as if this were the most normal thing in the world. He did the same when he came to describe his prodigious computer skills. By the fifth grade, little Bren's father was enrolling him in college level programming courses online. By the seventh grade he had taken numerous graduate level programming courses and was doing original work of his own.

Then his dad had passed away. They were a very religious catholic family, and when his mom was passing away several years later, he promised her he would go into the seminary.

Alyssa already knew of these events, but she let Craft describe them, as a check on the major's intel and to get some details filled in.

"With your scientific skills," she said, "this must have been a difficult choice to make."

"Yes. But I had made a promise. As you might expect, when I went to follow through on it, most people were pretty stunned. And concerned. They thought I was wasting a lot of talent, a lot of potential."

"And those arguments didn't sway you?"

"I really was spiritual," he replied. "Despite being enamored with science. Does that surprise you?"

"Not at all," said Alyssa, even though she wasn't being entirely honest.

"I felt as though, if God had a plan for me," continued Craft, "He would make sure I lived up to my potential." He had been making intermittent eye contact with Alyssa, but turned his full attention back to the road. "But it didn't work out. I left the priesthood very early on."

Alyssa raised her eyebrows. "Just didn't work out?" she said suggestively.

Craft sighed. "Sounds like you've already been briefed on what happened," he said. "I was hoping the major had skipped over that part. But you're going to force me to tell you anyway."

"You did say anything," said Alyssa.

"Okay, you win. It turned out that I had a libido the size of Texas. In my early twenties, I may have been the horniest young man who ever lived. A pretty grave character flaw when you've taken a lifetime vow of celibacy."

Alyssa couldn't help but smile. "Yeah, I've read your blog on the subject."

Craft nodded, and his expression was one of both amusement and embarrassment.

"Don't worry," she said. "I thought your blog post was excellent. And the science you included was very accurate, and very persuasive."

They arrived at their destination, the Bluegrass Waffle House, and were soon seated in a booth inside, requesting the most isolated one possible. They both ordered and then resumed their conversation.

Craft continued describing his life after the priesthood. How he had become fascinated with quantum mechanics and had devoted himself to this field, becoming accomplished very quickly. And how he had developed an algorithm that had ultimately earned him fifty million dollars. Alyssa had wondered if he would mention this.

So he had been rich, charming, and attractive. Not that Alyssa would ever put it this way to him. And he had no need to work. As young as he was at the time, he had put himself in an enviable position. Alyssa knew better than anyone that wealth didn't necessarily buy happiness, but she would guess he didn't have any trouble satisfying his oversized libido. She wasn't sure why this thought had entered her mind, but she pushed it away and focused on what he was saying, having already missed his previous few sentences.

". . . and it was at that time," continued Craft, "that I stumbled across a story about a man who had reportedly fasted for several years without any negative health effects."

"Negative health effects?" repeated Alyssa. "You mean like *dying*?"

Craft laughed. "Yes. I'm pretty sure the medical community considers this a negative effect."

It was then that Alyssa realized he was moving on to describe the next phase of his life, but had skipped over his fascination with The God Theory entirely. Had he done this on purpose?

Regardless, this was an important area for her to explore. It was this subject that was most likely to bring out the crazy in Brennan Craft, something he had hidden so beautifully up until this point.

The deluded could fool you. Right up until the point you switched the subject to the space program, and they began foaming at the mouth while insisting an immortal Elvis, who was actually an outer-space alien, shot Kennedy, who was actually a robot, before teaming up with the Freemasons and Illuminati to help NASA fake the moon landing.

Alyssa leaned in. "Before you skip ahead," she said. "What can you tell me about a book called *The God Theory*?"

23

There was a long pause as Brennan Craft finished the last of his pancakes and they both ordered coffee. Alyssa hadn't realize just how badly she was in need of caffeine, having only managed to take a single sip of her last coffee before all hell had broken loose.

"My compliments to the, ah . . . biographers . . . at your agency," said Brennan Craft. "They were very thorough." He considered. "I would love to discuss this theory in great detail, but it would take too long. And we have more pressing matters to discuss. Are you willing to take a rain check?"

Alyssa realized she must have looked disappointed at this, because the corners of Craft's mouth turned up into a reluctant smile and he added, "but just so I don't gloss over this part of my life entirely, let me give you at least a little background."

"Thanks," said Alyssa.

"*The God Theory* is a book written by Bernard Haisch. He and I have a lot of similarities. He is a successful and accomplished scientist. And he's helped make breakthroughs in the field of quantum physics, especially as this relates to something called the zero point field, which I plan to discuss momentarily. And like me, he attended the seminary."

"Really?" said Alyssa in amusement. "The seminary must be jam packed with brilliant physicists who are experts in quantum theory," she added wryly.

"Not as many as you might think," he replied with a grin.

"Well, I can see why you were curious about his writings."

"I didn't think I'd purchase the book," said Craft, "but I decided to give it a try after reading the reviews. The book was being lauded by a number of scientists. Seemed to resonate with them. Hit the logic centers of their brains in just the right way. But I was skeptical. I felt as though I was bright, and had given divinity a lot of thought. A *lot* of thought. I doubted he could possibly get me to see things in a new way, but I gave it a try."

"And you became a convert," said Alyssa simply.

"I became intrigued with the concepts presented," he corrected. "And came to believe they were valid. *Convert* has a more dogmatic nuance to it than I'd like to use."

"I'm pretty sure it doesn't," said Alyssa.

"Well, whatever the case, I just want to be clear that I don't believe in this dogmatically. These are a set of spiritual truths that resonate with me, that I believe are correct. But everyone is free to choose, and in fact, the theory encompasses aspects of a number of religions."

Alyssa frowned. If this was the part where he showed he was delusional and began foaming at the mouth, she had missed it.

"No one knows for certain what is really going on," said Craft. "All I know is that everything around us is astonishing. Impossible. We live in a universe so finely tuned for complex chemistry and life that the odds against it are greater than those of winning a thousand lotteries in a row. In a universe filled with exquisite microorganisms, voracious black holes, and trillions of stars, each of which can fit a million or more Earths inside. How can we possibly think that any view of God or creation can capture more than the tiniest hint of this reality?"

Wow, thought Alyssa. There was an inner passion and poetry to Craft's words, and she couldn't help but be somewhat swept up in his vision. People went about their day to day lives, not often considering the grandeur of creation, or the infinity of the cosmos. Perhaps that was why early man was so spiritual, because he looked up to stars each night. When was the last time she had spent any time star gazing, contemplating the countless diamonds of light, each representing incomprehensible furnaces burning for billions of years.

"So I don't pretend to know for sure what is really going on," continued Craft. "Our minds are too puny to grasp it even if it were shown to us. I am always amazed at the level of certainty those on both sides of the spectrum bring to the debate. I've met atheists who are absolutely *certain* a creator doesn't exist. Absolutely certain, despite the impossibility of the cosmos, thinking the very notion is the height of absurdity. Unable to imagine they could possibly be mistaken.

"And I've met practitioners of organized religions who are equally certain their view is correct. That cows are sacred, that this is self-evident, and who can't even imagine a cosmos where this isn't true. That Jesus was divine, refusing to allow for the *tiniest* possibility that the biblical accounts might not be absolutely accurate. And at the same time, ridiculing the beliefs of others."

Alyssa was captivated and found herself agreeing with Craft in every respect. Not only wasn't this the part where he revealed himself to be a crackpot, he was sounding more rational than the vast majority of people she knew. And now she was intrigued. For some reason, she suddenly believed that this God Theory would be more plausible and compelling than she had thought, when he did have more time to describe it to her.

Craft raised his eyebrows. "Okay to move on now?"

Alyssa nodded.

"So I was talking about fasting," said Craft, sipping at his coffee and setting the mug down gently on the table. "I didn't know it at the time, but I soon found out prolonged fasting has a following among any number of people across the world. Given the quality of your briefing, I'm sure you've heard of this."

"Yes. It's called Inedia. Or Breatharianism."

"Exactly. Inedia is just Latin for *fasting*. Makes it sound more sophisticated that way," explained Craft, flashing another disarming smile. "And Breatharians speak about living, not from the intake of food, but off light itself. Sounds ridiculous, doesn't it?"

"Very," said Alyssa simply.

"I thought so too. But when I read about it, a wild idea came to mind. One of the wildest, craziest ideas I've ever had. But let me back up." He paused, considering the best way to proceed. "We've spoken about quantum physics. The most successful theory of all time."

Alyssa smiled. This was an often used mantra in quantum physics, and exactly what she had told Major Elovic. Given its predictions had been so well verified, and given its role in underpinning computers and lasers and the like, however, this was absolutely true.

"And as you, yourself, described it during our lunch," continued Craft, "the quantum world is also quite insane. One consequence of the theory, which has been proven beyond any doubt, by the way, is something called the zero point field. Are you familiar with this?"

Alyssa had come across the concept in her readings. But she preferred to hear what Craft had to say about it. "I'm afraid not," she lied.

"Quantum theory reveals that there really is no such thing as a vacuum. In a sane universe, if you removed all matter and energy from a portion of deep interstellar space, you'd have a vacuum. But in our *insane* universe, this isn't the case. No matter what you do, there is always an underlying, seething froth of activity. Particles—energy—pop into and out of the void constantly. Randomly."

He paused. "This is called the zero point field. And if you do the math, you find that there is an incomprehensibly large amount of energy in every cubic centimeter of space. The universe has provided the ultimate free lunch, just waiting to be harvested." He stared at her intently. "Zero point energy."

"Go on," said Alyssa. So far this matched her understanding exactly.

"Collectively, this zero point energy is basically infinite. And it pervades the entire universe. It exists in interstellar space and in the empty spaces between atoms of your body. A cubic mile of space contains more energy than the lifetime output of our sun." He shook his head. "But, unfortunately, there's no way to tap into it. This energy flashes into and out of existence so quickly there's no way to grab onto it."

"How quickly are we talking about? A trillionth of a second?"

Craft shook his head. "*I wish*," he said in amusement. "No, it exists for far less time than this. Physicists have tried to think of ways to catch it, for obvious reasons, but have failed, and most have concluded it can't be done. Ever. Even so, NASA has been studying this area for years."

"If it's impossible, why does NASA waste its time?"

"Good question. I guess because the potential payoff is so enormous. But for years the zero point field really has become the ugly stepchild of quantum physics, locked in the basement. It is an annoyance. Since it is infinite and pervasive, it can be largely ignored, even in equations. And infinity can be such a pain in the neck to deal with, most think it's far better to have it brushed under the carpet. It has become a term physicists largely forget as they go about their daily business."

"I'm not sure I get it. You're saying that the zero point field affects us so little that physicists can all but ignore it. But if this energy is so all-pervasive, and nearly *infinite*, how is it that we don't *feel* it?"

"Good question," said Craft. "The only way I can answer is with an analogy. You've seen those giant industrial electromagnets, right? The puck-shaped ones with the circumference of a living room that are suspended from cranes?"

Alyssa nodded.

"Well, some of these exert a force so powerful they can yank a train car off the ground. A train car! But you could be standing right under one, directly in this immense energy field, and you wouldn't even know it was there. Provided you didn't have any steel on you, it wouldn't affect you in the slightest. A field can contain enormous energy, just waiting to be put to use, which we can't see or feel, and which doesn't affect us."

"Thanks," said Alyssa. "That helps a lot."

Craft picked up his phone, performed a few manipulations, and handed it to Alyssa. "I've pulled up an article with impeccable credentials for you to read. To confirm what I'm saying." One corner of his mouth curled up into a wry smile. "So you don't, you know, think this is all the ravings of a lunatic."

Alyssa had read enough to know the existence of the zero point field, as fantastic and counterintuitive as it seemed, was established scientific fact. Even so, she couldn't help but take a quick glance at the article. It was entitled, *Emerging Possibilities for Space Propulsion Breakthroughs,* and it had first appeared in a NASA publication, *Interstellar Propulsion Society Newsletter*, in July of 1995.

She scanned it quickly. A few sentences caught her eye. *Zero Point Energy is the term used to describe the random electromagnetic oscillations that are left in a vacuum after all other energy has been removed.* Overly simplistic, but essentially a good shorthand way to describe it, she decided. She went on to read the numerous experimental observations that supported its existence.

She read the final two sentences aloud: "If all the energy for all the possible frequencies is summed up, the result is an enormous energy density. In simplistic terms, there is enough energy in a cubic centimeter of empty vacuum to completely boil away all of the Earth's oceans."

Alyssa passed Craft's phone back to him across the table. "I really did believe you," she said. "But it's helpful to see this. NASA seems like a pretty sober organization."

Craft laughed. "Good way to put it," he said. He paused for a moment in thought. "Okay, let me move on to the next piece of the puzzle. I apologize for jumping around so much. But how familiar are you with the link between reality and consciousness?"

"Fairly so," said Alyssa. "There must be hundreds of books on the subject."

"So how would you describe this link?"

"Quantum physics has shown for a century that reality requires a conscious observer. I'm sure this is an inelegant way to put it, but a particle can be anywhere until you look at it. Then its wave function 'collapses' and it chooses where to be. In some sense, no consciousness, no reality."

"Nicely summarized," said Craft. "No one knows exactly why reality works this way. But it's driven scores of brilliant scientists crazy, including Einstein. A fairly recent idea is that we're living in the equivalent of a video game."

"Really? I hadn't heard that one."

"It actually makes sense in many ways. Imagine you had near-infinite computing power and wanted to create a virtual universe. Like Second Life, World of Warcraft, Sim City—that sort of thing. But on a much grander scale. This universe would be exquisitely tuned to support whatever characters were chosen to inhabit it. Like our universe is."

"Although this wouldn't explain how the programmer came to be," noted Alyssa.

Craft nodded. "A fair point. But dismissing this question for a moment, here's the part I find most interesting. In many of the virtual worlds that we've created for our computers, the reality only comes into being when a character in the world observes it."

"Say that again."

"The programmers don't waste computer power calculating and rendering images off screen. Why would they? But if you take your joystick, or whatever controller you're using, and march your character to the left, the landscape in this direction is instantly rendered. But not until your character *looks* in this direction, so to speak. When the character does, the landscape is calculated and rendered seamlessly, and presented to the character. Sounds familiar, doesn't it?"

Alyssa whistled. "Eerily familiar," she said. He had basically described how the universe was known to work. Reality was only rendered when it was observed. Particles were everywhere, until someone peeked, and then they took a discrete location.

"It's an interesting idea that is gathering more and more support in the physics community," said Craft. "But the point I'm really trying to make is that consciousness and the quantum realm are intimately connected. And even beyond this, many believe that consciousness *itself* is a quantum effect." He paused. "Would you concede that this is a view held by many prominent scientists."

Alyssa nodded. "Absolutely," she said without hesitation.

Less than a year earlier she had read a book about the progress of artificial intelligence, which discussed the concept of consciousness at length. Some believed a machine could never become self-aware. Could never truly marvel at the beauty of a sunset, create art, or take an intuitive leap. Because even if a computer could pass the Turing Test, fool someone into thinking it was human, it would simply be obeying a sophisticated set of programming, spitting out answers that could fool humans, but without true comprehension, and without freedom of choice.

One requirement of consciousness was that it be non-deterministic, non-algorithmic. And this was the very hallmark of the quantum realm, where inherent uncertainties and randomness reigned. So could it be that the magic required to make a lump of physical matter self-aware took place in the quantum realm? Did consciousness only arise when a collection of physical matter, like the human brain, became capable of harnessing *quantum* effects?

No less a luminary than Sir Roger Penrose, a giant of physics and mathematics who had worked closely with Stephen Hawking on the physics of black holes, was a chief proponent of this idea, theorizing that this quantum orchestra was conducted by tiny structures within neurons called microtubules.

"Good," said Craft, apparently satisfied that Alyssa was with him to this point. "So let me ask you this. What is light?"

"What is light?" she repeated, taken aback. "Where are you going with this, Bren?"

A smile flickered over Craft's face at her use of his first name. "Give it a guess," he said.

"Photons?" said Alyssa uncertainly.

"This is true," said Craft. "But in the broadest sense, light is electromagnetic radiation. What we commonly think of as light is just the portion of this radiation in the visible frequency range. But ultraviolet waves, radio waves, microwaves, X-rays, and so on, are all forms of light. Forms of electromagnetic radiation. And they are all carried on photons."

"I still think I'm missing your point."

"My point is that the sea of zero point fluctuations we just spoke about is electromagnetic in nature."

Alyssa considered this. "I get it now," she said finally. "You're saying the zero point field is actually a sea of *light*. Just not light in the visible spectrum."

"Exactly!" said Craft excitedly. "A sea of light with nearly infinite energy that pervades the entire universe. But some scientists believe it existed *before* the creation of our universe." He raised his eyebrows impishly. "Which brings me to the bible."

"The bible?" repeated Alyssa, blinking. To say he was jumping around was an understatement.

Craft grinned, obviously pleased by her confusion. "Are you familiar with the biblical phrase, 'And God said: let there be light. And there was light?'"

"Yes. It's followed by something like, 'And He saw that it was good.' You don't exactly have to be a biblical scholar to have heard that one. It's on the very first page. And it's probably the most well known single sentence in the bible."

"I would agree," said Craft. "But here's the thing," he added, clearly enjoying himself. "God created light on the *first* day. Any guesses when he created *the sun and the stars*?"

Alyssa's eyes widened, and she shook her head.

"*The fourth day*," said Craft enthusiastically. He paused for a moment to let the implications of this fully sink in. "Now isn't *that* interesting?"

"And then some," agreed Alyssa, finishing the last of her coffee.

"Seems like you'd need the sun and stars to have light, doesn't it? Most people read the bible and never think about this. But it's a discrepancy that didn't escape the notice of biblical scholars. The Kabbalah, often called Jewish mysticism, explains this discrepancy by saying that the light created on the first day was *different* than that created on the fourth. Not the kind of light we can see." Craft raised his eyebrows. "The zero point field, perhaps?"

Alyssa shook her head in wonder. Fascinating.

"Now this is just a fun exercise," said Craft. "I'm not saying the bible was divinely inspired. And I'm not saying it wasn't. And if it wasn't, I'm not suggesting whoever penned it knew about the zero point field. Maybe this is just the most glaring continuity error in the history of writing. But it *is* interesting."

Craft paused and took a deep breath. "So let me return to extended fasting. Inedia. These people claim to be living off *light*. Ridiculous. But my crazy thought was, *what if they really were?* But not sunlight. *The zero point field.*"

Alyssa put a hand to her chin in thought.

"We know it exists everywhere," he continued enthusiastically. "We know it contains nearly infinite energy. And we know the energy blinks into and out of existence far too quickly for us to ever grab hold of with our machines. But consciousness ties directly into quantum reality. As you've conceded, a number of prominent scientists believe our minds are quantum instruments. That consciousness itself is a quantum event. So what if some of these people undergoing prolonged fasts, without knowing it, are able to tap this infinite energy source? *With their minds.*"

The audacity of what Craft was suggesting was stunning. And yet Alyssa found it utterly compelling.

"We can't catch this lightening in a vacuum, so to speak, with any technology known to science," continued Craft. "But the mind is a quantum instrument. Something Nobel Laureate James Watson described as 'The most complex thing we have yet discovered in our universe.' So what if the mind can do what technology can't? Succeed where NASA has failed. Crazy, right?"

"Why do I have the feeling it isn't going to turn out as crazy as it sounds?"

"Just to circle back for a moment, fasting plays a big role in many religions. In fact, the word Breatharianism was first used to describe a fast-based lifestyle within Catholicism. One based on the idea that certain saints were able to survive extended fasts without sustenance. Muslims have their Ramadan, during which they only eat at night for the entire month. But what I find even more interesting is that Moses and Jesus—key players in both the old and new testaments—were *both* said to have survived fasts of forty days and nights."

Alyssa vaguely remembered that Jesus had fasted, but she wasn't aware this was also the case with Moses. "Both for forty days?" she said. "Pretty wild coincidence."

"Some believe forty-days was an ancient convention for saying, 'an extended period of time.' But either way, they both fasted for a very long time." He paused. "I'm not suggesting Jesus was divine or wasn't divine. I have no idea. But it's interesting to play with the idea that he could tap into the zero point field. Use his mind like a quantum lens. Tapping into an infinite ocean of energy and focusing it wherever he wanted. Fasting, walking on water—this would be easy for someone with this ability."

Alyssa marveled at the ease with which this man could make the impossible seem almost *reasonable*. His biography had been eclectic and his interests seemingly disjointed. But he had taken crazy events from his biography and woven them together to form a compelling tapestry that didn't seem so crazy at all. The loon who became obsessed with fasting to the point of almost killing himself was becoming less of a loon.

"The more I read," said Craft, "and the more I thought, the more I had to investigate this further. I tried extended fasts. Without success. As I'm sure you know."

"This might have come up," said Alyssa, fighting to keep a straight face.

"Okay, I'll admit. *Without success* may be an understatement. But I didn't let almost dying stop me. I took my nest egg and began to travel the world. Studying the best known cases of people who were undergoing prolonged fasts and still finding energy for their cells somehow. Still surviving. I did think this was a wild idea with little chance of being right. But I thought, if there was any chance I could figure this out, I could solve world hunger. World hunger! What if I could teach everyone to derive energy directly from the zero point field?"

"Might put some five-hour energy drinks out of business," said Alyssa in amusement.

"Not to be too biblical on you, but let me give you another item to chew on. These are all probably just interesting coincidences, but they are fun. The Israelites, after they were freed from the Pharaoh and wandered the desert for forty years, as described in the Passover story, were said to have been sustained by a substance called *manna*. Which came from heaven. *Manna* is thought to derive from an Egyptian word meaning, 'What is it?' Good question. But if Moses learned how to tap into the zero point field, perhaps he could have trained his people to do the same. Calling this mysterious sustenance bread from heaven wouldn't have been entirely crazy."

The waitress came over and refilled their coffees. They had now taken up a table for a long time and would need to leave a healthy tip. Still, Alyssa was riveted, and didn't want to interrupt Craft's flow. She had needed to use the restroom now for some time, but was determined to hold it until he was finished.

"So I set up a camp with my considerable financial resources, and brought a handful of people who I believed had legitimately fasted for extensive periods. I started in Afghanistan, of all places, because I found a few of the best fasters there. But I was paying big for security, and was planning to move the entire group, en mass, somewhere safer."

"Good call," said Alyssa dryly.

Craft smiled. "Anyway, I put the fasters I recruited through the wringer to see what made them tick. And I tried to pick up a unique, but characteristic energy signature from their minds. I scanned, and poked, and I studied DNA samples for years. I won't bore you with the exhaustive studies I did, and things I tried. But to fast forward, while I never did figure out the mechanism behind it, I was finally able to use it." A triumphant look came over his face. "I really can train people to channel energy from the zero point field with their minds."

"Incredible," whispered Alyssa. But while she would have thought this was a laughable claim a few hours earlier, she now found it, the greatest revelation in the history of science, to be so reasonable as to be almost expected.

"As I had guessed," continued Craft, "it's strictly an ability of the quantum-driven mind. Of the subconscious. The more belief you have that you can tap into this field, the better able you are to do it. Your subconscious picks up on your belief and turns it into reality. You have to have a very different sort of mind to really believe you can sustain yourself on nothing. But the fasters were some . . . unique . . . people to begin with. I mean, some of their reasons for fasting were seriously messed up. And to fast for years, having every confidence you'll survive. Well, that's pretty, um . . . special."

"Instead of fasting in the name of science like you did, you mean?" said Alyssa. "Intent on ending world hunger." She couldn't help but feel silly using this phrase, as though she were a contestant in a beauty pageant. *I want to end world hunger and bring about world peace.*

"Exactly," said Craft. "So in addition to the successful fasters, I brought in some minds that I thought were sharper, more rational. I ended up with a group of twenty. Fifteen of us couldn't fast without, you know . . . dying. But we were working on finding other ways to tap into the zero point field. And we had five fasters who were our guinea pigs. Who we verified could live, as far as we could tell, forever, without any food."

Alyssa had a sick feeling in her stomach that she now knew exactly where this was heading. It was a wild guess, but it felt right to her. She decided to ask a loaded question and see if her instincts were on target. "Anyone in this group stand out? You know, seem special in any way?"

Craft nodded. "Very good," he said approvingly. "As a matter of fact . . . yes. There was one. One of the five fasters. And he was *very* special. His name was Omar Haddad." A troubled look appeared on Craft's face. "Although lately, I understand, he goes by the name, Al Yad."

24

The moment Brennan Craft and Alyssa Aronson had entered the Bluegrass Waffle House, Santosh Patel had set up another call with the four other members of his team. Like him, they each had receivers in their ears and small mikes attached to their shirts. Each was in his own car, encircling their quarry at various distances.

Each member of Patel's team had lived in America for some time, but when they congregated it looked like the United Nations was in session. In addition to Patel, who was Indian, Suntai Ahn was Korean, Dmitri Volkov, Russian, and Bruno Haas a German. Hank Ridley was the only native born American in the group of five, and he had considerable experience fighting in other countries and with a variety of soldiers and mercs of different nationalities.

"While they're eating," began Patel, "we have some time. But we don't know how much, so we need to move quickly."

Patel paused. "Ahn, according to my phone there's a gun store five minutes from you. Get there immediately. Buy them out of blanks and distribute these to each member of the team. We'll need to use some live ammo during the early part of our campaign. But if this fails to take Craft out, we can't risk killing the girl during the shock-and-awe phase."

"Roger that," said Ahn.

"You don't really think this will be as challenging as Dr. Suave thinks, do you?" said Hank Ridley. The man who had hired Patel went by the alias, John Smith, but the team had taken to calling him Dr. Suave when he wasn't within earshot. They didn't care who he really was, as long as he continued to pay well. "You're the best marks man I've ever worked with, Santosh. Even if Craft really *can* take us out on sight, you'll have planted a bullet between his eyes before he even knows to look for us."

"Hard to imagine that's not true," replied Patel. He frowned. "But we're being paid five times our fee on this one, so let's not make any assumptions."

Patel paused. "Volkov," he said to the big Russian, "there's a hardware store nine minutes from here that's just about to open. Find it on your car's nav and go."

"Found it," said the Russian less than thirty seconds later. "Leaving now. What am I buying?"

"The most powerful chainsaw they've got. Along with gas for it."

"Chainsaw?" said Volkov.

"We may need it," said Patel. "They could be going anywhere once they leave the restaurant. The only destination that wouldn't be totally random, as far as we're concerned, is Bloomington, Indiana. Suave says that's where Aronson is from. Apparently he snatched her off the street there and brought her here."

"Still an unlikely destination," said Haas.

"True, but a better bet than anywhere else. They have no luggage, and by rights Aronson should still be in the hospital. If I were in her shoes, I'd want to return home. If only to set my affairs in order before going somewhere else."

"I agree with Patel," said Volkov. "We should be prepared for this. If they go somewhere else, so what?"

"Exactly," said Patel. "I've done a virtual recon of the route between here and Bloomington. Only backwater roads almost the entire way. Where there's not a forest there's a cornfield. Lots of opportunities. The chainsaw might come in handy if we want to isolate a kill zone." It was always best to eliminate as many variables as possible.

"Roger that," said Volkov.

"If they do try to return to Bloomington, this would be ideal for us," said Patel. "I've come up with a solid strategy." He shrugged. "If not, we'll have to plan on the fly. But there is one thing I'm sure of. For this kind of money, nothing is going to stop us from delivering Alyssa Aronson."

25

The moment of truth had arrived. When Craft had first asked Alyssa to leave the hospital with him, she hadn't been at all sure he would really tell her his connection to the man who was making the US and Syria so nervous. And if Craft did, she couldn't even hazard a guess as to what his connection to Al Yad would end up being. But the reality was stranger than anything she could have imagined in a hundred lifetimes.

"This is the information you were after, right?" said Craft.

"Yes. The government seems to feel that this Al Yad is the most dangerous man alive."

"He is," said Craft simply. "They're right to worry."

"I'm not sure what happened at my house," said Alyssa. "I'm told they only wanted to bring you in for an interview. You weren't targeted for anything you had done. You were just their best shot at getting some kind of handle on Al Yad. The major swears he doesn't know how it got out of hand."

Craft shrugged. "It was . . . unfortunate. And they did begin by politely asking me to join them. When I refused and tried to leave, they got a bit more forceful. When that didn't work, one of them tried to slow me down by shooting me in the leg and then taking out the car. It kind of snowballed from there. But I think your major is telling the truth. I don't think it was intentional. They just *really* didn't want me to leave."

Craft paused. "That's not to say I wasn't angry with myself for being so stupid. And upset that you had been put in harm's way. But I can forgive that." He flashed a good-natured smile. "What I *can't* forgive is that they ruined our date. I was having a *great* time. At least, you know . . . BTW."

"By the way?" said Alyssa in confusion.

"No. Before the war."

Alyssa laughed.

"So let me tell you about Omar Haddad."

"I don't understand," said Alyssa. "If you don't have any problem talking about him, why didn't you cooperate with the men at my house?"

"Because they're not *you*. I'd prefer no one knew about anything I'm telling you today. But you're critically important. I need you. So I'll tell you, and hope that you'll agree it needs to be kept secret."

"And if I don't?" said Alyssa.

Craft spread out his hands. "Honestly, I haven't thought that far ahead. I feel like I know you well enough to believe you will."

Alyssa studied him. He could have just as easily lied, but she believed he was being sincere. "Before you continue," she said, wincing. "I really need to use the restroom."

"Really? I'm finally at the part you're most interested in."

"Yes. I'm aware of the irony," she said with a grimace. "But I've been holding it for a long time now. And if my bladder explodes, killing everyone in this restaurant, your information won't do me any good."

Brennan Craft just laughed as she hurried off to use the facilities.

She returned a few minutes later, feeling relieved, at least with respect to her bladder. The pain killers the hospital had infused were beginning to wear off, and the stitches in her thigh and the slashes in her arm were beginning to whisper their presence to her. Before long they would be *shouting* their presence.

"Omar Haddad, or Al Yad, if you prefer, was the most impressive faster I studied," began Craft. "He had been an accountant in Syria and was visiting a relative in Afghanistan. He was somewhat religious, but not a fundamentalist. He just didn't know his favorite nephew was one of the top ten on the terrorist watch lists. He was almost collateral damage, as he tells the story, when they went after his nephew. He and his nephew made it to a cave. But our military bombed it back to the stone age, killing Omar's nephew instantly, and trapping Omar inside.

"Far above him there was a small vent, which provided some light and the air he needed. But there was no way out. There was some underground water, but no food. Two years later, Omar Haddad was found." Craft leaned forward. "He hadn't lost a pound."

Craft took a sip from his refilled cup of coffee and continued. "Omar stayed in Afghanistan while his story made the rounds and the authorities decided what to do with him. There was considerable confusion and red tape to get through before they would allow him to return to Syria. Which gave me the time I needed to learn of his story and recruit him. He was my first. And he was *not* a jihadist," insisted Craft. "In retrospect, one has to wonder what kind of mental toll being trapped alone in a cave took on him."

Alyssa had several questions, but decided not to interrupt.

"Ultimately," continued Craft, "I recruited others, as I mentioned. And I failed to find anything outwardly different about them. But they all had one thing in common: they never doubted they could live without food. Omar said that he never believed for an instant he would die of starvation. He flat out refused. He imagined himself feasting. Others have said similar things. They imagine they are being nourished. Most, by tapping into a sea of light, which, in their imagination at least, is in the visible range. But it's ethereal."

"So why didn't it work for you?"

Craft frowned. "I don't know. Somehow, I believed with my mind, but not my heart. I was the only one who understood the scientific underpinnings of what they were doing, what I was trying to tap. But you can either do it or you can't, to some degree. Just because you understand intellectually doesn't mean you truly *believe*.

"A few friends of mine bungee jumped one summer off the side of a bridge," he continued. "I researched the hell out of this, because they wanted me to join them. Basically, if you check your equipment and measurements, which you can do ten times to be absolutely certain, you're going to survive a bungee jump. Intellectually, I knew this. But I couldn't bring myself to do it. I knew in my head it would be okay. I just didn't believe it in my gut, where it counted."

"So that explains it," said Alyssa with a grin.

"What?"

"Why you didn't list bungee jumping as a hobby on your dating profile."

Craft laughed.

Alyssa was beginning to have an overwhelming feeling that the chemistry they had experienced during their date had been real. Brennan Craft continued to be brilliant, funny, good-natured, and thoughtful. And Alyssa's instincts told her he was equally drawn to her, even though she was aware this could still be an act on his part.

"Sorry," she said. "Didn't mean to interrupt. Go on."

"At some point I began to view the ability to tap zero point energy as a cross between a subconscious skill, and an autonomic response. And this was when I made my breakthrough. Because I realized that people *can* achieve some mastery over their own physiologic functions. Functions long thought to be involuntary, beyond their conscious control. Using biofeedback."

Alyssa nodded thoughtfully. This was ingenious, and made immediate sense to her. If you asked a man to raise or lower his body temperature, heart rate, or blood pressure while at absolute rest, he couldn't do it. But if you hooked him up to sensors that provided him with continuous feedback, *biofeedback*, at high levels of precision, he could begin to learn how. He could somehow train himself to affect these functions at will. As long as he could get feedback, so his brain knew whatever it was doing was working—or not working. It had been found that along with temperature and heart rate, brainwave patterns, muscle tone, and skin conductivity could be altered at will—once a person had been trained.

The people who were able to control these functions, eventually without the need of monitors, couldn't provide a recipe of how they were doing it to anyone else. There were no shortcuts. Each individual had to train themselves. Biofeedback had been used in medical practice for some time now, after it had been found that adjusting certain physiologic functions was beneficial for headaches and other maladies.

"That's why you bought scales," whispered Alyssa. "Not to weigh drugs. But as biofeedback monitors. So you would know if you were able to exert force on them using zero point energy."

"Nice intuitive leap," said Craft in delight. "You're even more impressive than I'd hoped."

Alyssa found herself delighted by the compliment, but didn't respond.

"We didn't use the scales at first," explained Craft. "Much too coarse a measuring rod. At first we were just trying to exert pressure that was the equivalent to the weight of a postage stamp. We had very fancy, very precise instruments we tried to affect. And we also used monitors that could register almost infinitesimal bits of electrical currents."

He paused. "Even at these tiny levels, it took me months of futile effort before I found the secret. A posture of the mind, a way of visualizing what you were trying to do, that is required. And one I can impart on others—although it still takes quite a lot of effort and time to begin to get it. But eventually, we were all able to tap into the zero point field, with various levels of proficiency. Using our minds as a quantum lens to focus and redirect the energy. Having no idea how we were doing it. And after we trained ourselves, we non-fasters were finally able to sustain ourselves on this energy, without the need for food." Craft gestured to his empty plate, which still smelled of maple syrup. "I do eat, as you know. But now it's a choice, not a necessity."

"If this is really true," said Alyssa. "It's beyond incredible. It utterly transforms what we know about the universe. And how we see our place in it."

"I *know*. Believe me, when I first managed to create a tiny electric current I was so excited, I'm surprised you didn't hear my celebrations all the way in Indiana. Ultimately we got stronger, although all but two of us defensively only."

"What does that mean?"

"Once our minds became trained and sort of, 'got it' a bit, and our belief increased, we found we could instinctively—and this is going to sound very stupid—create a force field around ourselves. Our own personal shields. You know, like the ones that protect starships on Star Trek."

Now this was pushing things too far. Exerting half an ounce of pressure on a scale was one thing. But a force-field? Ridiculous.

And yet, Alyssa couldn't help but flash back to her yard, where Craft had been caught in a crossfire he couldn't have possibly survived.

"Now this makes no sense at all," acknowledged Craft. "Force fields are popular in science fiction, but they are one of the most difficult feats known to science. I won't go into the physics or the energy requirement, but it's immense. Beyond immense. For us to achieve this, we have to be redirecting energy from the zero point field—quantum lensing, so to speak—at an efficiency of a billion trillion trillion times that required to nourish our bodies. And yet none of us could harness more than an infinitesimal fraction of this power for anything other than a shield."

"Why would that be?"

"It's unclear. But once you've trained your mind using biofeedback, and get more and more adept using the field, there comes a point when you generate a shield automatically. Involuntarily. When you're in imminent danger. The mind seems to react instinctively to threats, to work toward self-preservation. But harnessing energy for non-defensive purposes is a choice. Your life isn't on the line. You're just doing it to do it. Somehow the subconscious knows.

"Eventually, we each found ourselves protected by two levels of shield. The first became a maintenance level that is always 'on'. Like a second skin. The subconscious throws it up continually without a thought. If I'm slicing an apple and stick myself by accident, it's enough to stop the knife from breaking the skin."

"And the second level?"

"The second level only happens when you're being attacked. It's invisible also, and is thrown up about a foot away from the body. I don't know how your brain does it. And I don't know how it moves as your body does. But the subconscious quantum engine that is your mind is pretty miraculous. Who knows, perhaps we're not only tapping into the zero point field, but into the mind of God as well."

"Do we really need to get even more metaphysical than we're already gotten?" said Alyssa.

Craft shrugged. "There are miracles all around us. What's one more?" he said evenly. "Do you know what event I believe to be the most impossible, most miraculous of all?"

Alyssa thought about it for a second and then shook her head.

"The creation of a human being from the union of a sperm and an egg. Think about it. A single fertilized egg cell gives rise to many trillions of cells. Impressive enough already. But how do these trillions of cells know how to organize themselves into a human body? Into a human *brain*? How do they know where to be?"

Alyssa smiled stupidly. How *did* anyone take this for granted? How could a single microscopic cell possibly transform into an entire, immensely complex human being?

Craft continued. "Not only do various cells need to know where to be, they need to know *what* to be. At first they're all identical. Then, magically, certain cells begin to change, as stretches of DNA are turned on and off differentially. Some suddenly become heart cells. Others brain cells. Still others blood cells, or bone cells, or liver cells, or neurons. How in the world can this happen?" He shook his head. "If a microscopic grain of sand were to reproduce madly, resulting in a trillion grains of sand, and these grains began specializing, ultimately constructing an entire computer spontaneously, we'd call it a miracle. But a fertilized egg manages a feat much more impressive than this."

Alyssa tilted her head in wonder. *He was right.* He had such a unique way of looking at things. And his enthusiasm was contagious. "Okay, just so you know, you've officially blown my mind about ten times today."

"Only ten?" replied Craft, raising his eyebrows. "Well, don't worry," he added in amusement. "The day is still young."

26

More and more people had been piling into the restaurant during their lengthy stay at the table, and their waitress eyed them warily. Craft made a show of leaving a tip much greater than the entire bill was going to be and ordered more toast.

When the waitress had gone he said, "I also have offensive capabilities. They're feeble, but I can control them *consciously*—which is a nice change of pace. But even though I can conjure them up consciously, they are still driven entirely by my subconscious. I still have no idea how I'm doing it." Craft raised his eyebrows. "Would you like a demonstration?"

Alyssa looked uncertain.

"A very gentle demonstration, of course."

She braced herself. "Go ahead."

"I'm going to apply some pressure to your head. Just a slight amount."

His expression didn't change, but she felt an unmistakable tightening, pressing inward from both of her ears. "Amazing," she whispered. "It's basically telekinesis."

"Yes. But it has the potential to be so much more."

"Is that how you knocked the commandos unconscious in my yard?"

"Right. But this represents the full extent of what I think of as my offensive ability. I can clap you in the ears, so to speak, hard enough to knock you out for a short time. But that's about it."

"And bullets just ricochet off your, um . . . shield?"

"No. They don't bounce. They vanish. Near as I can tell, the shield is a wall of energy less than the width of an atom. But *what* a wall. The energy is of such potency that whatever touches it is consumed instantly. Like throwing an ice cube into the sun. Shoot a bullet at the shield and the bullet is vaporized as it travels into it, one microscopic layer at a time. We've done experiments. My belief is that nothing known to man can breach it. Including nuclear."

Alyssa nodded. At this point, she'd be foolish not to believe anything he said. If he told her he could pull an elephant from his ear, she'd back up to give him room.

"And saying it encircles me at about a distance of a foot isn't completely accurate either," he added. "It operates when and where it needs to operate. So if my back is to a wall and a bullet is coming toward my face, it will materialize in front of the bullet to stop it. But it won't vaporize the wall behind me. And it will vanish as soon as the threat is gone. It's not a dome. It's directional somehow. If I'm getting barraged from all sides, it will give me three hundred and sixty degree protection, but it won't touch anything beneath me. I won't melt a hole through the Earth and end up at the Earth's core—that sort of thing." He sighed. "If only I had a clue how I'm doing this," he added in frustration.

These feats required channeling massive energies, as well as a subconscious that was an absolute savant. But Alyssa was well aware of the power of the subconscious. If one's body was given over to it, it could perform feats the conscious mind could not. A pitcher could reflexively catch a blazing line drive aimed at his head before his conscious mind even registered that the ball had been hit.

"So you can't figure out the exact scientific principles you're using to perform these miracles. And you're frustrated. I get that. But you're also basically invincible. Which isn't such a bad thing to be."

"Not quite. I do have an Achilles' heel."

Alyssa was surprised he would admit this. She guessed that Achilles had avoided advertising exactly where his enemies needed to shoot him. She thought about it for a few seconds. "Sleep?" she said finally. "Unconsciousness?"

"Great guess," he said, and seemed genuinely impressed. "I certainly would have thought so. But no. As you know, the subconscious is alive and well and monitoring our surroundings far more than we realize, even in sleep. Deciding what is important enough to bring to our conscious attention. But training your mind to tap into the zero point field seems to enhance the subconscious significantly. It becomes immensely more powerful and vigilant than it would otherwise be. I'm more aware of my surroundings when I'm asleep, at a subconscious level, than when I'm awake."

"That makes no sense."

"We did experiments with rubber bullets. Try to shoot me, even when I'm *sleeping*, and the shield blocks it. If I'm awake, but my back is turned, and someone sneaks up on me and shoots me, my subconscious extends the shield once again. Even when I have no *conscious* awareness anyone is behind me. Once your mind realizes it can protect you, it clings to self preservation with an amazing tenacity."

"Isn't that dangerous for anyone sleeping next to you?" asked Alyssa, imagining accidentally rolling onto him in her sleep, and having her arm vaporized as his shield came to life.

Craft's eyes lit up and a mischievous smile came over his face.

"Wait a minute," protested Alyssa. "I wasn't asking because I'm interested, okay. Come on. It was strictly a scientific question."

"Of course," said Craft, managing to keep any trace of sarcasm or doubt from his voice. "But no need to worry. The subconscious can tell the difference between a threat and a . . . good friend."

Alyssa wondered if he had actually tested this theory with one or several women, but didn't ask. "So if sleep isn't your vulnerability," she said. "What is?

Brennan Craft blew out a long breath. "Omar Haddad," he said simply.

27

Eben Martin felt like an idiot as he stood with his legs spread, one foot on each of two laptops, and his arms spread and extended as far above his head as they could be, each index finger touching the bottom of one of two tablet computers suspended above him, providing the illusion that he was holding them up with the might of a single finger alone. He looked like a human letter-X suspended between four devices. Martin loathed every second that he remained in this position.

He smiled broadly.

"Perfect," declared the anorexic-looking professional photographer as he snapped dozens of pictures in quick succession of one of the most powerful CEOs in the world, dressed in business casual, although business casual that was impeccably tailored and was more expensive than a high-end suit.

"Now," continued the photographer, "I need a contemplative look. You're one of the world's wealthiest men, and a computer visionary, pondering the future of the web. Good . . . good. Excellent," he gushed, happily snapping away.

Martin continued standing, framed between the devices, and contemplated murder. Would anyone miss the chief photographer from Fortune magazine? Probably not, he decided.

Martin had been on the covers of numerous magazines during the past few years—and he was pretty damn sick of it. It was great for Informatics Solutions and for his image, but his personal celebrity was getting to be a nuisance, as were the endless creative poses that each magazine wanted him to assume for its cover.

"Now, let's get a serious pose . . . you've just been told—"

"Hold on one second," interrupted Martin. He pulled a phone from his pocket and pretended to read it. "Whoops," he said. "I have a fire that needs fighting. I'm afraid I have to call it a day," he finished, doing his best to pretend he wished it were otherwise.

"Mr. Martin," the man complained. "There were a few more poses I wanted to try."

"Really sorry about that," said Martin. "But I'm sure one of the many shots you've already taken will turn out great. I only wish I had more time. But, alas, the business world won't be kept waiting."

Martin offered to help the man load up his equipment, which had the desired effect of greatly accelerating his departure, as he was panicked into believing that if he didn't leave fast enough, Martin would commit the unpardonable sin of touching one of his precious cameras or lenses.

Two of Martin's key publicity people, Karly Rose and Susan Black, escorted the photographer through the outer door, leaving Martin alone in his private conference room. He had much to do, and wasted no time rushing through the door connected to his spacious office suite. Some CEO's of multibillion dollar corporations had eschewed lavish luxury so as not to seem to be elevating themselves too much above the rank and file.

Martin didn't share this view. He took the opposite approach. He wanted his office to be the size of a small apartment, and so lavishly furnished and appointed that it screamed opulence and power. He wanted it to be intimidating. And he wanted employees to aspire to improved offices as they moved up the ranks.

Martin fell heavily into his desk chair and spun it around to face his largest computer monitor, hanging in a recessed panel to his left.

There was an intruder in his office.

Martin's breath caught in his throat as he took in the situation. The man was tall and well-built, with a menacing air about him. He sat calmly at a small oval table that Martin used for working meetings with his executive vice-presidents, dressed in business casual as impeccable as his own.

Martin moved his hand to a small button under his desk, which would silently call for security, and pressed it gently.

"Sorry to surprise you like this, Mr. Martin," the man said. "But I was told you wanted to meet with me as soon as possible."

Martin studied his surprise visitor further. He was cool, confident, and conveyed a commanding presence. "How did you get in here?" said Martin casually, knowing he needed to stall for a minute or two until security arrived.

"My name is Turco," said the man. "Adam Turco. And I heard through the grapevine you were looking for a mercenary. The best in the business."

Martin's mind raced. He had sent his head of security, Randy Schram, on an urgent mission to recruit a mercenary. But Schram had been given strict instructions not to reveal who he was, and who Martin was by extension, until they had chosen who they wanted to approach.

"I realize," continued Turco smoothly, "that your man Schram wasn't ready to disclose his identity. Or yours. But when I heard a powerful player was in the market, my curiosity was piqued. So I took the liberty of learning who was behind it." He smiled serenely. "Easier to apply for a job when you know who's doing the hiring."

"I don't know what you're talking about," said Martin.

"I'm the best there is," continued Turco as if Martin hadn't spoken. "And I heard you were in a hurry. So to speed things along, I thought I'd apply in person. Demonstrate a few skills, just so you know I'm worth my ask."

Martin considered. The man had to be good. Because Schram was good, and Turco had traced Schram's feelers back to him in record time. And gaining access to his office like this was not supposed to be possible. They were on the fifty-eighth floor, the penthouse, and the executive offices were supposed to be secure. Visitors all required escorts, and the elevator wouldn't even travel to the top floor without a keycard. And even if there were no security, a surprise guest would need to make it past several of his secretaries and assistants to gain access to his office, which itself was not a simple task.

Martin shot a quick glance at the outer doors to his office and then returned his stare to Adam Turco. Turco caught his glance and smiled. "I temporarily disabled your silent alarm, by the way," he said casually. "So we won't be interrupted."

Turco paused. "So what do you say? Are you ready to acknowledge that you really are looking for a mercenary? And that I just might be as good as I say I am?"

Eben Martin blew out a long breath. He hadn't gotten to where he was by being indecisive. "Yes. I am looking. And yes, your skills are impressive."

"Thank you."

Martin texted one of his assistants that he didn't want to be disturbed until further notice. He then left his desk and joined Turco across the small oval table, but didn't yet extend his hand. "So what are your credentials?"

Turco told him. He was ex-special forces, a sharpshooter, and had been an integral part of a number of ops that were classified, but had involved gun battles against forces that had greatly outnumbered his own.

Martin studied him carefully. "You're experienced, you're qualified, and you've shown your initiative. But how do I know you can be . . . discreet."

Turco nodded. "You're very high profile. I understand that. But I've worked with other high profile people before. And you can think of me as Las Vegas. What happens between me and my client, *stays* between me and my client."

"Comforting," said Martin. "But not quite enough."

"I didn't think it would be," replied the mercenary. "The real answer is that I'm a pro. The best there is. With a code. And I charge a lot. Go with someone who will sell their services cheaply, and they'll sell you out on a whim. Also, when you partner with me, you partner with me for four-year blocks, during which time I'm yours. Exclusively. Which is nice, since I'm there in emergencies, and you'll never have to go through an exercise like this again. One you handled clumsily, if you don't mind some honest feedback."

"Go on."

"I charge three million dollars a year. At the end of this time, you can choose if you want to renew for an additional four-year period. You hire me on as your personal bodyguard, which isn't such a bad idea anyway. Since you're paying me extremely well, and on an annual basis, I'll want you to thrive in business and live to a ripe old age. And I'll be as loyal as a Golden Retriever during our association. Because if I'm not, I can't count on this money year after year."

Martin smiled. It was an ingenious offer. Charge a ridiculous rate, one so high as to ensure loyalty. Turco knew Martin was worth north of sixty billion dollars. So he had a lot to lose if his hired gun wasn't trustworthy. So much so that if overpayment was an insurance policy, it was well worth the premiums. Twelve million dollars over four years was rounding error for a man like Martin.

Turco went on to explain that at the start of the relationship, one million would be due immediately, and that he would hire additional men as needed, and pay them, so that only Turco would know Martin was running the show.

"Are you prepared to kill on American soil?" asked Martin when the mercenary had finished.

The man nodded without hesitation.

Eben Martin studied Adam Turco for an extended period, during which time his job applicant continued to appear relaxed and supremely confident.

"You're hired," said Martin finally, shaking hands with his guest. "Text me your bank instructions, and I'll have the money wired to you as soon as you leave. And there really is no time to waste. I assume you're ready to be briefed and to start immediately?"

"I am," said Turco. "I have a partner in mind, and can add him very quickly if necessary."

"Good," said Martin. He returned to his desk and opened a drawer, removing a manila envelope. He removed several 8 x 10 photos from the envelope, walked back to the table, and handed the top photograph to Adam Turco. "I'll also send the photos and information in this envelope to your phone," he said.

Turco studied the photograph carefully.

"This man is the reason you're here," explained Eben Martin.

"I gathered that," said Turco dryly. "So who am I looking at? And more importantly, what is he to you?"

"His name is Brennan Craft," said Martin simply. "And several years ago, we were very close friends."

28

The waitress returned with Craft's toast and placed it in front of him. The hostess was seating a young family one booth over, so Craft lowered his voice, not that anyone would understand, or believe, anything he was saying anyway.

"Omar was the strongest of us all," said Craft. "He was a natural. My guess is that one in a thousand, or one in a million, just happen to have a better knack for it. He did. I was the second strongest. The others could harness the field to varying degrees. I felt like I had pushed it as far as I could. I had taken careful and thorough measurements over many months, and I was going to write a paper and announce this to the world." He smiled wistfully. "Collect my four of five Nobel prizes and create a revolution unlike anything in history."

"But something happened to change this," guessed Alyssa. "Something involving Al Yad."

Craft nodded, and then frowned bitterly. "I was the second strongest, but other than the force field I generated without any conscious control, I could barely do anything at all. I could charge a cell phone or laptop. Exert a tiny bit of pressure on a scale. Or a skull. But Omar on the other hand . . ."

Craft stopped, and pain and loss were reflected in his eyes.

He paused for several seconds to collect himself. "While I was in the process of writing all of it up," he continued finally, "there came a time when Omar Haddad hit a tipping point of some kind. He was always the strongest, but suddenly his ability increased exponentially. It grew stronger by the day. He had cracked some kind of metaphorical sound barrier that none of the others in the group were close to cracking. And his success was a feedback loop. The more his power grew, the more belief he had—so the more his power grew. It was becoming alarming.

"I decided I needed to find a way to rein him in. And I realized that I couldn't go public with this, after all. What if there were others out there like Omar? Who, by the way, had rapidly begun losing his sanity."

"*That's* why you didn't want to disclose this to Elovic and his men," said Alyssa in sudden understanding. "If this leaks out and becomes widespread knowledge, anyone can use biofeedback techniques to awaken these latent capabilities. Possibly creating more Al Yads."

"Essentially," said Craft. "I had to make some breakthroughs in biofeedback techniques to get this to work, which won't be easily duplicated, but why take any chances? A single Omar Haddad—Al Yad," he amended, realizing that this name was Alyssa's preference, "is more than dangerous enough."

"Okay, but getting back to where you left off, he was beginning to lose his sanity," she prompted.

"Yes. He started to believe he was a god. And why not? This fervent belief in his own divinity certainly enabled him to wield the power of a god."

Alyssa swallowed hard. "Like, what are we talking about here?"

"We're talking about power that's immeasurable. Al Yad's transformation to his current abilities took about six months before leveling off for good. But no measuring instrument we could devise could survive the raw power he could throw off. He could willfully channel the zero point field with unbelievable bandwidth. If he wanted to, he could have powered the electrical grid of the entire US without working up a sweat."

Craft shook his head gravely. "But *I* was working up a sweat, I can tell you that. I was *freaking* out. He had begun studying Islam with a passion, and claiming he was The Hand of Allah, able to wield Allah's power. And he *could*. It's probably easier to be delusional when your delusion is *true*."

"Good point."

"And then he broke entirely. He was angry with me because I didn't want to help him grow even greater. And I insisted on testing him, which was annoying to him. Then he began ranting about punishing the infidel. More and more jihadist talk. I raced to find a way to defuse him, but failed."

Alyssa was spellbound. An alien spacecraft could have landed in the middle of their table and she wouldn't have noticed at this point.

"So the last strand of Al Yad's sanity broke, and he destroyed our entire camp. His goal was to kill off the only group on Earth who knew what was really going on. And who might—unlikely, but *might*—someday be able to challenge his power."

"But he failed, right?"

Craft was visibly distraught. "No," he whispered in horror. "He succeeded. All of the others were murdered."

He fought to get his emotions under control for several seconds. When he had, he continued, but his voice was strained. "Al Yad was able to direct energies that broke through their shields and vaporized them. They were annihilated instantly. I was the strongest, and somehow my mind, my shield, was able to hold out against him. But I knew—I *knew*—that I couldn't hold out for much longer. And I had no offensive means to strike at him. So I bluffed. I pretended to be bored. 'We can do this all day,' I said. 'But I'm invulnerable. Even to you.'"

"Since you're still here, he must have bought it."

"He did. But there's more. I told him I had just reached the same tipping point he had. That soon, I would be just as capable of wielding the zero point field as he was. So he could never kill me. But I had to get him to disengage and leave. So I told him to go, and do whatever he wanted. Use his power in any way he wanted. Amass wealth and glory and women. Build a religion. Wow followers with his abilities.

"But," continued Craft, "He knew I would recognize his handiwork anywhere. So I warned him that if I learned he had ever used his power for acts of terrorism—for mass killings, or mass destruction—or if he ever killed any world leaders, I would come after him. That I knew a way to become even stronger than him for short periods of time, and I would kill him. I said it with conviction, and he had respect for my intelligence and ingenuity."

"Which explains why he's built a following and threatened to destroy much of the world, but hasn't actually done it. Although it's hard to believe this bluff is still working, given his delusional state."

"I agree. We've been lucky. But this won't hold forever. Since this showdown, I've kept myself hidden, so he can't learn if I was able to make the breakthrough I boasted of. Or realize how close he was to breaking through my defenses. But my existence is the only thing holding him in check."

"And he can do what he's been ranting about?" asked Alyssa. But she already knew the answer.

"More. He can take out a city in the blink of an eye. He can wield enough zero point energy to make a hydrogen bomb look like a toy. And you can be sure he hasn't been sitting around, convinced he should change his ways. He's delusional, but very, very bright. He's been trying to find me. I've been monitoring his attempts. And when he does, he'll be thinking of a way to kill me. It won't take long for him to determine I still only have defensive capabilities. And then I'm vulnerable."

"How so?"

"He could entomb me inside a block of concrete, or trap me in a steel cage—or most anything else for that matter. And that's just one example of my vulnerability."

"Wouldn't your shield cut right through any cage?"

"Unfortunately no. If something isn't coming at me, if I'm not being *actively* threatened, I can't consciously invoke the force-field. It's sort of a panic reaction by my subconscious. Being trapped wouldn't be an immediate, visceral enough threat to evoke it. So I could be trapped for eternity. Or until my star pupil, Al Yad, decides to use zero point energy to launch me into the sun."

Craft rubbed the back of his head absently. "It sounds far-fetched, but he'll spare no money or effort. And when you can tap unlimited energy, many things become possible. If he's able to find me and . . .

dispose of me, then the world is at his mercy." Craft scowled. "Or at least what's left of it will be."

A chill went down Alyssa's spine. "So the men who interrogated me," she said. "You think they were sent by Al Yad, don't you?"

"Yes. Our government will stop at nothing to question me about Al Yad. And Al Yad will stop at nothing to learn my location."

"And he somehow got wind of our date, obviously. And wanted to know why you came out of hiding for me. The interrogation questions now make perfect sense."

"He probably has his fingers in the US government," said Craft. "He has the money to pay people off for access. And he has certainly hired the best mercenaries and computer experts. I've done a lot of things right, but putting my image on an online dating site was very stupid. I thought that since I'd rigged the system so my image wouldn't trigger automatic computer recognition, I was immune. I didn't consider that human eyes would be checking up on anyone with interest in *you.*

"Al Yad must have been ecstatic when he learned about you," continued Craft. "It gave him a lead and a recent location for me. The man who did all the questioning in the van is almost certainly the chief of military and intelligence for Al Yad's organization. His name is Tariq Bahar. Educated in Oxford England. Very gifted."

"Yep. Sounds like GQ."

"GQ?" repeated Craft.

"You know, short for *Gentlemen's Quarterly.* The high fashion men's magazine. He was quite dapper for a ruthless psychopath. He had a certain elegance. Anyway, he didn't give me his name. So that's how I thought of him."

Craft nodded. "I knew I might be putting you at risk by bringing you into this. But I thought it was something I had to do. I never imagined things would play out as poorly as they have. For that I am truly sorry."

"Look, Bren, I can't say it's been a pleasant week. I could have been killed at my house. And I really thought GQ—Tariq Bahar— was going to torture me to death. But I understand why you did what you did. And knowing about the breakthrough you've made is. . ." She paused in thought. "Well, let's just say there are no words for it."

"It's only a matter of time before I make a mistake and Al Yad finds me," said Craft. "And then finds out I'm still an ant to his T. Rex. So I've been searching for a way to even the scales. To become his equal. So trapping me and eventually killing me is no longer an option for him."

"Which is why *I'm* so important to you," said Alyssa. "Isn't it?"

"You've assimilated the situation with remarkable speed," said Craft in admiration.

Alyssa didn't feel like this was the case. Surreal didn't even *begin* to cover this conversation with Bren Craft. She was reeling from it all. It was too much to take in all at once. Too big. Too impossible.

No wonder Craft had wanted to bond with her before this came out. He needed her to ensure a madman with unlimited power, who wanted to unleash Armageddon on the world, continued to be kept in check. "And now it makes sense that you didn't explain why you needed me when I first asked. I have to admit, 'I need you to help save the world' isn't something I would have believed."

Brennan Craft rose from the table and gestured for her to do the same. "So let me try it now. I need you to help save the world. Are you in?"

29

"You don't need to answer me this second," said Craft, as Alyssa also rose from the table. "I know it's been a brutal twenty-four hours for you." He sighed. "Speaking of which—how are you feeling?"

While Major Elovic had asked the same thing days ago, the question felt different this time. Elovic had said it because it was almost socially expected of him. Brennan Craft because he genuinely cared for her welfare.

"A little weak. And I'm in some pain. It's fairly minor right now, but it's growing."

Craft produced a bottle from his pocket and handed it to her. "Prescription pain killers," he said. "I had some time to plan ahead while you were sleeping."

Alyssa smiled gratefully and read the label. She lifted a glass of water from the table in a mock toast and said, "To planning ahead," and then downed two of the pills.

After paying their bill, they reached the parking lot and Craft opened the door to let her in. She flashed back to their date. Did he consider this just a continuation, or was he always this polite?

"Where to now?" she asked.

"You could still do with some rest and relaxation. And it wouldn't hurt for us to get to know each other better. I was thinking we could hang out at a hotel for a while. Until late tonight."

She considered. "When you'd ideally like to pay a visit with me to my lab."

"Very good," said Craft approvingly. "Yes, ideally. But this will depend entirely on you."

Alyssa remained silent.

"What do you say?" prompted Craft. "We can find something near the woods on the outskirts of Bloomington. I really do love the woods as much as you do. Maybe a bed-and-breakfast."

The corner's of Alyssa's mouth turned up into the slightest of smiles.

"We'll get separate rooms, of course," he added quickly, having misinterpreted the smile.

"Of course," she repeated with exaggerated gravity. "I mean, what would be the point of ever sleeping with you now? Now that you've been gallant enough to tell me what I wanted to know without any strings attached."

"Between you and me," said Craft in amusement. "Gallantry sucks. But just so you know, if you ever did insist on sleeping with me some day, I'd probably let you. You know, out of politeness. But if we ever do become more than friends," he added, and the stopped himself. "Well, since we began the day with you hating me, I guess I'm making an assumption even to suggest we're friends. But, anyway, if we ever do sleep together, I'd like it to be because you really wanted to."

Alyssa nodded. "Between you and me," she said, "misleading someone temporarily because you're trying to save the world isn't the worst excuse for bad behavior I've ever heard."

"About the misleading part," said Craft. "I did choose you to get access to your expertise. But I also chose you for *you*."

Alyssa studied him for several seconds, but decided not to respond. "Why don't you finish your story," she said. "I know the punchline, but I'd still like to hear it out. And learn how I came into the picture, from your perspective."

Craft agreed, but first he conducted a web search and located a bed-and-breakfast about fifteen minutes outside of Bloomington. He activated the GPS navigation system and began driving.

"I spent many months exploring different strategies for stopping Al Yad or improving my own abilities," he said. "But I came up empty. But the one thing I felt sure of was that belief played a critical role in Al Yad's ascendance. Belief in his ability to fast forever and still survive. His increasingly delusional belief in his own divinity. He was naturally gifted for reasons that may never be clear. But it was the absolute belief in his gut that he could wield zero point energy like a god that allowed him to do so."

Craft frowned. "You'd think that my own success with the field would give me absolute belief as well. But it doesn't. Not knowing how I'm tapping into it must clash with the scientist in me. The rational me. My brain must consider it too much like magic to let me tear off the regulator and use zero point energy to its full potential."

"From my study of the subconscious, this isn't as surprising as you might think. But go on."

"So I wondered if I could be *hypnotized* to have this absolute belief. Like Al Yad does. But without the delusional part. Why not? The movies would have you think hypnosis can get a man to believe he's Elvis. But then I did research and learned this wasn't reality."

Alyssa nodded. She had told Major Elovic that Craft would have done his homework, and she had been right.

"But then I learned that Black Ops had a secret, leading-edge program in hypnosis. So I hacked in." He gestured to Alyssa appreciatively. "The techniques you've developed are complicated, but quite brilliant."

"Thank you," said Alyssa.

She had personally made several of the breakthroughs involved. They had learned how to isolate subconscious neuronal pathways associated with certain beliefs, and then nail these beliefs down using drugs, hypnotism, and through stimulation of neurons using oscillating electrical frequencies.

"It was the jackpot. Your advances could not have been more perfect for my needs. You weren't controlling people. You were improving the placebo effect. Your breakthrough was in getting a subject to believe in something strongly enough for this to translate into a miracle orchestrated by their subconscious. And an enhancement of belief was *precisely* what I needed. As long as a subject is willing, you can free up the full potential of his or her subconscious. Unleash the full power of the mind. As you said during your interrogation, the power of the subconscious is mysterious and immense."

"We really have done wonders in this area," said Alyssa proudly. "And yes," she added, nodding at Craft, "I should be able to easily instill an absolute conviction within you that you can harness the zero point field at any strength you want. But there is no guarantee this will work. There is always the chance something more is required. Something that only Al Yad possesses."

Craft sighed. "I know it's not guaranteed. But I'm convinced it will work. I thought you were perfect in the beginning," added Craft with enthusiasm. "And everything I've learned since tells me I was even more right than I knew. If anyone can help me strengthen myself to become invulnerable, even against Al Yad, you can."

He paused. "I know you're aware of this, Alyssa, but I found seven or eight of you who were almost equally adept at these techniques. As I said before, I chose *you* for a reason."

"Sure," said Alyssa with an impish grin. "Given why you left the priesthood, I think I know what that reason is. I'd be flattered," she added, "except most of the others are men."

"True, but Jana Sharp is in this group. And she could be a swimsuit model."

"So what's your point?" grumbled Alyssa.

"My point is that I didn't choose you just because you're a woman. Or just because you're attractive. I don't know if fate exists, but if it does, it operated this time. I don't care if there were ten thousand gorgeous women with your identical expertise. I would *still* have chosen you. Because we really are compatible."

"On paper."

"Before the commando raid from hell," said Craft, "I'd like to think we were compatible in *reality*."

Alyssa chose not to respond.

"So the rest you know. I stalked you, set up a date, and we went out. The other alternative was to call you out of the blue, and politely explain that the fate of the world was balanced on a razor's edge, and that you could make all the difference."

"Yeah. Probably not the best approach," she allowed.

"So I decided to get to know you. For you to know me. Develop a rapport. A trust. I hoped you could help me get to the next level, but I also hoped we could build a relationship. I wanted a gifted mind to share ideas with. A partner in the struggle against Al Yad. Which, ironically, he and I both see as the struggle of good against evil."

"Only his definition of good means cleansing the world of most of its inhabitants."

"Right. And his definition of evil is anyone standing in his way."

"Suppose I do this for you, and it works?" said Alyssa. "Can you defeat him?"

"Maybe. Although I'm not counting on it. But at minimum, I'd be a better deterrent. And if I alone can't defeat him, maybe I can train others. Good men and women. Altruistic. Stable. And maybe your narco-hypnosis can instill enough belief to make them all on par with Al Yad. So maybe two of us can beat him. Maybe three. Maybe fifty."

"My instincts tell me this would be a very bad idea. Playing with fire times fifty."

"I have some failsafe ideas, but let's table this for now." He paused and turned onto a narrow, two lane road. "But I ask you to think for a moment what it could mean for humanity. Imagine for a second we could harness this. That we could find some kind of failsafe to ensure madmen like Al Yad can't use it. Imagine the possibilities."

"I'm sure you've given this a lot of thought."

"A lot of thought," he said. "Energy is wealth. The two are one and the same. Think about how much money the world spends each year on power. Even if only a limited number of people could achieve Al Yad's level, they alone could direct energies to fill every power plant on earth. For free. What would it do for the world economy if every nickel spent by individuals, and corporations, for power could be poured into other pursuits?"

They drove under a spectacular canopy of trees that shaded the road they were on, but Alyssa didn't have time to admire the beauty of their surroundings.

"And hunger would be a thing of the past," he continued. "First, because no one would need food. But even if some did, this wouldn't be a problem. Desalination takes considerable energy. But with unlimited free energy, enough ocean water could easily be purified to sate the world's thirst. And for agricultural use, as well. The water could be pumped into fields at no cost."

Alyssa nodded enthusiastically. "And fossil fuels would be a thing of the past," she added. "You could power cars on your own."

Craft grinned. "If people really could harness the zero point field, they wouldn't *need* cars. Or even planes."

"Are you saying they could fly?" said Alyssa, her eyes widening.

"Al Yad can," he said simply.

Holy hell, thought Alyssa. Apparently Craft hadn't told her *everything*. "How does tapping into energy allow him to do *that*?"

"If you can control nearly infinite energies, there is almost nothing you can't do. Believe me, my shield uses billions of times the power needed for flight. I'm not sure how he does it, and neither is he. There are theories that the zero point field is involved in conferring mass and gravity to objects. But even if he's not doing it by controlling gravity directly, he can easily energize air molecules above and below him to achieve the Bernoulli effect. Which is what gives lift to airplanes."

"How fast can he go?"

"When I saw him last, a few hundred miles per hour. But my guess is that it's all a matter of training. There's no reason those who have learned to really harness the field shouldn't be able to achieve jet speeds. Or greater. And each of us could pilot a private space yacht, which we could power to near light speed. We could reach beyond our planetary cradle in a big way. Finally mange to avoid having all of the species' eggs in one planetary basket."

Alyssa's head was spinning. In addition to what Craft had said, the many billions spent on clean energy research and the study of global warming could be used for other pursuits. In fact, she realized, with unlimited energy, humans could create any climate they wanted. Air-conditioning a single room on a scorching hot day took considerable power. So air-conditioning the Sahara desert to a comfortable seventy-five degrees would take energy that was unimaginable. On the other hand, if a cubic centimeter of vacuum had enough energy to boil away all of the world's oceans, this was not at all beyond the realm of possibility.

Energy did indeed mean wealth. And made all things possible. "We could make a paradise on Earth," whispered Alyssa. "Even if only a fraction of the population could tap into the field."

"And if *everyone* could . . . . Imagine what this would be like. And we'd all be invulnerable."

"True," said Alyssa. "Of course, we'd still eventually die from heart failure, cancer, and the like."

"I'm not so sure about that," said Craft. "Since I've trained myself to channel the field, I haven't been sick a single day. My trick right knee hasn't troubled me in years. You know better than anyone that the scientific establishment is finally recognizing the true power of the mind to heal the body." He raised his eyebrows. "Well what if having a subconscious that can tap unlimited energy is all the mind needs to amplify the placebo effect a thousand-fold? What if tapping the field gives our subconscious the power it needs to heal the body completely?"

Craft shifted his gaze from the road and stared at Alyssa meaningfully. "We'd need to do many more tests, but my gut tells me this could extend life." He raised his eyebrows. "Maybe indefinitely."

PART TWO

"Our incomplete knowledge of physical reality enriches our human experiences by maintaining its novelty, its unanticipated outcomes, its newness. It allows us each to live our lives as a great adventure. What sense of satisfaction would a scientist derive from inquiry if the laws of physics were all clearly revealed as part of the act of creation? What joy would there be in searching for buried treasure if you knew all along where you hid it? It's the mystery that underwrites the joy of discovery."

—Bernard Haisch, *The God Theory*

"If you were God, could you possibly dream up any more educational, contrasted, thrilling, beautiful, tantalizing world than Earth? If you think you could, do you imagine you would be outdoing Earth if you designed a world free of germs, diseases, poisons, pains, malice, explosives, and conflicts so its people could relax and enjoy it? Would you, in other words, try to make the world nice and safe—or would you let it be provocative, dangerous, and exciting?"

—Guy Murchie, *The Seven Mysteries of Life: An Exploration of Science and Philosophy*

"The origin of the universe is the exact opposite of random. Our lives are the exact opposite of pointless. It is not matter that creates an illusion of consciousness, but consciousness that creates an illusion of matter.

—Bernard Haisch, *The God Theory*

30

Santosh Patel couldn't believe his luck. When Craft had driven north to nearby Cincinnati and then immediately west into Indiana, his hopes had risen. But now, an hour later, he was *certain*. They were going to Bloomington, after all.

Perfect!

Patel had taken a virtual drive of the entire route via computer, and had found the ideal spot for his needs. While he and the rest of the team raced ahead to this staging area, he had Hank Ridley hang back and continue following Craft, just in case. And they could use Ridley's car to transport Aronson once they had her.

Ten minutes later, Ridley reported Craft had stopped for gas, giving them even more of a lead, and more time for preparation. Patel couldn't have asked for anything more.

* * *

Alyssa still felt a little weak. And while the pain medication had kicked in, she was reeling from what she had learned from Bren. She was sure this would be the case for some time to come. It wasn't as if this was something one could wrap their mind around, no matter how long they had been exposed to it.

She stared out of the window at the beauty around her and pondered the possibilities that Brennan Craft had brought to life. She had grown up in Southern California, and while it was hard to complain about palm trees and perfect weather, a smattering of palm trees couldn't hold a candle to the magnificent woodlands she had been living in for the past two years.

No matter how many times she was immersed in the spectacular forests of Indiana, they never lost their power to captivate her.

Always majestic and serene. Teeming with life and vibrancy. A lush green haven from the artificial rush of civilization. A shaded wonderland of beauty whose cool, crisp air was infused with the pure oxygen released by each and every tree.

Some people loved the cities, with their culture, art, and endless opportunities for interesting social interaction. Some like the country; it's simplicity and wide open spaces. But Alyssa Aronson only truly felt at peace when she was surrounded by the mightiest of earth's living things. And with the possible exception of the Sequoia Forrest in Northern California, teeming with trees that made the tallest, thickest specimens anywhere else look like adorable little babies, no place was more majestic than the Hoosier National Forest, two hundred thousand acres of soaring central hardwood trees, primarily oak and hickory.

Alyssa decided she was as happy as she'd been in some time. The drive to Bloomington on narrow, two lane roads—one lane in each direction—was as scenic as any drive could be. She was well fed and well caffeinated, and she was with a man she admired and liked.

Best second date ever, she thought at one point, although she decided it might be a stretch to call it a date, even if Craft had taken her to breakfast. But at the same time, it was so much *more* than a date.

Her conversation with Craft never stalled, even after more than an hour in the car, nor did Craft's warmth or sense of humor. Elovic's description of this man had been deeply troubling to her, because it had badly shaken her faith in her own instincts. She couldn't believe Craft had fooled her so completely, or that she could have been so very wrong about him.

But she hadn't been. Her instincts had been flawless.

As she thought about this, she recalled something else she had wanted to cover with her new traveling companion. "Almost forgot," she said. "One last thing the major told me. He said it looked as though you were studying political and military choke points all around the world. He took that as yet another sign you were delusional. Is this true?"

"Is *what* true?" asked Craft, one side of his mouth curling up into a crooked smile. "That I studied political systems? Or that I'm delusional?"

"We already know you're delusional," said Alyssa playfully. "Anyone who accomplished what you did would *have* to be. But did you really research, you know, world domination?"

Craft nodded. "I did. To my great surprise, my bluff has continued to keep Al Yad in check. Not entirely, since he has still amassed quite a following and considerable power. But at least with respect to the devastating use of his abilities. But just in case he decided to use his power with pinpoint accuracy so as not to draw my attention, I wanted to get a sense of what moves he might make on the global stage. And monitor them."

"Makes perfect sense," said Alyssa. "I have to admit, after my meeting with Major Elovic, I would have bet my life there was no possible way you could explain everything I knew about you and your activities in a rational, logical way."

Craft laughed. "There isn't," he said. "Since when is using your mind to tap energy that flashes into existence for less than a trillionth of a second, without knowing how you do it, rational?"

"You've got me there," said Alyssa, deciding in that instant she was as content as she had ever been.

They emerged from the woods to find a long stretch of corn, dozens and dozens of football fields worth, on Alyssa's side of the car, while Craft's side looked out onto an endless expanse of eerie windmills.

Alyssa preferred the woods but found the cornfields awe-inspiring in their own way. The sheer scope of row after perfect row of proud green stalks, reaching skyward like perfectly aligned spears, protecting their nutritional gifts within a swaddling of green leaves, was breathtaking. She couldn't even begin to guess how many millions of ears each field produced.

The wind farms, on the other hand, were an eyesore. A blight on the earth. And they were becoming ever more plentiful in Indiana, as each turbine generated, not just energy, but irresistible tax incentives from the federal government.

The scale of the wind farms was daunting. Each turbine was a high-tech metal monstrosity weighing more than a hundred tons, with cylindrical bases the size of a large living room rising thirty stories into the sky. Near the top of these structures, three blades, each a hundred feet long, and weighing fifteen thousand pounds, swept a vertical area of almost an acre. And each turbine was anchored in over a million pounds of concrete and rebar.

There were hundreds of them, as far as the eye could see, each costing more than three million dollars. They were creepy in the extreme. Something about these towering sculptures was otherworldly and eerie. Unsettling. *War of The Worlds* Tripods come to life.

Craft was eying these monstrosities with an expression between awe and horror himself, and Alyssa realized one of the best things about Craft's discovery is that it would eliminate the need for these eyesores once and for all.

* * *

Santosh Patel was on his stomach peering around the base of the tapered conical skyscraper that was a modern industrial wind turbine. His sniper rifle was set in its tripod and he was ready for the op to begin.

On the other side of the cylindrical base, Bruno Haas was waiting with machine guns, filled with blanks, and dozens of flashbang grenades. Their cars were behind the base of the turbine, which was large enough to conceal them from the road fifty yards away. And Ahn had been in position for some time now as well.

"Craft is five miles out," said the voice of Hank Ridley in Patel's ear. "There is one car between me and him, about a quarter mile behind him. There isn't anyone behind me for as far as I can see."

Craft was driving at about forty miles per hour, so he was now approximately seven minutes distant. Patel checked his watch. "Ridley, catch up to the car ahead of you before he gets any closer to Craft. Blow out his back tire. And make sure your gun is silenced."

"Roger that," said Ridley.

"Volkov," said Patel. "Do your thing. Then get in your car and head this way."

Volkov acknowledged the command a mile to the west. He had chosen a mid-sized tree that was leaning toward the road, and at Patel's mark he started the chainsaw and leveled the tree in less than a minute. It toppled across the road with a satisfying thud, blocking both lanes, and there was no easy way around it.

Once Hank Ridley had disabled the car nearest to Craft's, the kill zone would be isolated for more than enough time, ensuring passing vehicles didn't become collateral damage, or worse, somehow interfere with the op.

Volkov killed the chainsaw and put it in a storage compartment in the back of his gray Ram pickup, whose front was muscular enough to resemble a mini Mack truck. He pressed gently down on the gas pedal, waiting for word from Patel to ensure his timing was precise.

31

Alyssa tore her eyes from the repugnant wind turbines and turned to a more pleasing view, the cornfield on her side of the car, seemingly close enough to touch. The corn, about eight feet in height, was packed in such dense and precise rows that if she viewed them from the proper angle, they created a strobe-like effect as the SUV flashed by.

Craft glanced at her and smiled. "Now that," he said in an exaggerated manner, "is *a lot* of corn. Amazing how these plants can turn dirt and sunlight into something so tasty."

"Indiana grows a lot of popcorn," said Alyssa. "I wonder if this variety—"

There was a sharp and startling *crack* from the direction of the wind turbines, like a giant whip being snapped, and a simultaneous boom sound that shook the entire SUV. The vehicle instantly lurched to the left, jamming Alyssa into her belt.

The front left tire had exploded into shrapnel!

Had the explosive crack been a gunshot?

Craft fought to hold the steering wheel straight and began to brake as smoothly as he could, somehow managing to maintain control, a cowboy wrestling a panicked steer to the ground.

The car came to a stop, and Craft opened his mouth to speak, but closed it again as another crack rang out and a hole appeared in the driver's side window, even with Craft's temple. Alyssa gasped from the shock, and her mouth remained open from the realization that if this were any other man, she would be wearing his brains right now. His shield must have vaporized the approaching bullet with superhuman speed and efficiency.

Before Alyssa could process anything else about what was happening, a series of explosions rocked the car.

They were deafening and bright as the sun.

"Stun grenades!" shouted Craft above the din.

Had the grenades been any closer, Alyssa was sure they would have been temporarily deafened and blinded. As it was, the explosions kicked up so much smoke it became impossible to see in the direction of the wind turbines, where it seemed like an army was stationed. Machine gun fire could now be heard, also coming from this direction.

"*Go!*" screamed Craft, having now fully recovered from the shock of the attack. "Hide in the corn! I'll take care of them!"

Alyssa hesitated, still partially paralyzed.

"*Go!*" shrieked Craft even louder.

Alyssa pushed her door open and bolted the short distance into the cornfield, her heart racing fast enough to keep pace with the staccato blasts of the machine guns behind her.

When she had put five or six rows of cornstalks between her and the road, she turned to look for Craft.

"Freeze!" bellowed a tall Asian man to her left, emerging from a row of corn. He had a gun extended and was on her in seconds, shoving his weapon into her side.

"Let's go," he said, spinning her around and pushing her deeper into the jungle of leafy green stalks.

But before she had completed the pivot, she had caught one last glimpse of Brennan Craft along a line of sight between two perfectly aligned rows of corn. He was striding purposefully over the brown dirt plain, toward the mammoth turbines and the assault force hidden behind them, his back to the road.

And just behind him, impossible to hear given the steady barrage of machine gun fire and explosions, was an imposing wall of steel that was the front end of a Ram pickup truck, bearing down on him at a speed of more than sixty miles per hour.

And it was accelerating.

***

Santosh Patel maintained his usual laser sharp focus and intensity, but inside he was *ecstatic*. The plan was working masterfully. The SUV had come to a stop within five yards of his estimate. Alyssa Aronson had bolted into the cornfield, away from the fake gunfire and flashbangs, exactly as planned, and at the precise location they had expected. He knew that he would hear from Ahn any second that he had the girl, after which they could get the hell out of there and collect their winnings.

The only thing that troubled him was the continued existence of Brennan Craft.

The man should be dead. Patel was an expert marksman. From a mere fifty yards, and with little wind, he could have hit Craft's head if aborigines had shrunken it to the size of a *baseball*. There was no chance he had missed.

Yet Brennan Craft didn't seem to have any extra holes in his head as he marched off the road and approached their position, not making any attempt to take cover. Either he knew they had been using blanks after Patel's first shot, or he just didn't care.

Patel saw Volkov's pickup barreling toward Craft like a guided missile. His timing on this had been perfect as well. Craft's body would either be hurtled thirty feet forward by the impact, or he would be slammed against the hard ground and crushed into pulp under the tires. Both Patel and Haas stopped firing their machine guns at the same time so they could hear the impact.

But they heard *nothing*.

One instant many thousands of pounds of truck was accelerating into Craft. And the next . . . it was *through* him, as though the truck were made of butter and he was a lava-hot blade. Craft's forward progress wasn't altered a hair. He seemed to be an ephemeral ghost operating in a different dimension than the truck.

But while Craft had been unaffected, the same couldn't be said for the truck. A two to three foot wedge had been cut cleanly through the entire vehicle, lengthwise, parting it like the Red Sea. It continued accelerating as though it hadn't hit Craft at all, not slowed or deflected in the slightest. It traveled forward for several seconds, two halves without a middle, as though the laws of physics refused to comprehend that the truck's left and right sides were no longer connected.

Finally the halves of the car lost their balance and crashed to the ground, skidding and rolling repeatedly.

Dmitri Volkov was thrown from the car in the first moment after the impact.

Or what remained of him was. A third of his body, lengthwise, had been removed with surgical precision. As though a giant guillotine had dropped from the sky, splitting him like bamboo from head to toe.

What the fuck? thought Patel.

What the fuck?

Ahn's voice shouted into his ear, "I've got Aronson!" it said, but this didn't even register as Craft continued to advance.

"I've got the girl!" screamed the voice again several seconds later. "Acknowledge!"

Patel shook his head to clear it. "Acknowledged," he said finally. "Get her to Ridley and get the hell out of here!"

Bruno Haas had had enough. As Brennan Craft continued to hurry toward their position, his progress inexorable, Haas sprinted for his sedan behind the base of the turbine, shouting for Patel to join him.

Patel didn't need to be asked twice. If you couldn't stop a man with a four thousand pound truck, tactical retreat was the only option. He threw himself into the passenger's seat while Haas frantically started the car and began racing away across the field of dirt and turbines.

Patel felt a moment of relief, but this was short lived, as seconds later Haas crashed down against the steering wheel as though he had been shot.

But he had not been. His entire head had been crushed. And blood and brain matter were seeping onto the floor of the sedan.

What the fuck? thought Patel again. He didn't tend toward this expletive, but it was the only response that came to him as he struggled to comprehend the horror show this op had become.

The car continued driving aimlessly across the eerie plain, slowly losing speed, as Patel dived across the seat and out of Craft's line of sight. Perhaps Suave's warning about this hadn't been so ridiculous after all.

Patel's mind raced, but he was all out of ideas.

What the fuck had they run into?

* * *

Two down, one to go, thought Craft as the driver of the sedan that had been hidden behind the turbine collapsed and the car rolled to a halt.

So much had happened so quickly that Craft hadn't had the chance to think. But now that the stun grenades and machine gun fire had stopped, and he was getting the upper hand, his faculties returned in full.

What was going on? This attack almost had to be Al Yad's doing. But if so, what was the point? The Syrian knew full well that these men couldn't succeed. Only Al Yad himself could possibly kill him. So why the assault?

Craft was just thankful they had been after *him*, and not Alyssa. He had only known her for a few days, and already the thought of losing her made him physically ill. The ambush had been planned with great precision, and the attackers had made sure to attack from his side of the car.

Craft stopped dead in his tracks as the truth finally penetrated.

They *were* after Alyssa!

Al Yad *knew* Craft couldn't be killed. So what other purpose could this attack serve?

But they wanted to keep Alyssa alive. At least for the time being. If not, the sniper shot would have been meant for her.

It was a brilliant plan. Make him think he was the target of an attack mounted solely on the left. Provide perfect cover for Alyssa to get out of the line of fire on the right. And then ambush her there as she moved out of the frying pan and into the fire, perfectly obscured from his sight.

The other man in the sedan had ducked down after Craft had taken out the driver. Craft had been intent on tracking him down as well, but instead now sprinted back toward the road and the cornfield on the other side, as raw panic coursed through his veins along with adrenaline.

An image of Alyssa, an incandescent smile on her lovely face, appeared in his mind's eye, and he somehow found a way to run even faster.

* * *

Santosh Patel slid out of the car from the floorboard and onto the ground, making sure the car continued to block Craft's view. He crawled beneath the vehicle and peered out.

Craft was sprinting full speed in the opposite direction!

Patel jumped up, opened the driver's door, and dragged Haas out of the car and onto the hard ground, his lips curling up in disgust at the German's bloody and disfigured head. He then quickly started the sedan, ignoring the blood and tissue on the steering wheel, and accelerated toward the cornfield.

* * *

Craft entered the green maze of corn, thousands upon thousands of closely planted stalks towering far above his head, which only intensified his panic. The air was thick with the smell of dirt and the musk of nearly ripened corn.

Finding Alyssa in this impenetrable forest was hopeless.

He saw a corn stalk that was slightly askew. Was he only imagining it?

No! Alyssa had managed to push or damage a stalk every so often, leaving a trail for him to follow. His heart surged with newfound hope.

A minute later he came to a narrow dirt road the farmer must have carved at periodic intervals through his field so he could reach each section by motorized vehicle. Craft raced onto this road just in time to see a car receding into the distance, about a hundred yards ahead.

He zeroed in on the driver, tiny in the distance, and imagined clapping him hard on the ears. The car suddenly careened back toward the paved road and out of his sight, cutting a random swath through the corn, and he could no longer see the man who was in the back seat with Alyssa.

Not wasting a moment, Brennan Craft rushed forward to locate the runaway car.

* * *

"Ahn, report!" shouted Santosh Patel into his phone, stopping the sedan he was driving just short of the corn. Although it seemed like forever, the attack had begun only minutes before.

"We had her and were driving away," replied Ahn immediately, traces of panic in his voice. "But Ridley just collapsed at the wheel. Unconscious but still breathing. We've veered into the cornfield and have rolled to a stop. I'm going to drive us out of here."

"No!" screamed Patel. "Change of plan. Leave the car *immediately*. Take Aronson and head back toward the paved road. Make sure Craft doesn't have a line of sight on you."

"Roger that," said Ahn.

Patel heard Aronson cry out, and realized Ahn was manhandling her, in no mood to be slowed down. He nodded absently in approval.

"How far did the car get before Ridley collapsed?" said Patel.

"About a hundred yards to the east of our original position."

"Okay, cut a perpendicular line to the road, and I'll be waiting for you there."

Patel drove an estimated hundred yards to the east and then exited the car. Minutes later, Ahn emerged with the girl, only nine yards away, holding a gun to her back and shoving her forward. Their coordination had been good, given the circumstances. Aronson had a welt on her face from where Ahn must have struck her.

Patel ran to join them. "Hurry!" he said to Ahn when he arrived. "Back into the field! There's only one possible way out of this."

Patel shot Ahn a grim look. "Just make sure you don't lose her," he added. "*Whatever* you do. She's our only hope of survival."

32

Patel scanned the field frantically in every direction, straining to catch a glimpse of Craft amongst the inexhaustible stalks. The fact that he couldn't was somewhat comforting, since it implied that Craft wasn't able to see him, either. They had become rats in the ultimate maze.

"*Brennan Craft!*" yelled out Patel as loudly as he could. "Stop moving! Now! Call out so I know where you are, or I kill your friend. You have three seconds. Three, two, . . ."

"You're bluffing," shouted Craft, thankfully still far enough to the west that he had no chance of spotting them through the thousands of intervening stalks of corn.

"Take another step and you'll find out!"

"You could have killed her at any time. You must have orders to take her alive."

"We do," replied Patel. "If she dies, we don't get paid. But if *we* die, we don't get paid either," he added pointedly.

"Leave her, and I'll let you go in peace. Kill her, and no power on earth will stop me from killing you."

"Good point," replied Patel after a moment of thought. "So I won't kill her, after all. I'll shoot her in the gut, instead, and then we'll run. Making sure you can't see us. You can come after us while she's bleeding out. Or you can get her to a hospital. Your choice."

There was a long silence.

"Say something so I know you aren't coming closer!" demanded Patel.

"I haven't moved," shouted Craft, and his voice did originate from the same location.

"Okay. Here's the deal. Retreat back to your car. Drive off. I'll watch you leave while my colleague stays in the corn with the girl. If you attack me, he'll shoot her in the gut. But if you disappear to the west, I promise not to hurt her."

"Can you make that promise for the man who hired you?"

"This is the best I can do, Craft. Take it or leave it. Gut shot coming in five seconds."

"I need to know she's okay."

Patel gestured to his captive. "Tell him!" he ordered. "Nice and loud."

Alyssa hesitated.

"Do you really think I won't shoot you?" he asked her.

Alyssa stared deeply into his eyes and found nothing but resolve. "I'm okay, Bren!" she shouted.

"Alyssa, I promise you," said Craft, "you're going to get through this. I'm going to get you back. I swear to it!"

"I know you will," she replied.

"Enough talking!" Patel hissed at Alyssa. He cocked his arm with the back of his hand showing and glared at her, sending a clear message that if she spoke again he would backhand her across the face.

"So we have a deal, then?" Patel shouted in the direction of Brennan Craft.

"Yes."

"Good," said Patel. "And Craft, I want to hear you call out every five seconds on your way to your car. I want to be certain you don't *accidentally* go the wrong way."

"You're making a big mistake. Give her up now, or I'll hunt you to the ends of the earth."

"Yeah, I don't think so," shouted Patel. "But it's about time I heard your voice growing more distant," he added.

33

Brennan Craft took deep breaths, repeatedly, in an effort to calm down and stay centered. Panic and self-recrimination wouldn't help Alyssa. How had she come to mean so much to him in so little time?

He drove off to the west as agreed. When he was out of sight he planned to wait five minutes and then return, but he came to a tree that was lying across the road and helped a man and his seventeen-year-old son push it enough to the side that traffic could get through, albeit single file.

The good news was that this truly was the road less traveled, and traffic was never heavy. The bad news was that the tree had been cleanly felled, and Craft had no doubt the men who had ambushed them were responsible.

They had been even better than he had thought. And whoever he had negotiated with at the end was nobody's fool. Perhaps Al Yad's time in Craft's camp had taught him the importance of surrounding himself with highly competent people. Craft had tried to instill this lesson, and others, in the entire group. He only wished this was one lesson Al Yad had failed to learn.

Craft returned to the site of the ambush and parked his car as far off the road as he could to let others pass. He raced through the field until he found the car which had first been used to transport Alyssa.

The driver was still slumped over. Craft pulled him from the vehicle and slapped his face several times. He began to stir.

A few minutes later he was fully awake, shocked to find Craft standing over him with this own gun pressed into his cheek.

"What's your name?" spat Craft.

"Hank Ridley," replied the man, having no interest in withholding information in this situation.

"And who are you?"

"I'm a gun for hire. A merc. Ex-special forces."

Craft wasn't surprised. These men were very high-end.

"Who hired you?"

"I don't know who he is. He calls himself John Smith."

"Describe him," said Craft.

None of Ridley's team had ever seen their employer, but a short description of his accent was all Craft needed. Not surprisingly, these men had been hired by Al Yad's right hand man, Tariq Bahar, whom they had nicknamed Dr. Suave.

"Where are your partners taking Alyssa Aronson?" growled Craft, his voice now guttural and his eyes gleaming like a predatory cat.

"I have no idea," said Ridley.

"*Where are they taking her?*" shouted Craft, and Ridley suddenly felt an intense pressure on his face, as if an elephant were resting its foot there.

"I don't know," said Ridley, finding it hard to move his lips. "I don't know. We didn't have much of a head start on you. Had to set up the ambush. Once we had Aronson, we planned to call Suave for further instructions."

Craft nodded. As much as he didn't want to believe him, he did. "Where is Suave now?"

"London. Don't ask me what he's doing there. This is all I know."

Craft's expression was tortured. *How could this have happened? How could he have let it happen?*

He had to get her back. Even if she hadn't been instrumental to his plans, he would move heaven and earth to save her. He had been in love before. And while he wasn't there with Alyssa yet, the trajectory was already obvious. And none of his other relationships had rocketed to this point nearly as quickly. This one promised to be the real thing.

If anything happened to her he would never forgive himself.

Hank Ridley was watching him with a calculating look, surely waiting for Craft to let down his guard so he could kill him, having no idea what he was up against.

Why are humans so despicable? thought Craft, allowing hatred to consume him, replacing the fear and helplessness he felt at the prospect of losing Alyssa Aronson. Barely repressing a powerful urge to unleash a primal scream, he wielded zero point energy to clap Ridley in the ears to knock him unconscious a second time.

Craft fought to control his now blinding rage. He needed to regroup. To check on the car and driver he had disabled on the other side of the road. And he needed to place an immediate call to Eben Martin.

But as he prepared to walk back to the road, he noticed that blood had begun dripping from Ridley's eyes and ears. *How could that be?* He felt for a pulse, and fell to the ground beside Ridley in shock.

The man was dead!

And he had killed him.

Craft reeled from the knowledge that he had taken a human life. He wasn't violent. In fact, he treasured all life. He had only wanted to knock this man out.

But a small part of him wondered if, in his rage, he hadn't accomplished exactly what he had set out to do, and a chill ran down his spine.

34

As soon as Patel confirmed that Craft's black SUV was finally out of sight to the west, he got behind the wheel of the car and shouted for Ahn, who emerged from the corn and shoved Alyssa Aronson into the back seat.

The road stretched on in a perfectly straight line as far as the eye could see. Patel sped off to the east, checking his rearview mirror nervously in case Craft had doubled back, and making sure to stay within the posted speed limit. The last thing they needed was police attention with a hostage in the back seat being held at gunpoint.

"Why are you doing this?" whispered Alyssa.

"Nothing personal," said Ahn. "But someone has a real hard-on for you."

Alyssa shook her head in disapproval at this turn of phrase. "Who?" she said simply.

"You're going to find out soon enough," he said. "So sit back and relax. Try anything cute and I'll shoot you in the chest."

She glared at him defiantly. "Nice try, genius. But did you forget I heard you admit you have orders to keep me alive."

Ahn flashed a humorless smile. "True enough. But we don't necessarily have to deliver you conscious." He bared his teeth. "Or uninjured. I'd keep that in mind—*genius*."

Alyssa turned away from him and broke eye contact. She had to relax and not do something stupid. Fight her justifiable fury at being passed around like a football. Provoking a ruthless mercenary could only make things worse for her.

Brennan Craft had promised to get her out of this. Craft was brilliant and resourceful, even without his quantum lensing ability. But could he find her? If these men made a single mistake, she was confident Craft would catch it. But if they made no mistakes, Craft could have the power of Al Yad and it wouldn't matter.

Ahn surveyed the road behind them through the rear window. "No sign of him," he said.

Patel nodded, and blew out a breath it seemed he must have been holding since Craft had driven away.

"What the fuck *was* that back there?" said Ahn, continuing to issue expletives and American slang with a slight Korean accent. "Jesus! We were driving off when Ridley just collapsed. That is some crazy, fucked-up voodoo."

"Yeah, *that* was the fucked-up voodoo," replied Patel sarcastically. "You were in the corn and missed it, but this freak *split a car in two*. Not to mention Dmitri Volkov. Volkov rammed him with his pickup and didn't disturb a single hair on Craft's head."

Patel glanced back at Alyssa. "Who *is* this guy? How did he do that?"

Alyssa looked confused. "I don't know what you're talking about," she said. "I never saw him do anything special. On the other hand," she added pointedly. "I was busy getting manhandled in an ocean of corn at the time."

Patel studied her in the rearview mirror for several long seconds, but decided not to pursue this further.

"Let's call Suave and find out where he wants his delivery," said Ahn. "I, for one, will be happy to get rid of this bitch and get on with my life."

"Amen to that," said Patel, removing a phone from his pocket.

The car lurched to the left as the left front tire exploded with a burst of sound. Patel's phone fell from his hand as he wrestled the car to a stop.

Déjà Vu. Alyssa would never forget the shock of being in a moving vehicle whose tire had been shot out, but just in case, she was being treated to a repeat performance. Except this time there were woods on both sides instead of corn and wind turbines.

As the car came to a complete stop, a bullet pierced a hole through the driver's side window and entered Patel's brain. The same would have happened to Craft if not for his freakish defensive abilities, but *Patel* was dead before his head hit the steering wheel.

Ahn pulled open the door on the passenger's side and yanked Alyssa from the car, but as he crouched down behind the car to protect him from whoever had shot Patel, he heard a sound and pivoted around, spinning Alyssa with him as he did.

A second man was on their side of the road, almost entirely hidden behind a tree. Only one of his eyes, and a hand gripping an H&K .45, could be seen around the edge of the trunk. The gun was pointed at Ahn.

Alyssa had never been a student of military tactics, but she didn't need a second demonstration to understand that an out-of-the-way two-lane road, with endless places to take cover on both sides, was perfect for an ambush.

"Drop it or I'll kill her!" shouted Ahn, using Alyssa's body as a protective shield.

A thunderous explosion blasted into Alyssa's ears, and at the same time half of Ahn's face was blown away, and his lifeless body crashed to the pavement behind her. Apparently, Ahn hadn't shielded himself entirely from the gunman behind the tree, who was either an amazing shot or who wasn't troubled by the possibility of hitting Alyssa.

She barely managed to remain standing as the shock and horror of Ahn's demise made her dizzy and caused her heart to pound furiously against her chest.

The man who had shot Ahn left the cover of the tree and approached her, his gun still extended.

Alyssa's breath stuck in her throat.

The team that had captured her in the cornfield had wanted her alive. But if whoever was responsible for *this* ambush didn't feel the same way, the man who was approaching might be the last thing she would ever see.

35

Eben Martin was tall, handsome, and charismatic, and having a net worth among the highest of anyone in the world seemed to greatly enhance all three of these attributes. Power and vast wealth couldn't make one taller and more handsome, but it certainly seemed that way to most people.

He was currently in a late morning meeting in his private conference room with the CEO and CFO of a Japanese multinational when his phone vibrated in his pocket. He had a number of settings he had programmed into his cell, and for this meeting he had selected one that would only ring through for a very select group of people, and then only after they had confirmed it was an emergency to a recorded message by pressing the number nine.

As the phone vibrated again, Martin said, "Excuse me," and checked it, interrupting the CEO, Masayasu Kobayashi, in mid-sentence. Kobayashi was one of the most venerated men in all of Japan. There were only a handful of people in the entire world who would dare interrupt him. Martin wished he didn't have to be one of them.

Martin read the name, Brennan Craft, on his phone, and his pulse quickened. Bren would never call in on his emergency line if it were not truly an emergency.

"Kobayashi-San," said Martin quickly, "I cannot apologize enough, but I must take this call. I'll make it quick. Please ask my assistant to show you around in the interim," he said.

Kobayashi and his subordinate rose quickly, hiding their distaste at this rude behavior, having not been treated in this manner since before they could remember. Martin completed a bow to the men that was at exactly the right depth for the occasion, something that had been drilled into him by his protocol experts, and walked through the door to his office, answering the call as he did.

"Bren, what's going on?" he said into the phone.

"We were ambushed!" shouted Craft. "I'm calling from the middle of a cornfield near Bloomington."

Despite the seriousness of the situation, Martin couldn't help but smile as this thought picture came into his head.

"Eben, they've taken Alyssa!" said Craft, his voice raw. "I thought your men were in place before we left the restaurant this morning."

"They were," said Martin with a frown.

"They sure weren't from what I could tell!" barked Craft. "It was a disaster. The ambush was orchestrated by Al Yad. And the men who carried it out were pros. I've completely lost her trail," he finished, unable to keep the panic from his voice.

Martin's phone vibrated again and he glanced down at the screen. It was Adam Turco, almost as if he had been cued.

"Hold on, Bren," said Martin. "My guy is on the line now. I'll patch us all on together."

Martin hit an icon on his phone to conference Turco in on the call and then answered. "Adam. What happened?"

"We ran into some trouble," came the immediate reply. "Craft and Aronson were ambushed."

"You saw it happen and you didn't intervene?" thundered Craft.

Before Turco could respond, Martin said, "Adam, that was Brennan Craft. He's on the other line. Brennan, this is Adam Turco."

"My partner and I didn't intervene," said Turco coolly, ignoring the introduction, "because we were following the instructions of your friend, Eben Martin. I was tasked to discover if you had a tail, and get rid of it if you did. To ensure you were off the grid once more. Eben told me if you did have a tail, there was *no way* they would attack. He's the boss, but I have to question his definition of the words, *no way*."

"Shit," said Craft. "Eben was just relaying what I told him," he admitted, taking responsibility for the bad intel.

"We had identified two men tailing you from the waffle house, but wanted to keep to the periphery until we were sure we had them all. The ambush took us too much by surprise to intervene in time."

"Even so," snapped Craft. "The attack dragged out for several minutes. So you did nothing?"

"No. We didn't do *nothing*," said Turco icily. "I was also told if the shit ever did hit the fan, Alyssa Aronson was my top and only priority. That if you were surrounded by a hundred men with machine guns, and she was about to break a nail, we should abandon you and see to her."

"Excellent!" said Craft, as quick on the uptake as always. Martin had passed on his exact instructions. "So can I assume from this, um . . . Adam, that you took off after her? That you know where she is?" he added hopefully.

"Yeah. I know where she is," replied Turco. "She's right here with me and my partner. Safe and sound."

Craft inhaled sharply in relief. "*Thank you!*" he said, his voice ecstatic. "I'll never be able to thank you enough."

"Uh-huh," said Adam Turco, not quite ready to forgive Craft's earlier accusations.

"Where are the two men who were with her?" asked Craft.

"Remember how these men were alive the last time you saw them?" said Turco. "Well, that's not so true anymore."

"Is Alyssa okay?"

"She's fine. A little roughed up from her abduction, but we didn't put a scratch on her."

"Well done!" said Craft with such palpable enthusiasm and relief that it was almost contagious. "If I could reach through the phone I would *kiss* you," he added. "Sorry about being kind of an asshole before. Eben told me he had hired the best. I should have had more faith."

"I really didn't hire him," said Martin, grinning. "The man sort of hired himself. He was so good he didn't really give me any other choice."

"We're circling back now," said Turco, ignoring the compliment. "Where are you, Brennan?"

"Would you believe the middle of the cornfield where Alyssa was first taken?"

There was a brief pause. "Okay. Get back to the road. I'll be there in about five minutes to reunite you with Alyssa."

"Fantastic!" gushed Craft appreciatively. "And sorry again."

"I accept your apology. But there is one thing you need to know."

"What's that?"

"If you try to kiss me," explained Adam Turco grimly, "I'm going to have to kill you myself."

36

By the time Craft discovered that he had also unknowingly killed the driver of the sedan on the wind-turbine side of the road, and was returning to his SUV, Adam Turco was just arriving. He pulled his silver Acura sedan over as far as possible toward the corn, behind Craft's vehicle. He and Alyssa exited the car and stood just outside the first row of corn.

When Craft reached Alyssa he threw his arms around her and drew her close. "Thank god you're okay," he said as several tears formed in the corners of his eyes.

A moment later they were kissing, at first tentatively and then hungrily, as if they were lovers who hadn't seen each other in years, their emotions heightened to a fever pitch by the assault and its aftermath.

Alyssa knew in her heart that this man wasn't faking his interest. He looked like he had been through an emotional wringer—because of his worry about her—and his tears of joy and relief were too heartfelt to be anything but genuine.

They didn't separate for several minutes. "In case I didn't answer this clearly enough before," she whispered into his ear when they finally had. "I'm in."

"I know you are," he replied happily. "And thank you." And with this, he drew her back into his arms and kissed her once again.

When they finally parted for the second time, Adam Turco looked at Craft and shook his head. "I guess you *really* needed to kiss someone," he said in amusement. "You made the right choice," he added dryly.

Turco held out his hand, and Craft shook it firmly. "I am forever in your debt," said Craft.

"No, that would be your friend Eben Martin," replied Turco with the hint of smile.

"What happened to your partner?"

"He left. His work is done. I hired him, but he doesn't know who I work for. I promised Eben I would be the only connection to him."

"And we won't need him?"

"Not right now. They threw everyone they had at you. Unless you know otherwise, there aren't any of this batch left."

Craft shook his head miserably. "They're all dead," he whispered. "All of them. I checked."

He shot Alyssa a troubled glance. "I don't know what happened," he said. "I must not know my own . . . strength."

Alyssa saw the concern and horror in his face. Apparently his ability to use the zero point field offensively had become somewhat stronger under duress. He had killed one or more of the attackers, and she could tell he was taking it hard.

Turco watched the exchange between his two wards carefully. "Not that I don't believe you could have taken these men out with your fists," said Turco sarcastically, rolling his eyes, "But you should know that Eben told me how you were able to survive."

Craft studied him warily. "How?"

"He said you've invented an advanced sonic weapon. A prototype. One that's directional."

Craft nodded, trying not to look relieved. "Yes. I wasn't aware he had told you. Apparently I used it on too high a setting."

"Well, don't mourn for these men *too* much. Trust me, they would have killed you without blinking." Turco opened the door to his car. "But we need to go. If we don't leave now, we risk that the party who ordered this ambush will locate you again."

Turco gestured toward Craft's SUV. "And I'm afraid you'll have to lose your car. They know it now, obviously."

"At least it's a rental," said Craft with the hint of a smile.

Alyssa insisted that Craft take the front seat next to Adam Turco and she slid into the back. Craft immediately called Avis, told them where to find their car, and hung up on a clerk who was in the middle of insisting that Craft couldn't just abandon the vehicle by the side of a road.

Alyssa smiled to herself. After all that had happened—mercenaries, explosions, machine gun fire, men dying, high-stakes negotiations—who else other than Brennan Craft would worry about the welfare of a rental car company?

Turco headed east, back the way they had come.

"We were headed to Bloomington," said Craft. "Which is west of here."

"I know. Eben filled me in."

"Are you really on a first name basis with Eben Martin?" asked Alyssa.

"He insisted," replied Turco. "Anyway, he told me you needed to rob a lab on the outskirts of the IU campus."

"I wouldn't put it exactly that way," said Alyssa from the back seat. "But close enough."

"I can get you back there by tonight. If you still want me to. In the meanwhile, we have a lot to do. First, we should clean the two of you up." He turned to Craft. "And Eben told me you wanted his help getting Alyssa a flawless fake driver's license and passport, under an alias."

Craft nodded. "Yes. Her ID was taken. And she can't risk returning home for her passport. I'll need another set as well. They can trace the SUV back to the fake license I used to rent it, so that ID is blown." He stared at Turco. "You can take care of that?"

The man nodded. "I'm well connected. Cincinnati is the closest major city, and I know someone there who can set both of you up."

"Not just the physical documents," said Craft, "but matching computer records as well?"

"Yes," said Turco. "You and Alyssa will waltz right through any airport. I'm told you're both immune to facial recognition somehow. A neat trick. Someday you'll have to show me how that's done."

Craft ignored this. "When your man is done with the ID's," he said, "I'll need his computer. I'll need to check out the security situation at Alyssa's lab for tonight's visit."

"That won't be a problem," said Turco. "But what's the rush? I don't know what you need in that lab, but if you can wait, you should. You have a powerful ally now in Eben Martin, and you're back off the grid."

Craft turned to Alyssa. "It's been an exhausting day already," he said. "And you lost a good amount of blood recently. Now that we don't need to do everything ourselves, we do have the luxury of waiting a few days. Would you rather postpone?"

Alyssa thought of the drive to Cincinnati they had yet to complete, followed by a busy afternoon, followed by a drive back to Bloomington, where they would have to wait until late at night to raid her lab. Then what? A drive to the Indianapolis airport?

Her overnight stay in a hospital had helped her recover from her blood loss, but she felt as though she had already been awake for forty-eight hours.

Please, she thought. *It's too much! For the love of God, we have to postpone!*

"I'll be okay," said Alyssa pleasantly.

How had these words come out of her mouth?

"Do what you think is best," she added, still unable to believe the voice she was hearing was her own.

"I can hack into your central computer system," said Craft. "But that won't tell me if the major has people watching your lab. He's sure to think I'm behind your kidnapping. And to guess that I might force you to return there."

"You should wait, then," advised Turco. "That way I can recon the building the night before. So you can know for sure."

Craft rubbed his chin. "Agreed," he said. "Instead, after we get our IDs, let's have Eben recommend a place we can hole up in for a while. He can meet us there."

"Eben's thoughts exactly," noted Turco.

They continued driving, mostly in silence. Alyssa didn't feel comfortable discussing their situation in Turco's presence. Eben Martin seemed to have considerable confidence in the man, and while she knew Martin hadn't shared Craft's secret, she wasn't sure how much else Turco knew. Until she was clearer on this, she would err on the side of keeping information confidential, and it was obvious Craft felt the same way.

After another thirty-five minutes, Turco stopped for gas and to use the restroom. Alyssa motioned for Craft to stay inside the car when their guardian exited. They would only have five or ten minutes of privacy, and Alyssa wanted to make the most of it.

"What the hell is going on, Bren?" she said, the moment Turco shut the door.

She hadn't fallen for a man this hard in years, and kissing him had been amazing, but that didn't get him off the hook entirely. "How did Eben Martin get involved in this?"

Craft sighed. "I contacted him a few days ago. You know he and I go way back, right?"

"No. I knew you licensed him the software he used to start Informatics Solutions. And that you cashed out for fifty million. But that's all."

"We grew up together. We were best friends. After I left the priesthood, we decided to form a company. Think Ben and Jerry. Or better yet, Jobs and Wozniac. That sort of thing."

"So what changed? Why didn't you end up at Informatics Solutions with your friend?"

"I came up with my crackpot Inedia theory. I shared it with Eben. Even at that time we knew that the informatics algorithms I had developed were, with all modesty, revolutionary. That a company based on this software could become the next Apple or Google. Eben thought it was crazy to give that up to chase a wild theory that had little chance of being correct."

Craft sighed. "I, on the other hand, had a gut feeling about it. And a growing compulsion to find out for sure. Maybe the better word would be, *obsession*. And how much money does one man need, anyway?"

Alyssa had any number of questions, but Turco wouldn't be pumping gas and using the restroom forever. "Did you stay in touch with Martin after you left the country?"

"No. I was completely absorbed by what I was doing, and I didn't want him trying to sweet-talk me into coming back. And he was a great friend. So if he had a problem he thought only I could solve, I would have felt obligated to solve it. After I had made my break-throughs, I wanted to keep them secret until I published."

Craft shook his head. "No, Eben was as surprised as anyone when I contacted him. But I brought him up to speed fairly thoroughly with a long e-mail message. I described how I had proven my theory. The situation with Al Yad, both historical and current. And my hopes that I could recruit you."

"But why? Why did you suddenly change your mind and decide to bring him in *now*? A titan of industry. A billionaire. When you've killed yourself to keep this absolutely secret?"

"I screwed up big by approaching you on a dating site," replied Craft miserably. "I put myself squarely back on the radar. I kicked a hornet's nest. Both with respect to the government, *and* Al Yad. I needed help. Powerful help. And I happen to have a close friend who's a billionaire, and who already knew my theories about tapping zero point energy. A man with nearly unlimited resources, who can pay to get top drawer IDs on the fly. Who has a private jet or two. And who could send men immediately to watch my back if I asked him to."

Alyssa had to admit that these were all good reasons.

"It turned out to be a good decision. I contacted him while I was lying low at the IU campus. I asked him to recruit some muscle in case I needed it. And I decided I needed it when you entered the hospital. I knew there was a chance Al Yad would keep tabs on you after he let you go. I had to be sure."

"You thought we might be ambushed? And you didn't *tell* me?"

"No. I thought if we were being followed, whoever was following would just . . . follow. I never in a million years thought they would attack. Al Yad, maybe, but not them. And if *Al Yad* attacked, we could have had an army protecting us and it wouldn't have helped."

"So you're sure the men who attacked us were sent by Al Yad?"

"Positive. I interrogated one of the men before he . . . died. The description of his boss fit Tariq Bahar to a T. "

"But why would *Bahar* be after me? He already *had* me."

"It's hard to fathom," agreed Craft. "All I can think of is that Al Yad heard a recording of your interrogation and figured out why I needed you."

"Then why not just *kill* me?" said Alyssa. "Much less hassle." She shook her head. "They went to *a lot* of trouble to capture me alive."

Craft shrugged. "Maybe Al Yad, as powerful as he is, thought that you could enhance his belief even more. Make him even better able to harness the zero point field."

Alyssa thought about this. They might never know for sure, but this was as good a conjecture as any.

"So why didn't Al Yad attack himself?" she asked.

"I don't know. Maybe he first wanted to learn if I'd grown as strong as I had said I would. I had guessed he would try to track me back to my base, so he could carefully devise a foolproof attack at his leisure."

"You mean, make sure he had enough concrete to trap you in?"

"Yeah, that sort of thing. But having his men attack when they did was the last thing I would have ever predicted." He blew out a long breath. "Which is one of the reasons I decided to bring Eben in. I've proven I can make mistakes."

A pained expression came over Craft's face. "And now you're involved," he said softly. "*I* may be invulnerable. But *you're* not."

Adam Turco pulled open the door to the Acura and seated himself.

Alyssa glanced meaningfully at Craft. "Before we go," she said to Turco. "I just realized I'm thirsty. I'm going to grab a bottle of water inside."

"I'll go with you," said Craft on cue.

Turco raised his eyebrows, but said nothing.

Once inside the small gas station mini-mart, Alyssa stood by Craft near a wall of refrigerated beverages, but made no move to take one.

"So you brought in one of the wealthiest, most famous men in the world," continued Alyssa. "And you had him hire mercenaries to watch our backs. And again, you decided this wasn't something I needed to know?"

"I was going to tell you. There was no avoiding it. But I had already drowned you with information. How much could I throw at you in one day? I thought I'd make sure we weren't being followed, and then tell you about Eben at the hotel while we were waiting to go to your lab."

Alyssa considered. This did make sense. They would need to wait until late at night, so he would have had plenty of time to fill her in as thoroughly as he wanted.

She removed a bottle of water for herself from the row of refrigeration units and handed another one to Craft, but didn't yet make her way to the register a short distance away.

"And you think you can trust Eben Martin with this? People with that kind of money and power always want more. And you're offering *infinite* power. It's the most potent secret—literally—in history. I don't care if he's your friend. You just offered the world's most irresistible bourbon to an *alcoholic*. He's not going to want to just sit on this like you are."

"He will," said Craft. "I promise. The Eben Martin I know is generous and compassionate to a fault. Some men rise to the top because they're ruthless psychopaths. Eben did it—with my software help—because of his talents. He is a very good man. The best I've ever met."

Craft paused. "Even so, I did share your concerns. I worried about how his success might have changed him. So I hacked into his computer. Read his private files. His private e-mails. Everything. At the risk of being inelegant, I spent a few days shoving a microscope up his rear. And he checked out. Same old Eben. As good a man as he always was."

While Craft paid for their waters, Alyssa decided she still wasn't certain how she felt about his decision to include Martin. But it didn't matter. She had no choice. It was done. And besides, she'd be in the hands of Tariq Bahar by now if Craft *hadn't* made this decision.

And now that Martin was involved, she would actually be meeting a man who had skyrocketed to the top of the business world and was the darling of the media, replacing Bill Gates, Steve Jobs, Larry Page, and Mark Zuckerberg before him.

Eben Martin was larger than life. She never imagined she'd have the chance to meet him some day. Or that when she did, he would only be the *second* most interesting, and powerful, man she would meet that week.

37

Al Yad rose from the polished marble floor and floated briskly to the picture window in his bedroom, looking out over the city far below. He pulled his vision back and surveyed the landscape halfway down the small mountain his compound crested, choosing one of several small boulders off in the distance and causing it to rise into the air.

He practiced his fine control every day, and it had improved. Yes, a god could destroy the entire world with a blink, reduce it to molten rubble. But a god should also be able to wield lesser force with the skill of a surgeon.

Al Yad unleashed pure energy at the boulder—almost certainly the same energy that formed his shield—and parts of it disappeared. They didn't melt. They didn't redden and then flow off like lava. They simply vanished in the maelstrom of energy—as if hit by a star trek phaser set to kill—their individual atoms torn from each other and dispersed into the ether at incredible speeds.

The boulder had now been reshaped into two perfect, joined tablets, a miniature version of the ones Moses might have carried down from Mount Sinai.

Thou shalt obey The Hand of God, thought Al Yad, and these letters burned themselves into the tablet in fine print.

This was one of many theatrical flourishes he had planned once he had finally nullified the threat posed by Shaitan, and took his rightful place as the ruler of the world, respected and feared as a god by every living person. He liked the idea of being original, but stone tablets containing ten commandments was an image seared into the collective consciousness. Besides, he would do Moses one or two better.

He would arrive at a stadium in front of a hundred thousand followers, with the few hundred million people he would let live watching on screens. And while rising from the heart of a raging orange bonfire at the center of the stadium, his white robes remaining immaculate, he would carve tablets from a giant block of granite spinning in the air. He would inscribe his new commandments while the world marveled at his power.

Although, at that point, the full extent of his power, and his wrath, would be well known by all.

The sixty inch television screen on the wall behind him came to life and announced that Tariq Bahar was calling in. Al Yad unleashed a force he thought of as a constrictive one, of pure weight and pressure, which might well have been an intensification of gravity, and the distant stone tablet was flattened to the thickness of a sheet of paper, as though a million ton steam roller had driven over it. Finally, he made it disintegrate into nothingness.

Al Yad faced the screen and accepted the call. Bahar's face appeared larger than life in front of him.

"Thank you for taking my call, oh Great One," he said in Arabic.

Al Yad waved a hand at him impatiently. "Report," he said.

Bahar winced, almost imperceptibly. "Forgive me, Al Yad, but the news is not good."

"How so?"

"I have failed you, Al Yad. The five men I sent to capture Alyssa Aronson did not report in, and I am unable to contact any of them. They are almost certainly all dead."

Al Yad noted that Bahar was all but cowering on his screen. But this had not been Bahar's fault. Al Yad had known this would be a long shot with Craft in the equation. He knew mere men could not defeat the incarnation of Shaitan on Earth, and that taking his demon mistress from him would require considerable fortune.

He could have reassured Bahar, but decided to let him roast further. "What was the strategy they used?"

"They planned an ambush on a backwoods road, oh Great One. With ample cover on either side. They planned to feign an attack on Craft's side, driving Aronson to take cover on the other side, where they would also be waiting. They understood the need to stay out of

Craft's line of sight. The plan was sound. I have no idea what went wrong."

Al Yad stroked his chin in thought. "What steps have you taken since?" he said.

"I've activated our closest available man, Great One. In Chicago. He'll travel to Indiana to inspect the ambush area. But the police will have been there by the time he arrives, so he won't be able to learn much. I'm having our best computer specialist hack into the local police department so we can get their report." There was a pause. "I'm also doing everything in my power to find them again."

Al Yad glared at him for almost a full minute, letting him twist in the wind against the might, and wrath, that this stare signified. He couldn't have Bahar getting sloppy. He couldn't have him thinking failure might be forgiven too quickly, even if he had done nothing wrong.

"You have served me well, Tariq," said Al Yad. "This is the only thing that has saved you from this failure." He paused for dramatic effect. "I trust that you will not fail me again."

Bahar shook his head vigorously. "No, Al Yad. Never. Thank you, oh Great One. You are as merciful as you are wise."

Al Yad nodded. "The lab this Jewish whore, this Aronson, mentioned during your interrogation," he said. "You know its location?"

"Yes, Al Yad. It is protected by advanced electronics and biometric scanners, but they try to pass it off as a harmless offshoot of a local university. They have made no effort to hide its location."

"Good. I want you to get a man to its vicinity, and have him surveil the lab after hours. If he sees either Craft or Aronson, you are to call in a team to tail them as before. But no further attacks this time. Until I say otherwise."

"I will set this up immediately, oh Great One."

"See that you do," snapped Al Yad.

38

Alyssa Aronson and Brennan Craft were now in possession of new sets of identification. They had thanked Adam Turco for everything he had done, and now found themselves in a limousine approaching the gated entrance to an isolated airfield at the Cincinnati Airport. This was part of the airport that precious few people even knew existed, but one that executives, the rich, movie stars, and dignitaries flew into and out of on a daily basis.

It was only a little past eight at night, but Alyssa was so exhausted that she barely managed to keep her head up as the guard checked their identification and waved them through. Their forged IDs had been as effective as advertised.

They were dropped off in front of an all white plane, the Boeing Business Jet 2, which they had been told was a customized 737, now the private property of Eben Martin. It had set him back eighty million dollars, but this represented a smaller proportion of his net worth than the average person spent on the family car.

Many millions of this total had been poured into the jet's elongated, thousand square foot interior, which was magnificent. It contained furnishings and art that would be at home in the finest luxury apartment, configured with two bedrooms, each with a private shower, a boardroom, a wet bar, and an executive suite. Leather chairs and couches—with hidden seat belts for takeoffs, landings, and rare bouts of turbulence—lacquered cabinetry, cherywood tables, elegant carpeting, and high end electronics and television screens were everywhere. The scent of garlic and pasta wafted through the jet, probably from a recent dinner prepared by the onboard chef that Martin had hired.

The two visitors were escorted to the boardroom and left alone to gawk at the brilliance of the design and furnishings of this flying apartment. They were doing so when Eben Martin stepped into the room and closed the door behind him.

"Bren!" said the billionaire excitedly upon seeing them.

The two men embraced in a warm hug a grizzly would envy.

"Welcome aboard," said Martin. "I didn't realize how much I've missed you until just this second."

"It's great to see you, too, Eb!" said Craft. "I didn't know you'd be on the plane."

"I wanted to surprise you."

Martin turned to Alyssa and extended a hand. "And you must be Alyssa Aronson. To say Bren thinks the world of you is an understatement."

"I told Eben you were above average in every way," interjected Craft with a twinkle in his eye.

Alyssa shook Martin's hand. "Nice plane," she said. "And thanks so much for your help."

In another lifetime, meeting Eben Martin inside a fantasy jet would have been intimidating. But after everything else that had happened recently, it didn't faze her at all.

"I'm just glad it worked out," said Martin. "You should both know that I've cleared my schedule for a week, and told my staff I was taking an impromptu vacation. The people on this plane will know nothing about you, and only know you by your aliases. We'll be landing in Florida, and then we'll take a helicopter to an island I own, where we can hole up. No one knows I own it, and I told my office I would be out of reach at an unspecified location. I told them I felt the need to get out of the limelight for a while." He sighed and shot Alyssa an apologetic look. "I know this is all a bit showy. Sorry about that."

"I'm not," said Alyssa. She waved her hand to encompass the small but lavishly appointed room. "It's going to be hard to go back to a middle seat in coach after this," she added with a smile. "And I've never known anyone with their own island."

"There are over a hundred and fifty thousand islands in the world," said Martin. "So it's really not that impressive. You can buy one for under a million dollars."

"You *can,*" said Alyssa in amusement. "But why do I get the feeling you *didn't?* Not that this is a bad thing," she hastened to add. "I mean, who wants to stay on a starter island?"

Martin laughed out loud. "I can see why Bren likes you so much," he said. "But there's a reason I told you I'll be joining you for a week. So you'll know we'll have plenty of time to get to know each other." He gestured toward the door. "But right now, we're kicking you out. You need to recuperate."

"I made sure Eben was aware of what you've been through," said Craft. "I didn't expect him to be on the plane, but I did make sure he put a doctor onboard."

Alyssa had a sudden urge to throw her arms around Brennan Craft and kiss him as passionately as they had done outside a cornfield in Indiana—a scene they had managed to repeat several times since then whenever they could get some privacy—but she restrained herself in Eben Martin's presence.

"So I'll take you to your room," said Martin. "After you shower and dress—Bren texted your size, and I've taken the liberty of providing an assortment of clothing for you to choose from—I'll send in the doctor. He'll check your vitals and fluids, give you any meds you need, and then leave you alone to get a good night's sleep."

Alyssa smiled wearily. "Sounds like heaven," she admitted. "But isn't Florida only an hour or two flight from here?"

"It is," replied Martin. "But once we arrive in Florida, we'll stay parked at the airport overnight so you can get a solid block of sleep. Given what you've been through the past day or so, it's a wonder you're still standing."

39

Eben Martin deposited Alyssa in her room and he and Craft took up in the main cabin, which was the jet's living-room equivalent. Martin left instructions that they were not to be disturbed, and then made himself a Tom Collins at the bar, fishing a lemon slice from several that had been pre-cut with a pair of small, gold tongs, and adding it to the glass.

Craft poured himself a Diet Coke and took a seat in a wide leather captain's chair that was so cushioned and comfortable, he seemed to melt into it.

Martin was surprised his friend looked so great after everything he had been through recently, and wondered if the ability to turn one's mind into a quantum lens had the effect of helping one stay . . . energized.

The billionaire took a sip of what looked like lemonade and sat on a beige leather couch across from Craft.

"So," he began casually. "Brennan Craft, in the flesh. Looks like you've been *busy*."

"You haven't exactly been running in place yourself," noted Craft.

"Just doing business," said Martin dismissively. "Nothing special. But you," he added, shaking his head in awe. "What can I say. Congratulations! What you've discovered is *incredible*. I should have known better than to doubt your instincts."

"Are you kidding," said Craft good-naturedly. "I would have checked you into a mental institution if you hadn't."

Craft spent the next hour bringing Martin fully up to speed, during which time the plane became airborne. Since Martin already knew what Craft had hoped to accomplish and the theory behind it, and had already read his thorough e-mail message, Craft didn't need to spend time on the basics. Instead, he could discuss the situation in more depth, and with more vibrancy, and fill in details.

Once the plane had leveled off, Craft demonstrated his personal shield. At Craft's insistence, Martin threw a heavy glass beer mug across the compartment at his head, as hard as he could, only to watch it disappear into thin air about a foot away from its target, and was told the same thing would happen if the mug had been a high energy laser or a nuclear missile.

Martin decided this was the coolest thing he had ever seen, and sent three more beer mugs to their deaths, just for the giddy thrill of seeing them vanish, before agreeing to move on. He had believed Craft when he described his capabilities, but intellectual belief was one thing. Seeing a demonstration like this was astonishing beyond words.

Craft spent considerable time describing Alyssa's work, how it applied to his situation, and how an accountant named Omar Haddad had turned into The Hand of God. It didn't take long for Martin to ask the obvious question: what was holding a deluded fanatic like Al Yad back?

Craft delayed answering for several minutes, first using the restroom and then pouring himself another Diet Coke. Finally he returned to his chair and faced Martin.

Martin could sense his friend was trying to come to some kind of decision, but had no idea what this might be. Martin knew Craft well enough to remain silent while his friend's mighty intellect grappled with whatever was troubling him. Even after not seeing Craft for many years, being with him brought back an instant flood of memories, and it seemed to Martin as though his friend had never been out of his life.

Craft finally blew out a long breath, signaling that he had reached a decision and was ready to continue. "What's holding Al Yad back?" he repeated. "Let me start with the answer I gave Alyssa when *she* asked this question."

What did that mean? thought Martin as Craft began telling him the story he had told his newfound female friend.

He remained silent until Craft was completely finished. "So this is what you told *Alyssa*," said Martin. "But I take it this wasn't exactly the *truth*."

His friend shook his head and looked miserable. "No. It wasn't. If it were, Al Yad would have come after me himself in that cornfield. Have you heard the old joke, I just flew in from Syria, and, boy, are my arms tired?"

"The version I heard wasn't Syria, but I've heard the joke."

"Well it isn't a joke for Al Yad. Except that if *he* had flown in, his arms *wouldn't* be tired. Because he can fly without moving them." Craft took a drink and set his glass back down. "Anyway, the point is the bluff I described to Alyssa would never have held him in check. He'd have nothing to lose by continuing to challenge me. To see if he could finally break me. And the fear that I might—*some day in the future*—have his level of power wouldn't stop him from the devastation he's so eager to unleash. And even if I did achieve his level of power, it's doubtful I could kill him."

"So what *is* the truth, then?"

"I told Alyssa that Omar Haddad had me totally freaked out. Although she likes to use the name Al Yad," said Craft as an aside. "More colorful, I guess. Anyway, this much is absolutely true. He did have me freaked out. I knew I had to have a mechanism to stop him. He was growing more deluded, and more powerful, by the day— both going hand in hand. I didn't have to be a genius to know where this was headed. I was listening to a man promise to cleanse the world of infidels while his finger was on the trigger of a thousand nuclear bombs. You can't see a train wreck like this coming and still sleep at night."

Martin nodded solemnly. The world was rushing by thirty thousand feet below them, and its inhabitants were blissfully unaware of the greatest threat they had ever faced.

"So I *didn't* sleep," continued Craft. "I worked around the clock during the months that Omar was falling farther and farther off the deep end. I found the certainty of a coming Armageddon—for which I would be responsible in many ways—to be very . . . motivational. I strained my brain to its limits." His face reflected a demonic intensity. "And finally I succeeded. I found a weapon that could stop him."

Martin leaned forward. "Then what are you waiting for?" he said. "*Use it.*"

"Thanks, Eben," said Craft, rolling his eyes. "That hadn't occurred to me."

"Sorry," said Martin. "So what's holding you back?"

"When I describe it, you'll understand. The only thing I could come up with was a feedback system. I won't drill down into the math and science of it, because you wouldn't understand it. I'm better at quantum physics than you."

"No doubt," said Martin. "You're better at quantum physics than *anybody.*"

Craft nodded to acknowledge the compliment and then continued. "I call my weapon—device really—the *quantum mirror*. Not because it resembles a traditional mirror in any way. But because, once it's deployed, any mind tapping into the zero point field has the energy it's harnessing reflected back at it. Imagine shooting a laser at a mirror and having a hole drilled in your chest by its reflection. The brain connects to the field, but instead of directing the zero point energy elsewhere, it flows right back to the brain. Like fire following a gunpowder trail back to the source. A personal shield won't stop it, because the energy follows the open connection between the mind and the field."

"Okay," said Martin. "I understand the principle."

"Once the device is activated, it catalyzes all quantum space within Earth's gravity well in a chain reaction. I was able to conduct a controlled test on a very weak version of it. And the kickback effect—the reflective effect—is extraordinarily potent."

"I thought you said your device started a chain reaction. So how did you conduct a controlled test?"

"The chain reaction requires a critical energy of deployment to achieve. Similar to a critical mass for a nuclear reaction. I made sure I was well below this threshold for the tests. Anyway, extrapolating from these small scale tests, if the device were fully deployed, any use of zero point energy whatsoever would cause instant death."

"Sounds perfect. Yet Al Yad is still alive. So I'm still missing something."

"What you're missing is that once you've used biofeedback techniques to build your skills, you reach a point at which tapping the field becomes automatic. Reflexive. I showed you my defensive shield, and told you about the first layer of defense that's always on."

Martin nodded.

"Well, you can't turn it off," explained Craft with a deep frown. "And the reflective matrix established by the quantum mirror device won't distinguish *how* the zero point field is being used. It doesn't matter if you're using it offensively or defensively. Purposely or involuntarily. For good or for evil. Once your mind sticks a straw in and takes a drink," said Craft, turning away and shaking his head in frustration, "it's game over."

Martin nodded. His friend had told him of the experiments he had done, showing that his subconscious had grown far more powerful than it had been before, and far more vigilant. "*Now* I get it," he said. "You deploy this weapon and . . ." He brought his finger tips together in front of his chest and then threw his hands apart, mimicking the sound of an explosion. "So long Brennan Craft."

"Thanks for the visual, Eben," said Craft, rolling his eyes. "That's really helpful." He sighed. "But, yes. It will kill me, too. And if I had activated it when it was first ready, I would have killed eighteen other people as well in my camp."

"Something Al Yad ended up doing anyway."

"Yes, as it turned out," said Craft gravely. "But prior to this I was racing to find a way for this quantum mirror effect to only reflect back energy when a mind *actively* directed it, rather than involuntarily. And I continued to work on the problem for some time after Omar became Al Yad. But there was no way. Tapping the field is *all* subconscious. Even when I'm able to consciously, *voluntarily*, direct it, it's my subconscious carrying out the order. I still have no idea how." Craft smiled humorlessly. "The only good news is that while

I was working on the problem, before Omar wiped out my group, I set up a fail-safe."

"Meaning?"

"I built a quantum mirror device large enough to catalyze the entire planet. Which would occur at the speed of light, by the way."

Martin was a student of physics himself, and knew that light could circumnavigate the globe seven times in a single second. "So basically, the effect is instantaneous."

"More or less," replied Craft. "I built it, and then I hid it. If I were to activate the device, the entire Earth would become toxic to any use of zero point energy. For about six hours. Then the effect would dissipate very quickly, and the field could be used safely once again."

"Where did you hide it?"

"Sorry," said Craft. "But that I can't share with anyone. I don't expect you to ever be captured by Al Yad. But the stakes are too high to take any chances. If he found it, he would destroy it in an instant."

Martin nodded. His friend was absolutely right. He shouldn't know.

"I set up the device so it could be activated remotely. By any cell phone. Dial its number and you connect to a computer housed within the device. If you then enter a certain code, the computer activates it."

Martin shook his head in wonder. He never ceased to be amazed at his friend's genius and ingenuity. "So after Al Yad killed your colleagues, and was a few minutes from doing the same to you, you played your quantum mirror card?"

"Exactly. My phone is always with me. And since I can power it myself," said Craft, raising his eyebrows, "it's always charged and ready. So before Omar managed to breach my shield, I told him about the quantum mirror. And I threatened to activate it. I told him to build his religion. Do anything he wanted. But if he ever committed terrorist acts, killed world leaders, that sort of thing, I would activate it. I would screw us both. A suicide pact." Craft's upper lip curled into a snarl. "And he knew I meant it."

Martin nodded appreciatively. "The ultimate stalemate."

"So this is what is *really* holding him back. Why he doesn't come after me himself. Because even if he wins, he loses. I have no doubt that he can kill me. He just can't do it fast enough to stop me from activating my device. And I've modified my phone. I can use zero point energy to boost the signal to a level no cell phone suppressor can overcome."

"So Al Yad needs to destroy your device before he can destroy *you?*"

"Right. Which explains why he didn't come after me himself in the cornfield."

"Everything's a field with you," said Martin wryly. "Zero point. Corn. It's all the same."

Craft laughed. "There's enough zero point energy in an ear of corn to boil away all the Earth's oceans. Fields within fields, my friend. Fields within fields."

"Well, now it all makes sense," said Martin. "You've done a masterful job of handcuffing our delusional friend." He shook his head. "But why not tell Alyssa?"

Craft lowered his eyes. "I didn't want her to think less of me."

Martin thought he understood, but wondered if his friend would acknowledge the situation openly. "Think less of you?" he repeated. "You've invented a brilliant deterrent. And you're the only one alive who could have possibly managed it, and we both know it."

"We also both know I should deploy it now. Don't we?"

Martin had his answer. Craft wasn't hiding from the cold reality. He sighed. "I love you like a brother, Bren. You know that. But I see where this argument could be made. Al Yad hasn't brought about the apocalypse—yet. But from what you've told me, he's killing scores of his own followers to demonstrate his supposed divinity. Or on a whim. And he's not growing any saner. Even if he never finds your device, at some point he'll grow too impatient, or snap completely, and destroy a major city. Or twenty."

"Yep. That's the analysis. And I *can* take him out now. But if I do, I go as well."

Craft paused and stared through one of the plane's windows into the black night outside. After an extended silence, he turned back to his friend. "I know I should do the heroic thing," he said finally. "But I can't. Remember when you guys were into bungee jumping? I couldn't do that either."

"No comparison," said Martin. "Who could blame you for not being in any hurry to commit suicide. It's nothing to be ashamed of."

"Other than I'm protecting one life at the almost certain cost of millions. The morally correct thing would be to activate it now. Rid the world of this threat."

"But you've been holding Al Yad in check. If the murder of millions was five minutes away, and certain, I have no doubt you'd . . ."

"Do the right thing?"

"Do the incomprehensibly difficult thing. But you're still kicking and he hasn't crossed your metaphorical line in the sand. And while you are, I know you're still searching for other ways to kill him. Ways that require less personal sacrifice on your part."

"Which is where Alyssa comes in. If I can get to his level, maybe I can beat him."

"God knows you have the far superior mind," said Martin.

"Alyssa worries that anyone with this kind of power is a danger. Including me. So if she knew about the quantum mirror, maybe she would refuse to help me get to the next level."

"Knowing that you could erase Al Yad from the picture at any time would certainly reduce the urgency of this move."

"Please don't tell her about the device," said Craft. "I'm still sorting through a number of possibilities, and I don't know where I'll land. But until I tell you otherwise, please keep this to yourself."

Martin nodded solemnly. "I promise." He downed the rest of his Tom Collins. "So you think if Alyssa helps you up your game you might be able to take him out?"

"Doubtful."

"He has to have some weakness," said Martin. He rubbed his chin in thought. "What about poison?"

"You're as sharp as you always were, Eben. Great thought. But it won't work. Liquid poison wouldn't get through his inner shield. The VX trick on the door handle that took out Alyssa's bodyguards wouldn't work. But gas could. It's the only thing that could. He still needs to breathe. Cut off his air, and he blasts through any restraint or barrier you could impose to get a fresh supply. Only an odorless, colorless gas, that he doesn't know is there until it's inside his body, could work."

"Then that's the answer."

"No. Al Yad knows this as well as we do. His fortress in Syria has a higher density of gas and poison alarms than any other place on earth. And just in case these fail, he surrounds himself with canaries. Inside cages with sophisticated respiration monitors and alarms. If this fails, he has long-range monitors that he's always wearing. "

"You're shitting me?" said Martin. "Canaries?"

"I would not shit you about this," said Craft with a wry smile. "He has them everywhere. From the intel I've seen, he tells his followers they're symbolic. Decorative. Naturally, he'd never tell them their real purpose."

"What about poisoning his food?"

"He's totally paranoid. He doesn't eat. Ever. He doesn't need to, other than for the flavor or social convention. The fact that he never does helps seal his divinity. Not that his followers need any more convincing."

This was a more daunting problem than Martin had realized. But Al Yad was just being smart. If you're invulnerable except for your heels, you don't go charging around in sandals like Achilles. You find the best heel protection money can buy.

Martin shifted on the couch, the ride so smooth they had no indication they were tearing through the sky at over five hundred miles per hour. "Bren, I know you've given all of this more thought than I have," he said. "But don't you think the world could use a second fail safe?"

"What do you mean?"

"I'm not trying to be pessimistic here, or a downer. But what if Al Yad finds a way to kill you that you haven't thought of? Or you die of a heart attack? You've told me you think tapping the zero point field confers health benefits. But are you certain it will prevent strokes and heart attacks?"

Craft frowned. "No. I *think* it will. But you're right, I can't be certain."

"Let's face it, Bren. If you were to die suddenly, the world would be at Al Yad's mercy."

"So you want me to give you the telephone number and code to activate the quantum mirror device? Is that what you're saying?"

"Yes. As a backup. Just in case. The stakes are too high. I know I'm asking you to put your life in my hands. But I think you should consider it."

Craft remained silent for some time, thinking. "You're right," he said finally. "But instead of putting my life in your hands, I'd like to think of it as putting *Al Yad's* life in your hands."

Craft wrote out a telephone number and code on a yellow post-it note and handed it to his friend. "Memorize this when we're done and then destroy it."

Martin looked down at the numbers, nodded, and then pocketed the yellow square.

"But let's get back to finding a way to kill Al Yad that *doesn't* guarantee my death," said Craft. "I told you that even if Alyssa's hypnosis—or placebo enhancement, whatever you want to call it— works, I don't think I can beat Al Yad. But what if two of us were at that level? Or fifty? At some point, I have to believe we could focus enough energy to overcome him. No matter how strong he is."

"I don't know, Bren. Now you've just multiplied the number of unstoppable people. And if absolute power corrupts, you could end up with a *worse* situation."

"That's exactly what Alyssa said," admitted Craft.

Martin smiled. "I really do like her already," he said.

"Just so you know, I agree with both of you. And I'm working on a solution. I'm sure you can grasp the paradise we could build if everyone could tap into the field."

"Yes, but even if we *all* become invulnerable, it just takes one Al Yad to destroy the Earth out from under us. A neutron bomb kills humans but leaves buildings. This would be the reverse. If we all had our own shields like you do, we could survive Armageddon but find ourselves living on a sea of magma and sulfur because a single asshole decided to play Dr. Destructo."

"I know that," said Craft with a pained expression. "But there has to be an answer. I don't believe that such a promising future will be forever out of reach because of the demons of our own nature. Of our own mental health. We need to understand human behavior better. Human psychosis. Or find some kind of regulator switch that only allows for peaceful, constructive uses of the field."

"It can't be done," said Martin adamantly. "There will always be those among us who will turn anything constructive into the opposite. Even if it's potential for destructive use isn't obvious. A violin seems about as innocent as you can get, but you could still use it to beat someone to death." He shook his head. "But in the case of zero point energy, the *destructive* uses are the most obvious ones.

"Thousands of murders are committed around the world each day," continued Martin. "If someone goes crazy, they can shoot up twenty kids at a school. That's tragic enough. But what if they could each destroy the entire world? You're envisioning billions of people, who are each their own weapon of mass destruction. We wouldn't last fifteen seconds."

"There has to be a way," insisted Craft stubbornly. "I agree with what you say. But I refuse to believe we have the genius and ingenuity to turn each of us into a veritable demigod, but don't have the genius to solve the most difficult problem our species has ever faced."

"Ourselves?" said Martin.

"That's right," said Craft. "And if it takes me a thousand years, I'm going to find the answer," he insisted.

40

While she was being tortured in the back of a van, Alyssa would never have believed that the next week of her life would be the best she would ever have. She slept a full fifteen hours on the impossibly comfortable queen sized bed on Martin's jet, and awoke feeling great.

As she had expected, Martin's island was majestic. It was about a square mile in area, with cliffs on one side, white sand beaches on the other, and a lush woods in between.

Near the beach end of the island, in a clearing in the forest, was a seven-thousand square foot home with a swimming pool, spa, and tennis court. Colorful, cotton-mesh hammocks were scattered around the grounds and surrounding area, each more than large enough for two people—as long as the two people didn't mind being somewhat entangled, which she and Brennan Craft did not.

The two visitors had taken up residence in the guest house, which, at three-thousand square feet, was considerably more spacious and opulent than Alyssa's own home. The first night there the two of them had made love repeatedly, alternating between wild abandonment and tenderness, and she already felt herself falling in love. Craft had more endurance and was more passionate than any man she had ever been with, and she wondered idly if the ability to harness an infinite sea of energy translated into the bedroom, or if he was just naturally gifted in this way.

Craft demonstrated his always-on second skin, as he called it, showing that no sharp or pointy object could so much as scratch him. Alyssa had wondered if he would be slippery because of it, but his skin felt perfectly normal against her body.

Despite Craft's assurances, Alyssa wasn't comfortable sleeping next to him. Not given Patel's description of what had happened to an entire pickup truck, and mercenary, that had hit Craft's shield when it was active. She helped Craft move a second, smaller bed beside the king size bed in the master bedroom, and when they had become too exhausted to talk or make love, she rolled onto it to sleep.

They spent their days on the beach, but it was also a working vacation for Craft. Even though it was an island, Martin had made sure to have all of the phone and wifi coverages, and advanced computers, necessary for him to conduct business here. So Craft tapped these resources to gather further intelligence on the activities of Major Greg Elovic, and also make sure he understood the electronic security measures that protected Alyssa's lab.

As he had expected, Elovic assumed Craft had been responsible for the gruesome killings of Alyssa's two bodyguards, and that she was most likely dead. Still, her retina scan or fingerprints would continue to gain her access to the facility, although the system had been programmed to alert Elovic the moment she used it. If Craft forced her to return to her lab, the major must have reasoned, this would enable him to pick up their trail.

According to Elovic's reports to his superiors, in his heart of hearts, he was convinced Alyssa had been killed. Now he was hunting for Craft more urgently than before, if such a thing was even possible. Capturing Brennan Craft to get intel on Al Yad had been one thing. But capturing him because he had almost certainly murdered one of their own was quite another. Elovic had become as obsessed with seeking vengeance for Alyssa as any cop had ever been over the murder of his partner, as Alyssa had insisted would be the case to Tariq Bahar.

During her second day on the island, Alyssa sent off a brief text to her parents, which Craft had made certain couldn't be intercepted, letting them know she was alive and well. She told them she would explain everything later, and that it was vitally important that they not tell anyone except her two brothers that she had contacted them, under any circumstances.

After this she spent all of her time resting on the beach, making love to Brennan Craft, and feasting on some truly outstanding cuisine, including fresh seafood from the area. She was soon feeling strong physically, and was as happy as she'd ever been. Her arm and thigh hadn't fully healed, but she no longer needed pain meds on a regular basis.

And she was having the chance to get to know Eben Martin as well.

Eben was amazing. Bren had been right about him. He was still down to earth despite his fortune: humble and self-effacing. He had a sharp wit, playful sense of humor, and was a great conversationalist. He also possessed the kind of compassion and kindness that couldn't be faked.

In many ways, Eben was similar to Bren, and Alyssa could see right away why they had been such close friends. She was falling in love with Brennan Craft, but she had a feeling that if there were an alternate universe in which she had met Eben Martin first—even if he weren't wealthy—she could have fallen in love with him as well.

On their fourth night on the island, after she and Bren had engaged in a particularly passionate session of lovemaking, Alyssa called up a thirty minute clip of one of her favorite stand-up comedians on the master bedroom screen, which took up much of the wall in front of the bed. She and Bren were propped up against the headboard, leaning against one another, and Alyssa had drawn the bed's burgundy satin sheet over her shoulders like a shirt, less because of any self-consciousness she had over being naked in Craft's presence, and more because of the chilly breeze coming from the bamboo ceiling fan overhead.

The comedian elicited plenty of heartfelt laughter from both of them, and when he had finished, Alyssa switched off the screen with the bedside remote. She turned her head and gave Craft a quick peck on the lips.

"Okay," she said. "Before it gets too late. You promised me a rain check, remember?"

Much had transpired since their conversation in the Bluegrass Waffle House in Covington, Kentucky, but after a few seconds of thought Craft remembered. "The God Theory," he said simply.

"That's right. Lay it on me."

Craft smiled and returned the quick kiss with which he had just been favored. "All right. But you really need to read the book. I won't do it justice."

"Deal," said Alyssa. "But in the meanwhile . . ."

Craft slid a few feet away along the headboard so they weren't touching anymore and turned his head to face her. "It's really fairly simple, actually. Reminds me of a marketing slogan from a board game I played as a kid: a minute to learn, a lifetime to master. So here goes: the first step is to postulate an infinite conscious intelligence. With infinite potential."

"That's pretty much the typical description of God, isn't it?" said Alyssa, unimpressed.

"True enough. But bear with me. Let's go on to postulate this infinite consciousness exists outside of space and time. In a way that is well beyond our possible comprehension. As you suggest, for want of a better word, let's call this infinite consciousness, God. I like that this God is postulated as being beyond space and time. *Independent* of space and time. If he weren't, then he would require a creator."

Alyssa considered this. So far, so good. This at least acknowledged something glossed over by many: that if a universe required a creator, one would think God would require a creator as well. "Okay," said Alyssa. "I'm with you so far."

"And I'll use the pronoun, *he,* for convenience. But I would never suggest that an infinite being who exists outside of space and time has a gender."

"What?" said Alyssa with a grin. "Is he like a Ken Doll down there?"

Craft laughed. "I sure hope not," he said. "But it wouldn't matter, even if he was . . . *supremely* endowed. Because there is only one of him. So if he did have this particular appendage, what would he do with it?"

Alyssa smiled. This was certainly something she had never considered before.

"Which leads me directly to God's problem," continued Craft. "If you think about it, since this postulated God is everything, he is also nothing. He isn't big, and he isn't small. He isn't great, and he isn't weak. There is no contrast. Like a kid who is an only child saying, 'I'm the smartest kid in my family, but also the dumbest. The nicest, but also the meanest. The most attractive, but also the ugliest.' All if this is true. When you're the only one, the only *thing*, you can't get any scale, any contrast."

Alyssa smiled. As usual, Craft had a way of explaining things she would have thought to be absurd in a very compelling manner.

"So this God has no way to get a sense of his own greatness," continued Craft. "Or a sense of anything." He raised his eyebrows. "And he certainly can't experience the bliss of making love to the most amazing woman in the universe. Like I have."

Alyssa beamed, but then caught herself and pretended to be alarmed. "If I find out who this woman is," she said playfully, unable to fully suppress a grin, "I'm going to kill her."

Craft leaned toward her and kissed her again, unable to help himself. "As you know, the book was written by a scientist named Bernard Haisch. He writes, 'God is infinite potential, but potential—infinite or otherwise—isn't the same as experience.'" Craft paused. "Still with me?"

Alyssa nodded.

"So God wishes to experience. He wants to transform potential into this experience. Haisch uses the example of a game. Playing it is far more satisfying than just reading the rules. Another analogy he uses is that of a man who has a billion dollars but isn't allowed to spend a penny of it. He has vast potential spending power, but can't actualize any of it. What good does money do you if you can never spend it?"

Alyssa thought of Eben Martin, the only billionaire she knew, and smiled. He certainly didn't suffer from the particular problem.

"So if you were this God, how would you rectify this problem?"

Alyssa thought for a moment. "Create a universe to enjoy?"

"But *how* would you create it?"

Alyssa shrugged.

"You can't create something in *addition* to yourself," continued Craft. "You're already all there is. The only way to create a universe is to *limit* yourself."

"Now you've lost me."

"Don't worry. Not for long. Let me switch gears for a moment to my favorite subject, light. How many shades of color are there?" he asked.

"Well, there are seven colors of the rainbow. But as far as shades go, there are basically an infinite number."

"Exactly. And if you combine all the infinite shades together, what do you get?"

"White light," said Alyssa, remembering that contrary to intuition, all wavelengths in the visible spectrum, combined in equal intensity, produced white light rather than black.

"Right again. But as Haisch points out, if the universe were made up of nothing but white light, you couldn't see *anything*. Again, no contrast. Just a fog of white. Why is the ocean blue? Because water absorbs all colors of light *except* blue. The color of the ocean isn't created from *adding* blue. But from *subtracting* everything *but* blue from the white light."

Craft paused. "Haisch uses a brilliant example. You remember the old-time slide projectors? Plastic slides have gone extinct, of course, but these devices are still used to project computer images up on a screen. But either way, turn these projectors on and they shine a strong white light onto the screen. But what do you *see* in this light?"

"Nothing."

"Right. Because there isn't any contrast. But this light has *infinite* potential. If you put a slide of Eben's island in front of the light, different wavelengths are subtracted out, allowing you to see green trees, blue ocean, yellow hammocks, and so on. By subtracting different shades of light from the white nothingness, you can create an infinity of different images."

"Very interesting," said Alyssa thoughtfully. "So Haisch is saying that God is this white projector light, so to speak. Infinite potential to create images. But by itself, nondescript. So that's what you meant by God creating the universe by limiting himself. God puts slides in his personal projector, so to speak, subtracting out bits and pieces of his infinite potential to achieve contrast."

Craft gazed at her appreciatively. "I couldn't have said it better. There are a few lines from the book I remember exactly, and one of these sums it up nicely. 'The process of creation is the exact opposite of making something out of nothing. It is, on the contrary, a filtering process that makes something out of everything.'"

This explanation did resonate with Alyssa, so long as she was willing to accept the postulate of an infinite God. An infinite God really couldn't experience anything, since he was *everything*. And a universe couldn't be something in *addition* to God, since God encompassed all. Thus the central tenet: the universe wasn't made from nothing, it was subtracted from everything.

"Haisch writes that 'by limiting the infinitely possible, you create the finitely real. In this way the infinite consciousness moves beyond sterile potential to actual creation—to *doing* rather than just *being*. He gets to act out and live out his ideas . . . his fantasies. He gets to spend his billion dollars.'"

"I'm surprised to find myself intrigued," admitted Alyssa.

"So God is experiencing himself, experiencing existence, through a lens that is the universe, and all living intelligences in the universe. Which, of course, includes us. He's limiting himself. Breaking himself into fragments so to speak. And making sure none of these fragments are omniscient. Because what fun is omniscience? Nothing can ever surprise you. It's more fun reading a mystery when someone hasn't spoiled the ending for you."

A playful smile came over Alyssa's face. "And it's more fun having sex when you aren't the only being in the room at the time," she said. "Infinite or otherwise."

"Amen to that," said Craft in amusement. "So once this postulated being of infinite potential limits himself," he continued, serious once again, "you get polarity. Which is an absolute requirement for existence, for experience. You can't have tall without short. Fast without slow. Up without down. And so on. Since our universe does have polarity, on the other hand, God can experience how powerful he is, how great, because there are things that are weak, and small. There is good versus evil. In versus out. Love versus hate. *Polarity*. Not just a fog of white. By breaking himself up into limited bits, God has created a rich tapestry of experiences. Or, as the great physicist Freeman Dyson observed, 'The laws of nature are constructed in such a way as to make the universe as interesting as possible.'"

"I'm guessing you believe then that at the end of our travels, each of us is ultimately reunited with the whole."

"Ultimately, yes. This way of looking at God, and how he solved his initial problem, makes sense to me. And I like the implications of the theory as well. This belief system encompasses many of the tenets of different religions. And if this is true, if we are all part of God, existing to help God experience existence, there is no need for prayer. No need for organized religion. Not that these both aren't welcome. But this isn't a requirement. And there is no heaven or hell. And no deity sitting in judgment. The only thing required of us is that we live and experience the richness of life and of contrast."

"But then aren't good and evil equivalent?"

"Great question. But the answer is no. Because Karma is a bitch. Because if you really are part of God, any pain you inflict is just being inflicted on yourself. But again, there is a need for pain. How could you experience pleasure if pain didn't exist? If everything was pleasurable, nothing would be. How could you recognize good if not for evil? You ultimately will be reunited with the whole in a non-physical realm. And there you will have to face and relive the pain and terror and hardship and cruelties that you inflicted."

This time Alyssa's face crinkled up in skepticism. "I understand what you're saying. But this still seems a little soft on cruelty and evil, don't you think?"

"Maybe. Again, Haisch explains it better and more thoroughly than I can."

Alyssa's eyes widened as she recalled something else Craft had said at the waffle house in Kentucky. "When you were expressing your awe at the ability of your subconscious to harness the zero point field, you suggested the possibility you were tapping into the mind of God, as well. Is this part of the theory, also?"

"Very good," said Craft. "You'd be above average, even in Lake Wobegone. I'll quote Haisch one last time: 'Just as creation can be viewed as a process of subtraction from the infinite rather than as an event in which something pops out of nothing, your personal consciousness can be viewed as a brain-filtered remnant of infinite consciousness rather than as a chemical creation of the brain.'"

"I have to admit," said Alyssa, "it's a very compelling theory. I'm not saying I'm prepared to jump on this bandwagon quite yet, but a lot of this makes sense to me. The part about tapping into the mind of God would normally seem especially hokey to me," she admitted. "But knowing that *your* mind can draw enough energy from infinitesimally short-lived fluctuations in the vacuum, and use this to stop a bullet—or a pickup truck—from hitting you, does make this more believable."

"Like I said in the restaurant. There are miracles all around us. What's one more?"

"You struck me as Zen when I first met you. And I can see why you would be like this if you really believed in The God Theory."

"Well, I do try to take things in stride. But I usually fail. I'm still a slave to certain wiring that evolved on this fascinating world in this fascinating universe. I believe that evil is an important part of experience. But I'll still do everything in my power to prevent it. I try to tell myself when I screw up that experience is experience, that contrast is important, that I wouldn't appreciate my success without failure. But most of the time this doesn't do any good. I can't take a laissez-faire approach to life, even if my beliefs would suggest I could."

Alyssa nodded. She knew what a difficult prospect it was to attempt to exceed the bounds of one's wiring.

Craft sighed. "And just because intellectually I believe in the afterlife," he added, "I still fear death. I'm still wired with a powerful survival instinct."

"Given all that's happening," said Alyssa. "That's a good thing. That's a very good thing."

41

Alyssa found it strange to be back in Bloomington, Indiana. Bloomington was still the same, but she was decidedly not.

It was difficult to even comprehend how much had changed in the short time since she had last been here, both with respect to her emotional life, and having her view of reality, and what was possible, turned upside down.

Martin had needed the Boeing and had sent her and Craft to the Indianapolis airport on a Gulfstream. After the Boeing Business Jet 2, flying in the decadent Gulfstream G650 seemed like slumming.

They waited in the bed-and-breakfast that had been their destination days earlier to get the go-ahead from Adam Turco. He had settled into his role as head of Eben Martin's personal security detail quite nicely, although from the moment he had assumed this position, he had been on loan to Brennan Craft, and had been told that orders from him were the same as orders from Martin himself.

Two days earlier, on Martin's island, Turco had supplied Alyssa and Craft with clean, untraceable phones, capable of sending and receiving encrypted calls, e-mails, and text messages. Even if these messages were intercepted, they would be nothing but gibberish, unless one had the decryption key. She and Craft were each given their own keys, seven digit numbers that when entered would transform the gibberish into English.

Turco had left the island two days earlier to perform reconnaissance on Alyssa's lab. As usual, he did an impeccable job. He first was able to identify four well concealed and well placed cameras installed in surrounding trees, pointing to areas of ingress into the lab. He had simply determined where he would place such devices if he were conducting surveillance, and was able to locate them in less than three hours, being careful in his approach so he wouldn't be caught by the very cameras he was trying to detect.

Turco had then reasoned that whoever was watching these cameras would be within a mile or so of the lab. Far enough not to arouse suspicion and near enough that if the cameras did detect Craft or Alyssa, the watcher could mount an ambush or follow them, even if they were in and out of the lab in a hurry.

A hotel or apartment would have been ideal, but the lab was outside of Bloomington, and there were no residences or hotels for nine or ten miles. Too far away to be certain that whoever was behind the surveillance could be roused from a sound sleep and make it to the lab in time for whatever they had planned.

So Turco drove the streets within a mile of Alyssa's lab building until he found what he was looking for. A blue industrial van marked *Kate's Florist & Gifts*, which had no windows in the back compartment, and which had been parked on a random curb, with nothing worth visiting in its vicinity. This was almost certainly where those conducting the surveillance were waiting and watching monitors, and eventually sleeping, counting on alarms to alert them if anyone approached the lab in the wee hours of the night.

Adam Turco camped out within binocular range, and sure enough, early in the morning, the van drove off. It had not been abandoned after all, which is precisely what he had expected.

Turco made sure not to molest the van in any way. If he had made his presence known, or had taken the van out, reinforcements were sure to arrive. Reinforcements who would now know with certainty that the lab was in play, and who would come in greater numbers and with greater caution.

So Turco chose to take out whoever was in this van just prior to the breach of the lab, so those behind this would have no time to regroup and recover. While Alyssa could have managed the breach herself, Craft had insisted on joining her. Given his ability to repel aggression, Alyssa decided she was glad that he had.

So she and Craft sat in the quaint, rustic bedroom of a bed-and-breakfast. For the first time in many days, they spent hours together in the presence of a bed and remained fully clothed.

Clothed, and anxiously awaiting Adam Turco's signal to proceed.

* * *

Turco parked his car several blocks away from where he had previously spotted the blue florist van and settled in behind a tight grouping of trees nearby, clutching a pair of high powered binoculars with a digital camera attachment. He arrived at seven p.m., expecting the van to return only after the last straggler in the lab had left for the night.

Sure enough, at about eight, the van appeared, rolling slowly to a stop in the same place it had parked before. Turco had counted on the driver being a creature of habit, and had made the right call. The driver had a scar on his chin and an eagle, talons extended, tattooed on his neck. He looked around to be sure no one was watching and slid open the side door of the van.

Turco was in perfect position to view the inside of the van, and he had been waiting for this precise moment. During the few seconds the side door was open he took over a dozen photos through the binoculars, which he sent to his phone for enlargement and study.

The driver was alone. Perfect!

The van contained a mattress, several monitors, a television, a thermos of coffee, and a bag with the words, Dunkin' Donuts, printed proudly on the side. Hanging on a hook against the back inner wall of the van was a Tavor assault rifle. Compact and ergonometric, the Tavor was currently favored by the Israeli military, and could pump thirteen rounds a second into anything unlucky enough to be in its way. Turco had tested this weapon himself, and while it had a number of positive attributes, he found the trigger heavy and clumsy.

Turco shrugged. *To each his own*, he thought.

Turco returned to his car and waited patiently. At just after midnight he cautiously approached the van on foot, cloaked in the darkness of a moonless night. He took a deep breath and rapped firmly on the sliding door. "This is the police!" he shouted. "Open up! Now!"

He rapped again, even harder, and then immediately dropped to the pavement and scurried around to the other side of the van.

Seconds later, as Turco had expected, a burst of machine gun fire screamed through the door where he would have been had he not repositioned himself.

The man inside threw open the sliding door the moment he stopped firing and jumped to the pavement, crouching low, searching ahead for other cops and for an expected corpse that would surely resemble bloody Swiss cheese.

As the driver looked to his right, Turco slid around the van to the left, his gun extended. "Freeze!" he barked. "Drop it!

No one was likely to be around for miles, and Turco doubted that his shouting, or even the sound of machine gun fire, would bring any company.

The man considered pivoting on Turco, but there was something about the assured way Turco had gotten the drop on him, and the utter confidence in his voice, that made him decide not to take this chance. He lowered the assault rifle to the pavement. Turco ordered him to kick it under the van, which he did.

Turco then ordered him to peel back his clothing and had him carefully remove a knife and gun this exercise revealed.

"Turn around!" ordered Turco. When the man was facing him he added, "Toss me your phone."

Once again, the driver did as instructed.

"Who do you work for?" demanded Turco, snatching the phone from the air.

The man hesitated for just a moment and Turco pulled the trigger. The slug missed the man's head by inches. "*Who do you work for?*" he shouted.

"I don't know who he is," came the immediate reply. "He contacts me and issues jobs. All I know is that he has a refined voice, maybe British, and pays very well."

"What instructions did he give you?"

"Surveil a lab building that's a mile or so from here until further notice. If a man named Brennan Craft, or a woman named Alyssa Aronson, try to enter, don't interfere, but contact him immediately for further orders.

"And you're getting paid by the night?"

The man nodded.

"What's your name?"

"Bobkoski. Carl Bobkoski."

"Okay, Carl," said Turco. "This can go one of two ways from here. Option one, I shoot you in the head." He let this hang in the air for several seconds. "Option two. You give me the contact information you have for your boss, and leave here now. Notice that in this option, you get to live."

"The contact information won't do you any good. You can use it to contact him, but you can't use it to find him."

"Good. Because I don't have any interest in finding him. It's useful to me to be able to contact men who need . . . professional help. And who pay well." Turco paused. "I need you to show me on your phone the contact e-mail and phone number for this man. It's not that I don't trust you," he added with a crooked smile. "It's just that I don't trust you."

Bobkoski considered.

"There is nothing to think about here . . . Carl. It's a win-win. You let my friends do their business in the lab without picking up a tail. So they win. I get potentially valuable contact information. So I win. And you can tell your boss that no one ever showed and keep doing this job until he tells you to stop. And since my clients will have already come and gone, you can find yourself a hotel nearby and take a vacation while collecting your paycheck."

Bobkoski frowned. It sounded good, but he knew there was a horrible catch. "When my boss finds out I played him, I'm dead. And so is my family. I don't know who he is, or who he represents, but he has a reputation. Rumor has it that a merc crossed him six months ago, and they're still finding pieces of this merc, along with his mother.

The man who hired me is *extreme*. On the reward side, *and* on the punishment side."

"He'll never find out. You know he's not sure the people you're watching for will ever strike the lab. That's why he's having you spend so much quality time out here."

"If you contact my employer, he'll want to know where you got his contact information."

Turco shook his head. Could Bobkoski really be this stupid? "He can *want* to know all he likes. But I won't tell him. True, I don't give two shits about what happens to you. But if I tell him, he'll know my clients visited the lab. I don't want him to know this. It might influence his decisions and boomerang back on my clients. And they're paying me quite well. Second, by not telling him, I look more impressive. Magicians never reveal how they do their tricks." He shrugged. "Besides, I may choose not to contact him, after all. Who knows?"

Turco had been more than patient, but his patience had now run out. "Look, you have three seconds to decide. When a man holding a gun at your head offers you two options, and the first one is instant death, you choose the second option. No need to even hear the second to decide."

Turco made a show of beginning to squeeze the trigger.

"I accept," said Bobkoski immediately.

"Good call," said Turco dryly.

* * *

Alyssa's phone vibrated and a short gibberish message appeared on the screen. She entered her seven digit decryption key and the message suddenly became readable. It was from Adam Turco, as expected. "Everything buttoned up. You have a green light."

Alyssa and Craft drove the twelve miles to the lab. Turco wouldn't be accompanying them during the actual theft, but they were comforted in the knowledge that he would be there, behind the scenes, making sure they weren't interrupted.

Alyssa entered her code to get into the building, holding her breath. Craft had assured her that she could still get in, and that he had seen to it that this wouldn't alert anyone, but it was still nerve-wracking.

The bolts on the door released and they entered the foyer. Alyssa touched a panel on the wall to reveal a recessed biometric scanner. She put her thumb on the glass and her eye to the scanner and was rewarded by the sound of a second set of bolts being released from the inner door.

They had made it!

Alyssa surveyed her lab with mixed emotions. She had been so proud of her work. So proud that she had morphed the program from something ugly into something that could revolutionize medicine. But that had been a few weeks earlier. Before Brennan Craft had come into the picture. Before everything had changed.

Now, if her placebo enhancing techniques resulted in unleashing the mind's potential to make use of the zero point field, these techniques might one day help to turn humans into demigods. And if Brennan was right, dramatically extend human health, vitality, and longevity. These were big ifs, without a doubt. But if this proved possible, the pot of gold at the end of this rainbow was the size of *Jupiter*.

She quietly led Craft through several rooms to what looked like a closet. Inside was the face of a walk-in steel vault, only slightly less robust than those found in banks. The drugs and protocols she needed were inside. She keyed in the combination, holding her breath one last time, and the thick steel bolts, the circumference of baseball bats, retracted smoothly with a loud *thunk*.

They were in.

Craft watched the door while she went to work, pipetting small aliquots of four different drugs into four separate plastic vials. She then added back water so no one would notice a volume change, so that their entry and theft would never be discovered. This would dilute the drugs a small amount, but all testing was surely being halted anyway in her absence.

When this was completed, she downloaded software to a flash drive, specifically an algorithm entitled, *Modified Headrush 188,* which she would later also store in the cloud for safekeeping.

They exited the lab without incident, leaving it exactly as they had found it, and met up with Adam Turco just outside the bed-and-breakfast at which they were staying.

"How many men were watching the lab," Craft asked him when they had reunited.

"Just one."

"Where is he?"

Turco shook his head. "I know you wanted to interrogate whoever was stationed here," he said. "I tried to capture him. But it didn't work out. I'm afraid he took whatever secrets he had to the grave."

"Damn!" said Craft, looking even more upset about it than he sounded.

"It could have been worse," said Turco.

"How?"

"He could have killed me instead," replied the mercenary dryly.

"Adam has a good point," said Alyssa, wanting to lift Craft's spirits. In the scheme of things, this was a minor setback. They were all but certain the surveillance had been ordered by Al Yad, anyway, and almost as certain the man wouldn't know anything else that was useful. "And you need to look on the bright side. We got what we came for. The mission couldn't have gone better."

Craft's mood visibly improved. "Yeah," he said. "You're right. I should focus on the big picture." He turned to Turco. "And you're *positive* we won't be followed."

"Positive."

"Then I'd call this mission an unqualified success," said Alyssa happily.

"I couldn't agree more," said Adam Turco with a self-satisfied nod.

42

Three days later, Alyssa Aronson and Brennan Craft arrived at their new base of operations in Costa Rica. Martin's personal island was exceptional, but it was still within the United States, and subject to heightened scrutiny when compared to Central America. And even though Martin had taken pains to ensure his island couldn't be linked to him, there were people he had dealt with when he had acquired it who knew. And while these were people he trusted, the stakes were too high to rely on trust.

Eben Martin would be the only person ever to know where Craft and Alyssa were located. Even Adam Turco, whom Martin had come to like and trust, was not privy to this information, although he at least knew the country they were in.

Costa Rica was a paradise. Located on the Central American isthmus, with a population just over four million, it bordered both the Caribbean to the east and the Pacific to the west, and featured over eight hundred miles of coastline. While it was sandwiched between Nicaragua to the north and Panama to the south, it had been a democracy since 1949, and was one of the most stable and prosperous countries in the region. Topologically, Costa Rica's altitude varied from sea level to over twelve thousand feet, and fully two hundred volcanoes made their home in this country, including several that were active.

Martin had bought a home for them in Costa Rica before they left, sight unseen, using an untraceable dummy corporation, based on a description on the Internet that read, "spectacular mountain retreat with breathtaking views."

While they had never visited the property, he and Craft had taken a virtual tour online, and it did not disappoint. They had purchased the estate for two million dollars, and Martin paid another hundred thousand to ensure the transaction was closed immediately.

A main house and guest house were situated on fifty acres just up from the base of a mountain. While the guest house was tiny compared to its glorious parent, it alone would have more than sufficed for their needs. The property was touted as a nature lovers paradise, and in this case the Internet hadn't lied. Paradise was the right word. They wouldn't have been able to touch this estate for even ten million dollars back in The States.

The main house was open and airy, with vaulted ceilings, limestone floors, and towering windows that provided panoramic views of the mountains, valley, and the Turrialba Volcano far off in the distance. The top floor of the three story structure contained an open-air balcony more spacious than any room in Alyssa's home back in Indiana.

Craft had immediately set up banking and Martin had seen to it that a hundred thousand dollars was wired in to get them started. Craft had retained a considerable percentage of the fifty million dollars he had made years before, but now that he was on the lam he was unable to touch it. This was when it paid to have friends so wealthy that they considered several million dollars to be pocket change.

Alyssa had originally questioned Craft's decision to bring Eben Martin onboard, but she had to admit he had done the right thing. And she didn't think this change of opinion had occurred because she had been seduced by luxury—private jets, islands, and spacious, glorious compounds with guest homes—but because strategic moves that would have otherwise been difficult or impossible to make became easy, and she was convinced that Martin was a very good man.

They settled in quickly and Alyssa went right to work performing her narco-hypnotic magic. Craft had expected she would need an EEG device, which could measure electrical activity in the brain and detect changes with millisecond resolution, but he learned that the video game start-up, HeadRush Virtuality, had improved the resolution and accuracy of EEG technology fifty-fold.

The HeadRush controller was expensive, and the company still only offered a limited number of games. But Alyssa didn't care about games. The system couldn't have been more ideal for her needs. When it had first come out, she had a team study it and modify it to her specifications.

Players wore tight mesh elastic caps that pressed an array of hundreds of BB-sized nodes firmly against their heads. An algorithm in the game controller would allow wearers to train the game to react to electrical patterns in their brains, allowing them to control game avatars using thoughts alone. Although the training was simple and could be accomplished in less than an hour, the technology behind the device was stunningly sophisticated, and hadn't been available anywhere in the world even a year earlier.

A specialist on one of Greg Elovic's other Black Ops computer and electronics teams had worked with Alyssa to develop software that could be easily uploaded into the game controller, allowing her to view the brain activity being analyzed by the cap's many nodes on a computer screen, and to modify the nodes to deliver electrical pulses to order as well.

This allowed Alyssa to identify key areas of the brain involved in the basic placebo response and combine drugs, hypnosis, and stimulation of these neuronal pathways to dramatically enhance the effect. Alyssa liked to think that great scientists invented technologies to achieve their goals, but never failed to modify existing technologies to suit their needs whenever possible. Why reinvent the wheel when there was so much else that needed to be done?

She and Craft had brought several HeadRush game consoles with them to Costa Rica, which each included two elastic skullcaps, and Alyssa successfully uploaded the software that she had retrieved from her lab, *Modified Headrush 188*. As the name implied, a hundred and eighty-seven iterations had been tried before the system finally worked with the precision and effectiveness that Alyssa had required.

They spent an hour calibrating the strength of Craft's ability to wield zero point energy, to get a baseline, and then Alyssa began. She had him wear the skull cap for almost an entire day, during which she mapped his brain activity when he was using the field, both defensively, without conscious control, and offensively—performing what he called feeble acts of telekinesis.

She also asked him questions about his level of belief, his certainty, that he could accomplish certain tasks, such as correctly adding two single-digit numbers, opening an unlocked door, and so on. Since his certainty was absolute in these cases, she was able to record his brain patterns associated with absolute confidence. She also had him focus on tasks he knew he could not do, like playing a perfect rendition of Beethoven's fifth symphony on the piano. Since Brennan Craft had yet to master chopsticks, his extreme lack of confidence was understandable.

Alyssa analyzed all of this data and then drugged and hypnotized him, all the while using the controller to stimulate different areas of his brain. She was confident she had done as good a job as possible. It would have been easier, and faster, to attempt to change his mindset temporarily, through the use of a hypnotic trigger, but her goal was to modify his subconscious permanently, once and for all.

When she had finished, Craft slept through the night to get the drugs completely out of his system, and then awoke.

"Are you ready to fully harness the infinite?" asked Alyssa confidently as soon as he had arisen, having been up already for several hours while he slept it off.

"Absolutely."

"Great!" said Alyssa cheerfully. "Let's do this thing. This is going to work. I've never been more sure of anything in my life!" she added passionately, wondering if Craft would guess that she had said this to help boost the placebo effect further, as a last effort to exert influence on his subconscious.

What she was really thinking was that she had done all that she could. That she thought the procedure had gone great, but she had no idea if it would work. And she was hoping like hell that it would.

But she had gone with, "I've never been more sure of anything in my life," having decided that, "I hope like hell this works," probably wasn't quite as inspirational to the mysterious, and all important, subconscious she was trying to reach.

43

Alyssa's techniques worked brilliantly.

Both Craft and Alyssa were euphoric.

He had been *right*. It was all about belief. If you were absolutely convinced a sugar pill would cure you, or convinced there was no limit to the energy you could seize from the zero point field, your mind could work miracles.

At first the increase in Craft's ability was modest, but measurable. Instead of being able to press down on a scale at ninety-six pounds of force, he could manage a hundred and eight. But even this slight improvement reinforced his belief that the narco-hypnosis had worked, resulting in further increases. Within days Craft's exponential growth rivaled even that of Omar Haddad, and in only two weeks he had maxed out, at least judging from his admittedly subjective assessment, since his ability to use zero point energy quickly became immeasurable.

During this growth spurt he and Alyssa celebrated wildly after each new milestone, as though he were a star gymnast after a flawless performance at the Olympics, and she was his beaming coach. Craft's success was Alyssa's success, and arguably, all of humanity's success.

Craft spent ninety percent of his waking hours practicing his skills, with Alyssa often an observer or a participant in various experiments he conducted, and the other ten percent in Alyssa's arms or making love to her. And while he actually *could* make the earth move during sex, no man in her life had ever been more gentle and attentive. And *tireless* didn't even begin to describe him.

Their feelings for each other continued to intensify, although neither said I love you openly. Alyssa felt as though she was in love but sensed Craft didn't want to go there this early in the relationship. But love was the elephant in the bedroom, or at least the giant cupid.

She wasn't sure why Craft was holding back, since she would catch him gazing at her when he thought she wasn't watching like a lovesick puppy dog. And she would swear there were times when he was biting his tongue—once literally—to prevent an expression of love from breaking through the fortress of his lips.

Why fight it so desperately? Here was a man who could stop a Mack Truck, but who was struggling mightily to fight the escape of three tiny words.

After the second week he concentrated solely on mastering different ways to channel the massive energies he now could harness. No one was more intellectually gifted than Brennan Craft, and he climbed the learning curve on different modalities of directing the energy, including precision uses that he thought of as fine motor control, with remarkable speed.

The energies he controlled were awesome, and scary. He would melt rock formations the size of houses before Alyssa's eyes, or make them vanish entirely, in addition to numerous other awe-inspiring demonstrations.

And he learned how to fly.

Craft believed he was actually modulating gravity when he did this, decreasing the affect of gravity below him to zero, while increasing the pull of gravity from the space ahead of him millions of fold, so that he was pulled in this direction. He was clumsy during his fist few attempts at flight, but after dozens of hours of practice over another two week period his technique improved dramatically.

He initially flew low to stay off any radars, and because significant increases in altitude brought bitterly cold temperatures. But he soon learned how to heat the air around him to whatever temperature he wanted, so this was no longer an issue as he tore through the sky like a human missile at hundreds of miles per hour.

And recently, Craft had become so proficient at flight he had been able to take Alyssa with him, not even having to touch her to direct gravity to propel her forward by his side. Not knowing, of course, how he was accomplishing this feat.

But while flying with Craft was indescribably exhilarating and wonderful, and should have brought their relationship to new heights, during the few weeks he had been flying, Alyssa felt that their relationship was backsliding. She was at a loss to understand exactly why.

But Craft was no longer the exact same man with whom she had fallen in love. And he began to treat her poorly on a number of occasions, in ways that were completely out of character. Yet on other occasions, she would still catch him gazing at her with a lovesick expression on his face.

It almost seemed like a fissure had appeared in his personality. That certain aspects of his behavior had become slightly . . . schizophrenic.

44

After Alyssa and Craft had been in Costa Rica for five weeks, Eben Martin came to visit. They had both been keeping Martin posted on their activities on a daily basis, but a visit was long overdue.

Before Martin left for Costa Rica, he changed his hair from black to salt-and-pepper gray, and applied a flawless fake mustache to match the forged passport Turco had acquired for him in the name Michael Emanuele, removing the mustache when he arrived at Craft's home in the mountains.

Martin brought a bottle of wine with him to celebrate, which Alyssa was sure had cost as much as her television, and they shared stories and laughs and had a great first night together.

Craft spent the next morning and afternoon demonstrating his abilities to Martin, who was even more blown away than he expected to be. Once again, no description of these abilities could do justice to the actual demonstrations.

Finally, in late afternoon, Craft lifted Alyssa and Martin simultaneously for a flight higher up the mountain. When they landed Martin was grinning from ear to ear and had the giddy look of a grade-schooler after his first roller coaster ride.

"That was *un-fucking-believable*," gushed the billionaire to his friend. Like Bren, he seemed to be a throwback to a more genteel time, and he quickly remembered himself and apologized to Alyssa for his language.

Martin had been so preoccupied by the idea of flying without an airplane that he had barely paid attention to his surroundings, but they finally sank in.

Craft had brought them to a hard-to-reach spot on the mountain that was unparalleled in its beauty. He had brought Alyssa here before, and they were convinced they were the first people to ever see it.

They were on a short bluff facing a wide, flat part of a river that flowed down the mountain. Thirty yards distant a glorious waterfall cascaded down a cliff face, framed by trees and tropical flowers, and surrounded by colorful lizards and birds that didn't know what to make of the three intruders to their realm.

The waterfall wasn't uniform, but was six or eight falls, separated slightly from each other, creating a wide, interrupted curtain of beauty shimmering down the cliff, two hundred feet across and fifty feet down. Sun peaked through the canopy at a dozen locations and produced localized rainbows of color through the mists. A Disney artist with the most vibrant of color palettes attempting to create paradise could not have outdone it.

"Flying is even better than you'd think it would be," said Martin, turning his head in a long arc, soaking in the magnificence of their surroundings. "But this isn't too bad either," he added, his voice awestruck. "Wow. Why do I feel like Lois Lane on a date?"

"I thought I was playing the Lois Lane role," said Alyssa with a twinkle in her eye.

"Yeah," said Martin. "I have to give you that. Way to rain on my parade. Now I feel like the third-wheel sidekick, *interrupting* Louis Lane on a date."

Alyssa laughed. "This place *is* supernaturally beautiful," she said. "And since I've taken the Lois Lane role, it occurs to me that Superman did have some big advantages in the dating scene. Not *only* could he fly a girl around, which by itself is a pretty appealing quality in a man," she pointed out, "but he was also able to get to perfect picnic locations." She raised her eyebrows. "On the other hand, Eben, Superman didn't have his own 737. I'm guessing women don't exactly hate that plane of yours."

"That really stings," said Martin, pretended to be hurt. "And here I always thought my success with women was due entirely to my charm and good manners."

"Well, I for one," said Alyssa, "think you'd do great on your looks and personality alone. Even if you didn't have a plane, and *weren't* a billionaire. I mean, even if you only had nine hundred and ninety-nine million dollars, there's still a chance you could get a girl."

The trio laughed, after which they lapsed into a long silence, basking in the beauty all around them. The waterfall gave off a steady roar, but the curtain was thin, so the rush of sound was loud enough to be soothing and exhilarating, but not too loud to make conversation difficult.

"This really is heaven," commented Alyssa, breaking the long silence. "Thanks, Clark," she said to Craft.

Craft arched one eyebrow. "Since we've been speaking of Superman," he said, "let me raise a subject I've been giving a lot of thought to lately. Our myths and our entertainment. Why is it that superhero stories resonate so much with us? Our species has been fascinated with these kinds of abilities since the dawn of time."

"I don't know," said Alyssa dreamily. "But I'm too busy gawking at the scenery to think too hard. Would I be right in guessing you have a theory?"

"Since I have a theory about nearly everything," said Craft wryly, "and I brought it up, this isn't much of a guess."

"Are you going to tell us?" said Alyssa.

"Okay. But only because I want to so badly," he replied good-naturedly. "Al Yad and I have shown that flying is possible. That any number of miraculous things are possible. I wonder if humans know in our souls that wielding zero point energy is our birthright. Maybe the collective subconscious of our species knows we should be unbounded. Maybe using our mind as a quantum lens is a skill that we somehow collectively forgot." He tilted his head. "Maybe one the creator *made sure* we forgot when he limited himself to create us. So we could experience the absolute exuberance we've been feeling at its rediscovery. Let's face it, we've all become giddy at being able to soar like . . . well, like Superman—without the outstretched arms."

"I haven't talked about The God Theory with you in some time," said Martin. "Does Alyssa know about it?"

"Bren explained it to me," said Alyssa. "And I read the book myself a few days later."

"Pretty interesting, isn't it?" said Martin. "Even if you don't subscribe to it."

"No doubt about it," said Alyssa.

Martin turned to his friend. "I know you believe that at a subconscious level, we may be able to tap into the infinite intelligence you think we're fragmented from. So what are you saying? That our superhero obsession is because we've all had subconscious glimpses of the glorious whole, during which we remember these abilities? Just enough to make us yearn to get them back?"

"Exactly," said Craft. "Making superheroes a dominant force in our entertainment and culture. And you have to begin to wonder about our mythology, also. What if people throughout history were able to access the zero point field at varying levels of ability? Jesus is a favorite example I've already given you both. But there are many others. Greek and Roman Gods. Zeus and Apollo and Poseidon. Norse Gods."

Craft tilted his head in thought. "Take Thor, for example. He was said to have a hammer that only he could lift. Right now I could do the same trick. By adjusting gravity, or using a modified form of telekinesis, whatever you want to call it, I can make a paperclip weigh a million pounds."

"Until *you* tried to lift it," said Martin. "Then you could return its weight to normal."

"Exactly. Even parts of our mythology that don't seem obvious can be connected to a quantum lensing ability. Like mythical characters who can hurl flames. Or sorcerers who can turn any moisture into ice. Because I can do that also."

Craft gestured at the river in front of them. "Watch this," he said.

A large, waxy tropical leaf formed itself into a green scoop and dived under the river. It rose a moment later, breaking the surface gently and floating to a position a few feet from Brennan Craft's face. A tiny puddle was now nestled at the base of this makeshift cup.

"All I have to do is force the water molecules to slow," explained Craft. "Everything is energy and forces."

The small sample of water instantly froze before their eyes. Craft held the leaf in place for a few seconds to make his point and then returned it, and the ice it contained, back to the river.

Alyssa whistled. She had seen any number of demonstrations of Craft's abilities over the past several weeks, but this was a new trick.

"Impressive," said Martin.

"I'm not saying these mythical figures were patterned after actual, historical ones. But I *am* suggesting it's at least worth considering."

Alyssa wasn't sure what to think, but she loved this side of Brennan Craft. The logician. The dreamer. Someone who could make the wildest theories seem tame. When he was like this he was the old Bren again, not the arrogant, unlikable man he had all too often become over the past few weeks.

"I don't know, Bren," she said. "It is an interesting theory. And we can't argue that Thor *couldn't* have been based on a real person, after all, since you can mimic many of his abilities. And *you're* real."

"Thanks," said Bren with a grin. "Being real is my best quality. Just don't say that around Pinocchio. It makes him jealous." He waved his hand toward Alyssa. "But sorry to interrupt. Go ahead and finish making your point."

"My point is that as interesting as this theory is, you still have to admit it's pretty farfetched, right? I mean, if there were people who could tap zero point energy, where are they?"

Craft shrugged. "Maybe this doesn't confer immortality after all. Or maybe a fragment of God's intelligence, greater than ours, has been assigned as a hall monitor and took them off the board. Called them home."

"Why would that be?" asked Martin.

"This is all wild conjecture," said Craft. "I know that. It's most likely crazy. But in the spirit of having fun with it, one answer is that they attracted the attention of the video game master. They discovered too much of the underlying programming and found some zero point energy cheats, like I have. So after a while the game master cried foul and they were removed."

Martin made a face. "Is this The God Theory or The Matrix?"

"No reason it can't be both," replied Craft. "And the zero point field gives us all a chance to be as powerful as our legends. In the past, our mythical heroes were solitary figures. But now we can envision a world in which all of us have these abilities."

"A matrix in which all of us are Neo?" said Alyssa.

"Exactly," said Craft with a grin. "Except without the karate skills."

The trio continued basking in their surroundings and discussing a variety of subjects for several more hours. They spoke at length of Craft's capabilities, and he felt certain that he was now as strong as he could get.

Finally, they decided to return home. As Craft was about to launch them into the air, Eben Martin caught his eye. "Okay, Bren," he began, his expression grim. "Let's say you *have* reached your peak. So here's the obvious question I've been too nervous to ask." He studied his friend carefully. "What now?"

"What now?" repeated Craft. "That's simple. I practice for a few more days," he said with a shrug. "And then I try to kill our good friend in Syria."

"I was afraid you were going to say that," said Martin unhappily as the ground quickly began receding below him.

45

Craft was out of the door at the crack of dawn, streaking through the sky at ever faster speeds and working on honing his skills. When Alyssa arose at eight a.m. and tramped out to the kitchen in her blue silk robe, Eben Martin was waiting to surprise her with omelets, toast, and hash brown potatoes. As she sat across from him and said good morning, he poured her a mango juice and coffee and slid them over to her. It was a breakfast fit for a queen. The aromas given off by these familiar foods made her stomach growl in anticipation.

"To what do I owe this royal treatment?" she asked as she took a drink of the thick yellow Mango juice and decided that ambrosia could not have been any tastier.

"I saw Bren fly out of here this morning. And when I say fly out of here . . . " He trailed off with a look of amusement.

"Yeah. It's not just a figure of speech."

"Still haven't quite gotten my head wrapped around it yet. But anyway, Bren was gone, I was up, so I thought I'd make you breakfast. To thank you for being such great company while I've been here."

Alyssa raised her glass of juice and tilted it in his direction as a salute. "Thanks," she said.

She continued to get a sense that Eben Martin was taken with her. Perhaps her father had been right, after all. Perhaps she had been cursed with only appealing to truly extraordinary men. She had dated dozens of men who were *not* truly extraordinary, and they never had the slightest trouble resisting her charms. If she were one of the industrial electromagnets Craft had described, they were made of cardboard.

She had only had close interactions with two men who fit her father's specification, Brennan Craft and Eben Martin, and both did seem to find her enormously appealing. Could it be that she didn't make the cheerleading squad because the other girls were too jealous, after all?

"How's it going back at Informatics Solutions?" she asked Martin.

"Fine. I surrounded myself with capable officers. I don't need to get back to run the company," he added with a smile. "I just need to get back before everyone realizes how well the company does *without* me."

Alyssa laughed. She couldn't believe how comfortable she had become around Eben Martin, and how he had yet to say or do anything that had changed her initial impression of him. While they ate, Alyssa decided to take the opportunity to discuss a few serious subjects that had been troubling her.

"So what do you think about Bren going after Al Yad?" she asked.

"I don't know," said Martin. "If he thinks he's now at the top of his game, I have to trust his instincts. And we've already been lucky that the Al Yad time bomb hasn't gone off. So days matter. *Minutes* might matter. The sooner Bren tries to kill a man who promises the streets of major cities will run with blood, the better."

Alyssa ran a hand through her hair, a look of confusion on her face. "I still don't quite understand why Al Yad has been dormant. I mean, all he has is the promise Bren won't bother him if he abides by Bren's line in the sand. And the threat that Bren knows how to become even more powerful than he is, and will kill him if he breaks the rules." She shrugged. "Is that your understanding?"

Martin blinked for several seconds, and then got a faraway look in his eye. "Um . . . yes," he said finally. "That's right."

Martin suddenly seemed distracted, but Alyssa decided to forge ahead. "So Bren goes to Syria and tries to kill Al Yad. If he succeeds, great. The apocalypse is averted. But if he fails, then what? Won't Al Yad know he was bluffing about being able to kill him?"

"I discussed this with Bren," said Martin, his full attention once again on their conversation. "If he fails, he'll pretend that killing Al Yad wasn't his goal. That Bren just wanted to give Al Yad a reminder that he was out there, and provide a demonstration that his power had increased dramatically. As he had said it would. Bren will tell him that, being a man of honor, he intends to continue to abide by their agreement."

"And continue to bluff Al Yad that he could kill him any time if he really wanted to, right?" asked Alyssa, bringing a forkful of omelet to her mouth.

"That's the gist of it."

Alyssa tilted her head in thought. Why risk having to feed Al Yad more lies if the initial lies were still working? Especially since it was so unclear why Bren's threat had ever worked in the first place. "I still think it's a bad idea," she said. "But since you and Bren are on the same page, I won't argue the point further. But there is one other thing to consider. What if Al Yad kills Bren?"

As much as the bloom had come off the rose with Bren, the thought of him being killed still hit her like a sucker punch to the gut.

"Bren thinks there's no chance of that," said Martin. "Maybe you baked *too much* belief into him," he added with a smile. "But I tend to agree with him. During their first encounter, Al Yad was at his full power and Bren was nothing compared to what he is now. And yet Bren managed to hold out against him for several minutes. Long enough to issue his, you know . . . his bluff. So worst case, Bren is still weaker. If so, he'll know before his shield is breached. Just like he knew the first time. And he can deliver his reinforced bluff with great vigor and enthusiasm and fly off."

"I don't know, Eben," said Alyssa. "I'm still nervous about it."

"You've seen what Bren can do now," said Martin, picking up a piece of toast and covering it with a thin coating of strawberry jam. "It's hard for me to fathom that he won't be able to kill Al Yad. He can vanish a mountain in an instant. I know Al Yad is supposed to be just as strong, but it's hard to imagine." He took a bite of the toast and set it back down on the plate. "But you've heard Bren whenever we suggest this isn't a good idea. There's no talking him out of it."

Alyssa took a deep breath. "Have you noticed any changes in him over the past few weeks?"

Martin paused for quite a while and picked at his eggs. "Maybe," he said finally. "But you've spent a lot more time with him than I have. So what do you mean exactly?"

"You know we're in love with each other," said Alyssa, although she was pretty sure this was no longer accurate. The truth was she *had* been in love with Brennan Craft, and was still in love with ninety percent of him. It was the other ten percent that had her worried. "We haven't exactly voiced it, but we don't need to." She exhaled loudly. "But as his power has grown, he's become shorter of temper. More agitated by little things. More arrogant. Less thoughtful and compassionate."

"I haven't been entirely blind to this," said Martin. "You're worried that this power is changing him. Absolute power corrupting absolutely?"

"He does have absolute power."

"Yes, but he's a good man. A very good man. It's probably just an adjustment period. Hard not to become more arrogant when you have the power of a god. I don't have his type of power, of course, but being a billionaire brings with it more power than you might imagine."

Alyssa smiled. "No. I think you'd find I can imagine it just fine. Although you've managed not to let it corrupt *you*. You're still the most decent man I've ever met, other than Brennan."

Craft had offered to instruct both her and Martin in his biofeedback techniques to get them on the road to using the zero point field. With Alyssa's narco-hypnosis added to the mix, the promise that they, too, could have Craft's power was out there. Both had elected to wait, perhaps instinctively wanting to see the affect this power would have on Craft. Their only data point was Al Yad, and he had lost his sanity. Craft was the only other exhibit in this trial.

"Thanks for the compliment," said Martin, a smile coming over his handsome features. "But I work at it every day. And believe me, I don't always succeed."

Martin paused. "Bren and I had an Israeli friend when we were kids, Eyal Regev. His father worked for the airlines and he was transferred to Mexico City. Given the exchange rate, money went a lot further there, and they could afford to have a live-in housekeeper. She did all of the cooking and cleaning. Eyal said that in the beginning, he found it awkward to have a live-in maid. He felt sorry for her, and that she shouldn't have to clean up after him. He vowed not to take advantage of the situation. But within six months, Eyal told me he would come home from school and leave a trail of clothing and books behind him on the way to his room, knowing the maid would follow and straighten up after him." He shook his head. "Power is insidious. It can't help but change people. Even if they fight it."

Alyssa marveled at this man. He wore the mantle of billionaire better than anyone she knew could possibly have done, including, she had to admit, herself.

"But Bren will be okay," continued Martin. "We talked about this stuff a lot as kids. During sleepovers. We'd talk about science, science fiction—real geek stuff—but we both thought we would tame the world someday. That we would be famous and wealthy. And we made a vow to each other. To never let our future success go to our heads. To still be good people. That even if we became prominent, to treat janitors the same way we treat dignitaries."

"And I'm sure he meant it. But he could never have envisioned *this*. Not what is happening now."

Martin swallowed another mouthful of toast and nodded. "You're right. What he has now is the ultimate level of power. Unimaginable. So it's understandable that it's changing his personality for the worse." He shook his head. "But I'm confident this will only be temporary. The Brennan Craft we both know will come around. I promise."

"I'm sure you're right," mumbled Alyssa.

But she was not sure. Not sure at all.

46

Brennan Craft flew into Tel Aviv, Israel on a commercial jet and made his way to the port city of Haifa, less than fifty miles west of the Syrian border. At nightfall he flew into Syria and to Al Yad's citadel, using his own motive power, staying low to the ground to avoid detection.

Since Craft's first encounter with Haddad, he had been in hiding. Scurrying like a rabbit. Off the grid.

Omar Haddad, on the other hand, had advertised his location. He hadn't diminished his lion's roar one iota out of concern for the attention it might attract. Craft knew his thought process well: gods didn't cower in fear, or anonymity. If anyone wanted to see him, they knew where to find him.

Craft had no intention of making this a fair fight. He would surprise Haddad as much as he could. If he could end this in an instant, before Haddad knew what had hit him, so much the better.

He doubted this was possible, though. Training one's mind to become a quantum lens enhanced the properties of the subconscious considerably, making it far too supernaturally vigilant and quick for surprise to work, as Craft had demonstrated himself when a surprise sniper bullet, and then truck, had failed to trouble him in the slightest. On the other hand, compared to the offensive forces he now commanded, these assaults had been as gentle as the brush of a butterfly's wing.

Al Yad's compound was perched on a flat at the top of a small mountain, and consisted of a dozen buildings stretching over many acres, protected by walls, razor-wire, and electronic surveillance. Al Yad may have been invulnerable, but his followers weren't, and these security measures would give him a heads up if they were being attacked, so he could more carefully determine the nature of his response.

So far, no attack had come. Al Yad's reputation, and following, were too great, and President Najjar had changed tactics. He was now going to great measures to appease him, not knowing why the uncaged cobra hadn't struck, but keeping him as calm and happy as he could.

Craft hovered high in the starry sky, his black clothing helping him vanish into the night, and made a careful survey of Al Yad's compound through high powered night-vision binoculars. The temperature had fallen quickly after sunset, but Craft kept the air around him at a comfortable seventy-four degrees.

Craft was well aware of the latest intelligence on Al Yad, and knew that only key players of Al Yad's cult were housed in this compound. Even so, they numbered in the hundreds.

After Al Yad had acquired the property, he had torn everything down except the central mansion, a magnificent stone and wood palace with arches featured prominently throughout, and five spacious inner courtyards, open to the sky and stars above.

He had then built homely concrete buildings, unappealing two story rectangles, behind his palace to house his followers. They had been painted white, but they were no more aesthetically appealing than bureaucratic offices or military barracks might have been.

Craft took a deep breath. He had stalled enough. It was time to act.

He flew slowly to the compound, counting on his approach and black clothing to elude detection. If the compound were attacked, the guards would be expecting jets from above or ground forces climbing up the mountain from below. They would not be expecting *him*.

Craft cleared the wall and inner razor-wire fence and touched down lightly on the ground, sending out a concussive blast to clear the area as he did so. He had learned to modulate this force better than before, and was certain he had rendered everyone within about a fifty-yard radius unconscious—without killing them. Dozens of men and women, including five machine-gun toting members of compound security, fell silently to the ground around him in unison, like bowling pins.

The main door to the palace was locked and cameras were pointed at visitors. Al Yad had lied and told his followers this was for the protection of his household staff, but Craft knew his vulnerabilities, his paranoia, and how he thought. This was a final deterrent in case someone made it through his outer perimeter, as unlikely as this was, and knew to bring poison gas with them. Not that the cult leader's birds and personal alarms wouldn't alert him in time to flee in any case.

Craft visualized the door cameras being vaporized with energy so great, the very atoms comprising them were torn from each other and flung to distant corners of the globe, and the cameras complied by promptly vanishing. The door lock also quickly gave up its battle to stay coherent against the incomprehensible energies that Craft directed its way.

Craft had memorized the plans for the palace and worked his way quietly and methodically from room to room, headed to the master bedroom, searching for his nemesis. The architecture of the structure was spectacular, and he loved its many archways, but it was sparsely furnished, mostly a sterile white, with endless bird cages comprising the principal decor, a unique style that Craft immediately dubbed *Early Canary.*

As he passed one of the inner courtyards a young woman spotted him. She was covered head to toe in a light blue burka, and Craft could only see her eyes, but these widened in alarm and he had no doubt she was about to issue a warning scream.

Craft reacted instantly, rendering her unconscious before she could utter a sound. She collapsed to the stone floor of the courtyard, but he reached out with zero point energy and cushioned her head before it made contact with the unforgiving surface.

Craft dispatched four additional men on his way to the master bedroom. When he arrived at the entrance, he listened carefully for almost a minute, but didn't hear voices or movement, so he slowly opened the door and stepped inside.

The room he entered was as spacious as a ballroom at a hotel. It was vaulted, two and a half stories high, and its white marble floor was polished to reflective splendor. The room was sterile like the rest of the residence, but undeniably impressive. Al Yad had walled off a small portion of the room on the left, accessible through another doorway, which doubtlessly housed his bed. Sixty inch television screens were hung like modern art on two of the walls, the only decorations. The room contained no furniture, and little else save an ornate wrought-iron chandelier hanging from the ceiling far above, and five of the ubiquitous gold canary cages atop white marble pedestals.

At the back of the room, facing the entry, was a raised level of white marble, veined with royal blue, perhaps five feet higher than the rest of the room and ten feet in depth, running along the entire back wall. Six steps, made from the same marble as the platform, ran along its entire length, like theatre stairs leading up to the stage at the Academy awards. In the center of the platform sat a heavy white and black marble chair, with a high back and elegant armrests.

The chair was simple but conveyed wealth, weight, and solidity, and Craft had no doubt it was the equivalent of a throne, although it didn't look particularly comfortable.

As Craft took it all in, holding his breath, he heard a familiar voice coming from the right.

Omar Haddad! The Hand of God himself.

The voice was coming from an archway that led to the palace's largest open-air courtyard, accessible only from this room. Al Yad was speaking to an underling in Arabic.

Craft crept closer to the archway, sneaking up on it from the side so he could stay out of sight of anyone beyond. He finally reached the edge and peered beyond it, catching a glimpse of the man to whom Al Yad was speaking. He had hoped this would be Tariq Bahar, but he was not that fortunate.

The cult leader's voice was unmistakable, although he had learned to control subtle vibrations in the air, and could give it the power and vibrato that made it seem like it truly was the voice of God.

Still speaking, Al Yad moved into Craft's line of sight, covered by the billowing white robes and headdress that had become his trademark.

Adrenaline surged through Craft.

It was time to strike.

He hurtled a torrent of pure energy at the man who had killed eighteen of his friends in cold blood, and who had promised to kill countless others.

Craft had no way to measure, but was certain this was the greatest amount of zero point energy he had ever controlled, all directed at a single point on Al Yad's forehead. The fabric of space itself couldn't contain it, and microscopic black holes punched through space-time a foot in front of the target before evaporating billionths of a second later, fortunately not massive enough to become self-sustaining.

Al Yad's shield had sprung to life to meet these energies before he had any conscious awareness that he and Craft even shared the same time zone.

The man standing five feet to the left of Al Yad burst into flames, but before the pain of this could register or the odor of his burning flesh could fill the air, he vanished into non-existence. The courtyard was plunged into darkness as all matter was annihilated within a twenty yard radius, vanishing entirely, while an outer circle of an additional fifteen yard radius beyond began flowing like molten lava.

Craft sensed that Al Yad's shield was weakening, but the man rocketed into the starry night sky to remove himself from Craft's focal point. Less than two seconds had passed since Craft's attack had begun.

Craft streaked into the air to follow, barely able to keep up as Al Yad accelerated to almost five hundred miles per hour, flying directly over miles of uninhabited desert before landing. Both men tapped the zero point field to throw off a path of light in front of themselves.

Craft set down ten yards behind Al Yad and launched another strike, but this time his adversary reacted with a strike of his own. Craft's own shield flashed into existence and instantly began to strain under a torrent of energy that rivaled that found at the sun's core, pinpointed to a single location.

Sporadic vegetation, scorpions, spiders, and all other desert creatures exploded into flames for miles around them, and a circle of sand almost a hundred yards in diameter, with the two combatants at its center, turned into glass—a transformation that only occurred at temperatures above four thousand degrees Fahrenheit. Even the glass's existence was short lived, as an instant later it vanished into nothingness.

The air itself around the two men was also annihilated in the face of the inconceivable energies being released, and new air rushed in to fill the void, a continuing process that caused winds to whip up around them like mini-tornadoes. Beyond this perimeter, the air didn't vanish, but any moisture in it boiled away, filling the sky with vapor and causing it to become blurry, like the air around a bonfire. A dense fog bloomed all around them, cutting off long-range visibility, despite the light thrown off by various fires.

Craft's head began to throb after less than thirty seconds from the lack of air and the exertion of marshalling incomprehensible energies to both attack and defend, and sweat began pouring from his body. Al Yad launched himself into the sky and landed several miles away to get fresh air, but this air was also annihilated the moment Craft landed and the battle was joined once again.

Sweat was pouring from Al Yad as well, and he finally broke down, unable to maintain both offense and defense simultaneously. His mind was strong, but not as strong as Craft's.

Al Yad turned his entire focus to bolstering his shield, which caused Craft's own shield to disappear, since he was no longer under attack. Focusing on defense was far less taxing, and Craft realized Haddad could always fly off again if he felt his shield begin to buckle.

Craft stopped his own offensive onslaught and the two men faced each other, neither one attacking or defending.

As expected, they had played to a draw.

The raging winds around them ceased and fresh air once again filled their lungs, although it was tinged with the odor of scorched sagebrush and sand.

"Trying to kill me, Brennan?" said Al Yad finally in lightly accented English. "Not very honorable, given our agreement. Although I would expect nothing less from the incarnation of Satan."

"I wasn't trying to kill you," said Craft. "I only wanted to prove a point. And hearing you speak of our agreement and honor makes me physically ill. Come on, Omar. Do you really expect me to believe you wouldn't kill me the second you had the chance?"

Al Yad shook his head. "You shall address me as The Hand of God, or Great One. Nothing less."

"Cut it out, *Omar*," said Craft derisively. "You are not the hand of god. You are an accountant who had some bad luck in a cave, and who is using the laws of nature to harness energy. Nothing more. Nothing less."

"I suppose I can't expect the Lord of Evil to recognize my true nature," said Al Yad. "And yes, I would kill you if I could. But I never agreed not to. I agreed not to cause mass deaths. You agreed, in return, not to harass me, or to activate your quantum mirror device."

Craft wondered how Haddad could continue to believe so strongly in his own divinity, while acknowledging that a complex device, based solely on scientific principles, could bring him down. Or how he could believe in his own absolute divinity and immortality, while recognizing the need to protect himself from poison gas. Humanity's talent for self-deception was truly inexhaustible.

"You really won't admit you just tried to kill me?" said Al Yad.

"If I wanted to kill you," said Craft calmly. "You'd be dead."

Al Yad laughed and shook his head. "No. You just gave it everything you had. I know. We've both reached the limit of our abilities."

"So even a god has limits?" said Craft, raising his eyebrows.

"Yes. For the time being," said Al Yad. "But in the fullness of time, I shall push aside these limits as well."

Craft noted Haddad's speech had become formal and somewhat biblical in its delivery, even in English. Perhaps he had become even more deluded than before.

"You came here to see if you could best me," continued Al Yad, glaring at Craft with unadulterated hatred. "And you've failed. So why are you still here?"

"I've come, not to try to kill you, *Omar*," he said, wanting to use this name as often as possible to irritate him, "but to get your attention. To remind you that I'm out here. Watching. Waiting. And that my threat still stands. You can gather whatever following and power you like, as long as no innocents are killed."

"The people I shall kill are not innocents," said Haddad. "They are *infidels*. They deserve the justice that I shall grant them."

"Come on, Omar," snapped Craft. "You know what I mean."

"So you've elevated your skills," said Al Yad. "I guessed why you had such great interest in Alyssa Aronson right away, of course. I see that this Jewish whore of yours managed to do what you've long wanted."

Craft bristled at the way he spoke of Alyssa, but forced himself to let it go. For now.

"She finally helped you achieve the self-belief necessary to match a god," continued Al Yad. Then, with a humorless smile he added, "Almost."

"If I were truly Satan, why would I need the help of a hypnotist?"

"We both are not of this realm. But we exist in this realm now, so we are burdened by some of its rules. You know this as well as I do."

Interesting, thought Craft. So this was how he justified the inconsistencies in his logic.

"You came here to learn if your new power was enough to kill me," said Al Yad. "And I have to ask myself, why? And the answer I get is that you're enjoying this level of power too much. I don't think you'll activate your device no matter what now. Because now that you've tasted the ultimate power, there is no way you would ever consider ending your own existence."

Craft shot him a condescending look. "I knew you before you became a mass murderer, Omar. And I liked you. But you've become nothing more than a pitiable, raving psychotic. You don't know the first thing about honor. Or about me. It is true that I am not eager to die. But violate the rules I've laid down and I won't hesitate. You're convinced that I'm Satan. Would Satan hesitate to do whatever was necessary to bring down the Hand of God? Think about it. Test me, and you'll be dead soon afterward. Man or God, you'll be deceased either way."

"I shall kill you someday," vowed Al Yad. "And I shall establish my kingdom on Earth. You are simply a minor irritant. It is only a matter of time. Allah is testing my patience. But I shall pass this test like I have every other."

"If it helps keep you in check to think so, Omar, then great. Just remember that if you step over the line, I will *end* you. I do love life. And I do want to keep living and share the potential of my discovery—*our* discovery—with the world. But if you've ever believed anything in that damaged mind of yours, believe this: I have zero tolerance. One wrong move and I end it. For both of us."

"I'm not worried," said Haddad. "Good will always prevail over evil."

Craft shook his head in amusement. "That's what I'm counting on, Omar. That's what I'm counting on."

And without saying another word, Brennan Craft shot into the sky and was gone.

47

Craft returned to Israel and flew on to Costa Rica by commercial jet, falling into a coma-like sleep during the duration of the flight as if he had been awake for a week. He could power his body with zero point energy, but restoring balance to the quantum lens between his ears took more time and rest. His mind needed the recharge that only extended sleep could provide, perhaps allowing it to temporarily reunite with the mind of the creator while in this unconscious state.

When he arrived back at his new home in the mountains, Craft described his encounter with Al Yad to Alyssa and Martin, although he had texted them the shorthand version before boarding the plane. When Alyssa was part of the conversation, Craft edited out the part of his discussion with Al Yad that had involved his quantum mirror device, but other than this he provided an accurate description of events.

The three of them all agreed that the effort had been worthwhile, and would help continue to keep Al Yad at bay.

The next morning, Martin returned to his offices in The States, having been absent too frequently of late, and having begun to get questions from key shareholders. Far higher stakes were in play than just the fate of a multinational corporation, but there was nothing more he could do in Costa Rica, so it made sense to return.

Alyssa called Martin several days later to let him know Craft's personality had taken a sharp turn for the worse. A very sharp turn. His failure to kill Al Yad had somehow sent him fully over the edge. Now he was arrogant, but also morose—and violent. He had flashes of temper that were truly terrifying in a man capable of destroying entire cities at his slightest whim. And he had begun treating her like dirt.

She told Martin she was no longer in love with this man. She was still in love with Brennan Craft. But she had begun to dislike, and fear, the imposter who had all too often lately been inhabiting his body.

Alyssa had made excuses for several nights in a row not to sleep with Craft, which made him even more irritable. He would berate her for hours at a time, and then apologize.

Brennan Craft was coming completely unhinged. It was undeniable. But was he following in the footsteps of Omar Haddad before him?

Several hours after her report to Eben Martin, Alyssa sat on a wicker chair on their balcony, watching the mountains and the local birds, trying to decide what she should do, trying not to panic, when Craft came in and sat beside her. He used his telekinetic ability to have the wicker chair reposition itself to face her, while he was in it.

"Alyssa," he began. "I've been doing a lot of thinking. And I've come to some conclusions. I won't beat around the bush. You know I was studying different types of world governments. Soft spots. Tipping points. I didn't lie to you. I was doing this to anticipate Al Yad. But I've decided I should do *more* than anticipate."

Alyssa had the urge to get up and run, but forced herself to remain calm.

"After I find a way to kill Al Yad," continued Craft, as if this were a given, "I think our species would be best served if I took over. Maybe at the helm of a world government, or maybe more behind the scenes."

Alyssa couldn't help but look at him uncertainly. "Really?" she said.

"I don't blame you for being skeptical. But humor me for a few minutes. Let me float a scenario by you. I don't expect you to jump on board, because I'm not sure of any of this myself. This is me thinking out loud, with a second brain in the room."

Something had changed, in just that moment. She had sensed Craft was losing touch with reality, and suddenly it seemed like the old Brennan Craft was back. The maniacal gleam in his eye was gone, replaced by the friendly, reasonable calm that she had come to know.

Before his . . . change.

On the other hand, what he was being reasonable about was the prospect of ruling the world. And as ridiculous as that seemed, with what she had seen of his abilities, it wasn't so ridiculous.

"Okay. What's your scenario?"

"Say we could put together a team of the finest men and women. Good people. We screen the hell out of them. No psychotics or psychopaths allowed. People with an unimpeachable history of caring and compassion. Then I train them to access the zero point field. And then *you*," he said, gesturing enthusiastically to Alyssa, "use narcohypnotic techniques to help them reach my current level of ability."

Craft spread his hands. "Then, when they're in place, we remove Al Yad from the board," he added, as though nothing could be simpler.

"From what you told us of your encounter with him, I didn't think that was possible."

"It is. I'm sure of it. It's a numbers game. At some point, if enough of us focus on him at once, we can stop him from fleeing and we can punch through his shield. But just for the sake of argument," he said reasonably, "let's just stipulate that we're successful."

Alyssa nodded.

"My dream is to transform humanity into something amazing. Into billions of individuals who are each invulnerable, long lived, and nearly all powerful. Capable of transforming the planet and eventually the galaxy. But our very nature stands in our way. Now I know your misgivings about putting this kind of power in the hands of even one more person. But if I—*we*—were pulling strings globally, we could marshal enormous resources to help discover how to use the field safely. Or identify those individuals who would be unsafe. Even if this work required generations to perfect."

Craft paused and studied Alyssa carefully, but she didn't respond.

"We also need to have tentacles everywhere," he continued. "Making sure others don't repeat my work. Until we're ready for them to. This isn't all that likely due to the biofeedback innovations

I pioneered, but you never know. But if the key to using zero point energy becomes widespread knowledge, our self destruction is guaranteed."

"Now that is something we can definitely agree on," said Alyssa, absently watching a bright yellow lizard scurry across the ground below and out of sight. She feared that even a single person capable of fully harnessing this power was enough to guarantee self destruction. Craft's recent behavior made this seem even more likely.

"Remember," said Craft, "with fifty of us able to tap the field, or one hundred, or two hundred, we really could pull global strings. By doing this gently, off stage, we could nudge the world in the right direction. Believe me, I have zero interest in running the world. My dream is to find a way for the entire species to use the field, and to prevent another Al Yad from arising. But being in a position of global dominance, it will be far easier to solve the problems I need to solve to fulfill this dream. And to monitor activity to make sure this secret is closely guarded until the time we can disclose it to all. And as an added benefit, I can be in a position to free the people of the world to achieve their potential."

"Through a dictatorship?"

"No. A democracy of a sort. In an ideal world, what purpose should a government serve?" asked Craft. Then answering his own question he said, "It should protect its people from internal and external dangers. It should help build infrastructure and help society run smoothly. It should police society so commercial interactions are conducted fairly. And it should help provide citizens what they need to excel, the infrastructure and means. And that's about it."

Craft rose and walked a few feet to the end of the balcony and then turned to face Alyssa.

"Once Al Yad is out of the picture, this would be our chance. To push the world into a single cohesive society. A world government. With me at the helm. Gradually. But the point is, *we* should be running the show. Either overtly, or covertly."

Alyssa tried not to stare at him as though he were mad, but this wasn't easy. She needed to humor him. He was unstable, and she couldn't risk rousing his ire. "Makes sense," she said.

"Come on, Alyssa. I know you a lot better than that. At this point you're thinking I'm a monster. So don't humor me *that* much. I want your honest concerns and criticisms."

"Okay," said Alyssa uncertainly.

She held her mental breath. How honest did he really want her to be? What might set him off, if she continued to humor him? Or if she was *too* blunt?

"If I were to be totally honest," she said, having reached a decision. "I'd say that you just want to replace Al Yad with a Western version. With you running the show instead of him."

48

A cool breeze blew across the balcony of their Cost Rican home, and Alyssa couldn't decide if the chill she was feeling was due to this, or her fear of how Brennan Craft might react to being compared to Al Yad.

"The difference," said Craft calmly, "is that I'm not a psychopath. Or deluded. I just want to unite the world under one leader and eliminate corruption as much as possible. I've never had interest in running anyone's life other than my own. And I would be *beyond* corruption.

"The level of corruption among world leaders is truly extraordinary," he continued. "And what we're aware of is just the tip of the iceberg. In countries with dictators, totalitarian regimes, this sort of thing, I'm sure you'd agree the psychopathy and corruption are rampant."

Alyssa nodded.

"But even democracies like ours are rife with corruption. The founding fathers had the right idea. They never envisioned professional politicians. They wanted citizen legislators, leaving their farms for a few years to serve their fellow man. A civic responsibility like jury duty. But under our current system, you almost have to be a megalomaniac to have interest in entering the sewer that is politics. And success in this realm requires that backstabbing, shamelessness, lying, and manipulation become an art form."

He returned to the wicker chair facing Alyssa and sat down once again. "Politicians take money from the citizenry, funnel much of it to themselves and their friends, and then use the rest of it to buy votes and to grow their power—which involves bigger and bigger government. Once a bureau is created it is never destroyed—like a malignant cancer. And government never invents the next great computer. Never produces. Only consumes."

Alyssa could tell from the way he was saying this that these were thoughts the old Brennan Craft had harbored. They were controversial, but at least coherent.

"We need someone running the show who is incorruptible. Who clears a path so that everyone can succeed to the best of their abilities. Who gives them the tools and environment to thrive."

"And you think you can decide what's best for everyone?"

"*No!*" said Craft fervently. "A *resounding* no. And that's why I'm better suited to the job than most. But before I explain this point further, let's first consider dictatorships and regimes. With little or no freedom or human rights. Cuba, Iran, Libya, North Korea, and numerous others. Will you at least concede that some kind of democracy, if implemented correctly, would improve the general level of well being in these countries?"

"Yes."

"So Western democracies like the US are the best system for the most people. The problem is that you can't force them on cultures who have no experience with them. Standard of living improves too slowly, and people unused to deciding their own fate can get lost. These societies can become an even bigger mess, because old habits die hard. You need to implement democracy in a way that quickly shows it's working, and have the power to make sure you continue to weed out the dense thicket of remaining corruption, and don't get backsliding."

Craft paused. "With this being said, let me get back to your question. Why do I think I can determine what is best for people? The answer is, I can't. But at least I *know* I can't. Politicians in democracies tend to think they're smarter than everyone else. That they know best how everyone should run their lives. If you think like this, government is always the answer.

"But there is as much corruption within government as there is within business. You find it in every human endeavor, even in the ivory tower of academia. But in government and bureaucracy, along with corruption, you usually find incompetence. Compare the US postal service with FedEx. Compare the government's attempt to establish a major website with Amazon. The government spent twenty times the money Amazon would have spent, to produce one twentieth the product.

"But unlike politicians and bureaucrats," continued Craft, "I don't think I know what's best for everyone. I think each individual knows what's best for themselves. Even those who didn't score as high on their SAT as I did," he added wryly.

"But you would admit we need *some* government?"

"Absolutely. We need to make sure there is a general fairness. And some agencies are vital. But even the ones that most people would argue are key watchdogs, protecting us against evil corporations overstepping their bounds, are most often too paternalistic. They can't help themselves."

"Can you give examples?"

"All day long," replied Craft. "But I'll limit myself to one. Take the FDA. The FDA exists to ensure unscrupulous pharmaceutical companies don't falsify data and put the public health at risk. A very important responsibility. But the agency increasingly goes beyond this. First, they are risk averse. If they reject a drug that could save hundreds of thousands of lives, most people never hear about it. But if they approve a drug that ends up killing a few dozen, they get their asses handed to them. So they have a bias toward rejecting drugs that could save lives. As a CYA maneuver."

Alyssa had some familiarity with the workings of the FDA, and had come to this conclusion herself.

"But that's not even the point," continued Craft. "Shouldn't I be able to decide for myself what risks I want to take? As long as I'm not putting anyone else in jeopardy? Most of us find a bee sting to be a painful, but minor, nuisance. But for a very few, it's fatal. There are small variations in our genes that account for these differences. So it's virtually impossible to have a drug that is perfectly safe for everyone. Especially hugely successful drugs given to many millions of people."

He paused to let this sink in. "Are you familiar with an old weight loss drug called Fen-Phen?"

Alyssa nodded. "Yes. But I don't know much about it."

"It was the most successful weight loss regimen ever developed. Killed appetites, and pounds seemed to melt away. But there were some deaths, and worries about heart valve problems in some of the people taking it. So the FDA rode in on its white horse and took it off the market. But should they have?"

Craft paused again to let Alyssa think about this.

"Isn't morbid obesity itself a grave health risk?" said Craft. "The drug carries some heart risk, but so does maintaining a weight of six hundred pounds! In fact, the health risks of morbid obesity are even greater. So how paternalistic should the government be? Shouldn't patients be given the tradeoffs on the safety and efficacy of a drug and be trusted to make decisions for themselves?"

This wasn't something Alyssa had ever considered before, but she decided he had a valid point.

"And everything in life is risky," he continued. "What if peanut butter were a drug? Millions of children think it's the world's most delicious food. But there are kids out there with peanut allergies who could die from it. Die from peanut butter! And there isn't a great way to know who is susceptible until the first time mom makes her child a sandwich. Just like with Fen-Phen. Millions of dieters loved it with a passion. Many lost hundreds of pounds, extending their lives by decades. And yes, some might have died from it. But I would argue many more have now died from the *lack of it*. And if Fen-Phen is banned, why isn't peanut butter?"

Good question, thought Alyssa. She had to admit, if peanut butter were a drug, it probably would be.

"And what about motor vehicles?" continued Craft, not waiting for an answer. "You're far more likely to be killed driving a car than taking Fen-Phen. So why hasn't the government pulled *cars* off the market?" he asked passionately. "Why? Because all of us know the risks of driving, and are willing to take our chances. We each get to decide if the benefits of driving exceed the risks.

"The same should be true for Fen-Phen. If I'm clinically obese and I'm told the risks, I should be able to decide if I think the benefit is enough. But I can't. The FDA has decided *for* me. Because they're smarter.

"I can't tell you how many people have begged drug companies to break the law and give them drugs that they believe are beneficial. Knowing the risks." Craft shook his head. "The government always thinks it knows what's best for everyone else. But people really are in the best position to run their own lives."

"Sounds libertarian."

"In many ways, yes. Western democracies, and specifically, capitalism, have led to the greatest levels of prosperity for the greatest numbers in human history. To the highest standard of living in history."

"But capitalism seems so . . . ruthless. So unfeeling."

Craft laughed. "I know its reputation. It does seem ruthless. Socialism and communism, on the other hand, sound great on paper. Sensible and compassionate. Everyone pitches in. From each according to his ability, *to* each according to his need. Fair and equitable. Utopia. Only human nature doesn't work like that. Every time it's been tried it's become a disaster. Because human's are selfish. They don't want to kill themselves so others can get a free ride. So *everyone* ends up losing."

"And you think this is a function of innate human behavior?"

"Yes!" replied Craft emphatically. "I was watching the news when I was about eight, and they were debating whether the wealthy in America contributed enough in taxes. One side argued that the rich, as a class, contributed more than ninety percent of total taxes collected. That about half of the country paid nothing in taxes, or *received* money in food stamps and welfare. Whereas the top earners, after all was said and done, had about half of their income confiscated by the government.

"The counterargument to this was that it wasn't fair that these high earners made so much. They could afford to give up even *more* of their income. And that they couldn't have possibly made their fortunes working hard and taking risks, like Steve Jobs. They could only have done so by cheating and stealing from others, or exploiting them."

Craft paused. "So I asked my father where he came out on the debate."

"And?"

"He told me to imagine I had a test in school and I studied for an entire week, night and day. My friend spent the entire week playing video games and having fun at the beach. I ended up getting an A, and my friend got an F. So what if the teacher said, 'it's not fair that Bren got an A and his friend got an F. So we're going to give you both C's. Still passing, right? So it's no big deal. Still plenty of cushion away from an F. The A earners shouldn't be greedy.'

"My father let me think about this and then asked me what I'd do the next time a test came around. How would I prepare for it? It occurred to me that if I knew I really couldn't earn an A, what was the point of killing myself? I told my father, and he agreed. In fact, he told me that soon the entire class would be getting Cs, and then Ds. And eventually Fs. Socialism at work."

Alyssa temporarily forgot to be afraid of this man. He had drawn her in intellectually. He was himself again. She didn't agree with everything he was saying, but he was presenting it rationally and with his typical flair.

"It's a great analogy," she acknowledged. "But what about the student like you who is naturally gifted? Suppose a student kills himself for a week, and still gets an F. While you party for a week and get an A. That hardly seems fair."

"It isn't. Which is why the tax code is progressive. And why it should be. Effort *should* be taken into account. You should help people who are less fortunate. You can't do pure capitalism. And you have to strive to guarantee equal opportunity. But if you try to guarantee equal outcomes, everyone loses. The more you take away from those who produce, whether their success is due to hard work or natural ability, the less they produce. And everyone is worse off."

Alyssa considered this but remained silent.

"And do you think the teacher is doing a favor for my friend in class who goofed off and got an F? What message does that send?" Craft shook his head. "You know from your study of human nature and happiness that we need accomplishment and achievement to have a strong sense of self-esteem. Dependency is a cancer that eats away at these things. And it's a vicious circle. Like an addiction. You know in your heart it's not good for you, but you can't break its iron grip. It seems better to get things for free and have endless free time than struggle in a job—even though ultimately you will grow and improve and feel better about yourself. The more handouts the less self respect, and the more miserable a person is.

"Still, it's human nature to want to be taken care of," he continued. "To want to be able to stay on the couch watching TV, not realizing how unfulfilling, how soul crushing, this really is. Give kids a choice between unlimited candy and vigorous exercise, and how many do you think will choose the exercise?"

"Not enough," said Alyssa.

"Exactly. Even though this will do far more to increase their sense of well being. But candy is tasty and exercise is hard work." He smiled. "And you know better than anyone that people are irrational. I'm sure you're familiar with the ultimatum game."

Alyssa nodded. The ultimatum game was simple and provided remarkable insight into behavior. Take two strangers and put them in separate rooms. Give one a hundred dollars and tell him he has to split it with the other. The split is entirely his decision. But the other person will be told the split, and will get to accept or reject it. If this other person accepts it, both will get their shares. If the other person rejects it, they both get *nothing*.

Remarkably, splits of seventy-thirty or worse were most often rejected.

This flew in the face of economic theory. The offering party was saying, "I'll keep seventy dollars and give you thirty." And the other party was saying, "No. Screw you. I'm rejecting this deal, even though I'll have to give up my thirty."

Why? Because the person rejecting the offer had a visceral feeling that the split being offered wasn't *fair*. That the person dividing it was being selfish and greedy, and they wanted to punish him. They were punishing themselves as well, but they were willing.

Economic theory would tell you that a rational person would take the thirty dollars every time. Forget the other party, the decision was simple. You get thirty dollars or you get nothing. With this logic you would take any positive amount.

But evolution hadn't made human wiring strictly logical. Cooperation was paramount to survival. So people were hardwired to punish those they didn't think were being fair. Yes, they were losing thirty dollars, but they were punishing the unfair party by making him lose *seventy* dollars. An imbecilic decision economically. Totally irrational. But part of the fabric of many people.

Craft continued. "Given our current tax code in the US, if we lowered taxes, everyone would be better off. There is an enormous body of evidence from around the world to support this. The gap between the rich and the poor actually gets wider when taxes are raised, and shrinks when taxes are lowered. This is counterintuitive. And many people refuse to believe the data, because their hearts tell them it can't be true. It's the ultimatum game all over again.

"So on one side they wave accurate data saying everyone is better off, and it's a proven fact—and they're *right*. And on the other side, they refuse to even consider that this is correct. And even those willing to acknowledge the accuracy of the data don't care. It still isn't fair.

"The people giving up thirty dollars *knew* that thirty was greater than zero. That they'd be better off letting the offering party keep their seventy. They just didn't care."

Alyssa couldn't argue the point. Even worse, people suffered from something called Confirmation Bias, which had been demonstrated time and again in numerous experiments. Once we formed an opinion or took a position, be it in politics, the worthiness of a television show, or global warming, we tended to filter new data, seizing on anything that agreed with our position and dismissing or ignoring anything contrary, no matter how valid. We would cling to our positions, even in the face of what should be incontrovertible evidence against them.

"And people like to think they're compassionate," said Craft. "Take the old adage: give a man a fish, feed him for a day. *Teach* a man to fish, feed him for a *lifetime*. Well, it feels *good* to give a man a fish. You're being generous, compassionate. Filling an immediate need.

"*Teaching* a man to fish, on the other hand, can be a longer, tougher process. But in the end, the gift of self-sufficiency is far greater than the gift of a single fish. You just have to find a happy middle-ground. Give a man enough fish not to starve, but don't let him off the hook, so to speak, on learning how to do it. Even if people call you an uncompassionate monster."

"So you would see yourself as a benign, libertarian dictator?"

"I'm not sure what you'd call it, but something like that. I'd give everyone the freedom to succeed. While directing some resources to solving the problem of using the zero point field more widely. Humans are motivated to work hard, knowing if they succeed they succeed.

"And I, and others we bring to my level, can eliminate poverty. We don't have to say how we're doing it, but we can make energy virtually free and unlimited. And if the world is united under my leadership, humanity would save trillions on military expenditures, which would no longer be needed."

Craft gazed deeply into Alyssa's brown eyes. "So what do you think?"

Alyssa had to admit he painted a nice picture. She considered her response carefully. "I agree with much of what you say," she replied after several seconds. "And who knows, the world just might be better off with you at the helm, helping level the playing field, giving people tools, and staying out of the way." She sighed. "But a dictatorship, benevolent or not, is still a dictatorship. I wouldn't want to be a part of it."

Craft's face transformed in an instant, as surely as if he had donned a mask. His warm, thoughtful, rational eyes suddenly burned with rage and his face reddened. Alyssa found herself desperate to get away from him, knowing she had flicked his switch from sane to something else entirely.

"*You are such a stupid bitch!*" he thundered, and the entire house shook. "How can I expect such a moronic bitch to understand the greatness of my vision?"

Alyssa shrank back in terror.

Several large boulders visible from the balcony shattered explosively, and jagged pieces of rock shot through the air, delivering shrapnel in all directions. Two colorful birds in the distance burst into flames and then disappeared entirely seconds later.

"*If you had a fucking brain in your head, you'd be dangerous!*" screamed Craft, his expression insane and predatory, like a snarling, rabid wolf.

The wicker chair Alyssa was in lifted from the balcony and hovered three feet above the landing while several trees below exploded into fragments that screamed outward in all directions. Several of the dagger-sized splinters imbedded themselves into the wall mere inches from Alyssa's head. She was too terrified to even scream.

"I should know better than to try to have an intelligent discussion with a dumb bitch like you!" he hissed in absolute rage and contempt.

Brennan Craft shot off the balcony and into the air, as Alyssa's chair crashed to the floor once again. "*You make me fucking sick!*" he bellowed.

"*I can't even look at you anymore!*" he added, and then streaked off into the sky as additional trees exploded beneath him.

49

Alyssa remained on the balcony as tears began streaming down her face. She had been in love with a perfect man. And now she was being forced to watch him transform into something unrecognizable. To watch him go insane.

Losing someone with whom you were falling in love was bad enough. Watching helplessly as he became a malevolent caricature of himself was even worse. She was at once heartbroken, nauseated, and terrified.

But mostly terrified.

She would be very lucky to survive him much longer.

Craft disappeared into the sunset, off to take his rage out on the local landscape and animal life.

Only weeks before she wanted nothing more than to make love to this man until the end of time. She had basked in his embrace, knowing they were barely able to keep from expressing their love for each other. Now all she felt was terror, and profound relief that he had left, even if temporarily.

She called the emergency number Eben Martin had given her, forgetting the time change and that she would be catching him in the middle of the night.

"Alyssa?" he mumbled in alarm the moment he answered, but quickly transitioned from groggy to alert. "What's wrong?"

She began sobbing into the phone as she attempted to speak, which drove Martin nearly mad with worry. "*Alyssa?*" he said. "Are you okay? Where's Brennan?"

She finally managed to get her sobbing under control. "Eben, he's gotten worse," she said. "I'm afraid for my life."

There was a long pause. "I am so sorry it's come to this," he said finally. "Bren seems to be going in and out of rationality. During our last few conversations he's been all over the place. Normal, wonderful, brilliant Brennan Craft, and then a raving lunatic—and back again. But I never thought *you'd* be in danger. Not with the way he feels about you. Did he threaten you?"

"Not with words, but with actions. He melts down and becomes consumed with rage. He curses at me. Calls me stupid. Shouts. While things explode and burst into flame. During this latest episode I barely missed being impaled by shrapnel from an exploding tree. We both know he could turn me into paste in an instant if he lost complete control."

"We need to get you out of there," said Martin.

Alyssa nodded vigorously as fresh tears began streaming down her face once again. "*Please*," she pleaded. "Do that. Get me out of here."

"I will. Hang in there. Humor him. Don't do anything to set him off. I'll think of a good excuse for you to come back to The States for awhile and book you on the first flight back. Then we can hide you from him."

"I loved him, Eben," she whispered. "I still love part of him."

There was a heavy sigh at the other end of the line. "I love him, too," replied Martin. "But he's sick. With power, maybe. Or maybe the human mind wasn't meant to tap into the fabric of the universe."

"I feel totally helpless," said Alyssa. "He's losing touch with reality and becoming more and more deranged. It's only a matter of time before he loses it permanently."

"This is disturbingly identical to what Bren said about Omar Haddad when he began to unravel. Bren described his growing fear, his growing certainty that if Haddad wasn't reined in, terrible things would happen. Bren's reliving this episode in his life, but from Haddad's side of the equation."

Alyssa wanted to respond but more tears poured down her face, preventing her.

"Hang in there, Alyssa," pleaded Martin, his deep concern for her welfare reflected in his tone. "You're an incredible woman, and you can do this. Get the tears out of your system—no one could possibly blame you for them—but then pull yourself together. Do whatever you have to do to humor him. Keep him from going critical. And I'll come up with a good excuse to pull you out of there. Just give me until morning here, okay?"

"Hurry," said Alyssa through her tears. "Please hurry, Eben."

50

Alyssa awoke to an empty bedroom. She had received an encrypted message from Eben Martin while she slept and quickly entered her decryption code. The message transformed itself into English:

I'm on my way there. I need to personally assess Bren and the situation on the ground. Can't wait to see you, Alyssa. Be strong. And careful.

Relief surged through her. Eben was putting himself in greater danger by coming here, but he knew Bren better than anyone, and he was also more resourceful and competent than any person she had ever met—well, other than Bren had been only a short while before. Eben would figure out a way to defuse the situation. And find a good pretext to get her away from Bren.

Great! she typed, and then thought better of it. She knew she was being selfish. She deleted this and started again. *Are you sure this is wise? You're flying into a danger zone,* she wrote, and hit send.

Three minutes later a new message arrived. *If Bren becomes another Al Yad, the entire world is a danger zone. Need to have a long face-to-face before he's too far gone. I'm confident I can reach him.*

I hope you're right, she texted. *Looking forward to seeing you. And thanks.*

When Alyssa entered the kitchen, Craft was reading a book on his tablet computer, but had pancake batter ready to go, along with plates, forks, syrup, butter, and chopped cheese and mushrooms, ready to construct a perfect omelet. He had taken a page from Eben's playbook, surprising her with breakfast.

When he saw her a tear formed in the corner of his eye. "Alyssa," he whispered. "I am so sorry about how I've been acting. I don't know what's happening to me. You mean the world to me. I can't believe I've been treating you like this."

"It's okay, Bren," she said, not quite able to make this sound cheerful. She had to keep him calm. To stay alive until Eben arrived to pull her out. "You're under a lot of pressure. I really do understand."

"*I* don't," said Craft miserably. "But I've been doing a lot of thinking. And I might know why this is happening."

He poured pancake batter into a skillet and turned on the burner beneath it. "I'm tapping into the zero point field around the clock. I have this second skin being generated, which is always on. I think this is just too mentally taxing."

"And you think that's what's driving you . . . She stopped abruptly and searched for better phrasing. "You know, having a negative effect on your behavior?"

"I'm pretty sure of it. But I can't shut it off," he said. "I need a break from the field. At least while I sleep. You need sleep as much for your brain as for your body. It gives the mind a chance to reboot. If you lose too much sleep, you eventually begin to hallucinate and go mad."

"Have you not been sleeping?" asked Alyssa with genuine concern.

"Not well. But even when I do, my brain is connected to the field. *It never stops*," he said, his voice suddenly wild. "I can't take it anymore!"

He paused for several seconds and collected himself. "But I had an idea," he said, forcing himself to be calm again. He flipped the large pancake to its other side with a tan plastic spatula. "Remember how you told me about the nocebo effect? The remarkable results you were getting? Is it possible you could help me disconnect from the field entirely? It's a subconscious, involuntary connection, as you know. But you said you were performing miracles stopping nervous ticks. Which are also wholly subconscious and beyond the voluntary control of your subjects."

"Interesting idea," whispered Alyssa, almost to herself. She tilted her head in thought. "Yes," she said finally, her enthusiasm growing. "Why not? Given our previous results, I think the chances of success are very high."

"Great!" said Craft. "I've become convinced that this is what I need to become myself again. I still need to retain my abilities to keep our Syrian friend at bay. But if I could get relief while I'm sleeping, this is all I would need. Maybe you could implant a trigger that would sever my connection to the zero point field for eight hours at a time."

"I don't see why not. You're right. We did this exact thing with nervous tics. We'd just have to reinforce certain neuronal pathways with electrical stimulation and hypnosis, using the new drug from our Lawrence, Kansas lab."

Fortunately, like the others she had selected, this drug could be delivered orally, so they didn't have to worry about Craft's personal body armor blocking a needle. Alyssa began to feel hopeful for the first time in weeks. Maybe she could get the man of her dreams back, after all.

She checked the current date on her phone while Craft slid a finished pancake onto a plate in front of her and began working on an omelet. "A new batch of this drug should have been completed about a week ago," she said. "Probably just finishing up quality control. Although my lab isn't scheduled to get any until the next batch is done."

"How much would it take?"

"Very little."

"What if I send you to Lawrence?" said Craft excitedly. "You could break in and get what we need. They'd never miss it." Without waiting for a response, he added, "Will this lab accept your biometric data?"

"It would have before I met you. I don't know about now, though."

"It probably still will. But I can restore you no matter what. I'm sure of it. I used your security access to leave a backdoor into the system." He paused. "Will you do it?"

She was desperate to leave, but pretended to weigh her decision. Finally, she nodded. "Absolutely," she said.

Craft blew out a relieved breath. "Thanks, Alyssa." He tilted his head in thought. "I'd ask Eben to meet you Stateside, but he contacted me early this morning. He's actually on his way here. So go with Adam Turco in case there's any trouble. Okay?"

Alyssa was swallowing a mouthful of pancake, but nodded her agreement.

"But do me a favor. Don't mention this to Eben."

"Why not?"

"He'll get nervous if he knows I'll be without my ability entirely. Even for short periods of time. He'll think it's too big a risk with Al Yad at large." Craft sighed. "So, please, just humor me. This is important. You can't mention this to Eben. Promise me."

Alyssa noticed the intensity returning to Bren's eyes and knew better than to challenge him further. "I promise."

"Good. Adam will be told to follow your orders as if they were Eben's. So I'll have you flown directly to . . . what's the nearest airport to Lawrence?"

"Kansas City."

"Right. I'll have Adam meet you in Kansas City and escort you to the lab. I'll make sure he knows not to mention this to Eben for the time being."

"When should I leave?"

"Immediately," said Craft. "Or sooner. I'll book you on the next flight. Pack a bag and I'll take you to the airport. I'll stay in Costa Rica to greet Eben. Unfortunately, you'll probably pass each other in the air. But with any luck, you'll return in a day or two with what you need to help me. If I could even get a few good nights of sleep, I think I'd be myself again."

"I'll be ready to go in five minutes," said Alyssa, almost gleefully. She had feared for her life and had no idea if Craft would let her out of his sight. Now she had a reason to leave immediately, blessed by him, and a chance to return him to sanity.

She quickly finished the breakfast he had prepared and retreated to the master bedroom, where she hurriedly packed a few days worth of clothing and toiletries.

When she was finished she checked to make sure Bren wasn't in the room and then activated her phone. *Great news!* she texted to

Eben Martin. *Bren wants me Stateside. And he even recognizes that he's losing his mind! A huge step in the right direction. I may have a way to help him through narco-hypnosis. No need for a pretext to get me away. Cancel your trip here.*

A minute later her phone vibrated and she decrypted the message. *That is great news! I am so relieved for you, Alyssa. But I just took off. I still need to assess Bren's mental state and have a heart-to-heart with him. I'll call you and let you know how it went. Have a great trip.*

Alyssa thought this was the end of it, but a moment later another short message appeared. Apparently, Martin had thought of one last thing he wanted to communicate. She looked down.

But Alyssa, no matter what, don't even think of returning unless I give you the word.

51

It had been a grueling day of travel by the time Alyssa arrived at the Kansas City International airport. It was ten at night when she met up with Adam Turco, and it was great to see a friendly and protective face.

Turco rented a car and drove her to Lawrence, home of the University of Kansas and their crimson-and-blue Jayhawks. She had spoken often with members of the Black Ops chemistry lab there, but she had never been to Kansas herself. She suspected she would find the state, on the whole, fairly flat and uninteresting, but the residents of Lawrence with whom she had spoken raved about the town, and were especially crazy for basketball.

Apparently the man who had invented the sport, James Naismith, had also founded the University of Kansas basketball program in 1898, and was the coach there for nine years. Ironically, the inventor of basketball was also the only basketball coach in school history, spanning well over a century, to ever post a losing record over his tenure.

Turco had already conducted a thorough reconnaissance of the lab, and reported that the coast was clear. Given Craft's superhuman ability with computers, and the backdoor access he had already established, Alyssa expected this to be a routine, in-and-out theft like the one in Bloomington had been.

Just as she was about to enter the lab, she tried to reduce the tension she felt by making herself smile at the absurdity of her situation. If what they were trying now failed to restore Brennan Craft to full sanity, she thought, at least she could survive as a professional thief while she was in hiding from him.

This was the best she could come up with, and it failed to elicit even the hint of a smile. Actually, it had the opposite effect, as it reminded her that she was now terrified of the man she had once loved.

And if they couldn't turn Craft around, she wouldn't be surviving as a professional thief for long. With two delusional men at large rather than one, who both also happened to be nearly omnipotent, and with no check on Al Yad once Craft went completely off the deep end, Armageddon would be just days away.

Alyssa's raid on the Lawrence lab went as well as she had hoped. Turco was in what Alyssa thought of as the getaway car, and watched the perimeter while she retrieved the compound they needed, which had been painstakingly resynthesized over the previous month. It was highly potent and stable up to two hundred degrees Fahrenheit, so she could carry it in a small plastic vial in her purse.

Just as she was finishing up in the lab, her phone vibrated, making her jump.

She finally smiled—at her own stupidity. She was pretty sure professional thieves remembered to turn off their phones while robbing highly secured buildings.

Eben Martin was calling. She would have loved to speak with him, but chatting on the phone while committing a felony probably wasn't the best idea. She declined the call, finished up, and rejoined Turco in the car, leaving the lab exactly as she had found it.

As Turco turned onto a main street she texted Eben. *Sorry, not private enough to talk. What's up?*

A minute later she received a texted reply, which she quickly decrypted.

Bren is worse than I thought, and deteriorating quickly. He's barely sane right now. His temper is even worse than you reported. I've never been this scared. He's demanding I help him take over the world. Really! Our only hope is that the real Bren is still hidden inside somewhere. If so, I have to find a way to reach him. And quickly.

Bile rose in Alyssa's throat and she suddenly found it difficult to breathe. Her fingers flew over her phone.

Bren didn't want you to know, but he thinks having his ability 'on' all the time is what's making him lose his mind. I know a way to temporarily strip him of his ability—at his command. Disconnect him entirely from the zero point field, even the always-on defenses he can't consciously control, for however long he wants. So he can sleep and his mind can rest. I have a technique, and drug, more powerful than what I used to improve his ability, so I'm very confident this will work. I'll call him and tell him I've got the drug, and will fly back ASAP.

A minute passed while Alyssa chewed her lower lip. Would she get to Bren in time? And would this actually help him, or had his condition become irreversible?

No!!!! came the emphatic texted reply. *Alyssa, you can't sever his connection completely. We need to talk first. There are things you don't know. Things you need to know. Crap. He's coming. Gotta go. Don't do anything until we talk.*

"Are you okay?" said Turco. "You look like you're about to vomit."

Alyssa tried to remove the queasy expression from her face. "I'm fine," she lied, as her eyes welled up with moisture.

Turco turned away from the road and studied her for several long seconds, but decided to leave it alone.

"I got us adjoining hotel rooms," he said, braking for a red light. "Your return flight leaves bright and early in the morning."

She nodded, still too stunned to speak. The world seemed to be spinning. How had it come to this?

They arrived at the Jayhawk Motor Lodge minutes later. Turco unlocked the door to her room and escorted her inside. Alyssa took in her surroundings with one glance. Small and basic, as she had expected, but at least everything looked clean, and the bedspread was a bright and cheerful yellow. She needed cheerful at this point. She had a feeling it was going to be a long, sleepless night.

"Thanks, Adam," she said, sitting on the side of the bed facing him. "I'm going to turn in," she added, wanting to be alone as soon as possible.

Adam Turco closed the door gently behind him and brought his hand toward her.

He was holding a gun.

Alyssa felt the strange urge to laugh. Were the fates really this cruel? Was the universe trying to remind her that no matter how bad things got, they could always get worse? Maybe it was just emotional weariness, but rather than feeling betrayed, outraged, or afraid, she just felt numb.

"What's this about, Adam?" she said tiredly. "What are you doing?"

"I'm really sorry, Alyssa. I like you a lot. I really do. But I've hired on with someone I think you know. Soft-spoken. Unplaceable accent, but mostly British. Ring a bell?"

Alyssa shook her head in disgust. "How?" she whispered.

"Long story. Let's just say I figured out who was so interested in you and Brennan and how to contact them. They were even more interested than I thought."

"So are you going to kill me?"

"No. This is a tranquilizer gun. With a dose that will put you out for four or five hours. I'll put you out and then tell my new employer where you are. He's only about an hour away. Neither of us were eager to meet the other. Trust and anonymity issues, I'm afraid."

"Eben Martin is paying you a fortune. Paying for your loyalty."

"That's the beauty of it. Because Eben will still be paying me a fortune. I'll just tell him they got the drop on me, and you were killed. It was tragic. And I'm being paid five million dollars for this. *Five million* dollars to do little more than shoot you with a tranquilizer and walk away. Simplest job ever."

Turco exhaled loudly, and for just a moment a look of concern flickered over his face. "I wish you luck, Alyssa Aronson," he said softly, pulling the trigger.

Alyssa fell back onto the bed and was unconscious in seconds.

Turco took a photo of her on the bed and sent it out as a text. His phone rang almost immediately.

"Satisfied?" he said upon answering.

"Very," came the reply.

"Good. She'll be out for four hours, and you're less than an hour away. When I see my bank balance increase by the initial four million dollars, I'll text you her location and where you can find the room key. And I'll give you the decryption key to her phone."

"And you'll make sure Craft and Martin think she's been killed?" asked Tariq Bahar.

"Yes. This is just as important to me as it is to you. I need to stay clean with my employers, so they don't ever find her or suspect my involvement. I bought ketchup and various meat products earlier. I'll photograph her in a heap on the floor, copious amounts of blood and other shit exploding from her head. Trust me, I've seen the real thing. I'll text the photo to both men in the morning, explaining that I found her this way when I tried to get her to leave for the airport." He paused. "They'll buy it. I'm sure of it."

"Good," said Bahar, unable to completely hide his excitement. "I'll wire the four million now. Check your account in five minutes."

"Acknowledged."

"We'll just need a small amount of intelligence from you over the next few days, as we discussed. When this has been accomplished, we'll wire in the last million, and our association will be at an end."

"My favorite kind of association," said Turco dryly. "Brief. And lucrative."

52

Alyssa awoke, lying on her side on what she suspected was a bed, and wondered what the *Guinness Book* had to say about the world record for the number of times being knocked unconscious over a span of a few months. And if she hadn't set a record for frequency, perhaps she had set one for variety, since four different methods had been employed.

She heard breathing and knew she wasn't alone in the room. She took a mental breath and opened her eyes.

She was greeted by a sight she had fully expected.

"Hello, Tariq," she said with a sigh to the man sitting in the hotel desk-chair watching her intently. The man she had once thought of as GQ. "I wish I could say I was glad to see you again."

Bahar had gone through her small leather purse, which had been turned inside out, and had removed her passport, the small plastic vial she had taken from the lab, and her phone, and had placed them on the small desk beside him.

"*Alyssa*," said Bahar, delighted that she was awake, and unsurprised she now knew his name. "How is my favorite prisoner?" He nodded toward her arm. "Looks like you've healed up nicely."

Alyssa turned her head again, and as she did so her hair didn't quite move correctly. She touched the side of her head. It was sticky.

Her heart jumped. Was it blood?

She removed her hand and inspected it anxiously. The tips of her fingers were red. But she didn't feel any pain.

"Just ketchup," said Bahar. "So your friends don't come looking for you. I got most of it off while you were asleep. But I'll require you to shower before we leave. So you're presentable."

Alyssa's pulse returned to normal. "Where's your sadistic asshole friend?" she asked wearily.

"Interesting question," said Bahar. "First, he isn't my friend. He's a necessary evil in my line of work. But if you must know," he added in a tone that was somehow ominous, "he's been working on his photography skills."

Bahar pulled a number of three-by-five photographs from his pocket. "You have two brothers, correct? Sam and Jeremy. And they each have two children."

He tossed the photographs in Alyssa's lap and waited patiently. Her face became ashen when she saw what they were: candid shots of her brothers, nieces, and nephews going about their daily lives. Her youngest niece, Allie, was six-years old, and the picture showed her with a pink sundress, smiling from ear to ear as she glided down a steep slide at a local park. Another photo showed Alyssa's eight-year-old niece, Eve, kicking a soccer ball in the front yard of her brother Jeremy's house.

"They look like a nice group," said Bahar icily. "It would be unfortunate if anything *bad* happened to them." He shook his head in mock concern. "Don't you think?"

Alyssa's heart began to hammer once again, and she glared at Bahar with utter hatred and revulsion. "You'd kill kids? Little girls? You are one sick asshole!"

"I would never kill a child," he said innocently. "It's difficult to find *anyone* who would. No matter how much money is on the line." He raised his eyebrows. "But the man who assisted me during your initial interrogation, Tom Manning. Where do you think he comes out on this? Would you be willing to believe he's the rare exception to this rule?"

"What do you want?" she snapped.

"Just your cooperation. There is someone who would like to speak with you. Someone in Syria."

"No kidding!" said Alyssa coldly. "Put him on the phone. I'll talk to him."

"He wants to meet you," said Bahar. "In person. So you'll need to accompany me back to Syria. Without ketchup in your hair. But just so you aren't tempted to create a scene while we're going through airport security," he added, gesturing to the photos once again, "I wanted you to know there would be consequences."

"I'll cooperate," she said. "You can call off your sick friend."

"I will. But in due time. Cooperate with us and they have nothing to worry about. You have my word."

"Is that supposed to be comforting?"

"I'm afraid it's the best I can offer."

53

The journey to Syria was a blur. Alyssa tried to sleep on the plane but with little success.

What could Al Yad possibly want with her now? He didn't want to lure Brennan in for an attempted rescue, because he had made sure Bren thought she was dead. Bren was unkillable, anyway, as he had demonstrated to Al Yad when they had fought to a draw.

Perhaps Al Yad was after information. But what information did she possess that would be useful to him at this point? Bren's location in Costa Rica? Maybe. Although given Bren's deteriorating condition, and her alleged demise, she'd be astonished if he remained there much longer.

She finally decided it was useless to try to guess Al Yad's intent. He was psychotic, after all, and his motives might be completely opaque to a rational mind. And she would find out soon enough.

The trip to the cult leader's compound was like a dream, and Alyssa felt as though she were having an out of body experience as she was ushered through the gate and onto the expansive grounds.

She was taken to the main house. Bren had done a good job of describing it. While it had never been built for a king, it was instantly recognizable as a palace rather than as a mere mansion. It was magnificent, but also white and sterile—apparently to symbolize purity and piety—and could have doubled as a bird sanctuary. At least one species was thriving because of this madman.

Alyssa was escorted to a bedroom on the opposite side of the palace from where Al Yad's master bedroom had been. And judging from the men walking around with power tools, he was no doubt still in the process of repairing the devastation Bren had wrought on that side of the residence in the initial moments of his attack.

She was left alone in the room, which was furnished with three white chairs and a white leather sofa. And the obligatory white marble pedestals with gold cages and canaries. While it wasn't as spacious as the master bedroom, which Bren had reported was the size of a ballroom, it was still one of the largest Alyssa had been in.

A guard had been posted outside. Not that she was naive enough to think she could escape.

She sat down on one of the lacquered wood chairs and awaited her fate.

54

Al Yad was ecstatic! More ecstatic than he had been since he first realized he was a god.

Alyssa Aronson had just been brought to his compound, and was waiting for him in what had become his temporary bedroom while his old room was being rebuilt. The four million dollar installment he had paid Adam Turco was the best money he had ever spent. It had not only bought him Craft's Jewish whore, but the key to decrypting her phone as well.

And this decryption code had proved more valuable than he could ever have *dreamed*. He was so close to being able to finally exert his dominion as a god that he could almost taste it.

He studied the phone of Satan's whore for the fourth time, still wanting to be sure he had read what he had read. His English was excellent, but one additional reading couldn't hurt.

He had read Craft's texted account of the epic battle they had recently waged in the desert with great interest. But this wasn't what had made him *euphoric*. This had happened when he read the recent exchange between Aronson and Turco's boss, Eben Martin—especially Martin's very last message.

The texts made it clear that Satan's incarnation on earth, Brennan Craft, was beginning to show his evil nature, confirming what Al Yad, in his divine wisdom, had always known about him. And the messages back and forth between the girl and the famous billionaire had grown increasingly frantic. Both were worried Craft would turn on them. Both thought he was going insane and would try to beat Al Yad to the punch with respect to reshaping the world to his desire.

Al Yad scrolled down and reread the last of Martin's texts the Jew had seen before Bahar had taken possession of her phone.

Bren is worse than I thought, and deteriorating quickly. He's barely sane right now. His temper is even worse than you reported. I've never been this scared. He's demanding I help him take over the world. Really! Our only hope is that the real Bren is still hidden inside somewhere. If so, I have to find a way to reach him. And quickly.

Al Yad scrolled down in delight to reread her reply again as well.

Bren didn't want you to know, but he thinks having his ability 'on' all the time is what's making him lose his mind. I know a way to temporarily strip him of his ability—at his command. Disconnect him entirely from the zero point field, even the always-on defenses he can't consciously control, for however long he wants. So he can sleep and his mind can rest. I have a technique, and drug, more powerful than what I used to improve his ability, so I'm very confident this will work. I'll call him and tell him I've got the drug, and will fly back ASAP.

When Al Yad had first read this, and then Martin's emphatic insistence that she not do anything until she had spoken to him, the only conclusion he could draw was that Craft hadn't told her about his quantum mirror device. Which was astonishing. And Martin had sent one final text, which Aronson had never read, that made this conclusion irrefutable: she knew nothing about the device.

Al Yad could easily guess the reason for this deception.

Craft must have suspected that if she had known the truth, she wouldn't have helped him get stronger. Once he disclosed he had a device that could stop Al Yad, she would realize that strengthening him wasn't necessary to thwart Al Yad's divine purpose.

And then Craft had lied to her to get her to temporarily sever his connection to what he called *the zero point field*. He had told her this would help him sleep. Restore balance to his mind.

It was brilliant! Craft could use his device on Al Yad while remaining temporarily immune from it himself. Craft might be pure evil, but there was no denying his cunning. And it would have worked if Al Yad hadn't intercepted Alyssa Aronson.

Not that there was ever any doubt that he would. The moment he heard the recording of Bahar's initial interrogation of her he had seen

the possibilities, had seen what this could mean. He was sure Craft
had also. He just had no idea Craft would choose to be so devious
about it.

But Al Yad had no doubt that when the drug had been resynthesized, Craft, or his whore, would travel to Kansas for it. He had made
sure that Bahar had assigned an entire team to surveil this lab.

When Turco contacted Bahar and offered his services, this was ic-
ing on the cake. With Craft in the equation, there were no guarantees
Al Yad could wrestle Aronson away from him. And had Al Yad failed
to do so, he would have been forced to kill her immediately, so Craft
couldn't use her.

But with Turco in the picture, someone Craft and the Jew trusted,
his odds of success had increased dramatically. And acquiring the
decryption code to the whore's phone had been an added bonus.

But the most earth-shattering bonus of all had come four hours
after Aronson had been in Bahar's custody. The proof that Allah was
merciful and just. That he loved Al Yad, Allah's personification on
Earth, and that he rewarded patience.

A final message from Eben Martin, which the whore had never
seen. Since Martin was almost certainly dead, the last message he
would ever send to anyone. A broad smile came over Al Yad's face as
he began reading it yet again, with all of the reverence reserved for
the holiest passages of the Koran.

*Alyssa, if you're reading this, chances are that Brennan Craft is
beyond redemption and I am dead.*

*I am writing this after returning from my first visit with you in
Costa Rica. As a failsafe. Bren is showing alarming signs, which both
of us have begun to notice. I worry he may be in the early stages of
heading down the path Omar Haddad headed down before him.*

*Hopefully, this won't be the case. But if this spirals out of control
in the weeks and months to come, and I end up dead somehow, this
message to you may be the only defense the world has against both
Bren and Al Yad. At this point, Bren is still himself more often than
not, but I like to plan ahead, and this is too important not to take
this step.*

Unless I reset the clock once in every twelve hour period, this message is scheduled to be sent to you automatically. And since I fully intend to reset it without fail, the fact that you're reading this means that Bren's condition has deteriorated to an alarming degree, and that I am either dead or incapacitated.

Bren misled you about the hold he has over Al Yad. You wondered why his fairly toothless bluff has continued to work all this time. The answer is that it hasn't. Bren invented a device he calls the quantum mirror, when Haddad was first turning into Al Yad. Within a few seconds of this device being activated, and for about the next six hours, some kind of anti-zero-point-energy matrix will encompass the entire Earth. During this time, anyone tapping into the zero point field is killed. Their very connection basically blows up in their faces. Or, rather, in their minds.

Bren threatened to use this quantum mirror if Al Yad didn't mind his manners. Since neither can stop tapping the field, even while they're sleeping, activating the device is an automatic death sentence for them both. Bren doesn't want to die, so he has been trying to find other solutions. A dangerous game, but I can't say I blame him.

Al Yad knows Bren can phone the device at any time and feed in a code to activate it. That's what's keeping him at bay.

When Bren was the good, sane man we had both come to love, he gave me the number and code to activate this device. As a backup. If he died somehow, I could use it immediately to kill Al Yad.

But given Bren's recent uncharacteristic behavior, I've come to realize I may need to activate this device while Bren is still alive. If he follows Haddad down the path of insanity, I'll have no other choice but to kill them both. It isn't a decision I would take lightly. But if Bren realizes I might take this step, there is a danger that he could take pre-emptive action so that I can't.

Which is the reason for this message. Since you're now reading it, the situation has gotten out of control. Bren must have gotten far worse, and I must have been too weak to kill my friend in time. I probably tried to save Bren from himself and failed.

So do not try to save him. You can't make the same mistake I must have made. Activate this quantum mirror device IMMEDIATELY. I know how hard this will be for you, but it is something you have to do. Just make sure you aren't anywhere near Bren when you activate it, or else you could be caught in the resulting blast.

As I write this, I know how much you care about Bren. If he's been able to hide his deteriorating condition from you, you may still care just as deeply for him when you get this message. But no matter what, you can't hesitate. You and I both know the man he was when you first met him would want you to do this.

Alyssa, you are an amazing woman in every way. Beautiful, brilliant, down-to-earth, funny, and hopelessly optimistic and romantic, despite your clandestine background, which turns most people cynical and distrusting.

I have to admit to being jealous of Bren since I've come to know you. I'm sure there are many men who could have fallen in love with you had they met you under the right circumstances, and I am one of them.

As a token of my admiration for you, and as penance for this terrible responsibility I am placing on your shoulders, I have made certain allowances for you in my will, which, since you're reading this message, will probably be read far sooner than I would have liked.

The telephone number and code to activate the quantum mirror follows. I can't possibly express how sorry I am that it has come to this. I can only hope that there really is an afterlife, and we can be reunited there someday.

In the meanwhile, rid the world of its two greatest threats, and go on and have the prosperous, happy life you so richly deserve.

Your good friend,
Eben Martin.

Al Yad read the numbers that followed and laughed out loud. He was aware that Allah worked in mysterious ways. He just wasn't aware that he had such a rich sense of humor—and of irony.

55

Al Yad decided he had reread these messages enough. It was time to visit his prize.

What had transpired after Aronson's last message to Martin was easy enough to deduce. Unlike her, the billionaire had known about the quantum mirror. So when she had texted him that Craft wanted her to temporarily disrupt his ability to connect to the divine, Martin had guessed Craft's intentions immediately. Martin's return text, insisting that she not do this, could not have been more emphatic.

And then Martin had made one last effort to convince Brennan Craft he should switch from the path he was on. And Martin had died for his stupidity. Without being alive to reset the clock, Martin's message had been sent to Aronson automatically, as he had planned.

But sent just a little too late.

Al Yad entered the room in which Alyssa Aronson had been waiting and floated to a landing in front of her, in full robes and headdress. As usual his close-cropped beard was neatly trimmed, he was well-scrubbed, and he radiated power and confidence.

He reached into the divine and caused the door to shut behind him. Unlike most, she seemed unimpressed. Since she was Craft's whore, after all, and had experienced this type of power, this didn't surprise him.

"Alyssa Aronson," he said in delight, making his voice supernaturally rich and resonant. He could tell from her reaction that the God-like voice he projected was intimidating. "Or should I say, Dr. Alyssa Aronson. I have been so looking forward to meeting you."

A flash of hatred came over her face but it quickly disappeared. She took several deep breaths, and Al Yad could tell she was forcing herself to tread cautiously. As well she should. He needed her desperately, but she had no way to know this. As far as she knew, insolence would be suicidal.

"Why am I here?" she asked, but calmly rather than defiantly.

He was impressed that she seemed prepared to keep the discourse civilized, whatever the reason. If she was willing to be civilized, he would be as well. Besides, he would soon need her cooperation, willing or otherwise.

"You are here to answer my questions," he replied. "After this, we shall see. There may be other services I shall require."

She shrank back, and he could tell she thought the other services he spoke of were sexual in nature. He was a *God*. Touching this diseased Jewish whore would be the last thing he would ever do.

"Follow me," he said, deciding not to disabuse her of the false and insulting conclusion she had drawn.

He led her to a nearby room. A bald man was waiting inside, near a table on which expensive, state-of-the-art polygraph equipment was resting.

"This is Aziz," said Al Yad, gesturing for her to have a seat across the small table facing him. "He is my lie-detector expert. Tariq tells me that this is the preferred way to be certain about the truthfulness of information."

Aziz spent the next ten minutes carefully hooking her up to the device, with the readout displayed on a computer screen in front of him.

"This will work best for our purposes," explained Al Yad. "I expect absolute truth at all times. Without fail. If you lie, Aziz and this device will know it. And one of your nieces shall die. Do you understand?"

He spread several photographs on the table, depicting members of her family, which Bahar had shown her earlier.

Alyssa swallowed hard, her hands involuntarily balling into fists. "Yes," she managed to croak out.

Al Yad waited impatiently while Aziz asked her simple questions to get a baseline reading: her name, age, sex, and so on, and then instructed her to lie so he could calibrate the system.

"She is ready, oh Great One," said Aziz in Arabic when he had finished.

"Use English, Aziz," he instructed. "For the benefit of our guest."

Al Yad turned to Alyssa and gave her a predatory smile. "Where is Brennan Craft?" he asked.

She told him the location of their complex without hesitation. Adam Turco had already indicated they were in Costa Rica, but even Turco had never been given their exact location.

Aziz, who was studying the computer screen carefully, caught Al Yad's eye and nodded. Given the threat to her family, Al Yad expected Aronson to be truthful unless something big was on the line. He turned to Aziz. "I shall assume she is being honest. If this is ever not the case, I expect you to alert me immediately."

"Yes, Great One," replied Aziz, this time in his heavily accented English.

Al Yad turned back to Alyssa. "Why did Craft seek you out?"

"He couldn't achieve the level of belief that you have. Belief in his ability to tap the zero point field. He wanted me to help him using narco-hypnotic techniques I've developed."

"What else did he want?"

"Nothing," she said. "I mean, I guess he also wanted companionship and that sort of thing."

"But nothing other than this?"

She shook her head.

The cult leader looked at Aziz questioningly, and the bald expert nodded.

Al Yad smiled. She really didn't have any knowledge of the quantum mirror. Outstanding! But just to be certain, he would explore this more directly. "Did he ever mention any devices he had built?"

After several seconds of thought, Alyssa shook her head. "I have no idea what you're talking about."

Al Yad studied her carefully. "Have you ever heard the phrase, quantum mirror?"

Alyssa squinted and searched her memory. "Never."

The puzzled look on her face was all he needed to see, but he again looked to Aziz, who nodded.

Interesting. Craft had pretended to be in love with her, but only so he could better pull her strings, better use her as the unwitting dupe she was.

"Why did you break into the lab in Kansas?" he asked.

"I was going after a drug there."

Al Yad pulled a small plastic vial from under his robe. "This drug?"

Alyssa nodded. "Yes. Brennan was becoming irrational. And he knew it. He thought it was because he could never turn his ability off. He remembered that I had achieved great success with involuntary nervous tics. He thought I might be able to strip him of his belief temporarily, so he could have a rest from the zero point field."

"And do you believe you could have accomplished this?"

"After my success improving his abilities, I have very little doubt. The drug you're holding is very special in this regard. With this and my proven protocols, I could have killed his ability to tap the zero point field for any length of time he specified, voluntarily and involuntarily. If I programmed this in, he would no longer be able to use zero point energy during this period, even if he wanted to."

"How have you and he been getting along recently?"

"What does that have to do with anything?" she snapped.

"Answer the question!"

Alyssa swallowed hard. "Not well," she said.

"I want specifics."

She turned away and lowered her eyes. "I'm afraid of him. I think he's a danger to me and to everyone else."

"Would you kill him if you could?"

She hesitated. "He *can't* be killed. So it's a pointless question."

Al Yad gestured meaningfully at the pictures of her young nieces and nephews, the oldest of whom couldn't be more than ten. He caused one photo to rise and hover in front of her face, depicting a girl of maybe eight or nine playing hopscotch on a school playground. "I can't believe you need me to remind you of how much is riding on your full cooperation," he said.

He returned the photo to the table. "So you have one more chance. Would you kill Brennan Craft if you could?"

Her eyes filled with moisture. "I don't know," she whispered. "Maybe. If temporarily severing his link to the field didn't work, didn't restore him to his former self . . ." She shuddered. "Then yes."

"Has everything she said so far been the truth, Aziz?"

"Yes, oh Great One."

Al Yad turned to Alyssa and barely managed to avoid grinning. Craft had planned to use this whore to destroy him, but he had intercepted her, and would now use her in the same way Craft had intended. Craft's plan had backfired, blown up in his face. The same way Craft's zero point field would blow up in his face when the quantum mirror device was activated.

Al Yad sighed heavily. "I'm going to admit something to you," he said to Alyssa. "I've come to believe I suffer from the same condition as Craft. For some time now. I can't sleep either. I need a break from this energy. Would you be willing to do for me what you were going to do for Craft?"

"I'm not sure I understand," she said, her eyes narrowing. "You want me to temporarily cut you off from the zero point field?"

"Yes. For eight hours. Just as you were going to do for Craft. I think it would do wonders for me. My mind is weary. I desperately need a break."

Alyssa paused to consider this request, obviously taken aback by it. "Okay, Al Yad," she said, surprising him by using this name. "If it might help you, I would be glad to do it."

"And you won't try anything deceptive? No tricks while I'm under the influence of drugs and hypnosis?" He paused. "Before you answer, know that I won't just trust you. That I shall first test the drug on one of my subjects. The same dose I will be given. Then I shall give irrevocable orders that your family is to be wiped out at some near future date. Orders that only I can countermand. When you're finished, I will watch a video of our session to make sure you haven't tried any deception. But even if you're clever enough to deceive me, unless everything goes exactly the way I want it to, I won't countermand the order."

He paused to let this sink in. "If, on the other hand, you do as you've agreed—nothing more and nothing less—I shall make the call to spare your family. Everyone will be happy."

He stared at her intently. "So now, under these circumstances, will you do what I've asked, and only what I've asked? No deceptions?"

Alyssa nodded. "I wouldn't have tried any tricks, even without your threats. Especially since I believe that Bren is right. This may well end up helping you. Helping all of us." She paused. "Besides, there *are* no tricks. Hypnotism can only work if the subject *wants* it to work. I can't plant any suggestions in your mind that you don't want to be there."

Al Yad turned to Aziz once again, who nodded vigorously. Everything she had said during the entire session had been the truth.

Outstanding! thought Al Yad once again.

He had Alyssa tell him what she would need to carry out the procedure, and the dose she planned to use on him, and then thanked her for her cooperation and called a guard to escort her to her quarters. She could bathe and relax while he used underlings as guinea pigs and made other preparations.

When she left, he turned one last time to Aziz. "Good work," he said. "You have served me well. I only wish you hadn't heard some of the things you did." He shook his head sadly. "But rest assured, Aziz, I shall see to it that your family is well taken care of."

And with that, the bald polygraph expert seized up and fell to the floor. Then, with another glance from Al Yad, Aziz's body disintegrated into its constituent atoms, and no trace remained that he had ever existed.

56

Only six hours later Al Yad was ready. He had waited a very long time for this opportunity, and he wasn't going to wait a second longer than necessary.

The drug Alyssa had taken from the Lawrence lab was very potent, and even after it had been diluted tenfold, the dose needed was only two microliters, an amount that could be drawn up into the very tip of a calibrated plastic needle. Al Yad had a physician dose three of his followers with five times this amount, and hours later they were still in good health.

During this six hour period, he also had several followers scour Syria, at the whore's request, for something called a HeadRush game controller and skull cap, which were very hard to come by in this part of the world. But they had found two of them fairly quickly, and paid the owners four times their worth to acquire them.

Apparently, Aronson also required specific viral software to modify the game system for her needs, but she had stored a copy in the cloud for safekeeping, which she could now access.

Al Yad also had two of his construction workers drive steel rings into the wall studs near his bed, to which he anchored leg irons. Then he had a table brought in, on which he set up a computer, also firmly anchored to the wall, and selected a pair of specialty handcuffs with a length of chain in between the cuff bracelets.

Finally, Al Yad had the Jew brought into the room once again. While she sat at the desk, ten feet from his bed, he had her handcuffed and placed in leg irons. He checked with her to make sure she had enough freedom of movement to do what she needed to do, and she assured him that while being restrained wasn't ideal, she could still read the monitor and use the computer to pinpoint the electrical stimulations she would need.

Al Yad thought the chances of her trying to attack him in some way were one in a million. Not only had she passed the lie detector test, but his threat to her family was real, and he was certain she believed him. Also, because of what the personification of Satan had told her, she believed that what she was doing might turn Al Yad back into the pathetic weakling of a man he had been before he had become a god. Something she badly wanted to see happen.

But even if the chances were one in a million, why take *any* risk with his immortality when the simple expedient of chaining her could eliminate this entirely?

Al Yad had also had a video system installed in the room, with the camera arranged to encompass both the desk and the bed. He would check the video to be sure Aronson had implanted the hypnotic suggestions she was supposed to implant, for the proper time lengths, and using the proper trigger words.

Finally, Al Yad assembled his eighteen guards, and Tariq Bahar, and let it be known that for the next twenty-four hours his staff and all workers were to be cleared out of the palace, and word was to be spread that anyone coming within fifty yards of it would explode into flame. He explained he did not want to be disturbed under *any* circumstances, without exception.

The guards were ordered to ensure no one stumbled near the palace, even by accident. Given that he had recently ended the lives of three randomly selected followers in truly horrible ways, in front of a large gathering, just to keep the rest appropriately awed by his power, he knew no one would dare challenge this edict.

After the palace had been cleared, Al Yad had a brief conversation with Adam Turco. Turco reported that Brennan Craft had just left Costa Rica in one of Eben Martin's Gulfstream jets, and was flying to a private airfield outside of San Diego, California. Craft had told Turco that his billionaire friend would not be accompanying him, but was staying behind in Costa Rica and would be out of touch until further notice.

This had brought a smile to Al Yad's face. *Out of touch until further notice* was a nice euphemism for *recently deceased.*

Turco had been instructed to meet Craft in San Diego, and soon thereafter to shadow someone named Robert Freund, who worked at a lab there, and report on Freund's daily movements and routine.

Al Yad had to smile yet again at the audacity of Brennan Craft. He had killed his friend Martin, was wantonly using Martin's private jet, and instead of wasting a moment mourning what he thought was the death of his Jewish whore, he had written her off entirely, and was about to abduct a man who was surely another expert in narco-hypnosis.

But no matter how quickly Craft was able to recruit this Robert Freund, he would be far too late. Al Yad had beaten Craft to the punch.

He blew out a satisfied breath. Brennan Craft, the incarnation of Satan on Earth, had absolutely no idea what was about to hit him.

57

Alyssa Aronson had spent over an hour mapping out what she called baseline pathways for Al Yad's states of belief and disbelief, and then she had drugged him. He was then under her spell for another three hours, although it seemed instantaneous to him.

He came awake and removed the skull cap from his head, lifting himself into the air to ensure he still had his divinity. He turned to the whore chained to a desk ten feet away.

"How did it go?" he asked her.

"It couldn't have gone better," she responded. "We can't know until you try, but my experience tells me you should now be able to temporarily disengage from the field. Provided that this is something you truly wanted."

Al Yad smiled. This was something he had truly wanted. As much as he had ever wanted anything.

He played back the video on the screen hanging on the wall in front of his bed. Most of it just showed the Jew studying her computer monitor. The actual part where she strengthened certain pathways, certain beliefs, or in this case, lack of beliefs, was fairly brief, and he fast-forwarded to these parts to ensure she hadn't planted any suggestions she wasn't supposed to have planted.

But he found no hint of trickery or deceit. All that was required for him to trigger the response was to be viewing an accurate clock while saying the English words, *mark one*, out loud. This would sever his connection to the divine, both voluntary and involuntary, for five minutes exactly.

If he confirmed that this worked as hoped, he could then view a clock and say the words, *mark two*, and this would have the same effect. But this time for eight hours.

He had been concerned that he might happen to see a clock from a different time zone and regain his abilities before the full eight hours had passed, but Aronson had assured him his subconscious wouldn't let him be fooled in this way. She had been certain that if he had wanted to be free for eight hours while undergoing hypnosis, and then later triggered this response, his connection with the zero point field could only be restored after this duration, as evidenced by an accurate clock in the proper time zone.

Al Yad took a deep breath and stared at the digital time on the bottom of his plasma television screen. "*Mark one*," he said aloud.

He gasped!

He had to steady himself on the side of the bed to keep from collapsing to the floor. His divinity rushed out of his body and mind with hurricane force.

Al Yad felt weak and powerless. Human. It was debilitating. A nightmare.

He tried to lift himself from the ground with his divinity and failed. He was unable to even lift a pillow. He stabbed himself gently in the arm with the tip of a knife, and bright red blood trickled out where he had poked a hole through his skin.

He glanced at the time. He had three minutes left.

He walked over and placed a heavy glass paperweight, in the shape of teardrop, on the desk, and freed the Jew's hands. He backed away fifteen feet. "Throw this at my stomach," he ordered.

Aronson didn't waste any time. She hurled the object toward him. It sailed through the air and hit him squarely in the gut. He had tightened his muscles, but it still hurt, and it still managed to knock the wind out of him.

He smiled broadly. *She had done it*. Satan's whore had done it! And not for Satan, but for him.

The digital clock advanced, marking the end of the five minute period, and power surged back into Al Yad, like divine breath being pushed into the lungs of a suffocating swimmer. He rose effortlessly to the ceiling and crushed the glass paperweight into nothingness. He was restored. Exactly as he had been.

"Satisfied?" said Alyssa.

Al Yad beamed. "Very."

"You heard my hypnotic instructions for the eight hour version," she said. "They were identical to the five minute one. So do you have any doubt that I've accomplished what you wanted?"

"No."

"Then call Tariq Bahar's psychopathic friend off my family," she said anxiously. "Like you promised. I've kept my part of the bargain."

Al Yad was tempted to have the merc kill off her entire family anyway, just to see her reaction, but he was ecstatic at the success of her techniques, and decided to honor his commitment. Not that it mattered. Her family would soon be dead anyway, along with billions of others, as he purged the world of infidels.

He placed a video call to Tom Manning, and the man's inhumanly proportioned body appeared on the screen above his bed. Al Yad noticed that the whore shrank back, involuntarily, even from the sight of Manning on the monitor.

"I'm countermanding your last order," said Al Yad. "The people on your list are no longer to be harmed. Please acknowledge."

Manning looked disappointed. "Acknowledged," he said.

"You'll be contacted if we ever need your services again."

Manning nodded and disappeared from the screen.

Alyssa Aronson radiated such palpable relief, Al Yad almost regretted calling it off. But no matter. He would soon turn this relief back into despair.

He could hardly wait to get started.

58

Alyssa had been holding her mental breath for hours. This procedure was the strongest she had in her arsenal, but the lives of people dear to her, of helpless children she loved, depended on the outcome. Given all she had witnessed since her fateful lunch date with a man who had called himself Theo Grant, she hadn't had a single doubt that Al Yad would carry out his threat without a second thought.

But it had worked!

She couldn't have asked for anything more. And Al Yad had done what he had promised. He had called off the grotesque psychopathic sadist she had called Tree Trunk.

She had been resigned to her own fate since she was brought here. Al Yad would either kill her or keep her as a prisoner, and no cavalry would ever come for her. But at least she would have the solace of knowing her loved ones were safe.

Her only hope now was that Bren had been right, and that a temporary reprieve from the zero point field would restore Al Yad's mental health. If so, he might let her live, and even let her return to Bren, so she could do the same for him.

It was unlikely this scenario would play out, but she seized on this tiny hope like a shipwrecked passenger clinging to a piece of debris in a raging ocean.

"It's a shame about Brennan Craft isn't it?" said Al Yad, and there was an undercurrent of malevolence in his tone. He had been civilized with her when he needed her to help him, but his body language suddenly conveyed a heightened cruelty that made her skin crawl.

"What do you mean?"

"He is evil. He is the incarnation of Satan. And now you've seen his true colors."

"Maybe he can be cured," she said. "Maybe giving your minds a break from the zero point field is all both of you need to . . . feel more like your old selves."

An icy smile came over Al Yad's face. "You stupid, stupid whore," he said. "Craft doesn't want to be *cured*. You've finally begun to catch a glimpse of his true nature. But he hasn't changed. He was playing you from the beginning. He was Satan from the beginning."

His invective and tone were getting increasingly hostile, and this reminded Alyssa of how quickly Craft had turned on her recently. But whereas Craft had once loved her and managed to take his rage out on inanimate objects, she doubted Al Yad would do the same.

"What are you talking about?" she asked.

"Did Craft ever tell you how he was stopping me from achieving my divine purpose? From purging the world of the impure?"

"Yes. He warned you he knew a way to become even more powerful than you, and that if you did this he would kill you."

Al Yad shook his head, a look of contempt and pity on his face. "He lied to you. He played you for the fool you are. He simply wanted to seduce you into doing for him what you just did for me."

Alyssa had never been more confused. "What? That's ridiculous. He wanted me to *strengthen* his abilities, not nullify them."

"You really are stupid, even for a diseased Jewish whore. He wanted you to do *both*. And if I hadn't intercepted you, he would have succeeded."

"I don't understand," said Alyssa. She bristled from the raw hatred and bigotry of his words, but she didn't have the luxury of taking offense. Al Yad seemed more out of touch with reality than ever. Perhaps his five minute stint isolated from the zero point field had made him *worse* rather than better.

"Let me *help* you understand," he spat. "First, you should know that your friend Eben Martin is now dead. At the hand of Brennan Craft."

Alyssa's eyes widened in horror. Could this be true? Given the deterioration of Craft's personality, Eben Martin had come to mean more to her than anyone else in the world.

"You couldn't know that," she whispered. "You're making it up."

"Am I?" he said.

He walked over to where she was seated and handed her a phone. It was hers.

"Take a look at this," he said, pointing to a lengthy message that was already up on the display. "It's from Eben Martin. It came in after Tariq confiscated your phone, so you never had the chance to read it." Then with a humorless smile he added, "Don't worry. I took the liberty of decrypting it."

Alyssa began reading and her stomach tightened. She forgot to breathe, and soon felt a suffocating pressure on her chest.

Her world began to shatter even more as she continued to read, finally managing to suck air into lungs that suddenly seemed paralyzed.

It *was* true. Eben was almost certainly dead. And Brennan had gotten worse.

Eben had designed the message so it would only be sent if he wasn't around to stop it.

The message described a weapon called the quantum mirror, and the lethal effect it would have on anyone tapping into the zero point field. Suddenly, everything became clear.

Al Yad had been right! Bren had been playing her from the beginning.

A tear formed in the corner of one eye. Brennan had never loved her. He had never cared about her in the least. It had all been a facade. So she could enhance his ability and also selectively strip it away. So he could kill the one man who could possibly stop him.

Perhaps Brennan had always been as evil as Al Yad portrayed him to be. As evil as Al Yad himself.

This information explained so much. Why Bren hadn't wanted her to tell Eben she was stripping him of his connection to the field. Eben hadn't known about her work on the nocebo side of the equation. But he *had* known about the quantum mirror.

So if she had told Eben, he would have connected the dots. He would realize why Bren wanted her to perform this particular mental surgery. So Bren could activate the device, killing his Syrian nemesis instantly, and leaving him as the only omnipotent being in existence.

Which is why, when she had finally texted Eben about this, he had been so adamant that she not perform this technique on Bren until they had spoken.

And this message explained the charade that Al Yad had just put her through. Now that Al Yad could sever his connection to the field, he could activate the device and kill Bren. He had turned the tables brilliantly.

The cult leader studied her carefully as she read Martin's message and pondered its implications, and correctly guessed when the full light of comprehension had crushed her spirit.

"So now you understand," he hissed. "The depth of Craft's deception. And your role in helping to change the world. All I have to do is trigger the eight hour period of dormancy you so helpfully programmed into me, and then phone Craft's device. I enter the code and Craft is gone.

"Now I know from our earlier discussion, when you were attached to a lie detector, that you now recognize his true nature and might even *welcome* his death." Al Yad shook his head. "But not as much as I will," he assured her icily. "Without him and the threat of his quantum mirror, I'll finally be free to carry out my divine purpose."

Alyssa felt as though the room were closing in, and at the same time she was being repeatedly struck by a hammer.

Eben dead. Brennan dead. The world at the mercy of a raving psychotic who was all but omnipotent. And the knowledge that she had been used ruthlessly, had been fooled into making it possible to end the stalemate.

Al Yad glanced at the screen above his bed and checked the time. "I'm afraid Brennan Craft is down to his last hour or so."

Alyssa didn't respond. Her head was down, and she looked utterly defeated.

"While the effect of the device is almost immediate," explained Al Yad, "Craft is a passenger on Martin's Gulfstream jet right now, headed for a private airfield outside of San Diego, California. I've

316 Douglas E. Richards

waited too long for this not to witness his death with my own eyes. I want the satisfaction of seeing it happen. And I want *you* to see it, too." He shrugged. "But don't worry. He'll be landing soon."

The cult leader placed another video call, and this time Adam Turco appeared on the screen high on the wall. "Give me a status update," he ordered Turco when the connection was made.

"Craft is still in the air, and still on schedule. He should be landing in sixty-eight minutes."

"Good. I want to know the moment his plane touches down. And have you tied a video feed into your binoculars, as you suggested?"

"I have," said Turco.

"Good. I shall see to it that Craft is struck down as soon as he steps onto the tarmac. Once you transmit video proof of his death, I shall have the final million wired into your account."

"If your hit team succeeds, you'll have your footage. If not, I will get you footage of Craft leaving in a car. Either way, I should get paid. It isn't my fault if your team fails."

"Agreed," said Al Yad happily. "But don't worry. There is nowhere in the entire world Craft can hide from this particular assassination attempt."

59

After Al Yad's brief call with Turco, he left Alyssa alone in the room. Alone with her fears. And her regrets.

She sobbed quietly for fifteen minutes. She hadn't cried in years before meeting Brennan Craft, save for during an occasional movie designed to evoke this reaction, but since this time she had shed tears more often than she had been forced unconscious.

She was almost grateful for the leg irons and handcuffs. Otherwise, she might well have curled up into a fetal position, trying to shield herself from a too-harsh reality, and beginning to lose her grip on it.

She lost track of time as she relived the events of the past few months, playing them over and over, looking for something she could have done differently.

But there was nothing.

Bren and Al Yad had both ruthlessly, and brilliantly, used her as a pawn to serve their own ends. Al Yad would win this particular game, but they both deserved to lose. If only there was a way to achieve this outcome. But there wasn't. Al Yad's connection to the zero point field would be severed for eight hours, and there was nothing she could do to restore it within the six hour period he would be vulnerable to the effects of the quantum mirror device.

Finally, an eternity in hell later, Al Yad reentered the room, his sprits as high as hers were low. He quickly established a video connection with Adam Turco. The wheels of the plane Craft was in had just touched down in San Diego, and the screen facing Al Yad's bed was now showing what Turco was seeing through his binoculars.

The sleek white Gulfstream taxied for several minutes and then came to a stop on an expansive field of concrete, riddled with dozens of small, private aircraft that were parked there, an eclectic assortment of small jets and propeller planes.

Brennan Craft appeared at the door of the jet as the stairs tele-
scoped down to touch the concrete. Not that Craft needed stairs, any
more than he had really needed a plane. His image was crystal clear
in Turco's binoculars.

Al Yad beamed upon seeing him standing there, his absolute hatred of Craft fueling his euphoria now. He stared at the time on the
bottom of the screen and said, "*Mark two.*"

Once again the cult leader gasped, even louder than before. This
time he fell to his knees as the subconscious tendrils he had planted
deep within the zero point field were ripped from their moorings.

"If you want the video of your hit-team's handiwork," said Turco.
"They'd better strike in the next two minutes. Once Craft is inside
the building he'll be out of my view."

"Don't worry," replied Al Yad, rising weakly back to a standing
position with a phone now in his hand. "The strike will occur in approximately one minute."

Al Yad carefully dialed the number Martin had texted to Alyssa,
looking to be in a state of absolute ecstasy. He established a connection with Craft's quantum mirror device, wherever it was hidden, and
entered the final activation code, pausing before the last digit.

"Allah Akbar," he said softly. *God is great.* And then entered the
last of the code.

Alyssa watched Brennan Craft on the screen in horror, but couldn't
look away. According to Eben's message, some sort of lethal matrix
would soon be racing across the globe at incomprehensible speed.
And the instant it crossed Bren's path, the defensive mechanisms that
had protected him so well would turn on him, destroying him utterly.

"Any second now," Al Yad assured Adam Turco as Craft stepped
off the lowest stair and onto the concrete field.

Alyssa gasped as a massive explosion filled the screen. It was so
violent that even the transmitted video of the event was nearly deafening and seemed to shake the entire room.

And Brennan Craft was at the very heart of it.

The man Alyssa had once loved had erupted into a furious orange
fireball before her very eyes.

60

The wall of flame shot a hundred feet into the cloudless San Diego sky, and a mini-mushroom cloud stretched even higher. Large pieces of the Gulfstream and small pieces of Craft's body flew toward Turco's binoculars, and if it had been filmed in 3-D, Alyssa might have ducked.

One second Al Yad's monitor was showing a living Brennan Craft, and the next, nothing but charred fragments of his body, a gaping hole in the concrete on which he had been standing, and a Gulfstream jet that had been obliterated. Five planes parked nearby had also burst into flames. As expected, the energy from the zero point field had traveled along Craft's mental connection, bypassing his shield, which had done nothing to protect him.

"Allah Akbar," whispered Al Yad again, closing his eyes and basking in the glory of this moment. No man had ever looked more blissful, or at peace.

"Holy shit!" screamed the voice of Adam Turco, and the screen went blank as he turned off the binoculars. "Too much heat," he said, and his breathing suggested he was running from the proximity of the blast. "What the fuck did you use on him? Napalm?"

"Your remaining fee will be wired to you shortly," said Al Yad, ignoring him. "This concludes our business."

Al Yad ended the connection and turned to Alyssa, who was hunkered down as low on the chair as it would allow, her eyes sunken and lifeless. She had passed her threshold. She was now broken, her will to live extinguished.

"Praise be to Allah," he said. "And now you see his true greatness. He caused a filthy Jew whore to be the instrument I needed to defeat my nemesis, the personification of Satan on Earth. Allah was testing me. To learn if I would do what needed to be done, make use of the likes of *you*, as distasteful as this was, to achieve my goal."

He paused. "Now the only question I have is what to do with you? I can keep you alive so you can witness the world become cleansed and purified. No part of the globe shall be spared. But I will begin with two countries, in particular, that I shall destroy entirely. Would you care to guess?"

Alyssa didn't respond. She had become numb, walling her mind off from horrors that she could no longer bear. His words barely registered.

"No? Then I'll tell you. America and Israel. I shall destroy them both. Wipe them off the face of the earth. Literally. I'm aware there are some pious Muslims in these countries, but this can't be helped. They have sinned by living in a cesspool of iniquity. By living among filthy infidels. And they shall pay the price."

He paused. "It is tempting to keep you alive, so you can see what you helped bring about. But I also have two other options. I can kill you now. Or I can have my men rape you and tear you to pieces."

Alyssa's eyes were rolled up in her head and they were no longer in focus as her mind desperately retreated from reality. She was aware of a sound coming from behind her, of the door opening, but she was far too numb to turn.

She vaguely caught a horrified expression come over Al Yad's face. His eyes widened and his mouth fell open.

But while her addled mind was still processing this strange sight, Al Yad collapsed to the floor, screaming, his skull crushed like a cracked walnut, trailing blood and brain matter behind it.

What the hell?

Alyssa couldn't comprehend what she was seeing. She had believed in Al Yad's invulnerability for so long, his collapse refused to fully register.

What kind of cruel joke *was* this? Had she finally gone mad?

Then a man rushed to her side, his eyes roving over her body frantically, assessing her condition. His expression morphed from one of panic to relief as he concluded that she had not been injured.

Alyssa Aronson had become Alice in Wonderland, finally completing her full immersion in the impossible world found through the looking glass.

Because the man was Brennan Craft.

And he was wearing the uniform of a Colonel in the US Air Force.

61

Craft leaned in to try to hold and comfort the shell-shocked women that Alyssa Aronson had become, but she shrank away in horror. He looked hurt and deeply saddened, but not surprised.

He walked the few yards to where Al Yad had collapsed on the floor and checked for a pulse. He knelt beside his vanquished enemy, and his face bloomed into the same display of ecstasy and relief Alyssa had seen on Al Yad's face only minutes earlier.

"We did it," he said triumphantly. "We ended this threat that I created. *You've* ended it, Alyssa. I've turned his brain to liquid, so there will be no coming back."

Alyssa's expression was totally blank. She might have been a zombie for all the emotion she displayed.

Craft removed the keys to her cuffs and leg irons from Al Yad's robe and gently freed her. She didn't protest as he escorted her to the white couch and helped her seat herself.

"I can explain," said Craft, backing away from the couch but still facing her. "I owe you that much." He shook his head. " I owe you *everything*. And if afterwards, you never want to talk to me again, I promise to leave you alone."

Alyssa nodded. So Craft had won after all. A surprise checkmate in the eleventh hour. But it didn't matter. The results would be largely the same, no matter who was the victor between the two.

But as Alyssa looked into his eyes, she saw the old Brennan Craft. The kind, gentle, compassionate man. Fully rational. It was this, more than anything else, that revived her sprit, thawed out her faculties so that she could be coherent, could think and feel once again.

"First," said Craft. "You should know that Eben Martin is alive and well."

Could it be? thought Alyssa hopefully.

Why not? She had traveled so far down the rabbit hole at this point, anything was possible.

"And I've misled you about some important things from the beginning. But I felt it was necessary."

"Like the existence of your quantum mirror device?" she said accusingly, finally coming back to life.

"There is no quantum mirror device," said Craft.

"Why are you still *lying* to me?"

"I'm *not*," insisted Craft, shaking his head vigorously. "The device was a bluff. The story I told you about the emergence of Omar Haddad to near omnipotence was accurate. He did kill everyone I was working with. And he was seconds away from killing me. And prior to this, when it became clear to me he was a runaway train, I did try to invent a quantum mirror device to stop him."

Craft paused, remembering. "But I failed," he continued. "Not only failed, but actually proved mathematically that such a device could never be built. But with only seconds left before Omar broke through my shield, I had the inspiration to use this as a bluff. I had worked on it enough to be very convincing about it."

Alyssa just stared at him, unblinking. Too much had happened for her to possibly digest it all.

"Let me go back to the beginning and work forward," said Craft. "I realized just before he was about to beat me that this would be the perfect bluff. I could keep him from killing me, and threaten to kill *him* if he became a one-man weapon of mass destruction. If I had a device that could kill him, he knew I would use it. He had just slaughtered my entire group. But this fictional quantum mirror device I described to him gave me a lethal weapon to threaten him with, and at the same time a credible reason why I would only use it as a last resort. Because it would cause *my* death as well.

"But I didn't know how long this bluff would hold. And with my feeble abilities, I was vulnerable, as you know. Who knew when he would call my bluff? Or just destroy a country or two because he couldn't help himself? So my original plan was as I described it to you. Recruit you to help me get to his level. So I would be a better deterrent, and even possibly kill him."

"Why didn't you tell me? About the device, and about it being a bluff?"

"I had planned to tell you about the device initially. To help you understand what was holding Al Yad in check. But I had already decided I could never tell you it wasn't real. If you were ever caught and questioned, I couldn't risk Al Yad learning it was a bluff."

"So what changed?"

"After we left the hospital together, I listened to the recording of your interrogation. And I heard about your nocebo work. Work that I wasn't familiar with. It blew me away. I almost fell off my seat when I heard you describe it."

Alyssa remembered being in the car while he listened to the recording through earbuds, and seeing him light up like a neon sign at one point.

"When I learned of this, my mind began to work overtime. I soon realized two things. One, I *couldn't* tell you the mythical tale of the quantum mirror device, after all. If I did, you would realize the potential of your therapy to temporarily suspend my connection to the zero point field. You'd add two and two very quickly, and be the first to suggest a way I could use the device, while remaining immune. End of problem. Al Yad is dead. And I'm still standing. But we couldn't use this strategy because the device didn't really exist. So I would be forced to tell you it was a bluff."

"Which you already decided you couldn't do, for fear Al Yad would get wind of it." Alyssa's faculties had returned in full. Craft's logic was a bit tortured, but also sound.

"Exactly. The second thing I realized was that your nocebo advance dovetailed perfectly with my bluff. Because Al Yad would no doubt hear a recording of your interrogation as well, and learn of this work. If it occurred to me that this would provide a means to become temporarily protected from the quantum mirror device—which he was convinced was real—it would also occur to *him*. And then I had my epiphany."

Craft caused one of the room's white chairs to glide through the air and land behind him. He sat down, still facing Alyssa, and continued. "I realized I might be able to find some way to fool Al Yad to strip *himself* of his abilities. Turn the invulnerable into something I could kill. But he'd only do this if he was convinced he could kill *me* by doing so. But as you so eloquently pointed out, these hypnotic triggers only work if the subject wants them to. I didn't have a plan at the time, but I felt sure I could come up with some way to orchestrate circumstances so he would feel in total control, and willingly give up his power."

Although the details were still fuzzy and she knew there was far more to it than this, Alyssa was finally able to glimpse the shadow of the Rubik's Cube Bren had managed to twist fully into place. She didn't know how he had managed it, but given Al Yad's lifeless body on the floor, she knew that he had.

She made a mental note never to play chess with Brennan Craft.

His face twisted into a picture of self-disgust. "But Al Yad acted before I had even begun to arrive at a plan. I never expected him to be so bold and decisive as to make a play for you that same day in the cornfield," he said bitterly. "But I *should* have. With all humility, I've made some good moves, but I was brain-dead on this one. *Of course* he wouldn't wait for me to orchestrate events. He knew he had to have you. He feared you would allow me to become temporarily immune from the quantum mirror, and he realized you could do the same for him. You were the key in the battle between us. I still can't believe I missed this."

"But at least you took precautions through Eben to make sure we weren't being followed. And because of this, his attempt to get me failed."

"Even so, I'll never forgive myself for not anticipating this move," he said with a deep frown.

Craft blew out a long breath. "But to continue," he said, trying to get himself past this mistake, "when we first met up with Eben after the ambush, I was still a long way from arriving at a plan. So I told him about the quantum mirror. But I didn't tell him it was a bluff. Which is the strategy I had planned to use with you."

Alyssa thought about this for a moment and nodded. "Because *he* didn't know anything about my success with the nocebo effect. Unlike you and Al Yad, he didn't hear the interrogation. So he wouldn't know there was a possible means to nullify the effects of this device. You know, if it were real. So you could tell *him*, without having to admit it was a bluff."

"Exactly. And the story I told you to explain what kept Al Yad in check was pretty feeble. You questioned it right away, and continued to question it. Eben would have also."

Alyssa nodded.

"At least Al Yad's play for you in Indiana made it clear that he had gotten the point. That the hook was baited. So I began to think about what would need to happen for Al Yad to make himself vulnerable."

Craft looked miserable once again. "But try as I might, the only viable plan I could come up with was a *nightmare*. I would have to play you, and use you, and send you to what could well be your death at the hands of a psychotic mass murderer. Without your knowledge or consent." He turned away and shook his head in disgust and disbelief. "And if this wasn't bad enough, I was already in love with you at the time."

There was a long silence in the room as this statement hung in the air.

"If you end up hating me for the rest of your life for what I put you through," he continued finally, "I couldn't blame you. I hate *myself*."

"But why?" said Alyssa. "Why couldn't you have just told me the truth? Told me your plan?"

"It was necessary. And it was your only hope of surviving. Your ignorance of the plan was the only protection I could give you against Al Yad. It freed you up to tell the truth, as you knew it, and avoid torture and failed polygraph tests." Craft curled his upper lip in self-disgust once again. "But it required that I make you fear me. Make you *hate* me. It was a horrible, despicable plan."

Alyssa stared deeply into his eyes and believed the pain she found there was real. "Tell me the details," she said.

"It was insidiously complex. An elaborate stage play. Al Yad had to think he intercepted you on his own, and that this was the last thing I wanted. But he was sure to be suspicious. And I've never met anyone more cautious. He would interrogate you thoroughly enough to find the tinniest *hint* of deceit. If you knew the plan was to strip him of his ability so I could kill him, you would never get through his interrogation without this coming out."

Alyssa nodded. She couldn't argue the point.

"And we were falling in love," continued Craft. "Imagine if I let our relationship go forward as it was. Imagine that you loved me. And then I arranged to have you taken by him. If you knew the quantum mirror device was a bluff, he would find this out, and all would be lost. If you knew about the device, but thought it was real, you would know why he wanted you to temporarily disable his ability. So he could kill me and get out from under the device.

"In this scenario, you would never do this for him. He would torture you. Torture and kill your family one by one in front of you. And you would still refuse to remove his powers. Because you would think this would end in my death. Killing the man you loved, and more importantly, leaving Al Yad free to kill millions." He paused. "Think about it."

Alyssa imagined being in this position and shuddered. "You're right," she said.

Al Yad would have done *exactly* as Bren had indicated. And she would have never given in, even so. Not if she truly believed millions of lives were at stake. Which she would have.

"So for this to work," said Craft, "Al Yad had to believe you knew nothing about the quantum mirror. He had to think I was manipulating you to temporarily free me from the field, by lying and telling you that I desperately needed to get some sleep. So *he* could pretend he wanted you to do the same for him. He had to believe you were a clueless rube."

"And for that to happen, I had to *be* a clueless rube."

"There was no other way. I needed you to help him. Help him destroy himself. Unless you were clueless this would never happen. If anything, this was the straightforward part of my plan. The complicated part was that I also needed him to have the activation code for this fictional quantum mirror device. Without knowing I was giving it to him."

"Why?"

"Imagine how the plan would go if I didn't arrange for this. You willingly implant a suggestion that lets Al Yad sever his tie with the zero point field whenever he wants. You do this because you have no idea he believes this will allow him to kill me. And you think it might actually restore his sanity. But then what?"

He paused for a moment and then answered his own question. "Well, then he would have to get me to activate the fictional quantum mirror device. So I would be killed while he was immune. And what's the best way for him to get me to activate it? The only way?"

Alyssa's eyes widened. "Cross your line in the sand," she said. "Goad you into it. Destroy a city or two. Then trigger his immunity and wait for you to carry out your threat."

Craft nodded. "He would reason that if he engaged in mass destruction, no matter how much I wanted to live, I would activate the device to stop further slaughter." He paused. "Then he would be safe, and I would be gone."

Alyssa was in awe of Brennan Craft once again. Not of his near omnipotence, but of his genius. His reasoning had been impeccable.

"So, again, finding a credible way to feed him the activation code to my fake device was vital. So he wouldn't think he had to engage in wholesale murder to make this happen. But it was one of the thorniest problems I've ever faced. The solution seems obvious in hindsight, but believe me, I pulled out my hair trying to figure it out.

"First, *you* had to believe I was becoming as big a threat to the world as Al Yad. To believe I could kill my good friend Eben Martin. To believe that severing my connection to the zero point field might restore my sanity—so Al Yad would come to know you believed this. And the timing had to be perfect. As you've guessed by now, I decided

I had to risk telling Eben that the quantum mirror was a bluff, after all. Because I needed him on board to pull this off."

Alyssa shook her head, feeling foolish. Of course Eben was involved. She should have realized this earlier.

"I had to make you think I had turned into a monster. The text Eben sent you, finally explaining about the quantum mirror and providing the activation code, had to seem absolutely legitimate. Like a desperation move. Al Yad had to have unimpeachable confirmation from you that I had become a monster. A danger to everyone. So much so that I would kill my closest friend. And that it would make perfect sense that Eben would send you the activation code and instruct you to kill us both."

This explained one of Al Yad's lines of questioning during her interrogation. He had read Eben's message and wanted to confirm things had gotten bad enough that she and Eben would consider killing Bren. Al Yad was as careful and thorough as Bren had expected him to be. For Eben's message to be credible, Al Yad had to believe Bren had gone insane and had turned on his friends. Which meant *she* had to believe it.

"So when you lashed out at me," said Alyssa. "When you went into a rage. This was all *acting*?"

Craft lowered his eyes. "It was the hardest thing I've ever had to do." He looked as though he might vomit or burst into tears at any moment as he remembered the role he had felt forced to play.

There was a long pause as Craft regained his composure. "Alyssa Aronson," he said finally. "I love you. I've loved you since the early days in Costa Rica. I wanted to shout this from the rafters. But I couldn't. It almost killed me to hold it in, but this would have only made things harder. For both of us. Because even then, I knew that I'd soon have to make you fear me. To curse at you and berate you. To make you think I had become deranged."

Alyssa wasn't sure what to say, so she said nothing.

Craft glanced at the time on his phone and sighed. "I'm long overdue calling Eben to tell him how it went. I promised him. He's extremely worried about you. So let's take a short break."

"How much time do we have in this room before someone realizes what happened?"

"Quite a while. I sent a concussive wave through the entire complex. We're the only ones conscious. So we won't be interrupted. And even when they awaken, if I know Omar Haddad, he made sure no one would come near this place during the eight hours he was disabled."

A minute later Eben was on the phone. "We got him!" said Craft. "It worked."

"And Alyssa?" said Martin immediately.

"She's fine. At least physically. I've started explaining to her what happened."

"Can I talk to her?" said Martin.

Craft handed Alyssa the phone and backed a polite distance away.

"How are you faring?" asked Martin.

"I don't know," she replied. "You and Bren have given me a lot to digest. So much of what I thought I knew is wrong. The last month has been a *nightmare*. And just when I was so deep in despair I almost lost touch with reality, Bren shows up here and throws everything I knew, and felt, and thought, into a blender."

Alyssa shook her head, her expression tortured. "Al Yad had me read your text. In the end, I was sure you and Bren were both dead," she whispered, a catch in her throat.

"I am so sorry, Alyssa. My text message may have been meant to be intercepted, but I meant what I wrote. I think the world of you. You are an extraordinary woman. Doing this to you was despicable, and I hated every second of it. But there are a few things you should know.

"First, Bren risked his life so that he didn't have to risk yours. He tried to kill Al Yad himself before he would consider implementing the plan that involved you. I told him it was too dangerous, too big of a risk. But he wouldn't listen. He was willing to try anything and everything to avoid doing this to you. To avoid treating you like dirt so you would hate him. And especially to avoid putting you in Al Yad's hands. This was the absolute last resort for him."

Alyssa nodded. She had wondered why Craft was so determined to risk everything to face Al Yad. Now she knew.

"And you should also know," continued Martin, "that as brutal as it was for me to mislead you, it was an order of magnitude harder for Bren. You weren't the only one calling me in tears. After he would pretend to fly off the handle, berating and terrorizing you, he would call me, and I'd have to talk him down off a metaphorical ledge. He'd tell me he couldn't do it anymore. That we had to scrap the plan. That he refused to put you in jeopardy. Refused to be an asshole to you one more time. I had to push him to remember the big picture. It took all of my persuasive abilities to keep him on track.

"He was *so* in love with you, Alyssa. Treating you like this was tearing him up inside. Afterwards he would leave you, not to go off and practice his skills, but because he couldn't let you see the agony this was causing him. *Really.*"

Just when Alyssa had thought she was emotionally spent—that her soul had been so torn by thinking she saw the world unraveling, her friends killed, and Al Yad prevail, that she had nothing left—Martin's words brought yet another tear to her eye.

"I know Bren doesn't expect forgiveness," said Martin. "He's well aware that you were the victim here. But I wanted you to at least be aware of the heavy toll this took on him, as well."

"Thanks, Eben," said Alyssa softly. "But I should go. Bren needs to finish filling me in, and we need to get out of here. But we'll talk soon."

"I look forward to that," said Martin. "And you may not have known you were playing such an important role, but you did make it possible to end the biggest threat humanity has ever faced. So thank you."

When the connection had ended, Alyssa turned to Craft. "Did you hear that?"

"Not Eben's end of the conversation." He was about to continue when he noticed Alyssa's eyes had moistened. "Are you okay?" he asked worriedly as she wiped a tear from her eye with the back of one hand.

Alyssa nodded, blinking away a few additional tears. "Go on," she said softly. "Tell me the rest."

Craft still looked concerned about her emotional state, but respected the fact that she didn't want to talk about it, and decided not to press her further.

While Craft paused to choose the best point to resume his narrative, Alyssa realized something else she had missed. "So Adam Turco was in on this, as well," she said. "Wasn't he?"

Craft nodded slowly. "Yes. Before Adam neutralized the man watching your lab in Bloomington, I told him to get Tariq Bahar's contact information from him. I didn't tell him why at the time, only that this might be useful later. Adam is a good man. He's a mercenary, not a saint, but he does have a code. Eben and I couldn't tell him the exact nature of the plan, but we assured him that although it was complicated, we knew what we were doing. And, most importantly, that you wouldn't be hurt."

"And that was enough?"

"Not by a long shot. It would have taken a lot of convincing to get him to throw any innocent party to the wolves, and this was especially true in your case. There is something about you, Alyssa. Your upbeat attitude. Your sense of humor. I don't know. But Adam likes you, and feels protective toward you."

Craft sighed. "He finally agreed because he knew how much I loved you. Not because I told him, but because he said it was painfully obvious. So the fact that I believed this was necessary, and that no harm would befall you, was convincing to him. Not that he didn't feel horrible about it, like the rest of us, and worry about how you would fare."

Alyssa thought back to the hotel room in Lawrence. Despite his apparent betrayal, Turco's face had reflected a deep concern for her welfare at the end. She hadn't known what to make of it at the time. Now she did.

"Adam played a critical role," continued Craft. "We convinced him that we were trying to accomplish something important, and honorable. He would have done it without a further incentive, but we insisted that he keep whatever money he could get from Al Yad."

"So you sent me running off to Lawrence, just when I was most desperate to get away from you."

A tortured expression came over Craft's face. "Yes. Knowing I was really delivering you to a crazed murderer with unlimited power." He shook his head in disgust. "For what it's worth," he said softly, "it was the hardest thing I've ever had to do."

Craft took a deep breath and then continued. "Eben and I had orchestrated events to ensure the timing was perfect. It had to be, on any number of levels. Especially for some of the key texts between you and Eben. Everything had to seem absolutely plausible."

"Did Eben even come to Costa Rica?"

"No. But we pretended you were crossing in the air, and that he was coming to confront me. For Al Yad's benefit and to set the timing. We had Adam deliver you to Tariq Bahar with assurances he would convince me you were killed, so I wouldn't come after you. Adam also gave them the key to decrypt your phone."

"Brilliant," said Alyssa. "So Al Yad could pat himself on the back that he was able to read the encrypted messages Eben sent to me. The same ones you so desperately *needed* him to read."

"Pretty clever, if I do say so myself," said Craft. "Eben's last message was key, of course. It made it clear you were never told about the quantum mirror, and reinforced that my friends feared me enough to try to kill me, so it would make sense that Eben was sending you the activation code. And because Adam was in on this, we knew exactly when they would confiscate your phone. So we could time the text so it would be intercepted, and Al Yad would be certain that you hadn't read it." A wry smile crossed his face. "Like I said, sometimes I make flawless moves, and sometimes I make mistakes that are stunning in their stupidity."

Alyssa thought he was being too hard on himself. Yes, he had screwed up by putting himself on a dating site, and by not anticipating Al Yad's gambit to capture her in Indiana, but that was all. For the rest he had played a perfect game of five dimensional chess.

"And the footage of you blowing up in San Diego?" said Alyssa. "Obviously you weren't in San Diego a minute before you arrived here."

"Eben had high-priced special effects people whip this up when Al Yad asked Adam to capture my demise on video. This request actually helped us, because it allowed me to time my appearance here. Adam texted me when Al Yad told him my death was minutes away, so I knew that he had invoked your hypnotic trigger and made himself vulnerable."

Craft sighed. "I would have liked to tell Al Yad how I had bested him. Rub his nose in it. He did murder eighteen of my friends. I would have liked to see the look on his face when I told him the quantum mirror had been a bluff, and that I had manipulated him into making himself vulnerable."

"Why didn't you? Once he triggered the nocebo effect, there was no turning back. Not for eight hours. No matter how much he might have wanted to."

Craft shook his head. "Probably. But I knew this would be my one and only opportunity to kill him. So I decided not to take any chances. To end him the first instant I could. Destroy the quantum lens between his ears. Just in case he had some quirk that would let him get out from under the block that you helped him impose on himself."

Alyssa nodded. It was sound thinking. And Bren's plan had been genius. A masterpiece.

And yet, he had put her through torture. He had been a terror, and had treated her like garbage.

But did he have any other choice? If the quantum mirror device had been real, he would have had the option of sacrificing himself to kill Al Yad. But it wasn't. Instead, after travelling to Syria and risking his own life, he had risked sending the woman he loved into the hands of a man he despised. A man who had murdered his friends and had tried to kill him.

Craft did this knowing that Alyssa might die hating him. Die thinking he had betrayed her and had never loved her. This had been agony for him. But he had decided no sacrifice was too great to stop Al Yad.

And if there had been some magical way for Bren to tell her his plan, and then erase her memory so she could still carry it out as the unknowing dupe she needed to be, would she have agreed to it?

She didn't even have to consider it. Of course she would have. Al Yad was an omnipotent madman. How could she have refused to do whatever it took to bring him down.

And if their roles were reversed, would she have done this to Bren? The answer was yes. She wouldn't have had any other choice.

And neither had he.

So while she wasn't prepared to forgive him this second, she knew that she would. Even in the brief time since he had arrived in Syria, she found herself drawn to him again. The magic was returning. His behavior had terrified and traumatized her far too much for her to fall back in love with him already, even knowing he had been only playing a twisted, but necessary, role. But she had little doubt that this would happen, and fairly soon.

"I have one last question for you, Bren," she said.

"Anything," said Craft.

"What in the world are you doing dressed in that uniform?"

62

Brennan Craft laughed out loud. "So you're not ready to believe that I've secretly been with the military all along? That I'm a colonel in the Air Force?"

"I don't think so," said Alyssa, breaking into a smile herself. "Yes, you've managed to screw with my mind beyond belief. But the military thing is where I draw the line."

"You are very wise, Alyssa Aronson," said Craft. "The truth is, I have never been in the military. But I'm wearing this uniform to help my country. There was one other thing happening behind the scenes when we were in Costa Rica. You know I continued to watch your Major Elovic. After you disappeared, he was more determined to find me than ever. So I thought it wise to keep tabs on him."

"Uh-huh," said Alyssa, having no idea where this was going.

"While I was doing this, I learned that Syria's President, Khalil Najjar, had all but begged the US to kill Al Yad for him. Al Yad had acquired such a following, and such a well-deserved reputation for omnipotence—not to mention that Najjar could no longer trust his own military—that he knew he couldn't survive a showdown. The US was able to wrangle a number of strategic concessions from Najjar on the promise they would take care of his Al Yad problem."

Alyssa shook her head in wonder. "Incredible," she said simply.

"Yes," agreed Craft. "Incredible is right. Fortunately, while hacking Elovic's computer, I was able to learn that the US was poised to strike. They had prepared a raid with multiple special forces groups, who would have significant air support, as well as missile support from both the air and sea. Najjar would cooperate fully and see to it that our forces were not interfered with. He was desperate. As desperate as only our omnipotent friend can make one."

"Did they make the attempt?"

"No. I couldn't let them. It would have been suicide. Scores of good men would have died for nothing. America wouldn't get the concessions Najjar had promised us, and our reputation would certainly get a black eye. At the same time, Al Yad's reputation would grow even further on the world stage."

"How long ago was this?"

"A few weeks. My plan was already underway. So I contacted Greg Elovic."

"No!" said Alyssa in astonishment. "You *didn't*."

"I did," he replied with a grin. "As you might imagine, the major was a bit surprised also. We had an . . . interesting . . . conversation. I told him you were alive and well. That I was aware of the pending strike on Al Yad and that it had no chance of succeeding. I told him I had invented an advanced weapon based on new scientific principles I had discovered. And that Al Yad had stolen one of only two prototypes."

"Elovic had already guessed you used some kind of advanced weapon to escape his team at my house," said Alyssa. "So this played right into what he already thought. And it also would explain some of the mystery behind the rise of Al Yad."

"Exactly," said Craft. "So I offered him a deal. I told him I knew of a way to counteract this new weapon. It was complicated, and would take some doing, but that in less than a month I would take Al Yad down myself. With Al Yad dead, the US would be a hero. Our international reputation would get a boost from pulling off what many observers were beginning to think was impossible. For very good reason. Because it was. I would defuse the biggest threat the world was facing, and President Khalil Najjar would be in our debt.

"In return, I asked the major to stop looking for me after I had killed Al Yad. And to give you carte blanche. If you wanted to return to your job and life, no questions were ever to be asked. You would get back-pay and treated like a queen. If you chose, instead, to stay off the grid with me, he would not only stop looking for us, but help us stay concealed."

"Very nice," said Alyssa. "If you really could kill Al Yad, he would jump at these terms—times a thousand."

"Well, being in the military, he did want information about this new breed of weapon I had developed. But I told him this wasn't going to happen. That I deeply regretted inventing the damn thing, and planned to destroy both prototypes and all of my plans. This was non-negotiable."

Craft paused. "But you're right, after I made this clear, he did fall all over himself to accept my terms." The corners of his mouth turned up into a smile. "I could have demanded that he buy you an island to rival Eben's, and I'm pretty sure he wouldn't have argued."

"And yet you didn't," muttered Alyssa in mock disapproval. "So now I know," she added, shaking her head. "Bungee jumping and negotiation: not your strong suits."

Craft laughed. "Well, the major did have one proviso. He agreed, as long as I could prove what I had claimed. And he still had to get his superiors on board. So he asked for a demonstration. For him and two of his superiors."

"And you gave him one?"

"Yes. One morning, when you were sound asleep, I left and flew to Nicaragua."

"Commercial? Or, you know, self powered? Zero point energy airlines?"

Craft smile broadly. "Self powered," he replied. "After I scheduled the meeting, I knew they'd be monitoring all commercial flights into Nicaragua. I figured when they didn't spot me at any traditional ports of entry, they'd have to assume I was already holed up in that country when I contacted them. A little misdirection to keep them off our scent."

Alyssa nodded appreciatively. "Very nice."

"I brought a fancy, bloated silver pen with me, making sure to conceal the brand name. It looked very high tech, believe me. And then I did a few tricks. I pointed the pen at a hillside and turned it into lava. That sort of thing."

"I guess the pen really *is* mightier than the sword?" said Alyssa wryly.

"This one sure was," said Craft with a grin. "And versatile. I told them the technology had other capabilities as well, but that I had done enough to prove I was telling the truth. And to prove that they had no chance against Al Yad. But as the inventor of the technology, I did."

"And this obviously convinced them," said Alyssa. She gestured at the body on the floor. "Good thing, too. Because you came through for them in a big way."

Craft blew out a long breath. "Thank God," he said.

"This still doesn't explain the uniform."

"Oh. Right. Well, let me tell you where we go from here. In a few minutes, I'll call Major Elovic. I'll send him a picture of Al Yad's body. And put you on the phone, so he can confirm you're still alive, and so you can authenticate that our target is truly dead.

"Then I'm going to call Najjar and tell him it's done. He'll send a man named Abdul Salib, who works for him. He's the only man loyal to Najjar who has ever met Al Yad and lived to tell about it. I'll explain that this compound is unguarded and everyone inside is unconscious. He'll come here and confirm that Al Yad is truly dead."

Alyssa nodded. This explained why Bren hadn't vaporized his nemesis. He needed him to be identifiable.

"I'll tell Salib the special forces teams responsible for this success are long gone," continued Craft. "But that I stayed behind to make sure Najjar knew the US had lived up to our end of the agreement."

"Wow. He and Najjar—and the worldwide intelligence community for that matter—are going to be scratching their heads forever, wondering how our special forces teams pulled this off. I mean, every resident of Al Yad's compound unconscious at once. No traces of gas or chemicals. And a dead man who was known to be invulnerable."

Craft smiled at the thought of the confusion this would bring. "Elovic thought if I succeeded, wearing this uniform while I placed a video call to Najjar, and met Salib, would lend an air of authenticity. I'll change out of it before I leave here, of course. The American military isn't exactly popular here, and I don't want to incite violence. But we'll get treated like royalty as we're escorted out of the country. Believe me, Najjar will be overjoyed."

"You know, Bren, if there really is an infinite intelligence who fragmented Himself to experience existence—to be surprised—you're more than holding up your end of things."

Craft laughed. "Yeah, it's been exciting. And emotional. But I wish some other fragment could have brought these experiences into the fold. It's been a little too taxing on this one."

"Before you call the major and Salib, tell me: was that stuff about you ruling the world just acting? Like the rest of it?"

"Yes. I'm a little worried that you even had to ask. But I guess I deserve that. This was just part of the narrative that we needed you and Al Yad to believe. You know, the 'Bren has become a power mad psychopath, bent on world domination' narrative. Again, an idea that Eben reinforced in his final text."

"No. I get that. But for much of that conversation, you forgot to be a jerk. And I had the impression that you believed a lot of what you said."

"You caught me. You're right. These are principles of governance to which I generally subscribe. In my fantasies, I'd love to see how prosperous the world could become if there were someone at the helm who would make things fair, give people what they need to thrive, and stay out of everyone's hair. But I'm not about to become a dictator. Benevolent or otherwise."

"So what now?" said Alyssa.

"My overriding objectives still remain. I want to find a way to impart the ability I now have to everyone—safely. And while I'm working on this, make sure another Al Yad doesn't emerge. Eben is on board for this. His money will be a good start. We can use some of it to begin programs and to identify and monitor the activities of anyone trying to duplicate my work.

"We haven't figured this out exactly, but at some point, we'd like to find a way to fill a significant percentage of worldwide energy needs free of charge. It's just a matter of establishing a big enough power plant and a way to transmit the energy cheaply. I can power up the entire plant repeatedly without much effort. And if you decide to join us, I'd still like you to consider bringing a handful of others up to my level. Beginning with you and Eben."

"I don't know, Bren . . ."

Craft held out his hands in surrender. "It would be your call entirely, Alyssa. If it will help bring you back into the fold, so that you can trust the power-mad me really was just an act, you can make *every* call."

Alyssa noted that he seemed quite sincere about this. Interesting.

"Eventually, I'd like to find select individuals who want to lead expeditions to some of the Earth-like planets we've been discovering over the past few years. They can power large starships filled with explorers. And I'd like to recruit others who can help us provide free energy. Finally, I have a kernel of an idea of how we might bring the vast majority of our species to my level, while ensuring they wield this power safely and responsibly."

"Seems impossible," said Alyssa. "What do you have in mind?"

"Are you familiar with the three laws of robotics?"

"Asimov's three laws?"

"Exactly."

"I've heard of them, but I don't know what they are. I just know that Asimov was the fictional father of modern robotics."

"He was. Many people in his day feared that if robots ever became widespread, they might turn on us."

"Yeah. Even more people fear that *now*," she said in amusement. "Have you been to any movies in the past few decades?"

"So I guess you're willing to concede the point," said Craft dryly. "Anyway, Asimov wanted his robots to serve as tools. So he imagined a robotics industry in which a prohibition against causing harm to a human being was etched into the very fabric of all robot brains. Even the *thought* of harming a human would paralyze them." He paused. "So I've been thinking, maybe there is a parallel with your work."

Alyssa considered. "So you think I could use hypnosis to program people with the human equivalent? The three laws of humanics?"

"Not exactly. But you'll need to evoke an enhanced placebo effect, like you did with me. Enhance their belief that they can control the zero point field. Is there any way to make this belief contingent? To combine this with other pathways of thought? So that subjects can only muster the kind of certainty they need to get to my level if their intentions are good. If they try to use the field for destructive purposes, their hypnotic enhancement vanishes. Is this a possibility?"

Alyssa considered this for almost a minute. "Maybe. We aren't there yet, but with a concerted effort with this as the goal, maybe. But the exact nature of the programming would be thorny. And remember, Al Yad didn't *need* to be hypnotized to achieve this level."

"We'll start with only the most stable people and monitor them."

"But the trick would be to define the parameters. We can't just link the ability to tap the field to a general prohibition against doing harm. Al Yad would have passed this test. He was convinced he was *helping* humanity. By destroying most of it."

"Again, he was seriously demented. But I take your point. I'm not saying it will be easy. Or that there aren't plenty of debates about the best parameter set. That is, even if it can be done. But it's worth thinking about. A grand bargain. We offer you omnipotence, but your ability disappears if you ever try to use it for ill, rather than good."

Alyssa looked skeptical.

"It's a long shot, I know," said Craft. "But is it more of a long shot than being able to tap into the zero point field in the first place?"

"Definitely not," said Alyssa.

"And besides, someone like you, someone who is far above average in every way, should be able to do this in a snap."

Alyssa grinned. "I'm also above average in my resistance to flattery."

"We'll have plenty of time to figure this out. But I wanted to at least start you thinking of the possibilities. Again, If you join us, you will have total say. There is no one whose ethics I trust more. Eben has already agreed to this."

Alyssa studied him thoughtfully, but remained silent.

"Look," said Bren. "It's your call. You can have your old life back, and then some. Elovic owes you a lot. But I'm begging you. Join me. Join us. You don't have to decide now. Take your time. After all, this is the worst time to ask for a decision. When you still have the bad taste of the asshole Brennan Craft in your mouth."

He made a face. "I may not have thought that last sentence out," he said with a grin. "Probably not the most artful phrasing I've ever delivered."

"Yeah," said Alyssa, fighting back laughter. "Kind of brings a thought picture to mind I'd rather not have." She paused. "But I know what you meant."

Craft suddenly became serious once again. "Alyssa Aronson," he said, staring deeply into her large brown eyes. "I love you. I love you more than I can describe. No matter what happens, no matter what you end up deciding, I will never stop loving you. And I will never stop regretting what I did to you. And if you join me, I will never stop trying to make it up to you."

Brennan Craft's lovesick puppy dog gaze was back. But more than this, so was *he*. His intelligence, warmth, and wit. His compassion. Absolute power hadn't changed him at all. Everything that had drawn her in like a black hole had returned.

She had been deceived and put through the wringer. But now that she had made it out the other side, she was beginning to feel euphoric. It had all just been a very bad dream. Yes, Brennan had trapped her in hell. But he had also waved a magic wand and transported her to heaven. The greatest threat the world had ever faced was gone. And the perfect man for her had returned. These rewards compensated her for the emotional trauma she had been forced to endure a hundred times over.

So she could either spend time bitterly recalling her stay in hell, and resenting Bren for it, or she could embrace the profound relief and joy she now felt at learning that this hell had been nothing more than a mirage.

The choice was obvious.

"I'll tell you what . . . Colonel," she said. "I'll give you a month to win me over. To remind me of what we had. And convince me that all traces of the other guy are truly gone."

Craft looked like he could float off the ground without the use of zero point energy. "Outstanding!" he said. After a long pause he added, "Would it be too forward to suggest I start this trial period off by reminding you of what it's like to kiss the old style Brennan Craft? I mean, only for a few minutes. We *are* a bit overdue making some important phone calls."

"Interesting proposition," said Alyssa with just the hint of a smile. "On the one hand, you did save my life." She raised her eyebrows. "But on the other hand, you were the one who put it in jeopardy in the first place."

She put her hands out in front of her, palms up, and moved them up and down, as though she were a human scale, carefully weighing the decision. Finally, she shrugged, and an incandescent smile spread across her face. "What the hell," she said, melting into his arms. "The world has waited this long to hear about the demise of Al Yad. What's a few minutes longer?"

"Al Yad?" said Craft giddily as he leaned in to kiss her. And his blissful, dreamy expression made it clear that, for just this instant, Alyssa Aronson really *was* his entire universe. "Who's he?"

FROM THE AUTHOR: QUANTUM LENS: WHAT'S REAL, AND WHAT ISN'T:

Thanks for reading *Quantum Lens*. I hope that you enjoyed it!

In addition to trying to tell the most compelling stories I possibly can, I strive to introduce concepts and accurate information that I hope will prove fascinating, thought provoking, and even controversial. I have conducted extensive research for all of my novels, but for the first time I've decided to touch upon this research further.

Although *Quantum Lens* is a work of fiction and contains considerable speculation, most of the main elements are based on our current state of knowledge. Naturally, within the context of a thriller, it is impossible for me to go into the depth each topic deserves, nor present the topic from all possible angles. I encourage interested readers to read further to get a more thorough and nuanced look at each topic, and weigh any conflicting data, opinions, and interpretations. By so doing, you can decide for yourself what is accurate, and arrive at your own view of the subject matter.

ZERO POINT FIELD AND ZERO POINT ENERGY: These are known to exist and have been proven beyond a reasonable doubt, although there is disagreement on the magnitude of zero point energy, with some scientists believing that we're missing an important principle in our understanding. The NASA article cited in the novel is real, and provides fascinating reading. I've posted an excerpt from this article below, after the *Other Books by Douglas E. Richards* section.

THE GOD THEORY: This is, of course, an actual book written by Dr. Bernard Haisch, and one that I highly recommend. Dr. Haisch is an astrophysicist who has authored well over a hundred scientific papers and was editor of the Astrophysical Journal for ten years. His groundbreaking work on the zero point field was partially funded by NASA.

Even if one disagrees with the thesis of *The God Theory*, the book offers a perspective on creation that is novel and thought provoking. The book also touches upon Dr. Haisch's work with respect to the zero point field, and why it is possible that this field is responsible for the very existence of matter, and how manipulations of this field could affect mass, inertia, and gravity.

THE MIRACLE OF A FERTILIZED EGG BECOMING A HUMAN BEING: Many years ago, I was working toward a PhD in molecular biology (aka, genetic engineering), utterly fascinated by the field. I eventually changed course, earning a master's degree instead, because, while I loved the science, I was horrible at lab work. *Horrible.* I was impatient and sloppy. And sloppy isn't a great thing to be when one is working with high levels of radiation, and a potent carcinogen called ethidium bromide whose sole purpose in life is to mutate DNA.

But in any event, my first graduate level course in Developmental Biology (i.e. how an egg transforms into an adult) blew my mind. Nothing in all of biology is more fascinating and miraculous to me. How can a single fertilized egg cell possibly contain all of the instructions required to construct an entire human, *and then be able to carry out these instructions with such perfection?* This single fertilized cell is the progenitor of *trillions* of cells, which differentiate along the way into different types. And each of these uncountable offspring cells need to know what to be, and where to be, to create the incomprehensibly complex universe that is a human being. But there's more. The system has to get energy and building blocks from the outside. How do we grow from an infant to an adult? We have to convert food into parts of our bodies. Food gives us energy, yes, but it is also our only source of building material. Our bodies must extract the raw materials we need for construction from such sources as ice-cream, meatloaf, and pasta, and then rearrange these raw materials into muscle cells, heart cells, brain cells, and so on.

The idea that a single fertilized cell could successfully transform itself into an adult human, including a brain with many billions of neurons and a consciousness, is utterly ludicrous. Impossible. There is no way this could ever succeed. And yet, all of us are living proof that it does . . .

HUMAN BEHAVIOR: The discussion of human behavior in the early chapters is as accurate as I could make it, and is based on my extensive reading, and my completion of a college course on human behavior. Genes do tend to shape beliefs and personality more than had been recognized in earlier decades, although environment does still play an important role as well.

HYPNOTISM: This is a very difficult area to research, as there is considerable misinformation out there, and it is hard to know which sources and people to trust. I read a number of research papers on the subject, and spoke over the phone at length to the ivy-league author of what many consider the definitive work in this area (who told me he preferred not to be acknowledged by name in the book). When Alyssa Aronson assures GQ that, "Hypnosis can't transcend volitional capacity," this is an exact quote from this world-leading expert (because I thought it sounded cool). All discussions of hypnotism in the book are accurate, to the best of my knowledge, including experimental results. This being said, the advances made by Alyssa Aronson and her Black Ops colleagues, with respect to the enhancement of subconscious belief and the placebo effect, are fictional.

TORTURE: This is obviously a controversial topic. I tried to convey the key points as accurately as I could based on my research, but as with all of these topics, interested parties should conduct their own research and decide which conclusions are valid.

THE PLACEBO EFFECT AND BIOFEEDBACK: Both fascinating, and both real effects. I was an executive in the biotech and pharmaceutical industry for many years before becoming a writer, and I have been involved with clinical trials of new medications, for which the placebo effect has loomed very large. I have also read extensively on the current state of knowledge. It has now been proven beyond a reasonable doubt that in many instances the mind is able to heal the body, using mechanisms that are not entirely clear.

INEDIA and BRETHARIANISM: Both very real, with numerous adherents around the globe, many claiming to have unimpeachable evidence of their ability to survive fasts of months and even years. According to the bible, along with Moses and Jesus, Elijah also fasted for forty days and forty nights, and a number of Catholic saints were said to have fasted for years, or even decades, (although they did make an exception with respect to partaking of the Eucharist).

THE ULTIMATUM GAME, CONFIRMATION BIAS, and THE LAKE WOEBEGON EFFECT: These are all real, and some of the most experimented upon phenomenon in the study of human behavior. After reading several books on these and other experiments, I have identified a number of common themes. Our memory isn't nearly as good as we think it is. We are influenced by far more than we imagine at the subconscious level. We are less in conscious control of our own decisions than we realize. We are far less rational than we think, and far more easily fooled. We are poor judges of probability. We are more biased than we think. And we ignore data that doesn't fit our preconceptions.

Other than this, we're practically infallible :)

QUANTUM CONSCIOUSNESS and QUANTUM PHYSICS: Many scientists do believe that consciousness is a quantum phenomena. A quick search will reveal numerous books on the subject.

Everything written in the novel about the quantum realm is based upon widely accepted, accurate science. Except, of course, the ability to wield zero point energy with one's mind. This isn't possible—that I know of :)

Note that no field is more mind-blowing, confusing, complex, and counter-intuitive than quantum mechanics, so the highly simplified and summarized account I've presented in the novel is akin to sticking a toe into an ocean of water. And even experts in the field often disagree about the implications of this theory. Albert Einstein and Niels Bohr, two fathers of quantum physics, had epic disagreements on many topics in the field for many years.

INDIANA UNIVERSITY: My parents and a number of my relatives are graduates of Indiana University, Bloomington, and I have visited the campus any number of times. While some liberties were taken with the locations of buildings and French restaurants, the supercomputer mentioned in the novel and Hogwarts-like limestone structures are real. This area of the world does have spectacular woods, endless seas of corn, and massive wind turbines big enough to hide ambushing mercenaries.

Finally, as mentioned, an excerpt from the NASA article, *Emerging Possibilities for Space Propulsion Breakthroughs*, appears after *Other Books by Douglas E. Richards*.

ABOUT THE AUTHOR

Douglas E. Richards is the *New York Times* and *USA Today* bestselling author of five technothrillers, including *Wired, Amped, Mind's Eye, Quantum Lens,* and *The Cure*. He has also written six middle grade/young adult novels widely acclaimed for their appeal to boys, girls, and adults alike. Douglas has a master's degree in molecular biology (aka "genetic engineering"), was a biotechnology executive for many years, and has authored a wide variety of popular science pieces for *National Geographic*, the *BBC*, the *Australian Broadcasting Corporation, Earth and Sky, Today's Parent*, and many others. Douglas has a wife, two children, and two dogs, and currently lives in San Diego, California.

OTHER BOOKS BY DOUGLAS E. RICHARDS
WIRED (see synopsis below)
AMPED (The WIRED Sequel)
THE CURE
MIND'S EYE (see synopsis below)
THE PROMETHEUS PROJECT (SF, ages 9-99)
    Trapped (book one)
    Captured (book two)
    Stranded (book three)
THE DEVIL'S SWORD (Thriller, ages 9-99)
ETHAN PRITCHER, BODY SWITCHER (ages 7-12)
OUT OF THIS WORLD (SF/Fantasy, ages 9-99)

WIRED SYNOPSIS: A *New York Times* and *USA Today* bestseller! The #1 bestselling Kindle book for an entire year in two major categories: technothrillers and science fiction.
Kira Miller is a brilliant genetic engineer who discovers how to temporarily achieve savant-like capabilities in all areas of thought

and creativity. But what if this transcendent level of intelligence brings with it a ruthless megalomania?

David Desh left the special forces after his team was brutally butchered in Iran. Now he has been reactivated for one last mission: find Kira Miller, the enigmatic genius behind a bioterror plot that threatens millions. But when Desh learns that the bioterror plot is just the tip of the iceberg, he is thrust into a byzantine maze of deception and intrigue, and he becomes a key player in a deadly game he can't begin to understand. A game that is certain to have a dramatic impact on the future course of human history. . .

MIND'S EYE SNOPSIS: A breathtaking new thriller about a stunning future that is rapidly approaching.

When Nick Hall wakes up in a dumpster—bloodied, without a memory, and hearing voices in his head—he knows things are bad. But they're about to get far worse. Because he's being hunted by a team of relentless assassins. Soon Hall discovers that advanced electronics have been implanted in his brain, and he now has two astonishing abilities. He can surf the web using thoughts alone. And he can read minds. But who inserted the implants? And why? And why is someone so desperate to kill him?

As Hall races to find answers, he comes to learn that far more is at stake than just his life. Because his actions can either catapult civilization to new heights—or bring about its total collapse.

Extrapolated from actual research on thought-controlled web surfing, Mind's Eye is a smart, roller-coaster ride of a thriller. One that raises a number of intriguing, and sometimes chilling, possibilities about a future that is just around the corner.

Emerging Possibilities for Space Propulsion Breakthroughs
Originally published in the Interstellar Propulsion Society Newsletter, Vol. I, No. 1, July 1, 1995. Marc. G. Millis, Space Propulsion Technology Division, NASA Lewis Research Center Cleveland, Ohio

"New perspectives on the connection between gravity and electromagnetism have just emerged. A theory published in February 1994

Douglas E. Richards

(ref 11) suggests that inertia is nothing but an electromagnetic illusion. This theory builds on an earlier work (ref 12) that asserts that gravity is nothing other than an electromagnetic side-effect. Both of these works rely on the perspective that all matter is fundamentally made up of electrically charged particles, and they rely on the existence of Zero Point Energy.

Zero Point Energy (ZPE) is the term used to describe the random electromagnetic oscillations that are left in a vacuum after all other energy has been removed (ref 13). This can be explained in terms of quantum theory, where there exists energy even in the absolute lowest state of a harmonic oscillator. The lowest state of an electromagnetic oscillation is equal to one-half the Planck constant times the frequency. If all the energy for all the possible frequencies is summed up, the result is an enormous energy density, ranging from 1036 to 1070 Joules/m3. In simplistic terms there is enough energy in a cubic centimeter of the empty vacuum to boil away Earth's oceans. First predicted in 1948, ZPE has been linked to a number of experimental observations. Examples include the Casimir effect (ref 14), Van der Waal forces (ref 15), the Lamb-Retherford Shift (ref 10, p. 427), explanations of the Planck blackbody radiation spectrum (ref 16), the stability of the ground state of the hydrogen atom from radiative collapse (ref 17), and the effect of cavities to inhibit or enhance the spontaneous emission from excited atoms (ref 18).

Regarding the inertia and gravity theories mentioned earlier, they take the perspective that all matter is fundamentally constructed of electrically charged particles and that these particles are constantly interacting with this ZPE background. From this perspective the property of inertia, the resistance to change of a particle's velocity, is described as a high- frequency electromagnetic drag against the Zero Point Fluctuations. Gravity, the attraction between masses, is described as Van der Waals forces between oscillating dipoles, where these dipoles are the charged particles that have been set into oscillation by the ZPE background.

It should be noted that these theories were not written in the context of propulsion and do not yet provide direct clues for how to electromagnetically manipulate inertia or gravity. Also, these theories are still too new to have either been confirmed or discounted. Despite these uncertainties, typical of any fledgling theory, these theories do provide new approaches to search for breakthrough propulsion physics."

Made in the USA
Columbia, SC
14 January 2023

10334152R00196